MANAGING MILLIE

RESCUED HEARTS OF THE CIVIL WAR ~ BOOK 3

SUSAN POPE SLOAN

WILD HEART
BOOKS

PRAISE FOR MANAGING MILLIE

"Sloan packs the narrative with suspense, and readers will find the endearing characters easy to cheer for, especially spirited, winsome Millie and her unflagging optimism in face of even the most trying of circumstances. This roller-coaster series finale doesn't disappoint."

— PUBLISHERS WEEKLY

"This poignant, beautifully written story shares the hardships and horrors Millie and Troy face as they struggle to survive the Civil War. The eye-opening realities will leave readers hoping and praying for the characters as they turn each page. Susan Pope Sloan knows how to whisk us into the action and the characters' hearts, and she keeps us there until the last page."

— DEB GARDNER ALLARD, AUTHOR OF *LOVE CALLS THE SHOTS*

"*Managing Millie* is a heart-wrenching story that takes you through the trials of the Civil War. You will laugh, cry, and experience heartbreak at times. Susan Pope Sloan is a masterful storyteller and will keep you turning pages until the very end."

— DIANA LEAGH MATTHEWS, AUTHOR OF *90 BREATH PRAYERS* SERIES, *HISTORY MADE REAL,* AND *FUN WITH WORDS*

"For those of us who haven't read anything about the Civil War since high school, *Managing Millie* is a great way to return to the time period. This is the third book in the Rescued Hearts of the Civil War series, and I would recommend reading all three. Each book sweeps us into the turbulent period through the eyes of compelling and complex characters. These are people who are casualties of war and who must endure its consequent hardships: women, children, and the elderly, man caught between politics and morality, etc. If you like lots of action, romance, and unforgettable characters, you will thoroughly enjoy *Managing Millie*."

— DEANNA RUTLEDGE, AWARD WINNING
AUTHOR OF *ON RUMOR'S DEADLY TONGUE*

"See, I am doing a new thing! Now it springs up; do you not perceive it? I am making a way in the wilderness and streams in the wasteland."

— ISAIAH 43:19 (NIV)

CHAPTER 1

*M*illie Gibson's whole world changed on account of a pan of dishwater.

She'd tossed it toward the rosebushes. And missed.

A hard freeze hit Georgia that night. The next morning, in her haste to return to the warm kitchen after visiting the outhouse, Millie skidded on the patch of ice beside the rose-bushes. One ankle twisted, and her hands flew outward for balance. Her frantic movements only delayed her fall. Her bottom hit the ground. Hard.

She struggled to stand, but pain shot through her right leg. Her wrist was swelling too. She crawled the remaining several yards to the house, feeling the rocks and stubble through her thin skirt, and at last collapsed inside the door.

Her stepmother turned from feeding wood into the kitchen stove. "Oh, dear. What happened to you?"

Millie stifled the urge to cry. At sixteen, she should be able to avoid such a tumble—or at least endure the pain. She'd experienced her share of mishaps over the years, often earning her pa's scorn for her clumsiness.

Lydia helped her to a chair and ran her hands over Millie's arms and legs. "I don't think anything's broken," her stepmother said. "But you'll be out of work for a few days, the way that hand looks."

Millie groaned. They could ill afford the loss of her wages. Even before Pa had been reported missing, the funds from him had dried up. She and Lydia together made just enough to keep the two of them clothed and fed.

Lydia wrapped a cloth around a bit of ice from the yard and laid it on Millie's wrist. "Hold it there while I get another for your ankle." She clucked her tongue. "Child, when you take a tumble, you do it with your whole body."

"How well I know." Millie's backside ached. She raised her skirt to examine her bruised knees. At least no one would see those. Her wrist and ankle, though. She groaned. Why did she have to be so clumsy?

Thank goodness for Lydia. She'd tended Millie with loving care since her marriage to Millie's pa. She never scolded or criticized, only admonished her to slow down and be more careful. Unlike Pa, who would berate her for the smallest infraction.

Lydia returned with another cold compress. "Let me help you to bed, then I'll bring you a biscuit and a bowl of grits." She looped Millie's left arm over her shoulder, and they shuffled to Millie's small bedroom, which backed up to the kitchen.

Millie sat on the bed, and Lydia helped her swing her legs over the rumpled covers. Millie couldn't suppress the groan when her injured members came in contact with the mattress. Lydia adjusted the quilts so Millie could spread them without causing her more pain.

"We should put a pillow under that foot. Maybe one under your hand too. Granny McNeil always said to let the blood flow away from the injury. I'll bring a couple from my room."

Within minutes, Lydia had wrapped Millie's injured limbs, brought her a few bites of breakfast, and made her as comfortable as possible. She stood by the bed and surveyed Millie's situation. "It's a good thing this happened on Sunday. I'll have time to prepare a pot of soup, so you'll have plenty to eat while I'm at work tomorrow."

Remorse increased Millie's discomfort. "I'm sorry you'll miss church."

Lydia waved away her concern. "I'd debated whether to go anyway, with it bein' so cold. There could be other icy places along the way. I'll get that soup on the stove and see what else we might fix so you don't have to move around much."

"Thank you for taking such good care of me. I'm sorry to be so much trouble."

"Shut your mouth. It's no trouble to take care of someone you love. I thank God you aren't seriously injured."

Millie closed her eyes as Lydia left the room. *Thank You, God, for Lydia. What would I do without her?*

Pa's decision to marry Lydia eight years ago had been a blessing. He hadn't done it to give Millie a mother after Mama died, of course. His primary consideration had been his own comfort, having someone to cook and clean his house and warm his bed. He'd also wanted a son, but that hadn't happened. Lydia suffered Cal's scorn as well as her own disappointment for that failure.

His last visit home—over a year before—had ended in harsh words between him and Lydia. After that, months passed without any word on his whereabouts. Then his name was printed in the list of those presumed dead at Chickamauga. The preacher had read it from the *Macon Daily Telegraph* a few months ago and offered his condolences.

Beyond that, nobody mourned Cal Gibson's passing.

~

January 28, 1864
Whitfield County, Georgia

*T*roy McNeil shivered, not from the frigid temperature but the sight of dozens of mounds that dotted the landscape below his position near Rocky Face. He'd heard rumors of recent skirmishes around Dalton, and this verified it. Fighting in the dead of winter.

A few miles behind him, more graves scarred the ground from last year's battle at Chickamauga. Scores of monuments to so many lost wagers, wavering hope, and shattered boasts of glory. Defeat dogged both sides.

A hawk soared overhead, its strident call interrupting Troy's silent vigil. Frustrated that his attempt to reach Union-held Knoxville had failed, he turned his steps toward the family home. Pa might not throw out a big welcome, but he wouldn't turn Troy away either. Ma and Old Liza would be glad to see him. He could avoid the rest of the family until spring. Maybe by next week he'd be able to sleep in the barn loft. That was, if he could avoid soldiers from both armies long enough.

He picked his way down the rocky terrain, his senses on alert for any movement that might mean a threat. Bears shouldn't be a problem this time of year, but wolves and bobcats could be on the prowl for easy prey. His greatest worry, though, walked on two legs and wore colors that blended with the winter gray. The dearth of green foliage increased his vulnerability, a man alone with no apparent means of defense.

Troy shifted the pack strapped to his back and pulled a strip of jerky from his pocket. A flock of geese honked as they flew overhead. He traced their movement as he tore off a bite.

"Hey, birds. You're goin' the wrong way. Winter's just gettin' started good." He kept his voice low by habit. You never knew when someone might be listening.

He tramped on, making note of familiar landmarks and the

sun's slow descent across the cloudless sky. He should make it to the state line in a couple of days. He'd go by Aunt Lydia's first, though, and see how she fared. Her and Millie. A strange sensation coursed through his veins at thoughts of Millie. He tried to ignore it, recalling earlier visits to his aunt's house and the blond hoyden who was her stepdaughter.

During his first visit after Lydia's marriage, the girl had followed him around asking persistent questions. He'd thought it crazy that a nine-year-old female would want to help him set rabbit traps and hoe up the garden. No other female he knew did that.

Later, when he went through that terrible phase of his voice wobbling from low to high, Millie had laughed at him. "I declare, Troy, you ought to make up your mind whether to sing bass or soprano. And what's all this stuff on your chin? You're fuzzy as a peach."

She'd learned to jump out of reach and hide behind Lydia's skirt, knowing what her punishment would be if he caught her. He knew her ticklish spots.

Those memories brought a smile. As much as he'd hated her teasing, he loved to hear her laugh and watch her face light up. Her blue eyes glimmered like a lake under the summer sky when she flashed that jaunty grin. Ah, she was a beauty, all right.

His smile faded. Last time he'd seen her, she'd been all grown up, with womanly curves and graceful movement. Even now, the recollection sped up his heartbeat and made sweat dampen his hands inside their gloves. With ruthless effort, he remembered what she'd said.

"I started at the mill last month." She spoke with a mixture of pride and dread in her voice.

"Why?" He'd glanced to where Lydia pulled a pan of cornbread from the stove and kept his voice low. "Are y'all needing the money? I can lend you what I have."

Millie placed a hand on his arm, and he felt a shock run clear down to his toes. "There's no reason I can't work. I've been blessed to stay at home and go to school till now, but Pa hasn't sent any money home in a few months. It's time I helped out."

Troy hated the idea of her going to the mill. He'd seen too many women worn down by the double labor of a job and home. In the few years Lydia had carried that burden, he could see how it dragged at her. But his funds wouldn't have made much difference. Lydia deserved better than what life had dealt her.

As it happened, he was at their house when the women came home with the news that Cal had been reported among the missing at Chickamauga. Millie's fate as a mill operative was sealed, at least until this war ended and Troy could return to a normal life. He couldn't reveal his feelings for her while he lived as a fugitive. By dodging the Confederate conscription, most folks in the South labeled him a coward and wouldn't think twice about turning him in.

A rumble announced a buckboard coming on the road. The driver wouldn't see Troy, who stayed inside the tree line. He stopped on a slight rise where a group of evergreens provided some cover and a welcome shelter from the persistent wind. As the wagon came into sight, Troy took a hurried inventory.

A mule pulled the conveyance, his pace steady but slow. The driver sat hunched over so only a floppy hat and dun-colored coat were visible, along with the booted foot propped against the box. There didn't appear to be any other occupants. Inside the bed, boxes lay higgledy-piggledy on top of some ancient furniture, as if the owner had thrown everything in without a care for how it landed.

As Troy pondered whether to show himself, the wind gusted, and several items tumbled over the wagon's side. The driver glanced back, calling the mule to a halt. "Whoa, there."

The stranger descended from the seat and limped to the back, grumbling at the delay.

Troy jerked to see the driver's boots covered by a dark skirt, and a long braid slipped from the hat. Without thought, he jumped from his hiding place and darted to the closest object in the road. He called a greeting as the woman noted his presence. "Looks like you're losing your load." He grabbed another parcel and carried it to the wagon.

Her wary stare gave way to a nod. "Much obliged, mister. I didn't see you back there."

Troy hoped his grin would put her at ease. "I just came over that hill about the time you passed. Saw your parcels bounce out and thought you might need some help. Where you headed?"

"Far south as I can git," she said. "Away from the guns and cannons. You from around here?"

"Pert near, a little farther down, west of Cartersville. I'm headed home for a visit. I'd appreciate a ride, if you wouldn't mind, as far as you care to go that way. I could hold down your wares."

Neither of them moved while she studied him.

"You got a name?"

"Troy McNeil. My folks live in Alabama, but I got kin in Campbell County. They'll put me up for a while. I expect they could find a place for you if you like to go that far, Missus."

"Mabel Tarvin." At last, she nodded and gestured to the wagon bed. "Hop on."

$\sim$

Campbell County, Georgia

*M*illie limped around the house, using the old cane Lydia found in the shed. The object must have evoked her stepmother's memories, as she'd run her fingers over the worn wood after she wiped away the dust.

"Cal wanted to give it away, but I convinced him one of us might need it one day. This cane, her Bible, and the old wheelbarrow are all I have left of Granny's things."

"Besides the house, you mean," Millie had said. Lydia never mentioned it, but the house, and the farm it sat on, had been part of Cal's attraction to Lydia. He'd hated paying rent on the tiny mill cottage. Ma's death gave him the opportunity to improve his living situation and get a younger wife, one he meant to control as he hadn't been able to control Millie's mother.

Lydia's smile didn't reach her eyes. "And the house. Clearing out her possessions was about the hardest thing I ever did."

"I remember Granny a little," Millie said. "She had the most remarkable laugh."

"That she did. It would tickle her to know that a young lady of sixteen would be the next one to use her cane."

Lydia had showed Millie how to hold it in her left hand. "It's fortunate your injuries are on the same side. It seems backwards, but you should put it on the opposite hand of the hurt leg."

She'd wavered at first but soon developed a rhythm so she could move between the rooms without much difficulty. After two days, she could even venture outside.

"Well, hello, Mr. Sun." She shaded her eyes as she stepped out the front door. She dropped into a rocking chair and leaned the cane against it. "Why did you let Mr. Frost trip me up the other day? I don't mind bein' away from the mill, but I don't like not bein' able to walk around without this stick."

"Who are you talking to, and why are you at home in the middle of the afternoon?"

Troy's voice came from the corner of the house as he sauntered into view and slipped the pack off his shoulders.

Millie's heart leaped, and she drank in the sight of him. His bare head revealed light-brown hair that drifted over his ears and melted into a reddish growth on his chin. Hazel eyes twinkled as he swiped the hair from his brow and stepped onto the porch.

"Troy McNeil, what are you doin' out here in the broad daylight where anyone can see you?" She hoped her scold would cover her joy at his presence—and remind him of the risk of being seen. Some people in this county would consider it their patriotic duty to report him to the Confederate Army.

"Who's gonna see me, Little Bit? Everybody's at work, either in the mill or on their farms. I just traipsed all over the road between here and Tennessee without seein' the first speck of Roswell Gray."

He settled in the other rocker with a sigh. "Ah, it's good to sit and rest."

"You've been to Tennessee and back? Then you didn't make it through the line to the Union camp." She shared his disappointment but secretly rejoiced that he wouldn't be so far away she might never see him again.

Troy gazed off into the distance. "No. I guess I left too late in the season. It started snowing, and I got turned around. A few folks let me stay in their barn or shed, but most were afraid to take a chance on somebody who didn't support the Confederacy."

She gestured to the coat draped over the rocker. "The coat your ma made didn't help?" Connie McNeil's clever idea had impressed Millie. With gray fabric on one side and blue on the other, Troy could reverse it anytime he found himself in a stronghold for either side.

"Not much. Everybody acted suspicious of a man traveling alone. Guess I'm lucky they didn't shoot me on sight." He stretched his arms overhead and turned her way. "Y'all got any food around here, or do I need to go trap us something to cook? And you never did say why you're layin' around the house today. Did you quit your job?"

"Whoa, one question at a time, please." She laughed at his puzzled expression. "We have food. There's a pot of potato soup on the stove, and no, you don't have to set any traps. I didn't quit the mill, but Lydia ordered me to stay home for a few days."

His brows lowered. "What'd you do?"

She flashed him a saucy smile. "I tried to skate on the ice out back last Sunday. My slippers didn't work so well as skates."

She waited for the crack of laughter to follow her flippant remark, but it never came. Troy gaped at her, his eyes skimming her body and finally landing on the low stool where her foot rested. He jerked his gaze back to her face.

"You broke your foot? You should be resting in bed." His face flushed crimson—the curse of a pale complexion, he'd always complained, letting everyone see his emotions.

She couldn't figure why he'd be angry or embarrassed.

"I, uh, I mean you shouldn't be up and around on it."

"It's not broken, only sprained. And I have Granny McNeil's cane to help me."

Troy blew out a breath. "That's good then." He looked away and appeared to collect himself, then smacked his hands on the arms of the rocker and pushed out of the chair. "Well, let's find some dinner. I expect Aunt Lydia will be home before long."

$\sim$

*T*roy prayed Lydia would be home soon. He didn't know how long he could be around Millie and act like nothing had changed since childhood. The difference in their ages had restrained a close relationship between them in years past. He'd brushed off her efforts to be his friend and treated her much the same as he did his younger cousins.

But she displayed all the signs of womanhood now. She wore her hair up, even at home, and she'd let down the hems of her skirts before she started working. He wouldn't even think about everything between those two points.

He stood rooted in place while she used the cane to get to her feet. It was rude not to help her, but he dared not touch her in his present state. She might chide him for his lack of chivalry, but better that than having her discover his feelings.

"Troy?" She paused in front of him and smirked.

Dear heavens. Could she discern his thoughts? He took refuge in ignorance. "What?"

"I thought you wanted to go inside and eat."

"Yeah, that's what I said."

"Well, move your big ol' self outta the way. You're standing in front of the door, and I can't get around you."

He fought to control the color seeping up his neck. "Oh, sorry. My mind wandered off there a bit." He pushed at the sturdy wooden door and gestured for her to precede him.

"Where did it go off to, some girl you met up in Tennessee?" Scorn filled her voice.

"No. Why would you say that?"

She shrugged. "You had a funny look on your face, one I ain't never seen before. I just figured it had something to do with a girl. After all, you are nineteen now, and Lydia's always warned me about older boys."

"Men."

"What?"

"Fellows my age don't like to be called boys. We're men."

"If you say so."

Millie thumped her way over to the stove and added a couple of sticks to the fire.

Troy followed at a safe distance. He'd been here often enough to know where they kept everything, and he hated to have Millie wait on him in her condition.

"Why don't you sit on the sofa and let me tend to this? You can just yell out what I should do."

Her eyes went wide. "I can manage well enough." She bypassed the sofa on her way to the kitchen. "Lydia put the bowls on a shelf I can reach. I'm going to fry up a batch of corn-bread because it's faster and easier than puttin' it in the oven. It'll be ready in a few minutes."

He jumped away when she came too close. He needed to get out of here. "Uh, I believe I left my pack on the porch. I'll get it and set a trap over at the tree line."

"But the food will be..."

He didn't hear the rest as he rushed out the front door, grabbed his pack, and beat a hasty retreat across the side yard. Streaks of pink in the west reminded him to hurry through his task. Folks would be heading home from the mill in minutes. Though most of them lived in the company cottages closer to work, a few still maintained their small farms on the outskirts. Lydia's home hadn't functioned as a farm for more than a decade, and Cal had sold off small sections now and then to supplement their income.

Setting rabbit traps also gave him a chance to check on something he'd noticed while they'd lounged on the porch. He couldn't say he remembered seeing a figure, but a movement among the trees had triggered his instincts. He'd honed his senses to detect danger so long, he was afraid he would never be at ease again.

Keeping his eyes and ears alert, Troy laid traps without conscious thought to the familiar task. He found a slight impression on the ground where a ring of pine trees created a ragged square. This was the place ten-year-old Millie used to claim for her "house" and swept clean so she could designate each room and dare him to mess it up. It would also make a temporary resting place for anyone who wanted to watch the farmhouse. Beyond that possible footprint, he detected no cause for concern. No need to imagine trouble where none existed.

As he started back to the house, a lone figure approached from the direction of town. He studied the stride for a moment to be sure. "Thank God." The words slipped past his lips as the sway of skirts danced around the woman's feet.

Lydia was home.

CHAPTER 2

*M*illie found the change in Troy's behavior puzzling. He'd acted natural enough when he first arrived, calling her by the nickname she used to hate but missed hearing when he was gone. Then, all at once, he'd started acting skittish and strange, even volunteering to finish preparations for supper and urging her to rest.

He missed the chance to tease or berate her for her injury and stared at her like she was a stranger. Maybe all those months of hiding out had addled his brain. He probably saw soldiers in his sleep. Once he'd told them about an old woman who chased him off her yard with a broomstick. Likely that wasn't the worst treatment he'd received.

Millie set the cane aside so she could lift the soup pot with both hands. "Now that I could use his help, he's not here." She limped the few steps to the table and set the pot on the scarred surface. She blew out her breath. "Now for the cornbread."

When she heard footsteps and voices from the front porch, she stopped her movement so she could listen. Recognizing Lydia's laugh and Troy's playful banter, she heaved a sigh of relief. Being in the house by herself all day made her jumpy.

She was ready to be around people again. Too bad Troy wouldn't be one of those. He never stayed more than a day or two. It wasn't safe for him to stay longer this far east.

Lydia entered the house first, a smile dancing about her lips. "Look what the wind blew our way." She tossed a fond smile at Troy, and he draped an arm over her shoulders.

"You know I couldn't pass up a chance to visit my favorite aunt."

"Oh, go on with you and your charming McNeil smooth talk." Lydia swatted his arm and focused on Millie. "And our girl has supper already on the table. I'm feeling spoiled."

Millie shifted as Lydia scooted around her to grab the plate of cornbread.

Troy sprang to Millie's side and pulled out a chair for her. "Here you go. Get off that foot for a while."

She sat while Troy and Lydia made quick work of washing up, then took their seats. Troy uttered a brief prayer of thanks, and then Lydia dipped out the first bowl of soup and handed it to him. Millie passed him the cornbread, glad to see him acting more normal.

Conversation lagged as they concentrated on their meal. The food dwindled, and Lydia pushed back her chair and filled the kettle at the stove. "I'll put on water for chicory if anyone wants some."

Troy jumped up. "I plumb forgot. I brought you some real coffee beans." He sorted through his pack and held up a tin. The contents rolled around inside as he handed the tin to Lydia.

"Truly? How did you come by such a prize?" She popped open the lid and inhaled. "Ah, that smells like heaven."

"Well, as to how I come by them, that's a secret. Let's just say I traded my strong arm for someone glad for the assistance." A smile played about his lips, but color crept up his neck.

Millie gathered the dishes and ignored her uneasy suspicions about his cryptic answer. Why should it bother her if he flirted with some woman miles away? He was a free man, her cousin-by-marriage even. She had no claim on him. Did she want such a claim?

Rather than answer that, she washed the dishes while Lydia ground the beans and got the coffee brewing.

Troy stood at the front window, his hands in his pockets, peering into the darkness. Was he thinking about the trade he'd made for coffee beans?

Millie wrung out her dishrag and resisted the urge to throw it at him. Good thing he'd be gone in the morning.

$\sim$

JANUARY 29, 1864

*a*fter a night of fitful sleep, Troy cast aside the blanket, slipped on his boots, and emerged from the secret room. Family legend said his great-grandfather had built it during the Creek War half a century earlier. In recent years, it had served as a storage area. Two years before when he'd been visiting, Lydia had shoved him into the hidden space and pushed an armoire in front of the door to hide him from a couple of conscription officers scouring the county.

Lydia turned from the stove, where a pot of grits bubbled. "Good morning," she said. "Millie made a double batch of biscuits so you can take some with you. We still have a few jars of muscadine jelly, too, if you want that."

"Sounds good. Where is Millie?"

"Getting dressed. It takes her a little longer these days, with her hand still healing, but she refuses to let me help her. She insists moving it will speed the recovery. I think she's tired of staying home with nobody to talk to all day. Too bad you can't stay longer and keep her company."

Troy's heart sped up double-time at the suggestion. As much as that appealed to him, he panicked to consider he'd have to continue hiding his attraction to Millie. "I need to keep moving. Planning to visit Ma for a bit, maybe go over to see how Uncle Henry's doin' since June passed." His words rambled while his gaze swung back and forth to keep pace with her movements in the kitchen.

Lydia set a couple of plates on the table and cocked her head. "I'd forgotten about that. You give him our love. If I can find some paper, maybe I'll write him a letter on Sunday. Well, come on and eat. You and I both need to leave shortly. I'm sure Millie won't mind if we don't wait on her."

They sat and blessed the food.

Troy strained to hear Millie's approach, hoping he'd at least get the chance to say goodbye. He was half-way through his meal when Millie entered the room and took the vacant chair. He kept his focus on his plate until Lydia spoke.

"Well, aren't you turned out nice today?" She got up to pour more coffee and patted Millie's shoulder. "You thinking to visit the school?"

Troy glanced up in time to catch Millie's flash of surprise. He might've missed it otherwise.

She picked up her spoon. "If I can make it up the hill. Miss Trotter would probably be glad to let me listen to the students read, if nothing else."

"That's very thoughtful of you. I need to scat now, or I'll be gettin' an earful from Mr. Tippins." Lydia rose and snatched her coat and bonnet. "Troy, it's good to see you again. Be careful out there and come back anytime you can."

She tied her bonnet strings as he stood and handed her the tin with her lunch. She reached up to pat his cheek. "You know we're always glad to have you." She turned her attention to her stepdaughter. "Don't overdo it today."

After she left, Troy shook his head and grinned at Millie. "Some things never change."

She gazed back at him with an expression he couldn't decipher. Then again, some things changed when you least expected it.

⁓

*M*illie dropped her head to disguise the heat rising in her face. All her efforts to show Troy she'd grown up, and he never noticed.

But what did she expect? Having known her most of her life, he'd probably always consider her a child. At least Lydia had provided her with another reason for dressing up so she wouldn't appear completely addle-headed.

Troy rounded the kitchen table and picked up the empty bowls while Millie poured water into the dishpan.

"Why don't you let me wash these?" he asked. "You don't want to mess up your pretty dress."

"I'm going to let them soak a while, then I'll wash them later. After I get back from the school." She added some soap and turned his way, hoping her face didn't reveal her feelings. "Is there anything you need before you go?"

His eyes flashed with some message she couldn't read before he answered. "Um, no. I think I have everything. I just need to grab my pack." He motioned toward the room behind him but made no move in that direction.

"Don't forget the bundle of biscuits and jelly." She tapped the package. "You'll be glad for them in a few hours."

When did things get so awkward between them? Was it because of all the time apart, or had something happened during his time away? How could they get back to their old ways of easy banter and bickering?

Millie lifted the food bundle and stepped toward him,

forgetting her injured foot until the pain made her gasp and reach for support. The package tumbled to the floor.

Troy caught Millie in his arms, his face close to hers. "Careful there." His gaze bored into hers, his warm breath grazing her cheek.

Millie couldn't tear herself away. She leaned into him.

"Millie." He whispered her name and tightened his hold. When his lips covered hers, she wilted like a sapling in July heat. She clutched his shoulders to stay upright while he pulled her closer.

He ended the kiss and pressed his lips to her cheek, her temple, her ear.

Millie's heart sang as Troy whispered sweet words against her skin.

"Millie, my sweet love. I've been thinking about you ever since I was here in the fall. Can't get you off my mind. I shouldn't have come back, but I couldn't stay away."

She didn't know how to respond. Didn't he know she'd loved him for years? She reveled in his confession but dared not speak and break the spell.

When his breathing slowed, Troy pecked the corner of her mouth and then pulled away, resting his forehead against hers. "Ah, Millie. What are we going to do?"

~

*H*e left as planned. What other choice was there? Staying in any place too long put him at risk of being found and sent to fight. The notion of killing anyone sickened him. He had no skills that would exempt him from service to the Confederacy. To announce his Unionist views would be a one-way ticket to hell on earth. Word was a new prison was being built in Andersonville, just a two- or three-day ride south of here. That was a place he had no desire to see.

He groaned. He'd had no business kissing Millie like that, letting his passion rule his head. When she stumbled into his arms, he should've set her on her feet and run out the door. But he hadn't. He'd yielded to the temptation, then had to force himself to leave before matters progressed beyond his control.

He kicked a stone in his path. "Stupid, that's what you are, Troy Harrison McNeil. A cad and a bounder to boot." He continued berating himself. Why, Millie was practically his kin. Not related by flesh, of course, but through Lydia's marriage to Cal.

Lydia would skin him alive when she found out. That brought him up short. Would Millie tell Lydia what happened? Did women talk about those things the way men did? He prayed they didn't. What could he say to excuse his behavior?

~

*M*illie jammed her lips together and forced back the need to scream again. No one would hear. Her gaze shifted from the unkempt man tugging on her hair to the long-handled knife in his other hand. His mismatched clothes—some from a uniform, others civilian—showed ground-in dirt. He smelled as though he'd tussled with an angry polecat.

"Now you just keep that mouth of your'n closed tight so's I won't have to carve up your purdy face or cut this long yeller hair." The man dragged her away from the front door toward the kitchen. He held the knife inches from her nose. She had no doubt he would use it.

She managed to nod. "What do you want? You're welcome to the food."

His black eyes glinted. He grinned to reveal a missing front tooth. "Now that's more like it. You and me are gonna get along fine, now that I finally have you to myself." He urged her toward the kitchen.

"I need my cane." It had slipped from her grasp and clattered to the floor when he seized her at the front door.

"No, you don't. We'll walk together, real close-like. I'll hold you up." He loosened his hold on her hair and wrapped his arm behind her. His fetid breath blew hot across her temple. His beard scraped the side of her face.

She shuddered as his leg pressed against hers and urged her forward. "Get that basket and fill it with what I tell you."

Millie hastened to comply, loading the basket with bread, jars of jelly, canned beans and tomatoes, plus the last onion from the shelves. She glanced toward the secret room and gave silent thanks that Troy had slid the armoire back to cover its entrance. The extra provisions hidden there would be safe.

"That all you got? I thought I smelt coffee last night."

Last night? He'd been prowling around since last night? While the three of them ate and chattered about old times, this ruffian had spied on them and planned his attack? How had they not noticed?

Millie huffed, hoping to dissuade him from searching the house. "Must be your imagination. I don't know how you think we'd be able to buy coffee."

He harrumphed but seemed to accept her explanation. "Put the basket on the table there." He propelled her in that direction. She set it down, glad to have her hands free again. She rubbed her sore wrist and prayed he'd take his leave.

Her captor tossed his knife on the table and pinned her arms to her sides with his tortuous grip. He turned her toward the hall and moved in the direction of the bedrooms. "Now we can have some fun."

CHAPTER 3

*P*erspiration beaded on Troy's forehead. He peered at the sky. The temperature rose as the sun climbed higher. He'd put on his coat when he set out, though the weather was mild enough. If he took it off, he'd have to carry it. No matter. The day promised to be a warm one, so he slipped off the pack and removed the jacket. Maybe he could hook it over his haversack. He liked to travel with his hands free. No telling when he might run across a fruit tree or a berry bush, even in winter. It stretched his food stores.

Troy came to a sudden halt as he remembered his traps back in the woods near Millie and Lydia's place.

How could he have forgotten? Those traps could make the difference between life and death for him. He'd been too wrapped up in what had happened and left in a hurry to escape the temptation Millie presented.

He reversed his steps, keeping as far from the house as practicable, and stomped to the place where he'd left them. One trap was empty, the bait missing, but the other yielded a plump rabbit. He held the furry creature aloft. "Where have you been eating, my fat friend? Somebody must have a winter garden hidden somewhere."

He examined the area for wild vegetation and froze at the sight of a cleared space—evidence of someone lurking in the woods. A frisson of alarm sizzled from head to toe. He searched farther back and found an empty tin next to a pile of pine straw. Someone had camped here recently. He'd better check on Millie before he left the area.

He didn't take time to skin and clean his prize catch, just wrapped it in a piece of cloth. He stuffed the traps in his pack and set off again. As he stepped from the woods into the sunshine, a woman's scream pierced the air. It came from Lydia's house.

Troy dropped his pack and sprinted to the house. The front door stood wide open.

Crouching below the windows, he crept down one side of the building and peeked around the corner. All clear there, with the back door firmly shut.

He neared the kitchen window and peered in. Nothing moved inside. He eased onto the back porch and put his ear to the door. The wood muffled any sound from inside, but he detected voices and scuffling. A man's harsh voice. The ring of a slap and crying.

Troy jerked open the back door and burst inside, all thoughts of stealth and caution gone. He grabbed a knife lying on the table. Three long strides took him to Millie's room, where she struggled in the grip of an intruder.

Troy's anger exploded. He launched himself against the man.

Troy's momentum carried them both crashing to the floor. The attacker howled in outrage. Troy drove the knife toward the stranger's back.

The man shifted, whipped his arm out, and sent the

weapon flying across the room toward the fireplace in the far wall.

Troy smashed a fist into the dirty face. He wrapped his hands around the sweaty neck and squeezed.

The man's eyes bulged as he fought against the pressure. Desperate fingers clutched at Troy's shoulders. One leg swept over Troy's as the stranger surged and flipped their positions. Troy's youth and quickness worked to his advantage as he used the same tactic to remain in control.

Millie's ragged weeping behind him flooded Troy with another wave of rage. The man attempted to wrestle free, but Troy pushed hard against him, gripping the miscreant's neck harder. Spying the poker at the edge of the fireplace, he lunged to reach it.

Quick to react to Troy's shift from him, the man scrambled away. He punched a fist into Troy's kidney. Turned to run. Troy launched after him, grabbed his feet, and yanked him backward. The man's hands flew out and slapped the floor. He bucked and twisted, reaching toward Troy's face. Troy landed a blow to his jaw, propelling him backward.

The stranger's head smacked the row of bricks at the hearth, the sudden thud overriding their grunts and growls. His black eyes rolled in their sockets, and his head lolled to one side.

It took Troy a moment to catch his breath and realize the fight was over. He bent forward to listen for a heartbeat. Nothing. He jerked away from the unseeing eyes.

Troy turned to check on Millie, who cowered near the wall, struggling against rope that circled her wrists. Her frantic gaze met his as he moved to loosen the knots.

"You're safe," he whispered, his clumsy fingers fumbling with the coarse fibers. "It's all right now, sweetheart. You're safe."

The knots gave way, and he gathered her in his arms.

She dissolved into racking shudders and sobs. "I tried...to fi-fight him...off."

Troy stroked the hair that tumbled down her back. "I know. I know. You did well. Thank God you screamed and I was close enough to hear it."

He should feel remorse at taking a man's life, but he felt only relief that Millie was safe. Maybe he'd regret it later. He knew he should, but she was all right, and for now, nothing else mattered.

At least, he hoped she was all right. He couldn't imagine how terrified she must have been. He ought to see if that monster had hurt her physically.

Her fists had knotted in Troy's shirt, but she let go when he shifted away. Glancing at the sight of her chemise beneath the gaping halves of her bodice, he groaned, his stomach filling with acid. Buttons dangled from the ripped fabric. He gazed back at her tear-streaked face, which wrenched his heart. He hated what he had to do now.

"Millie, I need to...I need to remove the body." He tilted his head toward the intruder. "So you don't have to see it. Maybe you can get cleaned up while I do that?"

Fearful eyes searched his face. She clutched his arms. "You won't leave, will you?"

He tugged her hands off his shirt. "Of course not. Is the wheelbarrow still in the old smokehouse?"

"I think so." As if suddenly aware of her dishabille, she crossed her arms over her bosom.

He leaned forward to kiss her forehead. "I'll be right back."

He squatted beside the lifeless figure and thrust his hands under the arms. Walking backward, he half carried, half dragged the man's body from the bedroom and dropped him by the back door. He sprinted across the yard to the smaller building that housed garden tools. It took a moment to locate and empty the wheelbarrow, then he rolled it to the house. Taking a deep breath, he lifted the body into the cart.

He called to Millie from the back door. "I'm closing the door behind me now, but I'll be back in a few minutes."

She peeked around the corner from the hall, clutching a robe over her torn dress. "Please, hurry." Her voice was small, bringing back memories of the little girl she used to be.

Emotion pricked his eyes. "I will. Sit and rest until I get back."

He closed the door and hauled the evidence of his act of violence into the woods.

~

Millie hobbled to the kitchen table and plopped into a chair. She stared at the basket of food she'd collected earlier and shuddered. Perhaps Troy could take it with him. But no, their stores were low. Somehow, she would find the strength to put those items away.

She'd disgorged her breakfast into the chamber pot after Troy removed the body. Chills had taken hold, so she wrapped her robe around herself. Not able to stay in that room any longer, she'd balanced against the wall as she'd shambled to the main living area.

Crossing her arms on the table, she put her head down. What would happen now? Should they report the incident? A harsh laugh escaped her mouth, the sound loud in the empty room. The only authority figures left in town were mill managers and one preacher. She couldn't imagine any of them wanting to take charge of the situation. Besides, most of them would consider Troy a coward for dodging the conscription. It would be a small step to label him a killer and send him to prison. No, she and Troy had to keep this a secret. Even Lydia mustn't know, for her safety as well as theirs. With the town's citizens divided in their loyalties, such an incident could shatter the fragile peace, and who knew where it would lead?

She didn't feel up to answering anyone's questions.

Millie glanced around, viewing the kitchen and pantry from her position. She and Troy would have to clean everything before Lydia came home. Make the house appear the same as it had a couple of hours ago.

She stood, searching for her cane. The sight of it brought back the man's harsh voice in her ear, the feel of his hands on her—

No! She pushed those thoughts away. She would not let them control her.

With cleaning in mind, she hobbled to the stove and set a pot of water on to boil. Determination gave her strength. There was much to do before sunset.

~

*T*he sun neared its zenith as Troy strode back to the house. He worried about Millie. How would she bear up after this? How dare that man do such a thing to an innocent girl like Millie?

If that man wasn't already dead, he'd hunt him down and kill him again. And it wouldn't be an accident this time.

He had to rein in his anger, no easy feat, if he wanted to concentrate on helping her recover.

He opened the door and called so he wouldn't frighten her. "Millie? Where are you?"

"Over here." She stood at the table, a worn robe over her clothes. He ached to fold her in his arms but feared what might happen. He wouldn't risk frightening her further.

With tentative steps, he moved closer. "Why don't you sit and rest? Just tell me what you need me to do."

She shook her head. "Troy, we have to get this place cleaned up. Anything he touched must be washed or wiped down. We can't let anyone know what happened today."

He stared at her, absorbing her words, and taking in her strained appearance. He'd never seen her so adamant. "Maybe we need to discuss this." He reached out to touch her but dropped his hand when she flinched. "You're in no condition to do heavy work, so you tell me what to do—"

"I've already figured it out. I'll get the wash water ready while you check the bedroom for any, um, evidence that needs to be removed."

Her blue eyes pleaded with him. "Can you take time to do that before you leave?"

"You know I will, but as to my leaving—"

"I don't want to talk about it right now. I've already got wash water heatin' on the back of the stove. You go start on the bedroom, please."

Troy hustled to do her bidding. Together, they cleaned or covered all traces of a disturbance inside and around the house. With the sun shining and a steady breeze from the south, the bedding dried in a couple of hours. The spot on the hearth where the stranger struck his head took some scrubbing, but it eventually yielded as well.

Millie stayed in the hall and gave instructions while he cleaned up the room. At last, she ventured in. Her glance flitted about, judging the contents, while tears clouded her vision. She still wore the robe over the damaged dress.

Troy joined her at the doorway. "Millie, darlin', you should probably change clothes. Looks as though you'll have to do some mendin'." He cleared his throat. "We also need to know how badly he hurt you and decide whether you require any doctorin'. Will you trust me to help you?"

He brushed the hair from her face and flinched when he saw a thin red line near one ear. Without thinking, he placed his lips on the spot, as if she were a child who believed a kiss would make it better.

The pain returned to her eyes. "He barged in and caught me by surprise. I gathered the food he wanted, so he'd leave. But then he...he bound my hands and dragged me into this room..." Sobs slurred her voice. She motioned toward the place the man had died. "How will I ever be able to sleep here again?"

A spate of tears cascaded down her cheeks, and Troy swiped at them with his thumbs. "Shh. You're safe now." He dropped his gaze to her neck where fingerprints reddened the skin. Her dress collar should cover them. His fingers feathered over the marks, and Millie's head tipped to allow the touch.

Her breath hitched, and his gaze returned to her face. "I'm sorry, darlin'. I didn't mean to hurt you."

Her hair swirled as she shook her head. "You didn't." She took a deep breath and gave him a tremulous smile. "You did a fine job putting the room back to rights. Thank you for taking care of...everything."

With effort, he stepped away from the temptation to hold her close. "I found a rabbit in my traps from last night. I'll go start it cooking while you change clothes."

~

*A*n hour later, Troy pulled his coat tighter over his damp shirt and knocked on the Tuckers' back door. Their place was a brisk ten-minute walk from Lydia's but closer to town, so he had to be cautious. He'd checked the windows to be sure Mrs. Tucker was in the kitchen alone. He kept watch to be sure no one had seen him while he waited for her to answer the summons.

She opened the door and turned away. Without speaking,

he helped her move the table and rug covering the trapdoor. "Have you eaten recently?" Her voice was low, though nobody was around to hear.

"Yes'm. I saw Samuel near the Tennessee line last month. He said tell you he's well."

Tears sprang into the tired brown eyes, but the wrinkles increased as she smiled. "He's a good boy. Like you, Troy." She stood back to let him descend into the chilly space. "There're several blankets, but I'll heat a couple bricks for you. How long will you stay?"

"Just tonight, thank you."

She turned, but he called her back. "I thought you ought to know, I'm pretty sure I saw somebody lurkin' in the woods near the Gibson farm. Y'all need to be careful." Maybe someone would search the area. If they found the man, they'd assume he died there.

Her eyes widened. Then she gave a brisk nod. "I believe I'll ask the home guard to check it out. You get some rest. I'll call you in the morning when it's safe to come out."

In the hidden basement, Troy set down his knapsack and spread the blankets over the single bed. He removed his boots and wiggled his toes inside the heavy socks Millie had pressed on him. It comforted him to know people like the Tuckers understood his feelings about the war. Not only that, but they also put themselves on the line by providing for the young men who held true to their convictions. He'd only stayed there once before, always preferring to stay with family. But Cal had been home then, and Troy didn't want to intrude and cause contention.

Mrs. Tucker would get someone to search the woods where he'd deposited the body. They should find it without much trouble. Hopefully, they'd assume the man had knocked his head on one of the nearby boulders. Whatever they did from there, it was out of Troy's hands.

Once he made sure Millie had recovered and learned how to defend herself in case of another assault, he would be on the road again. But his heart would remain.

~

JANUARY 30, 1864

*M*illie grabbed the knife before she limped to the back door. It was probably Troy, but she wouldn't be caught off guard again. During a sleepless night, she'd concocted all kinds of ways she should have defended herself.

She waved the knife in Troy's face as she opened the door. He grinned, but his eyes widened. "I hope you aren't planning to use that on me?"

She huffed and lowered her arm. "Not you, but likely anyone else who wears trousers."

"Good." He dropped his pack, pulled off his coat, and closed the door. "I decided I ought to give you a lesson or two in how to protect yourself before I leave. Guess I should've done it sooner." He gestured toward the hallway. "Let's move where there's no furniture or rugs."

Millie put down the knife and grasped his arm as he led the way.

"How's your ankle?"

"It aches some, but I can manage if I don't put my weight on it for long."

Troy nodded. "I'll try to be careful of it." He stopped between the bedrooms and faced her. "Now, there's a few places you should aim for whenever a man comes at you. His eyes, his ears, his beard if he has one, and his, um, crotch."

Millie ought to be embarrassed by that word. If it were

anyone but Troy, she would have been. This was too important to be priggish. "All right. What do I do?"

"It depends on how big he is and how he comes at you. You could poke his eyes." He demonstrated with his fingers. "You might box his ears." His eyes twinkled when he smirked. "There's a reason mothers do that. Be sure to keep your hand flat and put all your strength into it."

Millie considered, reaching her hands to cover Troy's ears. "I can do that as long as the man's not too tall."

"In that case, pull his beard or his hair if you can reach it. However, the most effective tactic is to jab your knee into his crotch. I'd rather you not practice that one, but let's see if you can remember the others."

They tried a few maneuvers with Troy playing the attacker. She was learning she had to act fast and not give the man time to trap her.

"What if I don't see him and he comes up behind me?" Millie leaned against the wall to take the weight off her foot.

Instead of answering, Troy pointed to her foot. "Your ankle hurtin' you?"

"A little."

"Let's go in here so you can prop it on the chair. I don't want you falling when I grab you from behind." He slipped his arm around her waist, and she leaned into him.

Millie's head lolled against his shoulder as she raised her eyes. He smelled of soap and bergamot. She grinned as they shuffled toward her room. "You smell like Mr. Tucker."

"Oh? And how do you know how Mr. Tucker smells?" He spoiled the frown meant to rebuke her when he waggled his eyebrows.

"He always hugged each child at church. I think he wore the cologne to cover the smell of tobacco, which the preacher didn't like. He gave the best hugs."

"Well, I give good hugs too." He drew her fully into his

embrace. The playful mood evaporated in a moment as he gazed at her and lowered his head. His lips touched her forehead, and Millie melted. She leaned forward to kiss his jaw and walked her lips closer to his.

Troy slanted his mouth to meet hers. Their breaths mingled in a gentle dance of giving and receiving comfort. Millie pressed closer, burrowing into the shelter of his arms, her safe place.

~

*T*roy's heart picked up speed. She had no idea how she tormented him. His hands slipped to her arms, prepared to push her away. In a moment. After he kissed her once more. She tugged his head, her small hands weaving into his hair.

He dragged in a breath. "Millie, you don't...I need to..."

She shook her head, her lips grazing his cheek. "I don't want you to go yet. Please."

Looking into her eyes, Troy noted the haze of desire and, behind it, the fear. What was she afraid of? That he'd hurt her?

"I need you, Troy." Her voice was soft and raspy. "I need you to make me forget that man yesterday. Help me replace that awful memory with a good one." She clutched his shoulders. "I love you. I've always loved you."

"Millie, you don't know—"

"Yes, I do." She didn't let him finish. "I know what I feel. Please don't deny me."

"Ah, darlin', I don't know how it happened," he said between fevered kisses, "but I love you too. I'm awful sorry I wasn't here to protect you from that monster. I can never make it up to you."

"Yes, you can, Troy." Her eyebrows dipped into a *V* above

eyes glinting with determination. "Right now. You can make it better. I want you to help me forget."

He hesitated, and she sighed into his ear. "Please."

Heaven help him, he couldn't deny her. But would he make matters better or worse? And how would he live with himself either way?

$\sim$

"The mill still lets out early on Saturday, right? I've gotta go before Lydia gets home." Troy stuffed the last bite of cornbread in his mouth and pushed away from the table. He shouldered his pack and embraced Millie for one last, lingering farewell.

"I wish you could stay." Millie's whispered words squeezed his heart. Did she realize how much he dreaded going?

"Millie." He kissed her forehead. "We should've waited, but with this war...I want you to know there's no one else but you for me. One day, when this trouble is over, I will make it official. If I knew Rev. Bagley wouldn't shoot me on sight, I'd go fetch him now." Someone had suggested the preacher might be a Confederate informant. Troy didn't think so, but he had to be careful.

She sniffed and gave him a watery smile. "I think he's still at his daughter's house in Marietta, anyway. I read that in Scotland, a couple is considered married just by saying so."

"Really? Well, then." He cleared his throat and held her hands in his. "I, Troy Harrison McNeil, take you, Millicent Anne Gibson, to be my wife. Will you have pity on this poor Alabama boy and accept him as your husband?"

Tears filled her eyes, but she dashed them away and nodded. "I will."

Forcing a lighter tone to cover his own emotion, he chided. "Oh, you have to say the whole thing. Say I Millicent..."

She swallowed and attempted a smile. "I, Millicent Anne Gibson, take you, Troy Harrison McNeil, to be my husband."

Troy placed a chaste kiss on her cheek. He shifted his knapsack and left by the rear door. No way could he look back. Her tears would wear down his resistance. He'd let the sun dry his own.

CHAPTER 4

FEBRUARY 16, 1864
CAMPBELL COUNTY, GEORGIA

*M*illie groaned as she rolled over and retched into the chamber pot. Would this ague never let up? She'd been sick all week, whereas Lydia had gotten over her illness in a couple of days.

Millie wiped her mouth and flopped back on the bed. Her stepmother peeked into her room. "You're still suffering with it?" Lydia asked. "Poor dear. Do you think you could keep down a bit of bread and some tea? I know that's all I could eat the first day afterward."

Millie shuddered and retreated under her blankets. "Maybe in a while. Right now, I just want to sleep." *And pray the nightmares stay away.* Hardly a night passed that she didn't wake up fighting off a phantom. The only way she could get back to sleep was to recite the Lord's Prayer or the twenty-third Psalm several times.

"Will you be all right if I go to work? I hate to leave you, but with this sickness going around, the mill is short-handed."

Lydia rolled a thick log onto Millie's fireplace. "I hope this cold spell breaks soon. We may need to get Reverend Bagley to help us take down another tree." She fastened her heavy cloak and pulled on her gloves. "I'll put on some tea to steep, in case you want to try it later."

"I'll be fine, Lydia. Tell them I'll try to come in tomorrow."

"Don't push yourself to do anything. I'll be home as soon as I can."

Millie waited to hear the door close, then wrapped the blanket around her and hurried through the house. She dropped the bar across both doors and scooted back to her bedroom. Ever since the attack last month, she'd been more cautious when she was in the house alone. The recent reports of stolen food across the area had convinced Lydia to add the extra protection on both doors.

Willing her stomach to remain calm, Millie poured the tea and grabbed an extra pair of socks before she headed back to bed. She closed the bedroom door to keep the warmth inside. The tea soothed her stomach. Cocooned within the covers, she settled down to sleep again, praying for relief from her ailment and dreamless sleep.

$\sim$

APRIL 10, 1864
CAMPBELL COUNTY, GEORGIA

*M*illie's sickness had finally passed, or at least it had become more manageable. She could eat most foods now, as long as she took small portions. Lydia might have noticed but didn't remark on her eating habits or her recent moodiness. However, she did mention Millie's blossoming figure, which had been slender but now showed definite curves.

"I'm so glad to see your health improving." Lydia closed the front door, and they set out on their walk to church. "The turn in weather certainly lifts my spirits. Did you notice the azaleas have started to bloom?"

Millie flung her arms wide and welcomed the sunshine on her face. "Yes. How glad I am to see spring come our way. Even with the war still going on, it gives me hope that things will improve before long."

Reverend Bagley's sermon carried a similar message. "It's no accident," he said, "that we celebrate our Lord's resurrection in springtime. He made the flowers to bloom and the animals to come out of their hibernation as a reminder to us that He is the giver of life. We can do nothing better than put our trust and our hope in Him."

Lydia and Millie returned home to a simple meal and tasks reserved for Sunday—needlework, mending, and sometimes letter writing. Millie longed to write to Troy, but Lydia would think it strange when they had no idea if he was with his parents or another relative. Besides, paper was getting scarce, and she didn't dare pour out her feelings in writing, in case the missive fell into someone's hands other than Troy's.

Millie stabbed her needle into a section of coarse bombazine and jumped when it pricked her finger. At the same time, Lydia clutched her middle and cried out. "Oh, my!"

"Lydia? What's wrong?"

Lydia deserted her chair and raced to her room. "Nothing bad," she called back. "I'll be right back. I just have to take care of something."

Millie sucked on her injured finger and waited. Should she check on her stepmother? She didn't want to intrude, but Lydia's abrupt agitation worried her. Millie laid down her project and slipped to the front bedroom door. She gave it a soft rap. "Lydia?"

"It's all right." Lydia opened the door, clad in her nightgown. She presented a wobbly smile. "I had a sudden attack of cramps and was afraid I'd soiled my clothes. I'm going to lie down for a bit. You know how it hits me at times. Perhaps resting will lessen the pain."

Millie nodded. "Can I get anything for you? A cup of tea or a hot brick for your back?"

"Either one would be wonderful, but don't feel you have to wait on me."

"You've taken care of me for years. It's the least I can do. Go on and lie down."

Millie stoked the fire in the stove and slid a flattened brick into the oven. She added more water to the kettle and measured out the tea. Waiting for the water to boil, she considered Lydia's discomfort. Poor thing. Lydia never knew when nature would pop up for her. She thought that probably accounted for her not being able to conceive a child. Millie's time, on the other hand, had been as consistent as—

"Wait," she said aloud. "What day of the month is this?"

The water boiled, and Millie poured it over the tea leaves. While it steeped, she ran to her room to search for the small book she used to record important information. She flipped through the pages until she found her last notation. January eighteenth? Had it been that long? What happened to February and March? What did this mean?

The words from a conversation she'd overheard at work last week came back to her. "I told Maybelle I bet she's in the family way, what with her bein' sick ever' mornin' and her bodice fittin' tight. Then she confessed her time was late, and I knew it. I was right."

In the family way? No, it couldn't be. It was that terrible bout of ague that messed up her system. It'd happened before, a few years ago, when everyone in town had experienced a similar stomach upset. Millie was sure everything would return to normal soon enough. No need to worry.

~

*I*solation gave a man too much time to think, and thinking could turn to worry if a man wasn't careful. Lately, Troy's thoughts bordered on worry as he recalled how easily that renegade had overpowered Millie.

The rage that had gripped Troy on that day concerned him. He'd never considered himself capable of killing a human. With few exceptions, killing was a sin. It was one reason he roamed around, avoiding those men who would coerce him into their ranks.

But then, without hesitation, he'd become a killer. And he didn't regret it.

Witnessing the life go out of that man didn't move him, not while Millie sobbed behind him. His attention had centered on the one he loved.

After dumping the body, Troy had wiped down the wheelbarrow and returned to the house. As he washed his hands at the kitchen sink, he recited a verse from the Psalms as a prayer and penance. "Hide thy face from my sins and blot out all mine iniquities."

He'd asked for forgiveness, but he couldn't find the remorse he ought to feel at taking a man's life. Even now, he'd do it again if he faced a similar situation.

Troy worked the pump behind Uncle Henry's house to wash off dirt from the field. He'd waved goodbye to Ma a month ago. Contention in the family had doubled when Paul came home minus half a leg, bitter and belligerent. His oldest brother glowered at everyone, even his two young'uns, but Troy was a prime target because of his refusal to fight for the South.

The battlefield had extended into North Alabama and Georgia, and Ma insisted he travel farther south to avoid the advance patrols. "But not too far south," she'd said. "I heard there's a lot of fightin' around Mobile Bay. Maybe you could stay a while with Henry or at Ellis's farm. I imagine either one of them would be glad to put you up. They can always use more help on their property."

Troy decided on Henry, who was older and alone since his wife had passed. Henry could surely use the help, with his family all scattered, although his fields mostly lay fallow. Besides that, Henry believed in his privacy and kept to himself. There wouldn't be a constant flow of neighbors dropping by his house as would be likely at Ellis's place. Less chance of Troy encountering neighbors while he was in residence.

A man of few words, Henry hadn't asked questions when Troy showed up at his door. "You can take the back room. If'n you can cook, you're welcome to whatever's in the larder. I'll eat anythin' you want to fix. Come outside, and I'll show you where I aim to plant this year."

Troy welcomed the hard labor and the luxury of sleeping in a bed. The mattress was lumpy, but it beat lying on the hard ground. He finally figured out how to use the stove and enjoyed the canned items Henry's wife had put up before she died last year. Though drought and marauding soldiers had plagued much of the South, the central part of Alabama escaped the worse of it.

Life almost seemed normal here, sheltered from the ravages of war. But things would never be as they were. Before the war.

Before he killed a man.

Before he fell in love.

His mind kept wandering back to Campbell County and the girl who'd stolen his heart. Who could have predicted the young'un who'd annoyed him for years would be the one he longed to see again?

Soon as he finished with Henry's planting, he planned to return and make certain she was safe. As the Union army moved steadily south, conditions could change without notice.

~

MAY 15, 1864
CAMPBELL COUNTY

*M*illie could no longer deny her condition. She'd discreetly let out the seams in her clothes, but it did little to hide her expanding middle. She didn't sleep well at night and could barely make it through the workday. The truth hit her hard when she felt movement inside. It filled her with fear and awe.

How could she tell Lydia, who'd yearned for a babe and been denied year after year? But Lydia was her only family now. How could she *not* tell her? But she couldn't reveal everything. Millie and Troy had vowed to tell no one about the attack, and she couldn't bring herself to name Troy as the father without telling the whole story.

Troy hadn't written since early March, when he'd let them know he'd arrived home safely. Millie had no idea where he might be now, and even if she did, it would be foolish to write him. How would he take the news that they'd created a child?

She grappled with how to handle this new dilemma. The child was Troy's, but nobody must know that until she could tell Troy herself. She alone bore the blame for her condition, for she shouldn't have pressed him to stay. Did she even deserve God's forgiveness?

After praying more than she'd prayed in her life, Millie accepted that she'd have to tell Lydia some half-truth. Lydia must have figured it out already, but she wouldn't ask Millie about it outright. Her friend as much as her stepmother, Lydia treated her as an equal. Her questioning glances carried a degree of hurt.

Millie shored up her courage on Sunday morning as they prepared for church. She leaned against the door to Lydia's bedroom and chewed her lip. "I have something to tell you. I should have told you sooner, but I just couldn't figure out what to say."

Lydia put down her hairbrush and gave Millie her full attention. "Then I'll save you the trouble. I believe we're going to have a wee one in our house before the year is out. Is that it?"

Tears pricked Millie's eyes as she nodded. "How long have you known?"

"Not as long as I should have. I kept finding other reasons for the changes I noticed." She bowed her head. "Perhaps it boils down to jealousy. I'm sorry I've let you carry this burden alone. Please forgive me." She stood, opened her arms, and Millie flew into them.

When she pulled back to wipe her nose and eyes, Millie forced a smile. "Thank you. I knew I could count on you, but I was afraid you might be angry or upset with me."

"Now, what good would that do? We must accept what's happened and go on. I must ask you, though, does the father know?"

"Not yet." Millie dropped her head. "I haven't been able to get word to him."

"Do you want me to help with that?"

"No. I will do so as soon as I can."

Lydia tilted her head and sighed. "You're not going to tell me who it is, are you?"

Millie pressed her lips together to keep from blurting the whole story. "I can't." She hated not sharing, but Troy was Lydia's favorite nephew, and Millie didn't want to affect their relationship.

Lydia patted her hand. "Well, that's not the most important thing right now. What we must do is make sure you stay healthy. You should probably quit work soon."

And take a chance on someone else catching her alone in the house? No, thank you. "I want to stay on at the mill as long as I can, Lydia. We'll have to put some money by for whenever the baby comes and I'll have to quit."

"Well, that's still a ways off. Maybe something else will work out before then. Too bad there's no doctor available. I'll ask around for a midwife 'cause you know I won't be much good when the time comes."

~

MAY 16, 1864
RANDOLPH COUNTY, ALABAMA

*T*roy cussed the cow all the way to the house. Pain and frustration tainted his language with colorful words he'd never used before. Pain from his broken leg—in two places, no less—and frustration that he'd have to postpone his trip to Georgia yet again.

Henry spent no time scolding him but left right away to fetch the closest doctor. The physician's assessment caused as much anguish as his examination and treatment.

The doctor spat a stream of tobacco juice into the yard before he rummaged through his black bag. He extracted a paper packet, which he pushed into Troy's hand. "I'd give you laudanum, but we can't get any 'cause of the Yanks blocking transportation. This here's willow bark. You can make tea with it and drink it to ease the pain." He winked at Henry, who stood nearby. "O' course, a shot of whiskey might help too."

Troy gritted his teeth. "How long before I can walk on it, Doc?"

"I'll leave you a crutch you can use for a while, but only for goin' to the outhouse for the next few days. After that, you can gradually be up longer, but don't put any weight on that leg until I see how it's mending. I'll come back around in three or four weeks."

Three or four weeks? That'd be mid-June. Troy rolled a few more of those choice words around in his brain. If he had a rifle, he'd go kill that blasted cow. After he killed the snake that sprang up and sent her into a frenzied fit. Of course, if he had a gun, he could've saved them all a harrowing afternoon and simply dispatched the snake with a well-placed shot. There were times a firearm came in mighty handy.

Troy abandoned his angry indignation at hearing the doctor's final warning to Henry. "You let me know if he develops a fever. The bones should heal fine, but that scrape bears watching. An infection could kill him."

With those comforting words, the doctor left the house. He must have let slip about Troy's mishap as he visited a nearby farm. Before long, each of Henry's closest neighbors came to gape and offer advice. With his current injuries, no one would go to the trouble of reporting his presence to the Confederates.

His most frequent visitor, motherly Mrs. Varner, brought her young son and three daughters, ranging from ten to sixteen. How they figured it was helpful to pile in on an injured man, Troy would never know. At least they did bring some victuals each time.

After a while, the novelty wore off, and their own chores kept them away. All except sixteen-year-old Becky Varner and Bobby Ray, her eight-year-old brother. Troy didn't mind the boy so much, but Becky's incessant chatter grated more and more.

Uncle Henry tired of it also and intervened at last. "Becky, you might as well stop coming over, makin' up to the lad and hopin' you'll turn his head. He's done lost his heart to a girl over in Georgia and aims to head back thataway soon's he's healed."

Surprised by his uncle's perception, Troy almost missed Becky's outraged expression. "Well, he should've told me that straight off instead of leadin' me on." She rounded on Troy. "I wonder how many more women you've played up to in all your gallivantin' around the country, Mr. McNeil. Guess you're just like the rest of the—"

"That's enough, Becky." Henry's usual good nature evaporated. "Now git on home, and don't come back till you can mind your manners."

The buxom brunette slammed out of the house, calling her brother from his favorite perch in the spreading oak tree. "C'mon, Bobby Ray. We got chores waitin' at home."

Troy rested his head against the rocker's back and sighed. "Thanks, Henry. I didn't want to insult your neighbors, but that gal was gettin' hard to take."

Henry sniffed and turned away. "Just like her mama, she'll latch onto a body like a deer tick if'n you ain't careful. Knowin' you plan to leave, I don't cotton to havin' her hangin' around here. With all the young men away, she might decide to settle for an old geezer like me."

~

JULY 8, 1864
CAMPBELL COUNTY, GEORGIA

*M*illie turned from the stove when a noise at the front door drew her attention. She'd left both doors open, hoping to let any breeze flow through while she prepared supper. Why had she let down her guard?

A Union soldier strode through the front room and into the kitchen. He halted when he saw her. Raking his gaze from her face to her bare feet then up again, he slanted her a seductive smile. "Well, hello there, beautiful. I came hunting for supper items, but I believe I've found dessert."

Millie raised the knife she'd used to peel the potatoes. Anger pulsed through her veins. "You Yanks have already stripped our garden bare, so just get on outta here. We ain't got enough to feed ourselves anymore."

He set his knapsack on the table and eased toward her like a bobcat stalking its prey. "I've lost all interest in the food you have. What I'm wantin' now is much sweeter."

With a sudden move, he knocked the knife from her fingers and gripped her arms. He pushed his face close to hers. "I always did like blondes with a little fire."

Millie's mind flew back several months to the day another stranger had held her captive. Desperation gave her the strength to wrestle from his grasp, but he grabbed her around the waist. She twisted around and punched his face.

"Ow, you little witch! You'll pay for that."

He held a fist to his bleeding nose and started toward her again. She backed against the stove. Her fingers found the cold frying pan, and she raised it.

Voices from outside called, and he spun around. Yanking his kerchief from his neck, the soldier pressed it to his nose. He snatched his knapsack but paused at the doorway and pointed his finger her way. "I'll be back for you, Miss High and Mighty." His gaze dropped to her belly. "Looks like you've been free with your favors before, and I don't mind takin' somebody else's place." Then he stalked away.

Millie sank into a kitchen chair and set the pan on the table. Shaking from the confrontation, she couldn't find the strength to rise for several minutes.

Lydia's voice roused her. "Millie? Millie, are you unharmed?"

She collapsed into her stepmother's arms. "Oh, Lydia, that awful soldier! Did you see him? Am I in trouble for hitting him? What will they do to me?"

"Shh, I don't expect you're in trouble." Lydia held her and stroked her hair.

Millie pulled back. "Are you sure? Did you talk to him?"

"No, I heard his friends yell for him to hurry before I got here. When he came out with a bloody nose, I figured you'd given him what for."

Millie nodded, but guilt nudged her. "I hit him when he tried to grab me. He said..." She sniffled as the tears started again.

"Never mind that now. His friends laughed at him and said he got what he deserved. So I don't think you're in trouble. He's probably too embarrassed to tell anyone a girl hit him, especially one he was trying to sweeten up."

Millie scoffed. "Don't know why he'd even try, since my condition is obvious now. I can't get into any of my dresses but this one. Guess we'll have to let out the seams in the others." She stroked her thickening waist.

"We'll do that soon. Now go wash your face," Lydia said, patting her cheek, "and let's see what we can find for supper."

Millie returned to the stove and her abandoned meal preparations. She splashed tepid water on her face, then rinsed the potatoes and diced them. She pulled the pot of warm water to the hottest part of the stove and added the three duck eggs she'd found at the edge of the marshy pond.

Lydia joined her. "I don't think they'll finish the repairs to your part of the mill until next week, so you'll be home again tomorrow. In fact, while I'm at work, I want you to gather up your things. Get ready to leave. We won't wait around here for the fighting to find us."

Millie dropped a potato in the boiling water and gaped. "We're leaving? But where will we go?"

Lydia shook her head. "Dunno for sure. I have a distant cousin down near Columbus where there's another mill. I'll see if I can find a name in Granny's Bible."

"But what about..." Millie scrambled for a way to pose her question. "What if...someone comes looking for us? How will they know where to find us?" Was her question too revealing? It was doubtful anyone would miss them except their neighbors or Troy. No other kin had visited since the war started over three years ago.

Lydia sighed. "I'll write to Pastor Bagley once we get settled, let him know where we are. I have a strong feeling we need to leave, not sit around and wait for something to happen."

Millie considered the plan. That might work. If Troy did come—though after all this time, she feared he wouldn't—he'd ask Mrs. Tucker, who could ask the pastor. But she'd leave a note somewhere in the house also. She alternated between cursing his prolonged absence and praying for him, figuring he must have fallen into some serious misfortune. Whenever he did appear, she aimed to give him a severe tongue-lashing. Right after they found a preacher—somewhere—to marry them proper-like.

CHAPTER 5

*H*eat lingered in the air, though the sun sank toward Alabama. In the distance, a thin stream sparkled in the dying rays, and three buildings huddled at the foot of a hill. Troy entered the nearest one and collapsed on the straw.

He stayed in Preacher Dan's barn whenever he passed this way. Dan had withheld his last name, saying it was best for all concerned to leave off family names until matters settled down. Somehow, Dan and his wife always knew when he happened to come their way and would bring him a plate of victuals. Other than the first time they'd met, they never spoke outside the pastor's property, merely nodded if they should see each other on the road.

Grateful as he was for the provision, Troy often wished he could get the man's opinion about developments in the area. Yesterday, he'd heard the Federals were closing in on General Johnston, who kept pushing south and west along the Chattahoochee River. Too close to Campbell County and East Alabama for Troy's peace of mind.

The barn door scraped open, and a figure eased inside. Troy stilled until he heard Pastor Dan's rich bass voice sing out, "A mighty fortress is our God." When he proceeded to the next line, Troy stepped into the aisle between the stalls. They clasped hands, then Dan pushed a warm parcel into Troy's chest.

"Good to see you, Preacher."

"I can't stay long. I have a hunch somebody's watching my movements, hunting for folks helping escaped slaves. Soldiers from both armies have been movin' this way. I'm surprised you didn't get caught. Are you traveling north or south this time?"

"Going to Campbell County to check on my kin." Troy bit into a biscuit and caught the oozing jam with his finger.

"I'll be heading that way to collect my sister and her young'uns from Hixtown. Get in the wagon at dawn, and I'll cover you with a blanket and straw, to be safe."

"I appreciate it. Does this mean the Federals are close?"

"Already camping south of Dalton, I heard. If you aim to join them, this might be your best chance. But have a care. You could get caught in the middle and end up somewhere you don't want to be."

"I understand. In case I don't get another chance to say it, thank you for everything."

Dan slapped him on the shoulder. "Just doing what I feel is right, son. See you in the morning."

JULY 9, 1864
CAMPBELL COUNTY, GEORGIA

*B*y noon, Millie had used every conceivable container available to pack their belongings. Lydia had gone into work to collect her pay and let the manager know she was leaving. Millie planned to leave a note with information on their whereabouts. Should she leave it in the house or with Mrs. Tucker?

She tore a page out of her journal. To preserve their secret, she kept her message vague. It wouldn't make much sense if someone else happened to find it first.

> *Dear T—*
>
> *Federals in town. Plan to go S to your kin in Col. Have news for you.*
>
> *Find me.*
>
> *Yours, M.*

Now, where to leave it? The secret room would be ideal, but she lacked the strength to push the armoire aside. Instead, she slid the paper into a drawer and closed it, leaving an inch of the paper sticking out.

"Please, God, let him find this and then find us wherever we are."

She went outside and dragged the old vegetable wagon to the front door, then started loading it with their baggage. The Saratoga trunk was heavy, but she managed to wrestle it into the vehicle by first emptying it and then replacing the contents.

She stopped to rest and gazed around the farm in a silent farewell. A bank of dark clouds gathered to the west, a warning of coming rain. She turned toward town to see whether she might spot Lydia.

A trail of black smoke stained the sky, and the air carried a hint of burning wood. Was that the mill? Burning?

Panic clawed up her throat, but a familiar figure hurried

down the hill. Millie left the wagon and motioned toward the smoke.

"What happened?"

Lydia glanced back the way she'd come. "The Union army's burning down the mill. I'm glad you're ready to leave, but you should've waited for me to put those things in the wagon. You oughtn't to be lifting that heavy stuff. Is anything left inside?" Lydia scanned the wagon's contents and wedged her lunch pail in a corner.

"Only your carpetbag. And you might grab Mama's old umbrella. It looks like rain's building to the west."

Lydia ran inside and returned with the last items. "Let's go by Ferguson's first and see if he has anything bigger than this wagon. We'll have to hurry, though, to get there before the army arrives at the sawmill. I don't care to run into that army major again."

"What major?"

"Never mind. It doesn't matter now."

Millie's anxiety grew. Would they get away in time? Would others be leaving town too?

"Oh, dear, the note for Reverend Bagley. Can we take it on the way? In case anyone comes looking for us, he—they'll know where we've gone."

Lydia shook her head. "I don't think it's going to make a difference now. That officer said for everyone to meet at the bridge by the sawmill."

Millie stared, trying to comprehend Lydia's words. "What for? Why does he care where we're going?"

"Because he said everyone working at the cotton mill was a prisoner. He's sending us all to General Sherman's headquarters in Marietta."

∾

*T*he sun had started sinking in the west when Preacher Dan dropped Troy near the turnoff to Hixtown. Dan pointed to a plume of smoke in the distance. "Looks like they got more than rain here today. Lightning must've struck something and started a fire."

Troy studied the sky. "It's either on the other side of town or dying down. Maybe the rain kept it contained to a small area. I'll keep an eye out. Much obliged for the ride, Preacher."

"You take care of yourself now."

Troy waited for the wagon to travel farther on. It was only a couple of miles to Lydia's house, so caution was called for. Pine trees edged the road and crowded so close together, it would be difficult for anyone to spot Troy moving through the dense foliage. Still, he weaved his way deeper until the road nearly disappeared from sight, choosing his steps with care in deference to his newly mended leg.

Besides shielding him from anyone's view on the narrow lane, the woods offered relief from the heat of the day. Welcome moisture dripped from the emerald leaves. Here in the shade, the scent of honeysuckle still lingered amid the more pungent pine. So different from the last time he was here when he'd tramped deeper to bury the evidence of his sin. He thrust the image away.

The house came into sight, but he waited and watched for any traffic around it. When he was convinced it was safe to venture out, he shouldered his pack and strode to the back door where he could peek in the window. He could see the kitchen and the hallway beyond it. No movement inside. He paced to the other side and noted the empty clotheslines. Of course, Saturday was a workday. Everyone must still be at the mill, although it used to let out early at week's end.

He rounded the house to the front porch. A yellow-striped lizard darted behind the rocking chairs where he and Millie had sat last time he was here. He couldn't stop the grin that spread across his face, nor the quickening of his heartbeat. Had she missed him as much as he'd missed her?

He reached the door and eased it open. After a quick glance around the yard, he stepped into the front room and dropped his pack. A rumbling in his stomach reminded him his last meal had been hours ago. He strode to the kitchen and opened the breadbox. Only a slab of bread about the size of his hand and a jar with an inch of apple butter, but it would do.

He tore off a big bite while he crossed to the pantry and peeked inside. A depleted sack of flour sat on one shelf, a half-dozen empty jars on another. The sight troubled him. Had they run out of food? Had one of the armies come close enough to raid the homes here?

He turned to the stove. No pan sat ready for cooking, and the water bucket was missing.

What was going on?

From the hallway, he saw that both bedrooms had been swept clean of personal items. He marched back to the armoire and pushed it aside before stepping into the secret room. That space seemed untouched since his visit last winter. He gripped the armoire to push it back in place and noticed a slip of paper sticking out of the top drawer. He pulled it out and scanned the note.

They were gone. How did the presence of Union soldiers figure into this? Had the women felt threatened or was the lack of resources to blame? What kinfolks did he have south of Campbell County? He couldn't recall, but "Col" had to stand for Columbus or maybe Colquitt, which was near the Florida line.

A noise at the door drew his attention. With the late-afternoon sun casting the person in shadow, Troy couldn't make out the man's face. But he clearly saw the outline of a hand holding a pistol—and heard its hammer click into place.

~

*B*y the time they reached Ferguson's sawmill, Millie's energy was flagging. Soldiers helped Lydia transfer their bundles from the vegetable cart to a wagon where other families had stashed their trunks and odd-shaped parcels. A couple of women and three small children also sat in the wagon.

A brief rain shower had doused some of the smoke and cleaned the air. Too bad it hadn't relieved the heat.

Lydia had set out to walk but encouraged Millie to ride. "You stay with our things. There should be enough room for you to sit here. Maybe you can take a nap."

Millie tried, but she didn't sleep much, thanks to the jostling of the vehicle and so many voices around her. When they stopped for everyone to refill their canteens and answer nature's call, she clambered from the wagon and hurried to follow the other women to a semi-private area. As she picked her way over the rough ground on her way back to the wagons, an auburn-haired woman caught up with her.

"You're Millie, aren't you? Lydia's stepdaughter?" Her warm smile set Millie at ease.

"Yes, I am."

"I'm Olivia Spencer. I worked at the mill last year and remember seeing you from time to time. You have such beautiful blond hair. You must get many compliments."

Millie's face grew warm. "Thank you. It does seem to attract attention." *Not always the best kind.*

A young boy ran up to Olivia as they neared the wagons. "This is my stepson, Wade. And here comes my cousin, Shiloh." She patted Wade's shoulder. "Did you go with Uncle Isaac to the men's area?"

"Yes, Ma. And I washed my hands, like you said."

"Good boy. Shiloh, this is Millie Gibson, and here comes

Lydia." Olivia gestured as she spoke. "We're all using first names since it seems we'll be traveling together."

An older couple joined them. Lydia introduced them to Millie as Olivia's aunt and uncle, Edith and Isaac Wynn. "I used to visit them with Ma when I was a young girl," Lydia explained to Millie. "Their son Thomas was a friend of my brother Ellis."

Millie smiled when Lydia then turned to Wade. "This must be young Mr. Spencer."

The boy denied her assumption with a shake of his head and serious eyes. "No, ma'am, I'm Wade," he said. "My Pa is Doctor Spencer, and this is my new ma." He gripped Olivia's hand and beamed up at her. "Can I walk with you a while, Ma? I'm big enough now."

Olivia pressed her hand to her heart and chuckled. "How can I refuse that smile? You'll have to stay right beside me, though, and not run ahead. These horses and mules aren't used to little boys getting close to them like Old Girl was."

"I'll stay with you." He turned to Lydia with the confident authority of a five-year-old. "Old Girl was our workhorse, but the soldiers said they needed her."

"Ah, I see." Lydia beamed at his explanation. Would life would have been different if Lydia had given Cal a son?

The call to move out again sent everyone scrambling. Lydia nudged Millie. "Did you want to walk now? I think I'll continue walking and visiting with Olivia. This brief rest has restored my energy."

Millie huffed. "I'll walk a while. It can't be any worse than bumpin' around in that wagon. Will you walk as well, Shiloh, or do you want to ride?"

The girl glanced at the older couple. "I'd be pleased to walk, if'n it's all right with y'all."

Olivia's uncle waved them all away. "You young people go ahead since you're all bound to go a-foot. We'll mind the belongings, not that they're going anywhere, packed tight as they are."

Lydia and Olivia put Wade between them, and Shiloh fell into step beside Millie. The young women strolled in silence for a while, neither yet comfortable with the other. How were they to navigate this unusual situation? Hundreds of people with no more than a passing acquaintance with one another. Now circumstances had suddenly thrust them into close quarters, traveling to a strange town. Would they be allowed to send any communication to their loved ones who were away?

Would Troy ever find her now?

Millie shook off her melancholy and attempted a normal conversation. "Tell me, Shiloh, how old are you?"

The question seemed to startle the girl, but then she smiled. "I turned sixteen last January. What about you?"

"I'll be seventeen in October, hopefully before this little one decides to be born." Millie rested her hand on her rounded belly. Did Shiloh notice the lack of enthusiasm in her voice?

Shiloh's eyes followed Millie's movement in surprise. "Oh, you're..." She paused. "Increasing, is that the word? Your husband is away to the war?"

Millie hardened herself to the reality. "I'm not married to him, but yes, he's away because of this stinking war." Maybe she'd let everyone think he was a soldier. That would avoid more explanations.

"So he'll wed you when he returns home." Shiloh pronounced the future as if she could see it, but they both knew her prediction was little more than a wish. So much could prevent it.

Millie refused to pretend. Recent events had soured her youthful dreams. "Maybe. If he survives the war. If he comes home. If he can find me. Who knows where any of us will end up in a few months' time?"

While other conversations went on around them, the two

outpaced the others, silent until Shiloh brought up a different subject. "What is this place where we're going now? Do you know it?"

Millie shook her head. "Marietta, I heard. All I know is what some of the men said while I was on the wagon. Seems the Yanks run off the Confederate troops that defended Marietta a few weeks ago. The railroad is what they wanted, I guess, so they can bring in their supplies from up north and cut off the Confederate supplies around Atlanta."

The war, always the war. Everything came back to the war.

"Reckon how long it will take us to get there?" Shiloh untied her bonnet strings and pressed a damp cloth to her neck.

"Lydia said it was nearly twenty miles, so we won't get there today. I guess we'll stop and spend the night on the road somewhere. At least we'll have guards posted to ward off any wild animals or robbers while we sleep."

Shiloh shivered. "Won't some folks decide to keep going and not stop on the road? Surely, we'll all meet up again after we get there."

Millie stopped and stared at her in disbelief. "Nobody has any choice in the matter, Shiloh. We aren't free to come and go as we please." Anger and frustration roughened her voice. "Didn't they tell you? We're prisoners of the Union army."

An older woman glared as she guided two children past them. Was the woman frustrated because Millie and Shiloh had halted in the middle of the road or because she'd overheard Millie's last words?

Shiloh lowered her voice to a whisper. "Prisoners? But why?"

"The cloth we made at the cotton mill is used to make blankets and uniforms and such for the Confederate army." She huffed. "I guess it wasn't enough for them to burn down the mill. They had to go and arrest all the workers. Of course, the families must go too. These soldiers here are taking us to their general in Marietta. They say he plans to send us away. Far away."

Her eyes rounded. "But I thought you said Marietta was just a few miles. We'll still be in Georgia, won't we?"

Did Shiloh also have something—or someone—she didn't want to leave behind?

"Not for long." Millie's anger dwindled into sorrow. "When we get to Marietta, they're gonna put us on trains heading north."

And she'd never see Troy again.

CHAPTER 6

*T*roy crushed the paper as he raised his hands and faced the man with the pistol. "Whoa there. I'm a relative of the people who live in this house. Who are you?"

The man lowered the gun with a nervous chuckle. "Troy McNeil? Is that you?" He stepped closer so Troy could see his face.

"Reverend Bagley?" Troy dropped his arms and reached to shake the man's hand. "It's been a long time, sir."

"Yes, it has. Several long, hard years for all of us. I suppose you've heard about our most recent trouble?"

"Not all of it. I came to check on Aunt Lydia and Millie, but I guess I've missed them." He displayed the paper in his hands. "If I read this note correctly, they've gone to visit a cousin somewhere south, maybe Columbus."

The minister shook his head. "That may have been their plan, but likely the Federals got here before they could leave. Soldiers ordered all the mill workers out of the building and set it on fire. Then they loaded 'em up on wagons and left a few hours ago. With a military escort, like common criminals. I heard somebody say they was headed east toward Atlanta."

Troy's breath rushed out. "That's a fine kettle of fish, ain't it?" He read the note again. "But maybe they left before the Yanks rounded up the workers."

"Maybe, but you won't know for sure unless you catch up to that party of wagons. Old man Ferguson might be able to tell you. They were all meeting at the bridge near his sawmill. Poor fellow, they burned it to the ground too."

Wagons. Lydia and Millie would've had to get a wagon to carry their stuff. Troy grabbed his pack and headed for the door. "I'll check at the livery first to see if the women purchased a wagon for their journey. If not, I'll see what Mr. Ferguson might know."

Reverend Bagley followed him onto the porch. "You do that, young man. I reckon I'll stay around here and keep an eye on things for a while. With only a handful of my congregation left in town, I'll probably have to move on as well. The soldiers left us little in the way of food, and hunger is a powerful motivator."

~

 *M*illie picked at the meal of beans and cornbread. She had no appetite for the food, but she had to eat for the sake of the little one nestled beneath her ribs. Getting upset did neither of them any good. Her outburst about being prisoners had shaken Shiloh, too, though the other girl tried to hide it.

She could tell Lydia worried over Millie's mood swings but hesitated to question her. She would confess all to Lydia, but it would have to wait until they had more privacy. Olivia had taken advantage of her status as Dr. Spencer's wife to remind Millie, gently and diplomatically, that she mustn't overexert herself. The others seemed to be giving her space and time to recover.

Everyone except Wade. With the great wisdom of childhood, he plopped down next to her and started sharing with her about his life on the farm. Most of the joys of farm life, for Wade, centered on the animals. His favorites were the two cats and the ancient horse.

"Mr. Smarty Pants, he's the boy cat. He's all black 'cept for white feet and part of his face and tail. He don't like me to hold him, lessen I got food. Mrs. Busy Bee is gray all over. Sometimes she sleeps on my feet."

He reached over his plate to pick a leaf off his shoe. "Old Girl, that's our horse, 'cept the soldiers took her away last week. She once found a nest of baby rabbits in the brush..."

He hardly paused to take a breath and rarely finished one story before he launched into another. The sheer volume of his repertoire soon had her smiling and shaking her head. She stroked his hair. "Do you ever wind down?"

He narrowed his eyes, and he puckered his lips as he pondered her question. "Don't think so. My Grammy that lived with me and Pa in town, she had a clock that needed winding, but I never did it."

Millie chuckled.

Shiloh grinned at their exchange and turned to tickle Wade on the neck. "Well, I guess you'd best be windin' up your stories for a spell. I see the soldiers are getting' ready to line up the wagons again. Maybe you ought to take a walk with Uncle Isaac over to the woods afore we get going."

"All right, I guess." He lumbered to his feet like an old man but then brightened. "Maybe I can ride with one of them soldiers again. That was fun."

"Oh, my, that boy." Shiloh shook her head in fond surrender. "He will wear you down once he gets going."

"He's great entertainment, though."

"Good to see you're feeling better. I 'spect you might be planning to ride the rest of the way and get off your feet a while."

"I suppose I should." She flexed her fingers. "My hands and feet feel tight, as though they might be swollen."

"Missy Livy might have some herbs to help. She tries to be doctor when the doctor's away." Her smile negated any implied criticism in the statement. Shiloh struck Millie as one of those souls who always saw the good in others.

"Why do you call her that? 'Missy Livy'?"

Shiloh's smile dimmed, and her eyes took on a faraway look. "When I come to the family as a child, she acted so much older than she was. Almost like a little grown-up. I guess she had to be, since her pa had put her in charge of her sister. Camilla was crippled, you see, and their mama had passed when Camilla was a little-un. They had a hard time finding folks to help while the pa worked his business, so finally he sent them to live with Aunt and Uncle. But Livy still took care of her sister until Camilla died. That was nigh on two years ago."

She paused and shrugged. "I jes' naturally called her Miss Olivia, but it usually came out 'Missy Livy.' I guess I ought to be more proper now, especially with her being married to Doc Spencer."

"Oh, I don't think she minds. I wondered if maybe her name was Melissa or something like that. Mine is Millicent, but everyone calls me Millie. Except Lydia when she gets upset, then it's Millicent Anne Gibson."

They laughed at her rendition of Lydia's strict voice. "I think all mams and daddies do that when they want to get your attention." Shiloh grinned. "I know mine did."

The innocent comment felt like a slap to Millie. Once, before he'd married Lydia, Cal had insinuated he wasn't her father. At her age, the comment had hurt but not made much sense. She only recalled it at odd moments. A girl ought to know who her parents were. She placed a protective hand over her swollen abdomen. *What will I tell you, little one? More lies? Or will I have the courage to tell you the truth?*

~

*N*obody answered Troy's call at the livery. Every stall stood open and empty. Numerous hoof prints marked the area, and he found a couple of warped boards and bent nails tossed aside. It seemed the owner had left town with the mill workers. Maybe he was related to some of them, or else he figured to go where he might find more business.

A few blocks past the livery, smoke still rose from the collapsed mill. The town's five-story landmark now lay in a tumble of smoldering bricks. Misshapen wood and metal stood in grotesque mockery of the great machines that had turned cotton into fabric the day before. The recent rain had merely dampened the destruction and created a residual hissing as portions of the structure continued to shift and settle with unnatural groans. The sharp scent of burned cotton irritated Troy's throat, but the eerie spectacle beckoned him closer.

He skirted the mill's perimeter without fear of discovery, his lone companion an old birddog that dared to sniff around the edges. "Probably looking for food," Troy said aloud.

His voice sounded foreign amidst the devastation. "What a waste." He spared the sight one last sweep and hurried on to the sawmill.

The Ferguson family roamed their yard like forlorn mourners. Losing their source of income must have hit them hard, much like losing a loved one. He'd never met the Fergusons, so he approached them as he would a stranger at a graveside funeral. He waited for the older man to turn his way.

"You can see we ain't got nothing to offer, if you're needin' lumber, mister."

"No, sir, that's not my aim. I just arrived in town and heard about what happened. Allow me to offer my sincere condolences."

Mr. Ferguson nodded his thanks, then seemed to shake

himself. "I expect you must be searchin' for some of your folks, then?"

"Yessir. My aunt, Mrs. Lydia Gibson. She's the widow of Cal Gibson. Perhaps you know her?"

"Yeah." He spat a stream of tobacco to the side. "Fact is, she was here right before the Federals rode up. Wanted to know if I had a wagon she could buy, I think. But I didn't have time to answer before those devils started torchin' my yard." Tears stood in the man's eyes, but he stiffened his jaw and muttered a curse.

Troy grappled for patience in the face of the Fergusons' loss. "Again, I'm sorry, sir. Do you remember if Mrs. Gibson went with the army or struck out on her own?"

"Oh, they caught her up with all the other workers. They warn't gonna let any of the women slip away. Said they was all prisoners, goin' to Marietta to be put on trains goin' north."

"Marietta?" Troy scratched his chin. "Don't know that I've ever been there." He'd always stayed close to the Alabama state line. "You know which way they went?"

The man gestured toward the bridge in the distance. "Just follow the road till you see the creek turn south. If you had a mount, you could catch up with 'em quick enough. Even walking, you'll move faster than that bunch, what with women and children on foot. They'll prob'ly hafta stop when it grows dark."

Troy shifted his pack and shook Mr. Ferguson's hand. "Thank you, sir. I pray you'll recover from your losses here."

"Hope you find your kinfolk. Have a care when you draw near that party."

Since the caravan had to be well ahead of him, Troy set a brisk pace for the first hour. Following such a large group required no tracking skills. Heavily laden wagons left clear imprints on the road, especially as he drew closer to the cavalcade. He slowed and dropped back when he spotted the rear guard. It wouldn't do to surprise a trigger-happy soldier so close to his destination.

With the sun sinking low behind him, Troy found a sheltered place to bed down for the night, confident the army would soon call a halt. He'd set out again at dawn and see if he could slip into their ranks without causing any commotion. They'd have to pass over the creek soon. Maybe he'd show up on the other side and act as if he'd been with them all along.

~

JULY 19, 1864
COBB COUNTY, GEORGIA

*M*illie regarded the swirling water with uneasiness. The creek didn't look deep, but appearances could be deceiving. She'd never been one of those brave souls who plunged into running streams.

"What happened to the bridge?" she asked.

"I don't know if there ever was a bridge." Olivia shaded her eyes against the sun's glare on the water. "Uncle Isaac said he never crossed here before. He always followed the Sweetwater Creek down to where it joined the river. But he wasn't going to Marietta either."

Early-morning sunshine promised another warm day, which would be welcome if any of them took an accidental dunking. All up and down the bank of the swollen waterway, the men on horseback carted women and children to the other side. Others helped guide the wagons through the swift current.

The soldier who'd carried Wade across the stream steered his horse their way. With one arm, he assisted Olivia to sit behind him and aimed the horse back into the creek.

Another soldier reached for Millie. She hesitated long

enough to search his face. Though he wore a crooked grin, his chin sported a full black beard. Not a face she recognized. She accepted his arm and swung up to sit in front of him.

So far, she'd seen nothing of the soldier who'd attempted to press himself on her a few days ago. The closest guards had been civil and kept a respectful distance, but caution had her watching for the one with a mole near his left eye. The one whose nose she'd bloodied. He might make good on his promise to settle the score or decide to renew his persuasion.

Her ride ended without incident on the far side of the creek, but fatigue and apprehension wore her down. She followed a line of women to a sheltered area, sat on a pine log, and yielded to the urge to cry. What would become of them? How would they survive this journey to a foreign place?

Comforting arms surrounded her, and Olivia's voice spoke in her ear. "It's all right. Go ahead and let it out."

Lydia soon found them. "What's wrong?" The concern in her voice added guilt to Millie's shoulders.

Though Olivia spoke to Lydia, her whispered words reached Millie. "Pregnancy doldrums, I believe. My husband has written reports about it. Somehow the baby inside upsets the body's humors, so it takes very little to bring on a spate of crying."

Lydia knelt in front of her. "Hey, honey. Is there anything I can do for you?"

Millie shivered but straightened and wiped away her tears. "No, I'll be fine in a minute. I just want to rest here a while." She needed to grow up and act like an adult. After all, she'd be a mother in a few months.

Shiloh joined them, and Olivia motioned to Millie. "Shiloh, maybe you can stay with Millie while Lydia and I go make arrangements at the wagon."

Millie turned to Shiloh as the others left. "I'm all right now. I guess the fear of crossing the river got to me." Shiloh had admitted her own dread on the other shore, so Millie felt safe in confessing to her new friend. She glanced around to find they were alone. "Where did everyone go?"

"There's some trouble over by the wagons. I think they caught a spy."

Eager to focus the attention elsewhere, Millie tugged on Shiloh's arm. "Well, let's not miss the excitement. Come on."

They reached the knot of people and wove their way through the gathering until they could see the center of the circle. Two soldiers held a young man. His head drooped on his chest, heaving from his recent exertion. He must have given his captors quite a fight. Blood dripped from his nose and bloomed at the corner of his mouth. Shaggy, light-brown hair covered his features, but Millie saw them plainly enough when the sergeant jerked him to his feet.

She gasped. Troy. He'd come for her.

The officer confronting him glared and slapped a gauntlet across Troy's face. "Where'd you come from, boy? Are you a spy or a Rebel deserter? I'll tell you now, I despise both and will treat you accordingly."

"I'm neither."

Troy mumbled the words, but the officer ignored his response. "Speak up, or I'll turn you back over to our welcoming committee."

Another slap accompanied his shout, making Millie jump.

Masculine laughter echoed around the soldiers' ranks.

Millie struggled to the front of the crowd. "Noooo! Nooo!"

Strong arms prevented her from reaching the officer in charge, but she thrashed and continued to wail. "Let me go. He's not a spy or a deserter. He's an innocent citizen."

The officer stepped away from Troy and addressed Millie. "You know this man?"

She cringed at the sight of Troy's bloodied face, his arms held immobile by a guard on each side. Troy didn't speak but raised his eyes, which seemed to plead with her. Did he shake his head? Why wouldn't he want her to acknowledge him?

"Yes, I know him." She choked on her words in the sudden quiet, but she continued. "He's avoided the war, refusing to fight his friends and family. He's got brothers on both sides."

A snort of disbelief answered her. "Then why is he here? Obviously, he had some reason for sneaking around our camp."

Millie glanced between Troy and the captain. "I guess he hoped to go north or join up with y'all."

Troy lowered his head. He neither confirmed nor denied her statement. Was he waiting for a moment to break loose while the soldiers were distracted?

Millie couldn't let that happen. They'd shoot him for sure. She blurted the only thing she could think of in his defense.

"Truth be told, he likely came for me." She dipped her head to hide her flushed face and linked her hands over her bulging belly.

Stunned silence reigned for a few moments. To Millie's left, Major Tompkins stepped forward. "Does anyone else here know this man?"

Murmurs and movement rippled through the spectators.

Lydia pushed into the circle. Three more followed. There should be others, but they were probably afraid to acknowledge the acquaintance. Millie couldn't blame them. Doing so might jeopardize their own safety.

Major Tompkins directed his next question to those who stepped forward. "As far as any of you know, has this man been a member of the Rebel military in any capacity?"

Each one gave a negative shake of the head or mumbled in a low voice.

Troy continued to stare at the ground and didn't acknowledge anyone. He seemed indifferent to the entire proceedings. Why didn't he answer, either to corroborate or contradict her testimony?

The major addressed the gathered crowd. "All right, then, we have no proof of spying activities, only the young woman's claim of an amorous encounter." He paused when some snickers interrupted him. "We'll treat him as one of the operatives arrested yesterday." Turning to his officers, he ordered them to put Troy with the other men from New Manchester but assigned an extra guard to watch him "for everyone's safety."

Soldiers hustled Troy to the edge of the crowd, and the spectators returned to their own affairs. Millie stayed, trying to make sense of Troy's behavior.

Lydia came over and wrapped her in an embrace. They stood there without speaking.

Olivia hurried to her side. "I just heard what happened. I'm sorry I wasn't here to be of any help." Edith and Shiloh joined them.

The unspoken show of support soothed Millie's shattered heart, but Troy's attitude puzzled her. Had he been searching for her? If so, why didn't he verify her claims? What message had he tried to convey in that moment when he looked her way?

CHAPTER 7

*T*roy dragged himself between the two older men near the rear of the cavalcade. The beating he'd endured, combined with a lack of nourishment, left him exhausted. It was the vision of Millie's stricken face, however, that drained him. She'd completely misunderstood what he'd tried to communicate. While he appreciated her rigorous defense, her words had not advanced his plans.

From his covert position, he'd seen her cross the creek with that Union man. The soldier held her much closer than the situation called for, and Troy's hackles rose. When they reached dry ground and she slid from the horse, the man's gaze followed her until she was out of sight. Troy must've moved or voiced his displeasure aloud because a minute later, he found himself clapped between two guards and hauled up the hill for his inquisition.

Now, as he was deep in thought, Troy's foot caught on an exposed tree root, and he stumbled into the man beside him. "Hey, watch it, mister." The fellow scowled at him and widened the space between them.

"Sorry, I didn't see—"

"Move along there, Lover Boy." The burly soldier behind took every opportunity to prod Troy. "We want to make Marietta by dinner time. But don't get any ideas about finding your lady friend there. You'll be staying with us until you get on a train heading north."

Troy sidled toward the man on his left. He appeared fit enough, but Troy had spotted the fingers missing on one hand. He'd probably been working in the mill since childhood. "Is that the plan, then? To send all these people up north?"

"That's what the major said, back at the mill." The man slanted a skeptical frown at Troy. "Name's Roy Gunther, shipping manager. You're not a mill employee. How'd you come to be prowlin' around and get caught?"

"I got into town late yesterday, went to check on my Aunt Lydia, and found her house deserted. Reverend Bagley told me what'd happened, but he didn't know if she was in this group or had lit out on her own. I wanted to be sure she was safe."

Mr. Gunther scoffed. "You should've been more careful. Now you're bound to be sent north with the rest of us."

Which suited Troy fine, since he'd been trying to get there for months. This wasn't the way he would have chosen, but it would suffice. The Lord indeed worked in mysterious ways.

In response to his companion, he merely said, "Yeah, I guess that's where I'll end up." The problem was, he didn't get a chance to speak to Millie. Would the soldiers still keep the men confined in a different area from the women and children? Maybe he could find her when they reached their destination.

He needed to convince the men in charge he'd wanted to join them all along. How long would he have to wait for that opportunity?

JULY 10, 1864
MARIETTA, GEORGIA

*A*t last, the caravan from Campbell County reached Marietta. The line of wagons stopped before a group of large buildings with expanses of green grass between them. Millie had never seen anything like it. "What is this place?"

A soldier nearby overheard. "It used to be the Georgia Military Institute." He sneered and ushered the women inside the closest building. "I'd say the cadets failed their final test when they deserted the place." He led them to a room off the main hall.

It had the appearance of a huge classroom, at least twice the size of the schoolroom at home. Desks lined the walls, stacked two and three high. In the middle of the room, trunks and baggage sat at odd angles, as if the handlers found them too heavy to carry farther. Around those, several families had spread blankets where they sat to rest or share a bit of food.

Millie didn't recognize anyone. And no sign of Troy. She couldn't hide her dismay. "How will we have room to sleep? There's already a bunch of folks here." Was Troy here too? Besides Mr. Isaac Wynn and another elderly man, she'd seen only women and children.

Open windows on two of the walls allowed for a breeze that might happen by, but the air felt close and stuffy. Various odors Millie didn't care to identify threatened to upset her touchy stomach. She covered her nose and dragged her valise behind her companions to an empty area.

Lydia dropped her carpetbag and sat on the bare floor. "As long as I can sit, I'll sleep. My poor feet are worn out."

Edith Wynn flapped her skirts to shake off the road dust. "I just want to change out of these clothes for a few hours. I wonder how far it is to the outhouse?"

Mr. Isaac gestured from his wife to the youngster pulling at his hand. "We'll go find out for Aunt Edith, shall we, Wade?"

Millie slumped to the floor between Lydia and Shiloh, exhausted from the heat and walking more than she was accustomed to. Lydia picked up a discarded newspaper and plied it like a fan to cool Millie's brow. She drifted into a light doze until voices woke her.

"These are the people Major Tompkins brought from the Sweetwater Mill. You say you got another place for them?"

"For some of them, anyway," a deeper voice answered. "Another train of wagons is on its way from Roswell. It should arrive shortly. We've located some vacant houses on the outskirts, but it's going to be crowded everywhere."

One officer approached them. "Ma'am?" He directed his words to Edith. "I'm Captain Griffin of the Seventh Pennsylvania, acting for Major Tompkins and Colonel Gleeson. If you folks can gather your things and come with me, we've a place where you might be more comfortable."

Soon they loaded into one of three wagons as others from New Manchester climbed into the other two. Captain Griffin waved a signal to the drivers as he paced back toward the building's entrance.

"For a Yankee officer, he sure takes an interest in finding us a decent place to stay," Lydia said. "The others seemed glad to be rid of us."

The vehicle lumbered through the town until it reached a quiet, tree-shaded road. Millie perked up at the sight of several large townhouses. The wagon stopped before one house with stone steps and a wide porch. The front door stood open as if welcoming them.

Each woman grabbed her own bags and followed the driver to the gate. Some of them started to explore the house, but Millie got no farther than the settee in the well-appointed parlor. Would Lydia chastise her if she put her feet on the nearby hassock? She took the chance.

Fatigue dragged her toward sleep until the clatter of more wagons outside heralded additional arrivals. Lydia and Olivia descended the stairs and went to the door.

"Are the Federals bringing more folks here?" Lydia asked.

Olivia kept her voice low. "That's what it looks like, but I don't know any of those people."

Curiosity urged Millie to her feet, but she lingered in the doorway as the others drifted to the porch. The same officer who'd brought them here helped several women descend from one wagon. He led the last young woman to the porch.

He offered them all a brief smile. "Ladies and gentlemen of Roswell"—he gestured from the newcomers to Millie's group—"these folks are from the Sweetwater Mill in New Manchester. I regret you will have to share these living quarters for a day or two, but I think you'll find them more agreeable than the military academy where your fellow workers are staying."

He turned to address the soldiers who hefted large bags of foodstuff. "I believe the summer kitchen is accessible through the rear door."

Millie gaped at the quantity of flour, cornmeal, salt, and lard. At least the captain didn't plan to let them starve.

The officer gestured to the soldiers still unloading the wagon. "Private Jones and Private Allen here will assist you as needed. I'll try to check on you again tomorrow." He bowed and hurried away while the strangers started to introduce themselves.

A gray-haired woman stepped closer to greet Millie. A young girl clutched her hand. "Hello. I'm Ada Anderson, and this is my granddaughter, Sarah Grace." She tugged the girl forward.

Millie nodded and smiled at the child. "Nice to meet you, Mrs. Anderson. I'm Millie Gibson. What a pretty name you have, Sarah Grace."

Mrs. Anderson pointed to a dark-haired boy. "That's her

brother, John Mark. It seems he's already met a friend."

"Wade Spencer," Millie said. "He's Olivia's stepson. Olivia is the red-haired lady, and the other one is my stepmother, Lydia."

"Oh, they're talking with Rose and Celeste Carrigan. There's my daughter, Emily, coming up the steps, and the old man is J.D., my husband."

So many names and unfamiliar faces. Millie felt obliged to act as hostess, since they'd arrived first, but the task fit awkwardly. "I suppose we'll all learn each other soon enough. Maybe we should move inside and figure out how to go on."

Ada Anderson nodded. "I'll be glad to sit in a place that doesn't move and jostle a body. Thankful we arrived ahead of the rain."

Millie followed the others heading indoors. A slight breeze carried the clean scent of rain, and sprinkles warned of an impending summer shower. Did it mean a blessing was on the way, or more trouble? She paused at the threshold and glanced up the street. Where was Troy? Would the Federals give him shelter and a place to rest?

~

*P*ropelled by a push from behind, Troy stumbled to the wall. He put out a hand to halt his movement and turned around to address the stocky soldier who sported a droopy mustache. The same one who'd poked him in the back when Troy's steps dragged. "What happened to my pack?"

The soldier snarled. "What pack?"

So this was how it was going to be. "I had a knapsack with my things. Nothing valuable, just a change of clothes, a canteen, and a bit of jerky." He motioned to the half-dozen men who sat on the floor, weary from their journey to Marietta. "You let all these folks bring their stuff. Don't see why I can't have mine."

The man yelled to his companion, who sauntered in and added a couple of sacks to the pile of baggage. "Hey, Ned, you seen this fellow's knapsack?"

"I don't think so," Ned began before he noticed Troy. "Oh, you mean the one we dumped out? The one with the love note in it?"

Troy's fists curled at his side. They were goading him, trying to see how far they could push before he struck back. Nothing new, but he had trouble curbing his temper sometimes. "You can have the contents, but I'd like to get my pack. It was a gift from my parents."

Private Ned spread his mouth in a grin that revealed a couple of gaps in his teeth. "Oh, we took everything in it already. We're taking bids on who gets the love note." He pulled a paper from his pocket. "I'm keeping it safe until everyone has a chance to bid."

He unfurled the paper and read in a loud voice. "'Dear T.' I guess that's you, big man, huh? 'Federals in town.'"

He grinned at his comrades. "That's us. She says she plans to go south to your kin in 'Col.'" He looked up from the paper. "Now I don't know where 'Col' is, but I don't think she's gonna make it, if she was amongst the workers we rounded up. Now, here's the good part. 'Have news for you. Find me.' The way I read it, that could mean she's spyin' and passin' messages on to you."

He waved the paper in Troy's face but pulled it back when Troy reached for it. "I think you could be spies, both of you." He faced the other way. "What you think, boys?"

Troy gulped but stood his ground. "You heard what the major said. I'm to be treated the same as these other men. There's no sign I've been spyin'. Matter of fact, I just arrived from middle Alabama. Far as I know, there ain't no action there on either side."

Ned sneered in Troy's face. "Ah, but your girl was here, right between us and Johnston's army. Maybe she's the one who gathers the information and passes it on to you."

Dear Lord, what tales they could concoct out of a simple note. Why had Millie given misleading information? And why not write exactly what she meant rather than such a cryptic message soldiers could interpret half a dozen ways? Did she mean to protect him by sending him in the wrong direction? How could he keep the suspicion away from her?

One of the aging mill workers shambled closer and handed Troy his knapsack. He must have spotted it when he retrieved his own baggage. "Ah, Sergeant, leave the boy be. It was plain to everyone that gal and this young man been doin' some serious sparking. If she was a spy, she'd've left him to his fate 'stead of speaking up like she did."

Warmth spread from Troy's neck into his face. Had Millie gone back on her word and told what'd happened? Was everyone in Campbell County privy to their private relationship? Lydia's face, when she'd stepped out on his behalf, swam before him. He'd read the disappointment in her eyes and dropped his head. Troy might never recover her good opinion. He might as well stay wherever the Federals sent him when the war was over.

He hadn't protected Lydia and Millie by staying silent. His life had just become more complicated.

∽

JULY 11, 1864

*I*f Millie had thought life would calm down once they reached Marietta, she soon discovered it wasn't to be.

That same Union officer came by the house the next evening, and a guard caught a thief stealing from the kitchen.

When the thief turned out to be a young woman who was a runaway slave, the women rallied around her and implored Captain Griffin to let her stay at least for the time being.

Mrs. Edith and Shiloh herded the runaway, who gave her name as Dorcas, into the kitchen to feed her while Rose discussed the situation with the officer.

Millie approached Olivia in the yard. "What will happen to her?"

"We're hoping the captain will let her travel north with us when we go. She's fortunate she picked this house with people who don't hold much with slavery."

"I don't know anyone who has slaves." Millie gazed at the woman, intrigued by her smooth, dark skin, which she'd seldom seen at home. "Of course, this is my first time away from Campbell County."

Olivia frowned as she observed the newcomer. "She's going to need more clothes. Hers look like they're barely holding together."

Millie considered the girl's size. "She might fit into some of mine that I've outgrown. I had in mind to try to let out the seams, but the fabric won't hold up to much sewing. I'll go see what I can find."

She met Celeste Carrigan at the back door. Though a few years her senior, Celeste had soon set Millie at ease with her sweet smile and easy-going nature. "Hey, Celeste, come help me see which of my clothes might fit Dorcas."

They opened Millie's carpetbag and pulled the contents out. They found two dresses and a petticoat that should work. Millie added the mended chemise and bodice she'd been wearing that fateful day in January, glad to get them out of her possession. Maybe she could find a way to earn enough money for replacements in a larger size. It felt good to be able to help someone in need. Could that be what people meant when they said it was more blessed to give than to receive?

When Shiloh brought Dorcas upstairs after she'd eaten and washed up from her perilous journey, Millie handed her the clothes. "You can use the chemise and petticoat for your night rail until we get a chance to find something better."

Dorcas blinked away tears and held the garments to her face. "Oh, miss, this here's fine as I ever had. I thank you most kindly."

Millie's eyes misted in response to the girl's obvious gratitude. *Yep, giving feels pretty good.*

Rose directed Dorcas to the bed she'd prepared. "I hope you'll be comfortable here. We're all rather crowded."

Surprisingly, the crowding didn't bother Millie. As an only child, she'd lived a rather isolated life with few friends her age. Perhaps that was why she'd gravitated to Troy, first seeing him as someone to emulate, since he was three years older. In time, her admiration had grown into love. What other discoveries would life hold for her?

~

*T*he next day brought rain, so Rose and Celeste conducted lessons for the children inside. Millie stood next to Emily Anderson as the Wilson children—neighbors of the Carrigan sisters— dashed into the house so they wouldn't miss them. "Y'all don't take the summers off from school?"

The petite woman shook her head. "We don't have a school for the mill workers' families. There used to be one, but they couldn't keep teachers."

Rose recruited all the adults to help. Even Dorcas got involved, lining up the students for a game. By the end of the activities, Millie knew everyone's name, and they all enjoyed cookies that Edith and Ada brought from the kitchen.

At last, the rain let up enough for the Wilson offspring to

return to their assigned housing next door. Millie helped pick up the dishes, then trudged upstairs, hoping to lie down for a while. Or maybe she'd go outside and ask one of the soldiers where Troy might be. Would they know?

Rose's voice drifted down the stairwell. "Let's see what we can find for Millie."

She popped her head in the room where she'd planned to sleep. "Did I hear my name?"

Rose smiled at her. "Yes. Just in time. Because you gave so much for Dorcas, we got permission to see what will fit you from this chest." She led Millie to the armoire and started rifling through the sturdier garments.

Stepping back, Millie exchanged a glance with Celeste. "What do you mean, you got permission?"

Rose drew Millie to her side and lowered her voice. "Didn't Lydia tell you about the soldier in the cellar?"

"No." This was news for concern. Her experience with soldiers didn't recommend them. "What's he doing in the cellar?"

Celeste gripped Millie's arm. "Shh...he's not a Union man. This house belongs to his family. Sergeant Morgan took a furlough to check on his folks, then hid in the cellar when he discovered the town filled with Yankees. He'll be returning to his unit soon as it's dark."

Rose raised her eyebrows at that news. "He's going back tonight?"

Celeste nodded. "It's too dangerous for him to stay any longer, he said. Too many people around."

"That's the gospel truth." Rose directed Millie toward the tall cedar chest. "Come on, little mama. Let's see what we can find here for you."

They delved into the armoire, rejecting several lovely silks and satins, though each woman found something among those to admire. Soon they had a pile of items for Millie to try on.

Skirts, bodices, full dresses, even petticoats and shifts littered the surfaces of both beds and every chair in the room.

Lydia came to the door, Olivia and Dorcas following closely. "What's going on here?"

"We're finding clothes for Millie." Rose turned, and her brow furrowed as she regarded Dorcas. "Hmm. We should search for things to help Dorcas pass through the guards." She started pulling open bureau drawers.

Olivia and Celeste joined in the hunt.

Lydia seemed perplexed. "What are we looking for?"

"A wide bonnet, gloves, bits of lace to bring that neckline up higher," Rose muttered as she continued searching through a box of fabric remnants.

Millie joined in, giggling. "This is the strangest shopping I've ever done."

After supper, Edith encouraged Millie and Dorcas to don some of their new clothes so the women could see which items needed alterations. Millie happily complied, feeling lovelier than she had in months, despite her expanding waistline. She even smiled at the boys who ran past, trying to show the little Anderson girl the frog they'd caught.

She and Dorcas stood in the parlor as the other women fluttered around them and admired their finery. A knock at the open door drew her attention. And there was that Union officer again, staring at them. Millie gasped, and everyone's focus shifted to him.

"Well, now, don't you look different." He directed his words to Dorcas, then he flashed a smile around the room. "I see you ladies were able to find more suitable clothing for our young friend."

Millie's exuberance bubbled into speech. "We found that some of my things were perfect for Dorcas, and I was glad to let her have them, knowing I won't be able to use them for a while, if ever again. Then like a blessing from heaven, I learned

Sergeant Morgan said we could take whatever we needed, and I found these wonderful things..."

She stopped suddenly and glanced around at the others. Heat flooded her face.

"Sergeant Morgan?" the officer asked. "I don't recall a soldier by that name among the guards. He told you to take whatever you wanted from where? When did this happen?"

Olivia stepped forward and put her arm around Millie. "I believe the name wasn't Morgan but Munsen. He's one of the guards who escorted us from New Manchester the other day." She frowned. "No, maybe it was Monroe. I'm sure it started with an *M*. Is Morgan what I told you, Celeste?"

Celeste bit her bottom lip. "I thought that was the name. Could be I misheard it."

Rose stepped up beside Celeste. "Well, whatever his name was, the point is we were concerned about making use of anything we found along our journey, and Mrs. Edith said she thought it would be all right to take what we needed but no more. After all, we'd be glad for anyone who entered our houses to do the same."

Several nodded, and Isaac Wynn, bless his heart, added his wisdom. "None of us can take any of this earthly stuff with us to the next life, anyway. We might as well share with one another while we're here."

Captain Griffin issued another smile. "Well, I'm glad you found what you needed for Dorcas. My superior officer seemed to think leaving her here was a good choice for the moment. If a higher commander should decide differently, I'll let you know. I feel satisfied I can trust you all to take care of her."

He glanced around the room. "Now, where did John Mark go? I have good news for him about his arrowhead. I want to tell him before I leave since I may be gone a few days."

Millie's shoulders relaxed, but she pressed her lips together.

She'd nearly landed them all in the suds. Best keep her mouth shut from now on.

As she and Lydia prepared to retire later, Millie apologized for her blunder.

"Don't worry about it." Lydia smothered a yawn and crawled onto the bed. "Olivia's quick thinking smoothed it over, and you saw how everyone stuck together."

"Yeah, that was amazing." She compared that show of loyalty to the reluctance of her lifelong neighbors to speak up for Troy. "It also helps that Captain Griffin is besotted with Miss Rose." Millie stifled a chuckle. "What a strange mixture we are. Families from two different places, a Confederate soldier, and a runaway slave all in the same house. And a Union officer keepin' watch over us. How much stranger can things get around here?"

The following morning, Lydia told her they'd found the Rebel in the cellar burning with a fever.

"Oh, my." Millie put a hand to her chest. "What will we do?"

Lydia shrugged. "All we can do is keep an eye on him. We have little in the way of medicine, and we don't know what caused the fever, so we must tread carefully. I'll take a turn stayin' with him, and so will Olivia and Emily Anderson. Mrs. Edith and Mrs. Ada will continue to oversee the kitchen and the housework so there won't appear to be anything different. The best we can do is give him time to heal with sleep and rest."

Time, folks said, was the great healer. But the longer he stayed here, the greater was his chance of discovery. Which put them all at risk.

CHAPTER 8

July 13, 1864

A sharp kick to Troy's midsection roused him from a deep slumber. It was the first time he'd slept soundly since arriving in Marietta two days before.

"Get up if you want any grub before you get on that train," a rough voice said. "We don't coddle prisoners."

Troy rolled over with a groan. Did that attitude apply to the women too? How would Millie hold up under such harsh treatment? If only he'd arrived in Campbell County a day or two earlier, perhaps he could have helped her and Lydia get somewhere safer.

He reached for his pack and stood. The considerably lighter weight renewed his aggravation. They must think he'd hidden coins or messages in the seams of his clothes, which had been confiscated. He'd heard that women sometimes used such a method to hide their valuables. A quick examination of his belongings would disabuse them of that notion. Troy was fortunate the seams had held together this long.

He followed the other men to the facilities designated for

morning ablutions and then to the assigned dining area. He carried his biscuit and bowl of grits to a table where four other men bent over their food.

One man made a face after tasting the thin gruel. "Crazy Yanks don't know how to cook grits." He pushed his bowl away.

Troy agreed with the pronouncement but shoveled in his own food. He'd learned to be thankful for anything edible.

"Best to eat it, anyway, Sam," another man said. "Once they put us on that train, there's no telling when we'll get to eat again." He pointed to Troy. "So, what's your story, son? I ain't never seen you at the mill, though my cousin was one who stood up for you. Abe Fincher, by the way." He extended his hand across the table, and Troy shook it.

"Troy McNeil. My aunt and her stepdaughter are mill employees. I stopped by on my way from Alabama to check on them and learned from Reverend Bagley what happened."

The man who complained about the food—Sam, was it? — peered at Troy through narrowed eyes. "You a Union sympathizer?"

Troy's jaw clenched, but he met Sam's gaze full-on. "I'm a man of peace." Even as he spoke the words, his conscience taunted him. *Some man of peace. You're a killer.*

Sam smirked. "Is'at what they're calling cowards nowadays?"

The other men froze as Troy stood and leaned across the table to glare at his accuser. "I don't know. What did they say about you?"

Sam's florid complexion darkened as he rose to his feet, sputtering. "Why, you—"

"Glad to see you men are finished here." A Union lieutenant strode to their table. "Grab your gear and get outside. There's a wagon ready to take you to the train depot."

Troy slung his knapsack over his shoulder and took long

strides toward the door. As Pastor Dan would say, sometimes the best defense was a hasty retreat.

He climbed into the rickety wagon bed and sat behind the driver. While they waited for the others to join them, Troy let his gaze wander. Now that he was on his way north—the goal he'd tried to accomplish for several months—a sense of melancholy tempered his eagerness. He might never see Georgia or Alabama again. His parents or brothers. Aunt Lydia or Millie. The thought squeezed his heart. The fleeting look he'd had when Mille came to his defense the day before yesterday had only increased his longing.

Perhaps now he could write to her without fear of being caught by Rebel forces.

But where would she be? What had happened to the women when they arrived in Marietta? With so many wagons coming and going, and the building where they were crammed with people, he'd not seen them even from afar.

While he ruminated, the wagon filled. The driver flipped the reins and called to the mules in their traces, "Walk on, lads." Troy grinned, glad he wouldn't be the one walking.

The vehicle lurched forward and clattered over the bumpy road. The sun intensified as it rose into a clear sky, but Troy faced a shadowy future.

∾

JULY 16, 1864

*M*illie didn't know whether to laugh or cry. Instead, she stood in appalled silence, along with everyone else who'd run from the house, while Corporal Jones stared down the empty road.

Captain Griffin had dropped by to see if their group had been sent north while he was away. He barely said his hello before they heard a commotion outside. Hooves thundered close by, then someone shouted, "Hold, thief!" and they'd all spilled outside to see what the trouble was.

Captain Griffin called to the private. "Langley, what happened here?"

The soldier raised his head and stood at attention, obviously expecting a reprimand. "He got your horse, sir."

Captain Griffin strode forward in outrage. "Do I understand that someone stole my horse? No, not *my* horse, mind you, the *Army's horse*, while two Union guards sat on their..."

He glanced at the women crowding behind him. "While you sat on this porch?"

"Yessir." Langley stiffened but kept his gaze steady. Pink tinged the tips of his ears.

People from the nearby houses emerged, bending over the porch rails as they searched for the cause of the uproar. Everyone followed the scowling corporal's progress as he stomped from his position on the road to report to the captain.

"I couldn't get off a clean shot, sir, not with him riding through the yards and into the trees. As the senior guard here, I take full responsibility. I should've kept the horse within sight instead of letting him graze beside the house."

The captain ran a hand down his face. After a moment, he turned to the group behind him. "Do any of you know who would dare to steal an army mount?"

While the others stood frozen, Phoebe Wilson, the older girl from next door, pushed her way forward. "It must've been that Rebel soldier what was hiding in the cellar here."

Millie went cold. How did Phoebe know about Sergeant Morgan? They'd all been careful to keep his presence hidden. She gripped Shiloh's hand and followed the others into the house at Captain Griffin's command.

The officer called the three children to stand before him.

Clever, but they don't know anything.

She had to give him credit. He admonished the children to tell the truth and promised no one would punish them. Thankfully, they hadn't seen or heard any indication of Morgan's presence.

Captain Griffin dismissed them and called for Dorcas, who swore she knew nothing about Sergeant Morgan being on the premises. She must not realize he was the one who gave permission for the clothes they took.

The officer moved on to Phoebe. "So, what do you know, Miss Phoebe Wilson?"

The girl licked her lips, then pointed to Rose and Celeste. "I saw them two coming out of the cellar before supper today. They looked guilty, like they's hiding something, so I snuck back after they come inside. I went in the cellar to see what was down there and saw that man, and where he'd been sleeping on a pallet."

Captain Griffin kept his eyes on the girl. "And he had on Confederate uniform?"

Phoebe hesitated, as if debating on whether to lie. "Well, no. But why else would he be hiding out down there?"

The captain shrugged with apparent unconcern. "He could be a deserter from either army, or just a no-account thief, hunting a place to rest. He could have gone in there after Miss Carrigan and her sister left, after seeing them come out, like you did."

Phoebe's nostrils flared, and her eyes shot angry sparks toward Rose and Celeste. "No! I tell you, they was hiding him. There was a blanket and a pillow and...and a stack of dirty plates near the door."

Captain Griffin waved her away, and Phoebe joined Dorcas and the children on the front porch. Millie's heartbeat sped up when he motioned to her and Shiloh, who sat with her on the settee. What should she do? Telling the truth would get them all in trouble. At least she could say she'd never seen the man.

Lydia intervened. "Millie had nothing to do with this."

Olivia joined her and took all the blame. "Captain, I'm the one who found him and took care of him."

Millie caught her breath when Rose stepped beside Olivia. Would she stand with the others? It was plain to everyone that Captain Griffin was smitten with Rose, and the feeling might be mutual.

"He was too weak to move," Rose said, "sick and exhausted from walking for days."

All three women stopped talking when the officer raised his hand for silence. Millie held her breath.

"All of you were in on this?" His gaze passed over each member of the group.

Edith Wynn tried to bring reason into the discussion. "Really, Captain, how could we turn a man out of his own house?"

"His house?" The officer crossed his arms and scoffed at the notion. "The owner of the house was hiding in his own cellar? Then apparently, he was a Confederate soldier, as Miss Wilson said."

Rose licked her lips. "When he heard the Union Army had taken Marietta, Sergeant Morgan traveled from Virginia to check on his family, not realizing they'd already fled the town."

She motioned toward Lydia and Olivia. "The three of us found him when we went to the cellar looking for put-up stores. He was asleep but wakened long enough to tell us who he was. We thought to let him sleep to regain his strength before setting out again."

Captain Griffin trained a fierce frown on her. "That's called aiding and abetting the enemy."

Rose lifted her chin, her face flushed. "What does it matter? We've all been labeled as traitors and taken as prisoners anyway. Deprived of our livelihood, moved from our homes, we're just biding our time here until your army can ship us out." She took a deep breath. "We did not ask for this war. We have no cause to refuse help to anyone in need, no matter what color they wear."

Millie stared in awe at the slight woman. Rose jeopardized her relationship with the captain to stand up for all of them. Would it do any good?

Captain Griffin turned away and headed toward the door. He looked back and said, "I thought I'd earned your trust. Now I see I was mistaken."

Millie's heart plunged as Edith embraced Rose and the others offered what little comfort they could. Emily called the children inside, and Millie helped Shiloh and Dorcas get the young ones settled for the night.

Downstairs, the older adults discussed their situation, but Millie's dismay devolved into anger as she got ready for bed.

What did that bossy officer think they were supposed to do, turn a sick man over to him? She was tired of men ruining her life. Cal had criticized her. That awful stranger attacked her, and then Troy stayed away for months. Even after she stood up for him, he'd ignored her. She was through with trying to please them.

She pounded her pillow, annoyed with it too. It was getting harder to find a comfortable position for sleeping, and she still had three months to go.

∿

JULY 16, 1864
CAMP CHASE, OHIO

*A*fter three days on and off trains, Troy yearned for a good long walk in the woods. What he got was a short walk from the depot to the Union Army Prison at Camp Chase.

Their numbers had grown with each stop along the way—

Chattanooga, Nashville, Louisville, Cincinnati—mostly with prisoners from Alabama, Mississippi, and Georgia from what he gathered as he listened to their conversations. A few men in line ahead of him had their possessions taken, their money exchanged for a receipt they could use at the camp store.

The man behind Troy snorted. "If that sutler is anything like the Roswell Mill's company store, they won't get much for it."

Troy surrendered his empty knapsack and then requested an audience with the camp commander. The sergeant sneered at him. "I'll be sure to pass that message along."

Each prisoner received a set of clothes and a blanket. The guards divided the men into three groups and marched them in different directions. His group passed rows of tents, which Troy supposed housed the Union trainees who milled about the area, and arrived at Prison Two, which the guard said stretched over several acres. Rows of wooden barracks lined both sides of a road wide enough for a wagon to pass. Trenches had been dug between the road and the buildings for drainage.

The officer who led Troy's group stopped to explain what the prisoners could expect. "You'll get two meals every day, breakfast an hour or two after sunrise, and dinner in late after-noon. A cook is assigned to each mess area, with supplies of meat, flour, coffee, and such. If you work, you'll be paid in full rations. Right now, work consists of digging ditches to drain the water away from the camp and shoring up the prison walls."

He stepped to the door of one building. "We provide you with soap to bathe and wood for your stoves. This prison has two wells, one for cooking and drinking water, the other for washing."

The guard called out the names for the first barrack, then moved to the second building. A dozen men were assigned to each, where the cots were stacked three high. Thankfully, Troy's assigned barrack stood near the well that supplied the drinking water. As soon as he finished the dinner, he retired for the night, more exhausted from the jostle of train travel than he would've been from walking all those days.

So many questions ran through his mind about this new situation. How soon could he get an audience with the commander and take the oath of allegiance? Even after that, what would he do? He'd need to find some work to provide for his living. All he knew was farming and odd bits of woodwork and smithing, which had supported him in his travels, but he could learn something else.

How could he find out about Lydia and Millie? The Federals said they'd be sending all the workers north, but where would they put the women? On the train, he'd learned that the Roswell mills had suffered the same fate as the one in Sweetwater. That meant hundreds of workers, mostly women, might be scattered from Kentucky to New York or beyond.

Troy needed a plan, but his brain refused to function. Now that he was beyond the reach of the Confederate Army, what was he to do? Three years he'd spent dodging the conscription, only to find himself a prisoner of the army he believed in.

How much longer could this war last?

CHAPTER 9

"*D*o all babies take so long to be born?" Millie blurted between contractions. She hardly had time to catch her breath before the next one hit. Then she had to push.

"First-time babies usually take the longest." Olivia wiped Millie's face and stroked her hair.

Back in June, she'd anticipated giving birth with only Lydia and a midwife in attendance. When the Union army sent them to Marietta, this group of women had banded together and were now as dear to her as anyone. They'd become her family as they settled in the refugee house in Louisville—two hundred miles from home.

From her place at Millie's feet, Edith guided the process with calm assurances. "You're doing fine. We're almost there. Hold on a minute."

Millie clenched the sheets as Lydia mopped her brow. Edith shifted her position. "Now, one more push."

Millie gathered her strength and bore down, determined to finish this job. She'd never been so exhausted. At last, she sank into the pillows at her back, happy to hear a baby's cry amid glad exclamations from the other women.

"You've got a girl."

"Listen to her, tellin' the news."

"Not much hair, just peach fuzz on her head."

As Millie struggled to stay awake, Lydia and Olivia huddled over the newborn. *Please, God, let her look like Troy.* "Can I see her?"

"Yes, ma'am."

The baby calmed down as Lydia lifted the sweet bundle and laid her in Millie's arms. With trembling hands, Millie peeled back the blanket to peer at the tiny, heart-shaped face. Dark eyes stared back at her. No question, she was Troy's. The fair complexion and long fingers affirmed her lineage. Before Millie could inspect the legs and toes, her daughter complained with a healthy cry.

Lydia called to their friends at the door. "Come meet my granddaughter. I think she's gonna be a singer. She's got the lungs for it."

Rose, Celeste, and Emily stood back as Ada showed Millie how to help the baby nurse. With some coaxing and encouragement, she soon succeeded and marveled at the love that surged through her for this tiny life.

"Have you decided on a name?" Rose asked.

The baby grasped her finger as Millie gazed at her. "Amelia." She lifted her eyes to Lydia. "I think she should have your middle name. Amelia Ruth."

Lydia laughed. "That's a mouthful for such a tiny girl. Maybe we should call her Amy until she grows into it."

She hesitated over what to say about the baby's family name. Amy Gibson or Amy McNeil? Maybe nobody would ask.

Maybe Troy would show up one day and make the decision for her.

Where was he? Did he have any idea where to find her?

~

OCTOBER 27, 1864
CAMP CHASE, OHIO

*D*ark clouds threatened to send the small gathering indoors, and the wind gusted now and then, but the sun held its own. Autumn decorated the ground with leaves of red and gold. It brightened the unending browns of the prison camp and carried a breeze of hope to the weary inhabitants.

Troy stood at attention while Sergeant Jake presented him with a rifle. "Welcome to the Union Army, Private McNeil."

Pride and wonder surged through Troy as they saluted each other. Three months he'd waited, hoped, and prayed. Finally, he was no longer a prisoner. Finally, he would be able to defend the cause he believed in, for the sake of his lifelong friends, Jem and Pansy.

Though his family had slaves, Pa would have released them if not for the law against it. Neither he nor Ma tolerated their mistreatment. Simon's vocal opinions on the matter had caused problems with some neighbors, so he'd left home for the North at sixteen, then joined the Union forces in sixty-one. According to various reports, his brother now languished in Libby Prison.

Troy waited until all the others in line had received their weapons, then pivoted to congratulate his fellows. Of the four who were former prisoners, two would be leaving for assignments elsewhere. He and Walter Dykes would continue at Camp Chase as guards. He was thankful to be in a position that didn't require him to shoot anyone, though the rifle was standard issue.

When he'd finally been granted an audience with the prison commander, Troy explained his views on slavery and how he'd avoided the Confederate conscription.

"I thought if I could get far enough north, I could find something to do to help the Union cause without havin' to fight my friends and neighbors."

General Richardson pursed his lips while he listened, never revealing his thoughts. When Troy ran out of words, he shuffled toward the door. "Well, thank you for hearin' me out, General. I reckon I'm finished now."

"How would you feel about guarding the prisoners here?" The general's question drew him back. "You'd have to carry a gun to ensure their respect, but I doubt you'll need to shoot anyone."

At last, Troy had croaked his acceptance. "I'd be right honored, sir. Thank you."

Now with the induction complete, Troy shook hands with his new roommate. They ducked into their shared quarters as the first drops of rain fell. Walter leaned his rifle against his bunk. "After weeks of training in the heat, I'm glad the cooler days are upon us."

Troy removed his coat and stretched out on his bed, his feet hanging off the end to keep from soiling the blanket with his new boots. "Yeah, but I'm wonderin' how cold it's gonna get in a couple of months. This is farther north than I've ever been."

"Just be glad we're here and not in the crowded barracks of Prison Two anymore. At least the general assigned us to a different section." Walter sat at the desk they shared and pulled out a few sheets of paper. He examined the pencils in the drawer, then opened his penknife and started shaving the end of one.

Troy rolled to his side and propped his head on one hand. "Yeah, although we still might get some taunts from the prisoners for goin' over to the other side. I guess they'll settle down after a while. You going to write to your wife now?"

Walter grinned. "Yeah. Gotta let her know I'll be sending some money home in a couple of weeks. With Atlanta under Union control, she oughta be able to buy whatever they need now."

A wave of sadness washed over Troy. As much as he didn't agree with Confederate politics, he hated to hear about more destruction so close to home. According to the reports going around, Sherman was burning his way across Georgia while Grant battered Virginia. How long could General Lee and President Davis hold out with such vicious attacks on both fronts? Would they wait to surrender until the South was totally destroyed?

"I won't be long at this," Walter said. "Don't you need to write some letters to your folks or that gal back home?"

"I'll write to Ma tomorrow." He rolled onto his back and stared at the ceiling. "As for Millie, I don't know where she is. Maybe Ma has heard something, although I doubt it. All I can do now is pray that she's safe, wherever she may be." His heart quailed at the notion of never seeing her again. He'd find her somehow. He'd use whatever resources the Union Army offered. Surely, someone could tell him where the Federals had sent her.

$\sim$

November 7, 1864
Louisville, Kentucky

*I*t's funny how people come into your life, disappear for a while, and then return without warning. Millie gazed out the second-floor window of the refuge house, holding the baby to her shoulder and thinking over recent events.

Two weeks after Amelia's birth, Captain Griffin, now a major, found them in Louisville and began a serious pursuit of Rose Carrigan. Millie and the other women had noticed the attraction between those two from their first meeting in Marietta. She'd figured their friendship was over, though, when someone stole the officer's horse and he blamed them for harboring a Rebel. Then, out of the blue, Rose told them she'd received a letter from him, and the relationship was salvaged.

Millie tried to bury her envy and be happy for her friend. The major had cared enough to seek out Rose's location when he was hundreds of miles away. How silly of Millie to expect Troy to find her when he obviously hadn't cared enough to write much when she was still at home. Or to acknowledge her on the road to Marietta.

She shifted Amy to peer into the tiny face. "He has no idea what he's missing, does he, sweetie? At least I have you and Lydia. We'll be fine without him. Just us girls."

Millie jumped when a hand gripped her shoulder. "Millie, we're going outside now. I thought you wanted to meet Doctor Spencer."

"Oh, yes."

Lydia reached for the baby so Millie could don her shawl.

And now, two other men from their past had arrived in Louisville. Doctor Spencer had treated her a time or two as a child back home. He'd also set Troy's arm when he broke it several years ago climbing that big oak to untangle their kite. It was the first time she'd met him. The rest of the family had come as well, but she'd had eyes only for Troy.

Millie hadn't met the other man, but Sergeant Seth Morgan had certainly influenced all their lives back in July, hiding out in the house in Marietta and stealing Captain Griffin's horse.

She fell into step beside Lydia as they moseyed down the hallway and toward the stairs. The others were far enough ahead not to hear if she kept her voice low. "I heard Olivia weeping last night. Did you find out what happened?"

Lydia paused at the top of the stairs where a beam of light brightened the dark wood. "Her father was at the house they visited yesterday. Olivia hadn't seen him since he sent her to Georgia years ago. She was quite shocked to find him here with his new family."

Millie wanted to ask more, but Wade's excited voice carried back to them. "C'mon, y'all! My pa's over there."

She scuttled after Lydia, eager to witness the boy's reunion with his father. Behind them, Dorcas rushed from the house in time to see Wade leap into Doctor Spencer's arms. The guards who'd escorted him from the prison stood back while the man embraced his wife and son. Olivia's aunt and uncle hovered nearby.

"How did the doctor know his wife was here?" Dorcas asked.

Lydia chuckled as they strolled to the bench where they could enjoy the meeting but not disrupt it. "Remember when I went for a walk yesterday? I was over at the depot when a group of prisoners arrived. Doctor Spencer was one of them. I didn't recognize him at first, but Sergeant Morgan was there too. When he said the name, I remembered him."

Dorcas stared in wonder. "If that ain't jes' like the Lord's workin'. But who's that comin' this way?"

Millie turned her attention the way Dorcas indicated, and Lydia gasped. "Oh my, that's Seth, uh, Sergeant Morgan."

Amy began fussing, and Lydia stood. "I guess she doesn't enjoy sittin' still. I'll walk her around a bit." Lydia's course led straight to the sergeant.

Millie and Dorcas exchanged looks of surprise. "I wonder what that's about." They continued to chat and sneak occasional peeks at Lydia, who joined the mysterious Sergeant Morgan a few yards away from their bench.

"Ever since Marietta, she's been different, not talkin' as much and seemin' more withdrawn," Millie said. "I thought it was just the circumstances, but now I wonder if that man might have something to do with it."

Dorcas hid a grin behind her hand. "It might bear watchin' if'n he's gonna be here awhile."

When Amy's fretting became so loud that Millie could hear from where she sat, she rose from the bench. "I guess I'd better go feed her." Dorcas stood to follow, but Millie protested. "You stay and enjoy an hour of leisure. You don't get many of them."

She crossed the yard and reached for the baby. "I think she's hungry again."

Millie bounced the baby while Lydia made the proper introductions. "Millie, you never got to meet Sergeant Morgan when we were in Marietta. Seth, this beautiful girl is my step-daughter."

Millie smiled. "So you're the one who stole Major Griffin's horse. Someday I'd like to hear how you accomplished that, but right now I've got to feed the little one. Nice to meet you at last, Sergeant."

She let her smile fade as she slipped inside the house. The element of attraction between Lydia and Sergeant Morgan was hard to miss. Lydia deserved another chance at life with a good man. A better man than Cal had been. She wasn't sure if Sergeant Morgan could fill that position, but he'd been generous and encouraged their group to take whatever they needed from his home in Marietta.

If they ever saw the end of this war, maybe he and Lydia could be happy together. That thought gave her pause. What would she and Amy do if Lydia left?

"Oh, I'm just borrowin' trouble, ain't I?" She spoke to Amy as they entered their room, now empty with everyone preoccupied downstairs or outside. "When will I learn to stop dreamin' of some perfect tomorrow and live for today? As long as we have food and shelter and friends around us, I should...no, I *will* be grateful."

~

NOVEMBER 8, 1864
CAMP CHASE, OHIO

*T*roy saluted Sergeant Jake as the man hustled toward him and Walter. It was time to pick up the prisoners' rations and distribute them among the barracks of Prison One, but Jake's hurried approach indicated a change in the routine.

"Good morning, men. I need one of you to report to Captain Gallagher. You can decide which of you should go. You'll accompany him into town to provide security at one of the voting locations."

Troy glanced at Walter, who usually spoke for them both. "I'll go. McNeil can handle the distribution. Are you expecting trouble with the voting, Sergeant?"

Jake passed a hand over his beard. "Possibly. Not everyone's in favor of President Lincoln getting re-elected. Some folks blame his policies for the war lasting so long."

Walter nodded. "I'll get my rifle and head on over, sir." He ducked inside the tent, returned with his weapon, saluted Sergeant Jake again, and strode away.

Troy took a step toward the supply tent, but the sergeant held him back. "We're not providing food today, McNeil. Orders from General Richardson."

Dumbfounded, Troy forgot himself and blurted his questions. "No food? But why?"

Sergeant Jake lifted one eyebrow. "Because we're ordered to do so, soldier."

"Yes, sir." Troy snapped his lips together, chagrined at his lapse. He straightened his spine and saluted. "What do you need me to do, then, if that duty is off my schedule, sir?"

"Take some time for yourself. Clean your rifle. Write some letters. Then make your rounds early." Jake appeared to be agitated by the change in orders. He paced away, then returned. "Are you a praying man, Private McNeil?"

Troy blanched, knowing he'd let down somewhat in that area since he'd joined the army. "Yes, sir, although I could do more of it."

"Couldn't we all? While you're praying, then, you might send up a word for our Union men in prison down in Andersonville. Their treatment affects how we're able to provide for the men here. We will respond in kind. And don't forget to pray about this election. It could greatly affect the outcome of this war."

Troy swallowed at the implications. How did it help anyone for each army to retaliate every mistreatment? How was his brother Simon being treated? According to Ma's latest letter, they hadn't heard from him in months.

"I will, sir," Troy said. "It's hard to claim we're loving our fellow man, as we've been told to do, when we're aiming rifles at each other."

"You have the right of it, son. I hope to have better news for you tomorrow." He walked away, his usually brisk pace slower, as if he carried a heavy load.

Ducking inside their quarters, Troy retrieved the Bible he and Walter shared. He'd put this unexpected spell of leisure to good use. It was time he did some serious thinking and praying for someone other than himself and those he loved.

November 8, 1864
Louisville, Kentucky

*T*aking their turn at laundering for the soldiers, Millie and Shiloh started at dawn so they could finish by midday. The sun chased a chill from the air as they neared the end of their task. Birdsong added a cheery note, and splashes of red and gold on the trees brightened the yard.

Millie stooped to lift another shirt from the basket at her feet, then paused with it in her hand. Noise from the street sounded like more than traffic passing by. "Do you hear that?"

Both women hastily pinned up the last of the garments, picked up their baskets, and rushed inside. Edith met them at the base of the stairs.

"I'm glad you girls are done with the laundry. I want you to stay in the house until all the commotion dies down."

Shiloh protested. "But it's my turn to fetch the children from school."

"Not today. I've already asked Isaac and Mr. Anderson to do that. They'll be better able to protect them if it's needed."

Millie grasped Edith's arm. "What's happening? Why would they need protection?"

"Today's election day," Edith said. "Lieutenant Goodson says they've put twice as many guards at the polls all over town. I guess some people get mighty worked up about the candidates."

Millie started up the stairs. "I wonder if we can see anything from the upstairs windows."

Shiloh followed, worrying out loud as they went. "Lord, have mercy. There's already enough trouble in the world with this war. We don't need fightin' in the streets."

Lydia already stood at the window in the room they shared. She turned as they entered. "What's all the noise about?"

"It's election day," Millie said. "We heard men shoutin' and what sounded like a bunch of horses goin' down the street."

Shiloh peered out the glass. "Mrs. Edith said they're

doubling the guards all over town. She's sending the men in my place to get the children from school. Do you think there'll be trouble?"

Millie remembered hearing some comments from the guards. "Heaven only knows. That McClellan fellow has strong support in this state. The Kentucky governor is determined to keep the opposition away from the voting polls. He even arrested the Lieutenant Governor and a judge, had them deported to Virginia."

Lydia put an arm around Shiloh, who was visibly shaken. "Now, the voting has nothing to do with us. We're out of that on two counts, being female and being Southerners. We should be fine as long as we stay inside and off the streets."

Millie picked up Amy and dared to stir the pot again with her next words. "But those suffragists keep fighting for women to get the right to vote and get more education like the men. I'd like to go to one of their meetings and see what it's like."

"Honey, those women have been working on it for years and haven't made much headway." Lydia turned her gaze back to the window. "I reckon they never will, not as long as men are the ones voting on their proposals."

"What they have to do is convince the men to vote for it." Millie flashed a smile at them. "You know, use their charms to persuade their husbands and...other menfolk."

Lydia stared at her, seemingly shocked by Millie's boldness.

Millie pressed her lips to keep from laughing. "Oh, Lydia, you forget I worked in the mill too. All the women in spinning loved to talk about how they kept their husbands in line. They provided an education nobody ever learned in school."

Lydia recovered and laughed. "Well, I didn't know you were paying such close attention. Maybe I should have come to you for advice."

CHAPTER 10

November 16, 1864
Camp Chase, Ohio

*P*risoners' rations had resumed, much to Troy's relief. The men in his charge looked as though they couldn't afford to miss much food, and it didn't improve anyone's attitude. Walter returned from his assignment to report that the election had proceeded with no major altercations.

A few days later, several more prisoners arrived to swell the numbers at Chase even more. Among them, a doctor, Captain Evan Spencer, according to Sergeant Jake. This was good news for the prisoners and their keepers alike, since they'd lost their last physician when smallpox raged through the camp. Troy was glad to have missed that episode. Reports said more men had died from disease than from the battles these last four years.

New arrivals, however, could be bad news. Some of them instigated fights or upset the relative peace when they brought tales from the field. Others challenged the prevailing hierarchy among the prisoners. Troy had learned to tread carefully lest he add to the unrest by displaying his unique circumstances. Many of his fellow Southerners sneered at his opposition to secession and resented his presence in the Union Army.

One fellow assigned to Prison One worried him. Sergeant Morgan of the Georgia Eighteenth Infantry brought his reputation with him. Rumor had it he was a mite unhinged and had a nasty temper. Walter pointed him out. From a distance, the fellow appeared to be average in size and as sane as the rest of them. Looks could be deceiving, though.

It was best for Troy to avoid close association with anyone from Georgia or Alabama, if possible, including Sergeant Morgan and Doctor Spencer. More and more, he followed Uncle Henry's advice to keep his eyes and ears open, but his mouth shut.

He chuckled at the direction his thoughts had taken. That sounded like some verses in Proverbs he'd read last week and remembered learning at Mama's knee.

Of course, Pa's favorite proverb was the one about using the rod to drive foolishness out of the child. Pa had been tough on all four of his boys, though Paul, as the eldest, claimed he and Simon endured more than Rupert and Troy. That may have been true when they were younger, but the war had changed the family dynamics. Simon and Troy were the renegades who sided with the Union while Paul and Rupert followed Pa's fierce loyalty to the South.

Ma had a more objective viewpoint, having been a teacher. She'd always encouraged them to consider a matter from all sides and not go blindly along with the crowd. In following that advice, Troy had alienated a few people. His entire family had earned a reputation for independent thinking. Simon liked to say they argued well, but they loved well too.

Troy's thoughts circled back, as they frequently did, to Millie.

Especially at night, when the camp settled down. Whether on watch or lying on his cot, he relived every moment of that fateful time last winter. Guilt still dogged his thoughts, though the man's death had been an accident, and he tried to imagine what he could have done differently. If only he'd waited to leave later...or turned back sooner...or seen the man before he entered the house. He wouldn't contemplate what might've happened had he not gone back at all.

Then he'd remember their sweet parting. He could close his eyes and see Millie, hear her voice, taste her lips. Did she relive it too? Did she ache to be in his arms the way he ached to hold her? Or had she found someone to replace him? She'd been sheltered in that small mill town all her life. She had no knowledge of how the world was, how cruel it could be.

He could only pray for her safety—and hope she didn't hate him for not acknowledging her when she'd defended him to Major Tompkins back in July. Did she understand he thought he was protecting her? If the major had decided Troy was a spy, anyone associated with him would also fall under suspicion.

≈

November 16, 1864
Louisville, Kentucky

*W*hat a week. Millie collapsed on her bed and prayed that tomorrow would usher in calmer days. So many comings and goings had upset Amy's schedule, and she expressed her unhappiness with frequent bouts of crying. Motherhood was so much harder than Millie had expected it to be.

It had started yesterday morning, when Olivia went to the prison, expecting her husband to take the oath of allegiance and join them at the refugee house. She'd returned alone and distraught.

"I can't understand why he's so insistent on not taking the oath," Olivia said. "It's not as if he's against the Union. He's a doctor. He can use his skills anywhere."

Millie couldn't help but overhear as Lydia and Mrs. Edith tried to soothe her.

"Your husband told Isaac he feels God directed him to delay taking the oath. Evan feels his Hippocratic oath means he tends the greatest need, and the prisoners need him most right now." Edith moved her hand in circles on her niece's back.

Lydia offered Olivia a fresh handkerchief. "He seems to have a special connection with Sergeant Morgan, like he needs to be near whenever Seth—Sergeant Morgan—goes into a rage."

That worried Millie. She didn't want to see Lydia involved with a man who had frequent bouts of temper. Maybe she should discourage their friendship.

At least one possible calamity had been avoided. Sergeant Morgan and the doctor had left town without running into Major Griffin. No telling how much worse the day could have gone if those two had faced each other after Morgan stole the major's horse.

In the afternoon, Major Griffin had roused the entire household when he couldn't find Rose to take her for a drive they'd planned. At least that mystery pulled Olivia out of her depression. She and Lydia found the major's discarded note in the office trash can.

After hours of waiting and praying, Rose returned safe and unharmed.

"But what happened?" Millie asked after Rose went upstairs.

Major Griffin's concern bled through his brief explanation. "Unfortunately, Rose's former associate at the library bribed the guard here to kidnap her." He glanced at the others who'd gathered. "I hope you all will see that she rests. This ordeal has taken a toll on her. I'll plan to check on her Sunday and escort her to church if she feels up to going."

The incident revived memories of Millie's own traumatic experiences. How safe were they here if a guard could carry off such a crime?

Faced with uncertainty, Millie turned to prayer as she never had before. Going to church was difficult with an infant, so she pulled out the Bible that Lydia had brought with them. Dorcas rocked Amy and listened to Millie read it while the others went to church on Sunday. The next day, an unexpected answer came to her prayer for safety.

Rose approached Lydia and Millie as soon as Amy went down for a nap. "Ladies, I have a request to make of you. Celeste and I plan to go with Major Griffin to visit his family in Indiana. Celeste suggested maybe y'all could stay at her employer's house. You could help with the cleaning and cook-ing. Mrs. Coker—the woman she works for—is worried Amy might get sick, with there not being any heat in the refugee house."

"But what about when Celeste returns to Louisville?" Millie asked. "Won't it be too crowded with all of us there?"

Rose laughed. "Dear Millie, that house has seven bedrooms. It's bigger than Sergeant Morgan's house in Marietta. Honestly, I think Mrs. Coker misses having her family there. She treats Celeste like a family member, and I'm sure she'll do the same for y'all."

Millie sighed, caution warring against her excitement. "As long as she can abide Amy's crying spells, it sounds like a wonderful idea to me."

On Wednesday, she and Lydia packed their few possessions and made the move. Major Griffin borrowed a wagon to carry them and their baggage. The company bound for Indiana proposed to leave on the morrow. Mrs. Coker assumed her new role as guardian and declared herself Amy's adopted great-grandmother.

While Major Griffin tended to the horse and wagon, Celeste led Millie and Lydia upstairs to the rooms they would occupy. "You can use the wardrobe and the chest of drawers for your clothing. Hattie will show where to find clean linens for the beds."

They retraced their steps to the parlor and exchanged amused glances at the sight of Mrs. Coker cuddling the baby.

Lydia expressed her gratitude again for the opportunity to winter there. "You mustn't hesitate to ask me or Millie to do any chores. We're both capable, and except for my days at the bakery, have nothing to occupy our time besides caring for Amy."

Mrs. Coker waved away her concerns. "We'll figure it all out."

When Millie asked about Mrs. Coker's grandson, Lieutenant Gideon Hart, the older lady waved away her concern. "Gideon's on the mend, so Herbert will resume his usual household duties. As for that grandson of mine, we'll soon put him in his place."

~

DECEMBER 27, 1864
CAMP CHASE

*G*ray clouds blocked out the sunlight as Troy followed his roommate to the commander's quarters. An icy drizzle prompted him to pull up his coat collar and snug his kepi toward his ears.

Walter set the ladder in place, climbed it, and unhooked a dried spray of greenery over the doorframe. He dropped the prickly frond into Troy's waiting arms. "Didn't we just hang these boughs the other day?"

"Yeah, but the general says they have to come down today. Says it looks more like a dance hall than a prison." Troy added the branch to the growing pile outside.

"Did nobody tell him whose idea it was to put them up in the first place?"

Another bough muffled Troy's answer. "His wife won't be visiting again for a while, so it's safe to remove all the decorations." He tossed that branch toward the pile in time to catch the next one. "Christmas is over, anyway, and it's a mite depressing to fancy up a prison when everyone's dreaming about being home for the holiday."

"You're right about tha—yeow!" Walter dropped the knife he'd been using to pry the nails from the wood. It landed point-down in Troy's outstretched hand just below his thumb.

Troy's cry vied with his comrade's as he jerked the blade from his skin. "Watch it, Walt. That knife nearly took off my thumb." He tugged his kerchief from his neck and wrapped it around the bleeding appendage. He fought off the sudden dizziness that accompanied the searing ache.

Walter scrambled down the ladder. "Sorry, McNeil. A splinter buried itself under my fingernail. I don't think I can get it out, and you need to get a proper bandage on that cut. Let's head over to the doctor."

The throbbing pain overshadowed his discomfort from the frigid dampness. "Maybe this sleet will stop by the time we get done there, and then we can finish up."

They abandoned the chore and hurried to the infirmary.

Blessed warmth greeted them as they pushed inside the building. Two rows of cots lined the center aisle, and nearly every bed was occupied. Besides a few moans from some of the occupants, the room was silent. A skinny boy crossed toward them. "You fellas need something?"

Troy extended his hand. "Got a cut that might need stitchin' here. And Walter has a splinter in his hand. If the doctor has a moment."

"He's in his office. I'll get him."

Moments later, the lad returned with a tall, dark-haired man. His spectacles perched on top of his head accented the gray at his temples. A tremor of alarm shot through Troy, but he couldn't figure out why. Maybe he'd developed a revulsion of doctors. Truth to tell, his last encounter with the one at Henry's last summer had precipitated all that happened since.

The doctor eyed them. "What's the problem, men?"

Walter showed him his finger. "If you can get this out for me, Doc, I'll get back to taking down the commander's decorations. McNeil's hand might take longer."

"If you'll both follow me, we'll get you fixed up. My instruments are in the back room."

Five minutes later, Walter left, and the doctor fastened his attention on Troy. "Your name's McNeil?"

"Yes, sir. I reckon it only needs a few stitches," Troy said.

"This will sting." The doctor's warning coincided with a squirt of something that burned Troy's hand and made his eyes water. A flash of silver tugged at the skin's ripped edges, but the doctor kept talking.

"Where you from, McNeil?"

Troy snorted. "Alabama." He should've known this man—a Confederate officer—would detect his accent.

"I thought you might be. Whereabouts?"

"A little place called Wedowee, not far from the Georgia line." He guessed the doctor's aim was to keep his mind off the pain. This wasn't Troy's first experience with that tactic.

"Is'at so? I'm from Georgia myself, near the Alabama line." He appeared to expect a certain response—or did Troy imagine it?

Troy pulled his hand back as soon as the doctor tied off the thread. "Thank you, sir. I need to get back and help Walter finish removing the decorations."

Doctor Spencer halted his retreat. "When you finish with that, Private, I have a favor to ask. There's a man in Prison One, a fellow Georgian. I need you to bring him to me so I can check on him. His name is Seth Morgan. He might balk, but you can threaten him if you have to."

Something about the request raised Troy's suspicions, but he had no reason to refuse the doctor. "Yes, sir, I'll return in a bit, then."

He rushed out the door, heedless of the cold rain now mingled with snow. He wasn't sure it was the same doctor who had set his arm several years before, but Troy wanted to avoid any questions as to why he'd joined the Union Army. The man seemed to see right into his mind.

∼

DECEMBER 27, 1864
LOUISVILLE, KENTUCKY

*M*illie bounced her fretful baby as Lydia wished their housemates a good time on their ride.

"You should have gone with them, Lydia. You'd enjoy riding in the sleigh through the snow."

"I don't think Celeste and Lieutenant Hart need another chaperone. They have Rose and Major Griffin. I would feel out of place. Besides, I can help you with Amy."

"I think she'll settle down as soon as she's fed. Hattie's idea about letting her breathe the steam helped."

"Go on, then." Lydia urged Millie toward the stairs. "I'll wash enough diapers for tomorrow before I go up."

Millie climbed the steps to her room and settled in the rocking chair to nurse the babe. She marveled at the love that surged whenever she gazed at her daughter. At two months old, Amy already displayed a distinct personality. She demonstrated traits Millie attributed to Troy, who wouldn't be able to deny her. If he ever got to meet her.

This morning's hard freeze brought back memories of that January day when she'd slipped on the ice at home. Her sprained ankle had kept her out of work, so she'd been there when Troy showed up. In recent months, she'd refused to let her thoughts linger on those days. Now she took time to examine each word, each look he'd given her. How amazed she'd been to find he felt the same pull of attraction as she did. Did he still care for her, or had time and distance made him forget?

Amy's gurgle interrupted her musing, and Millie smiled at the sweet picture she made. Her soft breaths issued from pink parted lips, and a milk bubble formed in the corner of her mouth. For all the reasons Millie might hate to think of the events that led to Amy's conception, she couldn't regret the precious result of them.

She wrapped the blanket more snugly around the little body and laid her in the middle of the bed. She'd heard Lydia mount the stairs a moment ago. With no word from Troy since July, she no longer felt bound to the promise they'd made. Surely, she didn't have to worry about any retribution for that man's death here in Louisville, surrounded by Union supporters and the Union Army. Her fear for Troy's life had kept her silent, but her silence had created a rift between her and her stepmother.

She'd overheard Celeste ask Lydia if she'd had any news of Troy. Millie should warn Lydia not to get her hopes up for their reconciliation. Now, while they weren't surrounded by dozens of strangers, it was time to share her story with Lydia.

CHAPTER 11

December 27, 1864
Camp Chase, Ohio

*T*roy nudged the prisoner forward with the butt of his rifle.

"Where are we going, Corporal?"

"Over to the infirmary. Get a move on. I ain't got all day." He spoke as little as possible because of his distinct accent.

The prisoner spoke over his shoulder. "Is Doctor Spencer all—"

"You'll soon learn everything you need to know. Keep walking."

Troy couldn't tell what he didn't know. The doctor's request had struck him as odd, but the commander treated the doctor like a respected captain, though they served in different armies, and he expected his subordinates to show Doctor Spencer the same respect.

After the doctor had sewed up his hand, he'd asked him to bring the half-crazed sergeant from the Eighteenth Georgia infantry to his office. Under threat of punishment, if necessary.

With such a strong directive, Troy figured he'd better approach the prisoner with caution.

Snow on the ground slowed their pace to a careful trek. His uneasiness increased with every step, but soon the infirmary came into view. As they neared the building, Doctor Spencer pushed open the door to his quarters and beckoned them inside.

The doctor pointed to a couple of chairs for his visitors while he propped on the corner of his desk-cum-laboratory. "Before we get to proper introductions, allow me to explain why I asked the private to bring you here, Seth."

"Let me guess." The sergeant smirked. "You had a premonition I'd get into trouble today, and you wanted to save your bandages."

The doctor gave Morgan an expression that reminded Troy of his mother, raised eyebrows and a frown. He continued as if the prisoner hadn't interrupted. "A couple of guards came to me this morning with minor injuries related to their duties. When I heard the other guard call this man's name, it caught my interest because he already seemed vaguely familiar."

He switched his attention to Troy. "I believe I set the arm you broke a few years back while you were visiting relatives in New Manchester, Georgia."

Apprehension sent a chill down Troy's back. Had he heard tales about Troy's resistance to the conscription? Though Doctor Spencer seemed to be a decent fellow, some Southerners were obstinate in their loyalty. Troy pushed those thoughts aside. What could they do to him in a Union prison? "I didn't think you'd remember. That was six or seven years ago."

The doctor chuckled. "I probably wouldn't have remembered except your Aunt Lydia has everyone in the Confederate army looking for you."

"She does? Why?" Apprehension escalated into alarm. Had

something happened to Millie? Why would Lydia give his name to the men he'd been avoiding?

The prisoner gawked at him. "*This* is Troy McNeil, Lydia's nephew? He was right under our noses?"

While the doctor nodded, Troy spun to face the other man. "How do you know Aunt Lydia? And just who are you, anyway?"

Evan Spencer cleared his throat and completed the introduction as if they were meeting in someone's parlor. "Troy McNeil, meet Seth Morgan. Your aunt was in the group that stayed in Seth's house in Marietta, along with my wife and family."

Troy's confused glare bounced from Morgan to Doc. He still clutched the rifle, but the business end of it pointed at the floor.

"How'd they end up in his house?" Troy addressed the doctor and pointed to Morgan. "And how'd they meet him there if he's Confederate? The town was overrun with the Union Army when I was there last summer."

The doctor held up his hands. "I know you have a lot of questions. Give us time to explain, and you'll see." He motioned for Morgan to begin.

A weary sigh preceded the sergeant's explanation. "When I heard the Federals were moving into North Georgia, I applied for a furlough. It finally got approved in July, so I headed home. I had to wait until dark to reach my house in town."

Troy tapped his foot with impatience as the prisoner scratched his head. "Unbeknownst to me, the Union had burned down the mills over in Roswell and New Manchester and put the workers on wagons to take them to Marietta."

"I know about that," Troy said.

Morgan paced to the stove to warm his hands. "As I understand it, most of the workers were women, and the army soon ran out of room for them and their families at the Georgia Military Institute. A cavalry officer found the houses on my street deserted, so he brought several wagonloads of folks to stay there until their turn to board a train heading north."

The man's meandering explanation made no sense. "I still don't see how—"

Morgan scowled. "I'm gettin' to it. It was close to dawn when I reached my street, and I could see the guards walkin' between the houses. Our old root cellar was partly hidden by overgrown bushes, so I hid in there and went to sleep. When I woke up, I found three women going through my family's canned goods. One of those women was Doc's wife, one was from Roswell, and the other one was your Aunt Lydia."

No mention of Millie. "But you said the workers and their families stayed there. Were they there alone? No one else was with 'em?"

Doctor Spencer answered. "My son was with my wife, as well as her aunt and uncle and cousin. There were two families from Roswell, and Millie was with Lydia, of course."

The doctor's penetrating gaze raised prickles on Troy's skin. His heart raced. "How was she? Millie, I mean. How is she doing? Do you know?"

"Yes, she seemed fine when we saw them in Louisville, back in November." He challenged Troy with his watchful stare. "We also got to meet your beautiful little daughter."

Daughter? The word pulsated through Troy's mind. He must have misunderstood. "Daughter?" he asked. "How can I have a daughter?"

～

DECEMBER 27, 1864
LOUISVILLE, KENTUCKY

*M*illie knocked on Lydia's door and twisted the knob at her call to enter. "Amy's asleep. Can we talk a few minutes?"

"Of course." Lydia set aside her brush and started braiding her hair. "I've missed our quiet times together. Should we go downstairs and make some tea?"

"No." Millie reached out a hand to keep Lydia in her chair. "I'd rather stay here, where we won't be interrupted or...or overheard."

"All right. What do you want to discuss?"

Millie swallowed and sat on the edge of the bed. "I want to tell you what happened. Back in January of last year."

"All right." Her hands dropped to her lap as she shifted to face Millie fully.

"I should have told you before, but we decided to keep it between us, Troy and me."

"I see," she said, but her brow puckered.

Millie picked at the pilled cotton on the bedspread. "You remember I'd sprained my wrist and my ankle. I was recovering, so I was home when Troy visited. After you left for work the next morning, I lost my balance somehow. Troy was right there, and he caught me."

How was it she blushed at this part? She closed her eyes and plunged ahead. "He kissed me. But that's all that happened. Then he left. I think it scared both of us." She chuckled, recalling again Troy's shaky breath, how he'd smiled and set her gently in the chair.

She took a deep breath. "What happened next is difficult to tell. I was so—I'm not sure what the word is—excited that Troy felt the same way I did. After he left, I guess I wasn't paying attention, and somebody caught me unaware. He grabbed me—"

"Someone came into the house? Who was it?"

"An escaped prisoner or a straggler from one of the armies, maybe." Millie's voice shook as she relived those moments. "He was dirty and evil-looking. He had a knife." She put a finger at her neck where she could still feel a faint scar.

She rushed on as Lydia gaped, obviously astounded.

"I thought all he wanted was food. I filled a basket and thought he'd leave. But then he...he forced me down the hall and into my bedroom." Her breath grew shallow as she remembered the helpless feeling. "He tied my hands and pushed me toward the bed."

Lydia's hands flew to her mouth as she gasped. "Oh, Millie. I'm so sorry. I thought—"

"Please let me finish." She pushed the words past her lips, swiping at the tears on her face. "His intention was clear, but by some miracle Troy came back. He grabbed the man and threw him on the floor. They fought." She drew in a deep breath. "The man hit his head on the hearth, and he died."

"I'm confused. Are you telling me this to say..." Lydia's voice squeaked, and she paused to inhale. "Amy *isn't* Troy's daughter?"

"Oh, she is. The man never... And you can see she has Troy's eyes and chin."

"Yes, but that means..." Lydia's voice hardened. "If Troy took advantage of you at such a time, I'll—"

"No! It wasn't like that. I promise."

Millie stretched out a hand to halt the threats. "Troy helped me clean up the house so nobody would know, not even you, to protect us all. If we reported it, they might've turned him into the Confederate Army. People might turn against us. And I...I couldn't stand for people to pity me." She took a deep breath and pushed on. "He stayed at the Tuckers' that night and came over the next day to teach me how to fight back if anyone else accosted me. He was so sweet, and we.... I take all the blame."

The tears welled despite her struggle. "I begged him to love me. I wanted to wipe out the memory of the attack, to replace it with the feeling of being loved for myself instead of the object of some man's lustful intentions."

Lydia moved to the bed and wrapped Millie in her embrace. "I have to say it surprised me to learn the two of you felt that way about each other. I never guessed it was Troy until you spoke up when they captured him on the road to Marietta."

"Well, at the time, I thought he loved me." Millie sniffed and willed the tears to stop. "I'm not so sure anymore. He ignored me when I stood up for him back in July. And he's made no effort to find me since then. Anyway, I wanted you to know what happened. Also, to warn you not to get your hopes up that he'll marry me, even if you find him. I don't know how he'll react when he learns about Amy."

∼

CAMP CHASE, OHIO

*T*roy waited for the answer to his question while Sergeant Morgan stared.

The prisoner chuckled. "I guess you'd better explain it to him, Doc. You're much better at that kind of thing."

The doctor choked off a laugh. "With my son being only five, I'd not planned on such a conversation for some time. How old are you, Troy? Didn't your Pa ever talk to you about—"

"I know how babies are made, but..." He glanced toward Seth Morgan and steeled himself to ask his question. "Don't it take more than one time?"

The prisoner barked a harsh laugh and stalked to the window.

Troy's face burned. "I heard Ma, a few years ago, tell Aunt Lydia not to lose hope, even though she'd been married a good while."

Doctor Spencer ran a hand through his hair. "Sometimes, for some people, it does take longer. But not always. Anytime you lie with a woman, there's the possibility she'll conceive."

The doctor kept talking, but Troy's mind wandered. Had Millie known that? Was it why she urged him into her bed? Not that he'd needed much convincing, crazy as she made him. Was *that* the news she'd referred to in the note he'd found at the house?

A baby?

"You should write a letter and let them know you're here," Doctor Spencer said. "Seth has the Louisville address where they're staying."

Troy fisted his hands. He wasn't much good at writing, though he tried to let Ma know how he fared from time to time. Could he trust Seth Morgan—the supposed lunatic who raged like a madman at times but joked with Doctor Spencer as if they were bosom friends?

If it was true, if Troy had a daughter, if he'd left Millie in such a predicament without her even knowing where he was or how to reach him, he'd better write that letter without delay. He wouldn't consider the possibility the child could be the result of that low-life's attack. Hadn't Troy arrived in time to quash that likelihood?

He shuffled his feet and addressed the sergeant. "So...you have Aunt Lydia's direction. Can you help me write a letter?"

Seth glared at him, then shifted his stare to Doctor Spencer. "Why me?"

"Because you have nothing better to do," the doctor said, "while I have more patients than I can handle."

"Doc, you have more patience than any man I know."

Troy caught the play on words, but he waited for the man to

answer. Morgan scrubbed his face, tugged his beard, and sent Troy an irritated frown. "I'll have to get her letter from my stuff in the barrack. How do you propose we do that without drawing everyone's attention?"

Troy hitched a shoulder. "I suppose I could drag you here again tomorrow. Would you be all right with that, Doc?"

The doctor had turned his attention to cleaning some instruments on his desk. "I don't have a lock on the door, so all you have to do is walk in. It might help if Seth developed a cough or a rash of some kind, so you could say he needed medical attention. I'll leave it to y'all to figure that out."

A nod from Seth sealed the agreement. "I guess you'd better escort me back to my hotel, then, Private McNeil. Maybe Doc can find some coffee to offer us tomorrow." He tossed the teasing remark toward the doctor.

"I hear ya, Seth. You just brace yourself for the cold walk over and be glad to get out of the wind." He grinned at them. "I leave it to you to figure out how you're going to tell Mrs. Gibson you found her nephew."

❧

JANUARY 23, 1865
LOUISVILLE, KENTUCKY

*M*illie bundled Amy in a warm blanket, then settled the baby in the old pram that Lieutenant Hart brought from the attic. After several days of brutal cold, everyone was eager to enjoy a day of milder weather.

Millie pushed the metal contraption while Celeste and the lieutenant walked behind her on the path to the park. They passed a few others out to enjoy the sunshine, and Millie returned the smiles and nods, along with the occasional comment about her "precious baby." At the park entrance, Millie spotted Lydia coming toward them.

"Oh, I'd have waited on my errands if you'd mentioned taking a stroll." Lydia smiled, but her gaze darted away.

"We'll be glad for you to join us now." Celeste removed her hand from Lieutenant Hart's arm and gestured to the center of the park. "The lieutenant was going to show us the ornamental pond."

"Actually," Millie said, "I think I need to rest a bit. I haven't done much walking since we left Georgia. If Lydia doesn't mind staying with me, we'll wait on that bench while y'all go on."

Celeste protested. "Oh, but—"

"I think that's a grand idea." Lydia reached for the pram's handle. "I'm a bit winded myself. We'll be happy to sit and enjoy the fine weather."

Lieutenant Hart grinned as he placed Celeste's hand on his arm again. "Very well. We won't be long."

"Take your time." Lydia wheeled the baby carriage to the bench and sat.

Millie followed. How to ask her questions? "How far did you get on your walk?"

"I had no destination in mind, but I wound up at the Turners' house. Rose was on her way to the post office, so I went with her."

"Did you have a pleasant visit?" What a dumb question. Those two were good friends. Of course, they'd enjoyed a chance to chat. Millie chided herself for being out of sorts.

"We did." Lydia angled to face Millie. "As it happens, I asked her advice about something that concerns you."

Uh-oh. Was there a note of worry there? Surely, Lydia hadn't shared the story of Millie's attack.

"I had another letter from Seth. He's found Troy."

A chill swept over Millie. She lowered her eyes to her clenched fists. "And how is he?"

"He joined the Union Army. He's a guard at the prison in Ohio."

Bitterness overrode Millie's momentary relief. "Well, that's just dandy for him. He's got what he wanted and forgotten all about us, I suppose."

Lydia touched her shoulder. "We don't know the whole story. Troy must have been in the first train load sent north. It seems there were some captured Confederate soldiers mixed in with the mill hands 'cause they went straight to Camp Chase. Troy convinced the commander he'd never been part of the rebellion, and they let him join up and stay on there as a guard. That way, he shouldn't have to shoot anyone."

Millie glanced to the side, her emotions see-sawing with this new information. Anger, relief, confusion. "Did Sergeant Morgan tell him about us? Where we are?"

"Of course, he did. It seems Doctor Spencer recognized Troy's name and remembered tending to him a few years ago when he broke his arm."

"Why didn't Troy write instead of Sergeant Morgan?"

"He did. There's a note for you back at the house. I just wanted to tell you that much before I give it to you."

A note for her. From Troy. Millie's heartbeat sped up. What would it say? Did he know about Amy? She both dreaded and longed to read it.

"Shouldn't Celeste and Lieutenant Hart be back by now?"

~

JANUARY 26, 1865
CAMP CHASE, OHIO

*T*he wind whipped at Troy's back, freezing his ears beneath his kepi. Even his fingers felt the cold, despite the thick army-issued gloves. He ducked between two

127

buildings and knocked at Doctor Spencer's office door at the far end of the hospital.

"Enter."

Troy gripped the knob and pushed inside. The doctor glanced up and nodded but continued writing at his desk. Troy set his rifle in a far corner and backed up to the struggling fire. Moments later, the door opened again, letting in a blast of cold air.

Walter Dykes stuck his head inside. "Here's your patient, Doc." He spoke to Troy as Seth Morgan entered. "You'll take him back, I guess?"

Troy nodded as his gaze flitted over the prisoner who'd become his link to Millie. Brown hair stuck out from the dark-green toboggan of questionable origin—probably the prize in one of the camp's rat-killing contests or the abandoned possession of a prisoner who made his final escape into eternity. The guards overlooked the exchange of possessions as long as it didn't upset the peace. "Yeah, Walt. I'll see he gets back in time for his dinner."

"I'd say those look like snow clouds out there, Doc. You'd best build up your fire." Seth stalked over to the fireplace to warm his gloveless hands. He turned to Troy. "You have news?"

"Yeah, I reckon you might want to hear it before you go trying to skedaddle back to Kentucky and get yourself killed." Troy had been keeping an eye on Seth since his last letter from Lydia revealed information about the man who'd murdered Seth's wife. Ironically, he was at the Union Army prison in Louisville where Seth had been three months before. "I was cleaning up near the commander's office and overheard him discussing his recent orders. General Grant plans to start releasing prisoners again as early as next week."

Seth glanced at the doctor. "He's sure the Federals have all but won the war, then."

Doctor Spencer tossed his pen on the table. "The Union's

locked down all the South, except for Virginia. It's just a matter of time before Richmond falls as well. The South is out of food and low on men to put on the front lines. It's wintertime, and sickness kills as many as the enemy does, on both sides." He leaned against his desk and crossed his arms. His posture spoke of bone-deep weariness.

Seth lifted his chin and directed his question to Troy. "So when do you expect this to affect us here?"

Troy grinned. "What you really want to ask is how soon can you get on your way to Louisville, right?"

Seth lifted his hands, palms up. "And what about you? Will you be able to take leave and head that way?"

"I have a plan." For once, Troy was the one to take the lead. "It might work, and it might not, but it's worth a try."

The doctor joined them at the fireplace, keeping his voice low. "With Dr. Fisher here and finally well enough to tend to the remaining patients, I won't be needed as much. Knowing they plan to release a good number of prisoners, perhaps General Richardson can be convinced to let me go in the first wave. Troy's going to ask to accompany us to Kentucky to be sure *you*"—he poked Seth in the chest—"my half-crazed patient, will stay in line and not attack anyone along the way."

Seth ran shaky fingers across his chin. "I'm willing to go along with that. Tell me what I need to do."

Doc draped his arm across Seth's shoulders. "Nothing, my friend, except be ready to leave at a moment's notice. And don't get into any trouble before we leave."

"Who, me? I've been a model of good behavior, I'll have you know."

Doc Spencer snorted, and Troy chuckled. He clapped Seth on the shoulder. "As much as I hate to admit it, your reputation may work to our advantage here. The commander's been expecting you to go on a tear ever since you arrived. He'll be glad to see the last of you."

"Dang!" Seth snapped his fingers and grinned. "I wondered why all those bluecoats avoided me."

"There's nothing scarier than a man who doesn't fear anyone." Troy pinned him with a serious eye. "I'll have to warn Aunt Lydia to tread softly around you."

"Nah, I never direct my anger at women." Seth waved away Troy's concern. "They know how to hurt you without using their fists."

CHAPTER 12

*J*anuary's gift of a few sunny days had vanished with the arrival of February. Snow and sleet kept everyone indoors, huddled near their fires.

The paper fluttered in Millie's hand as she read the message Troy had scrawled on it. "They're coming here." She whispered the words, though no one was around to hear. The letter said he planned to leave Ohio the next day with Sergeant Morgan and Doctor Spencer. They would go to Frankfort first, since Olivia and Wade, Doc Spencer's wife and son, had moved to her father's home.

Millie couldn't decide whether to hold onto her anger for his prolonged silence over the last year or to forgive Troy and act as if nothing had changed. How ridiculous. Of course, everything had changed.

Either way, Amy needed a new gown for her first meeting with her father. She grew more every week. It was time to dig into the trunk they'd brought from Georgia.

131

Millie peeked around the door to Celeste's room. "Celeste, will you listen for Amy? She's asleep, but I need to get some things out of a trunk in the attic."

Celeste looked up from her needlework. "Of course. I'll be here for a while."

Millie climbed the stairs and opened the attic door wide to let in as much light as possible. Their trunk should be nearby since it was a recent addition. She found it right away, but it was locked. She studied the metal lock and tried to remember where she'd last seen a key.

When nothing surfaced, she explored the other trunks for ideas. Two of them had keys sticking in their slots, and she tested them for fit. The second one produced a satisfying click. Millie released the two clasps at either end and raised the lid. Setting aside some kitchen items, she dug to the bottom and pulled out the box with her name on top.

As she'd remembered, the box contained several baby gowns, bonnets, and tiny stockings, items she'd worn years ago, set aside by her mother. Millie removed the box and carried it to her room for further exploration.

She sorted everything by size and color, seeing what would be best for church. When she lifted the pink bonnet to put with the matching gown, it crinkled. Frowning, Millie opened the material to find a folded paper pinned inside. It was a letter, addressed to her.

October 20, 1852

> *My dearest daughter Millicent Ann,*
>
> *Today you are five years old, and I fear I may not live to see you turn six. The doctor says my lungs will never improve, so I must set my house in order.*
>
> *He has no idea how hard that will be, but I begin by writing to you, my heart, though it pains me to do so. To put it plainly, you should know that Cal Gibson is not your father.*

If you've waited until you have a child of your own to open this box, as I instructed, you will know what a hard man Cal is, so maybe you will understand why I ran away in the first year of our marriage. I went to visit my Aunt Myrtle in Alabama, telling everyone she was very ill and I had to help her out for a while. I stayed there all winter, using the bad weather as an excuse to keep from returning home. I was so unhappy with Cal, I let temptation in the door with a young man there who showed me kindness.

In early March, Cal fetched me home, and I knew I had to stay with him because I was in the family way. I never told Cal, and I guess he thinks you are his child because he never mistreated you too bad.

Now I must confess my sin to him and to your real daddy, or else take the secret to my grave. I don't know which would be the best thing to do. But I wanted you to know when you are old enough to understand. Your real father has his own family now, but if you should get in a desperate way and need someone, you can find him in Randolph County, Alabama. His name is Ellis McNeil.

All my love,
  Mother

Millie's head spun. Cal wasn't her father? And was this Ellis McNeil the same as Lydia's brother Ellis? She needed to talk to Lydia, but she was working at the bakery.

Amy woke up babbling and cooing, then started pushing at the pillows surrounding her on the bed. Millie put her mother's letter next to the one from Troy, two problems to be set aside until after she tended to the baby. Perhaps Lydia would have some wisdom to share.

She found no opportunity to speak to Lydia until they retired for the night. Millie secured Amy in her bed and slipped into Lydia's room.

"I have something to show you, something I found this morning." She stifled the tears that threatened and sat on the edge of Lydia's bed. "It was folded into a tiny square and pinned inside the pink bonnet amongst the baby clothes set aside by my mother. As you know, she gave me strict instructions about not touching those things until I needed them. I thought it was because she didn't want me to play with them and risk soiling them when I was younger."

Millie extended the paper to Lydia. "It seems there was another reason."

Lydia took the letter and sat in the chair close to the lamp on the dresser.

Millie stared at her lap, her hands twisting a worn ribbon between her fingers.

Lydia finished reading and refolded the paper with care.

"Do you think this Ellis McNeil is your brother?" Millie held her breath.

Lydia took her time answering. "My brother lives near Randolph County, but there are other McNeils in the area. Eighteen years ago, I was ten, and Ellis would've been about nineteen, so it's possible. But let's not dwell on that."

Millie surged from her seat. "How can I not think about it? If my father is your brother, then that makes—"

"It makes me your aunt." Lydia's smile looked forced.

Millie tried to smile in return. "Yes, that's true. And it would make Troy my cousin."

～

FEBRUARY 4, 1865

A heavy knock at the front door interrupted the friendly chatter in Mrs. Coker's parlor. Besides the gray skies threatening to drop icy rain or snow, it was much too early in the day for social calls. Millie whispered to calm Amy, who'd fallen asleep but startled at the noise.

Herbert's firm steps echoed in the entry as he went to discover what news might affect their cocoon of safety. "Why, Miss Rose, er, Mrs. Griffin, I beg your pardon." His voice carried to the other room. "May I take your cloak, and yours as well, gentlemen?"

Lieutenant Hart stood and advanced to the parlor door, prepared to intercept the visitors. Lydia and Mrs. Coker put away their knitting. Millie tucked the sleeping baby into the cradle beside her chair.

Celeste hurried after the lieutenant to greet her sister. "Rose? Is anything wrong?"

"No, dear." Rose clasped Celeste's extended hands at the threshold. "I just accompanied these gentlemen to show them the way here. You remember Sergeant Morgan from Marietta?"

Millie tried to peer past the bodies blocking her view, her heart picking up speed. Troy would be with him. What would she say to him? How would he react when he saw her and Amy?

"Seth? You brought Troy with you?" Lydia surged from her place on the settee.

Millie caught a glimpse of the men as Lydia embraced her nephew. "Troy Harrison McNeil, I ought to strangle you for worrying us so. And here you've been with the Union Army all this time."

Troy hugged her briefly as she scolded him, but his gaze drifted over her shoulder and connected with Millie's. Conflicting emotions kept her immobile. Joy, wariness, hurt, and an aching loneliness. While introductions went on around them, Millie could only stare at Troy.

He looked...good. The uniform accentuated his shoulders, broader than she remembered, and his beard had filled out. What was he thinking? How did he see her now?

Lydia took Troy's arm and pulled him farther into the room. "Come over here and meet your daughter."

Troy stared down into the cradle, a look of wonder on his face. And then his gaze moved to Millie. He cleared his throat. "Millicent."

Her heart dropped. Why was he so formal? Millie lifted her chin. "How are you, Troy?" Amazing that her voice didn't quaver in tempo with her heart.

Lydia stepped away from Troy, leaving them to navigate their reunion without her.

Millie focused on Troy as he lowered himself next to the cradle. His long fingers plucked at the blanket to reveal Amy's face. He studied her while Millie held her breath.

"She's so small." His voice conveyed wonder.

Millie laughed. "She's nearly doubled her weight since she was born, according to the scales at Mr. Turner's store. We weigh her and measure her on the fabric table every time we go there. It was Rose's idea."

"Clever." He traced the baby's hairline down to her chin. "Do you think she favors me? I can't tell."

"Wait till you see her smile. She looks just like you." Millie's voice dropped to a whisper. "I prayed she'd look like you. The old folks believe a bad experience can affect a child's looks."

His eyebrows lowered. "Millie, I don't care who she favors. She's my daughter."

～

*T*roy was captivated by the infant who'd already stolen his heart. "What did you name her?"

"Amelia Ruth, but we call her Amy."

"Amy McNeil. I like it." He ramped up his smile and turned to Millie. Her answering smile seemed strained.

He searched her face for condemnation. His conscience

said he deserved it for what she'd endured the past year because of him. How could he make it up to her? He was due back at Camp Chase in a few days. Even if the war ended next week, his two-year commitment to the Union Army still held, and he had no idea where they'd send him. "Millie, we need to talk."

She gazed into his eyes. "Yes, we do. I can ask Lydia or Celeste to take care of Amy if you want to go somewhere private."

He shook his head. "Not enough time right now. I have to go with Seth to the prison in a bit. How about if I come back tomorrow? We'll see if the weather will allow for a walk or ride if I can borrow a carriage."

"Maybe after church—"Amy's pitiful wail interrupted Millie's reply.

Troy jumped in alarm. "What's wrong? Did I scare her?"

"No, silly. Babies cry all the time." She reached into the cradle and lifted Amy out. "I think she needs a fresh nappy."

The woman who closely resembled Mrs. Griffin, who'd directed them to the house, turned to Millie. "Here, let me take care of that. You two keep visiting."

Some unspoken communication passed between the women as Millie handed the child to her friend. "Thank you, Celeste. Call me if you need anything."

Celeste moved toward the stairs, speaking to the baby in a soothing voice. Millie glanced across the room but directed her words to Troy. "How did you get a furlough so soon after joining the army?"

Troy followed her gaze to where Seth and Lydia conversed in quiet tones. "A couple of things happened about the same time. Seth found out the man he was hunting down was in the prison here, and I overheard the commander say he had orders from General Grant to start releasing prisoners in February. Doc Spencer decided he could leave his infirmary to the other doctor. He told the colonel I'd just become a father—" He paused, still awed to claim the title. "Anyway, Doc said he needed my help to keep Seth in line on the trip to Frankfort."

Millie tilted her head. "Olivia's father owns a mercantile in Frankfort, right? And he's married to Luke Turner's mother?"

"Yeah, and he had to bring some supplies to the store Luke runs here in Louisville, so we caught a ride with him yesterday."

"So that's how you ended up at Luke's house. I guess Rose recognized Sergeant Morgan from our stay in Marietta."

Troy grinned. "Yeah, they told me about finding him in the cellar and him stealing Major Griffin's horse."

"It's funny now, but it terrified me at the time." Her eyes grew wide. "You won't report him to the army, will you? He showed us kindness, even let me take some of his departed wife's clothes."

"Don't worry." Troy patted her hand, then curled his fingers around hers. "I won't tell anyone."

The woman named Celeste returned with Amy, but Rose announced that it was her turn to hold the baby.

Suddenly feeling awkward, Troy cast about for something to say. He breathed a sigh of relief when Herbert rang a little bell to catch everyone's attention from his place in the doorway. "Hattie says for everyone to gather in the dining room for luncheon."

Troy stood and offered his hand to Millie. She raised her eyebrows but let him assist her.

"Will you need the cradle for the baby?"

Millie smiled. "No, one of us will hold her. In fact, several of us will probably hold her during the meal. She's happy to be with almost anyone. Even Major Griffin held her when he was here."

"Do I get to hold her too?"

"Of course." She glanced at his uniform. "But you might

want to wait until you've finished your meal. She's started reaching for whatever you have in your hand, and if she grabs it, you might end up with food on your jacket."

"Maybe I'll wait until later then. I wouldn't want extra decorations on my uniform when we visit the prison."

CHAPTER 13

illie met Celeste's questions when she came downstairs after nursing Amy. Rose and Lydia had socks and gloves for the prisoners, so they went with the men to the prison where Sergeant Morgan would confront his wife's killer. Mrs. Coker sat dozing in her favorite chair while Herbert helped Hattie polish a few silver pieces. Millie propped up the baby with several pillows and sat beside her on the settee.

Celeste dragged the hassock over to join them. "You and Troy seemed to get along well today. What did he say about our sweet Amy?" She wiggled the baby's cloth doll and elicited a watery chuckle.

"He claimed her as his daughter. Which is plain to see, but I wondered if he might try to deny it." Millie lifted a shoulder. "He wants to get together tomorrow to discuss our situation."

"Good. I'll be glad to watch Amy if you need me to. And what did you think of Sergeant Morgan? He acted quite interested in Lydia, don't you think?"

"I suppose they've become friends of a sort." Millie tugged Amy back when the baby leaned too far to one side. "They exchanged a few letters while he was in Ohio. She was determined to find Troy, and he's been searching for the man who killed his wife."

"And each of them has lost a spouse, so that gives them common ground. I'd guess they're about the same age too." Celeste flashed a speculative smile. "Hmm. There could be something brewing between them."

Millie stared at her friend. "Do you think so?"

"I think the sergeant is hoping so. The question is, what will Lydia do about it?"

Mrs. Coker's snores intensified, and the younger women stifled their laughter. "Should we wake her?" Celeste asked. "It's not long to teatime."

"No, let her sleep. I hear her sometimes at night when I'm up with Amy. She must not rest well. Do you think all of us staying here is too much for her?"

"If it is, she wouldn't admit it. I think she enjoys having people around." Celeste regarded the older woman. "You should have seen her when Rose and I first approached her about working here. She bristled like a porcupine, but only because she was scared and lonely. Now she's warm and generous."

"She's surely been good to us. It almost feels like family." Her thoughts centered on that word—family. It no longer meant what it had in the past. The circle shrank and expanded as people came and went out of their lives. What if Celeste was right about Lydia and Sergeant Morgan? Would they stay or leave? More critical to Millie, would Troy now join as a permanent member?

141

"*W*ednesday? But that only gives you two more days to prepare." Millie pulled her bonnet strings away from the baby's grasping hands as they descended the church steps.

Troy chuckled and took Amy from her arms when they approached the borrowed wagon. "Here, let me have her while you climb up." When Millie settled on the wagon seat, he handed her the child. He took his place, jiggled the horse's reins, and set them in motion.

Millie marveled at the change in him, not only the physical maturity, but his increased confidence. His time in the army already served him well.

"Lieutenant Hart and I plan to go to Mr. Turner's house later to discuss possible strategies with him and Seth on presenting his case about his wife's murder." He glanced at Millie. "Which means our time today will be shorter than I'd planned, and the weather isn't the best for a drive. Is there someplace at Mrs. Coker's where we can talk in private?"

Millie twisted her lips. "Everyone usually naps on Sunday afternoon. There's the old nursery room. I guess that would do."

They ate luncheon with the other residents at Mrs. Coker's house, then left a sleeping Amy with Celeste and ascended the two staircases to the nursery. Millie set the brace of candles on a child-sized table and pointed to a couple of rocking chairs that had seen better days. She chose one and waited for Troy to open the conversation.

He sat and cleared his throat. "I hardly know what to say, except I'm sorry. I had no idea that you...that we...I mean—"

"That we could make a baby?"

Troy's ears turned red, and he gripped the back of his neck. "Yeah. From what I'd heard over the years, I thought it must take a bunch of tryin' for most people."

Millie chortled. "I guess we're not most people."

He smiled. "Guess not." He shifted in his chair. "I didn't mean to stay away so long, but after that day, I figured we needed some time apart."

"Because you thought you'd get caught by the Rebel Army, especially if that man turned out to be one of theirs."

He huffed and shot to his feet. "Not only that. What happened when we were alone together, well, I didn't think I could be near you without wanting to repeat it. And we ought not to until we could get a preacher to marry us."

Millie stared as he paced. "You were near me yesterday and this morning, and you appeared to be perfectly fine."

"We've been surrounded by people, and thank God for that. I'm not so lost to propriety that I'd dishonor you with a public display."

She took a deep breath, stood, and touched his arm. "There's nobody here now..."

He jerked away. "Millie, please. Don't distract me. I'm trying to apologize and ask you to forgive me. I've wrestled with this for the last year, and more so since I found out about the baby. I can't imagine what you had to endure."

Pain lanced Millie's heart, sparking a backlash. "What I had to endure? Do you mean the weeks of being sick and not knowing why until I heard someone at the mill wonder aloud what was wrong with me? Or maybe having Lydia look at me with hurt in her eyes because I didn't confide in her? Believe me, that was worse than the physical pain of childbirth." She forced back her tears. "But worst of all was wondering why you didn't come back and why you didn't even acknowledge me when the Federals caught you on the road to Marietta. It was like I meant nothing to you at all."

She spun away and headed for the door, but Troy reached her in a few long strides. He pulled her into his arms. "Millie, I'm so sorry. I didn't know." He whispered in her hair. "Even last summer when you came to my defense, I didn't know. I was hoping you wouldn't say anything. I didn't want you to get in trouble with the Federals. I had your note in my knapsack, and it wouldn't have boded well for you if they charged me with spying."

Surprise stopped her tears. She lifted her head. "You found my note?"

"Yeah, on the same day y'all left. Reverend Bagley came by to check on the house and told me the Federals had arrested all the mill workers." He ran his hands over her arms. "I followed and hoped I could catch you alone or maybe blend in with the other men. It didn't work out that way."

"But you'd been gone so long, since February. Without any word from you, I was afraid you'd been killed or apprehended or hurt..."

He pressed a kiss near her temple. "At first, I didn't know what to say in a letter. We kept hearin' about battles in North Georgia, and Ma got upset whenever I mentioned goin' that way. So I went to Uncle Henry's and helped him with the plantin' on his farm. Got myself a broken leg that took forever to heal." He pulled back to peer at her. "I wrote you about that. Asked a neighbor to mail it while I was laid up."

She shook her head. "We only got the one that said you made it home."

He frowned. "Hmm. Anyway, it was late June before I could walk much at all. That's when I finally left Alabama. I nearly went crazy when I got to the farm and found the house empty."

Millie's lips grazed his jaw. Troy groaned and protested even as he pulled her closer. "Millie. We can't." He kissed her eyelids. "We've got to talk."

She pulled his head down for a proper kiss. "We talked. You explained, and I forgave you."

"And I forgive you, but we still—"

"Wait a minute. You forgive *me*? For what?" She reared back to stare in his eyes.

He sighed and dropped his arms. "For tempting me beyond reason, as much today as you did a year ago."

"So what happened that day was my fault?"

"I didn't say that. It was my fault. I should've left immediately after we cleaned away all the traces. Instead, I sought an excuse to see you again."

She hung her head. "I did beg you to stay."

"I should've been strong enough to deny you. I was weak. And angry. I failed to control myself...with you *and* him. He treated you like a...a piece of trash. I *wanted* to kill him. I committed the very sin I didn't want the army to force me to do." He met her gaze with troubled eyes.

"You were trying to protect me."

"Didn't do a very good job of it." He paced away, then turned back. "I'm still not—"

The baby's unhappy cry halted his words, and Millie whirled to see Celeste at the top of the stairs. She hurried to meet Millie in a few steps and handed her the sobbing child. "I'm sorry. She woke up crying and wouldn't be consoled."

"It's all right." She nestled the baby close. "Shh, little one. Mama's here."

Rather than add his own words of comfort, Troy glanced about as if hoping to find an escape. "Lieutenant Hart is probably ready to leave. I'll be back later today or tomorrow."

CHAPTER 14

*T*he restaurant bustled with activity. On each table, a vase of flowers and sparkling dishes sat atop a white tablecloth. A waiter led Millie and Troy to a corner, seated them, and presented each with a menu. Having never been to a restaurant before, Millie marveled at the abundance of food on the tables they passed. Except for men in uniform, one would never know the war still raged to the south and east.

The fancy atmosphere didn't seem to bother Troy. Moving with ease, he looked as comfortable here as at Lydia's kitchen table. Had he always been so confident, or had he gained that polish recently? His looks hadn't suffered during their time apart either. He'd spruced up in civilian clothes that Lucas lent him while the Turners' housekeeper cleaned his uniform.

She glanced around the room. "How did Rose know about this place?"

Troy peered over his menu. "Mr. Turner suggested it. Mrs. Griffin asked him if he could recommend one when we were talking this morning."

"Are you sure you can afford their prices?" Millie had worn her best outfit, but the few women in the room dressed as if they had wealth to spare. Despite that disparity, she wouldn't embarrass Troy with her country manners.

Troy laid his hand over hers on the table. "Don't worry about it. I've been saving all my wages, and it's worth whatever the price to get you to myself, away from the others, for a couple of hours."

She couldn't control the warmth that seeped into her face. She slid her hand to her lap as the waiter came to take their order. Troy selected the day's special, and Millie echoed that choice, since she'd been too distracted to read the menu.

After the waiter left, Troy cleared his throat and fiddled with his fork. Was he nervous, after all, to be in a fancy restaurant? Or was his unease because of her? Had Rose suggested he bring her here to propose?

"This is really nice, Troy." Millie traced a line of stitching in the tablecloth. "Thank you for bringing me here. It is good to get away for a little while."

Troy unfolded his napkin. "At least we shouldn't be interrupted here, and we need to make some decisions before I have to return to Ohio."

The waiter brought their food, and Millie swallowed her questions about what those decisions included. While they enjoyed their roast beef, potatoes, and a vegetable that looked like overgrown pole beans, the conversation centered around Amy's latest developments—how she'd started sitting up but still tended to lean to one side, and the way her babbling had increased. Millie thrilled to hear Troy declare Amy to be the smartest and most beautiful baby he'd ever seen. He was as proud as any father she'd met.

When the waiter brought them dessert and coffee, Millie dared to broach the subject. "You said we needed to make some decisions, but I confess I'm not sure what you mean."

Troy swallowed the bite of pie and laid his fork aside. "Millie, I signed up for two years. I'll be posted at Camp Chase until the war ends. If that happens before my time is up, the prison will close, and they'll send me somewhere else to finish out my time."

Millie cut into her slice of pie. "Where would that be?"

"I don't know. Could be anywhere. Out west, up north, or even back to the South to help rebuild. The thing is, I don't know if it'll be somewhere suitable for a family. I can't be sure whether I can take you and Amy with me."

Did that mean he wanted to go alone? Millie touched her napkin to her lips to keep from answering right away. "What are you trying to say, Troy?"

He took a sip of coffee. "We have to decide whether to get married now or wait until I get my orders."

"I don't understand what one has to do with the other."

Troy heaved a sigh. "What if I'm sent to an outpost where savages attack the settlers? You and Amy could be in danger, or I could be killed, and you'd be there alone with a baby. I don't want to put you in a position like that."

His comment felt like a rap on the knuckles. He must consider her an ignorant child. And a whiny one. She lowered her eyes and fiddled with the napkin in her lap. "So your answer is to go without us?"

"Not unless it's necessary. What I'm saying is maybe we should wait until I know more."

She reached across the table to grip his hand. "That shouldn't keep us from gettin' married now, while you're here. We have a child."

"Yes, but I can't take y'all back to Ohio with me. There's no place for you to stay where I could keep you safe."

"I understand that." She struggled to express herself. "Amy and I could stay here for now. Everyone says the war is nearly over. When the prison closes, we can join you then."

The waiter paused at their table. "Excuse me, sir. Do you care for more coffee?"

"No, thank you. We're ready to leave." Troy tossed some money on the table and rose. He helped Millie with her cloak and shrugged into his overcoat.

She frowned but allowed him to escort her into the waning sunlight. Her heart beat fast. Did he really think any of the reasons he'd mentioned could justify not wedding her now that he had the chance? Millie opened her mouth to ask but shut it when another woman called Troy's name.

"Troy McNeil! Is it really you? What are you doing here in Kentucky?" The spunky brunette grasped his free arm and tugged him close before she acknowledged Millie's presence. "And who is this, a relative of yours? Last time I seen you was when you was laid up at Henry's with that broke leg."

For all the woman's questions, she didn't pause to give Troy time to answer. The more she talked, the more rigid he stood, and the hotter Millie's anger percolated. How well did he know this woman who treated him so familiarly?

$\sim$

*T*roy didn't need to look at Millie to witness her growing anger. Her grip on his arm increased steadily. Finally, Becky stopped for a breath, and Troy groped for the manners his mama had taught him.

"Millie, this is Becky Varner, a neighbor of Uncle Henry's. Becky, this is Millie, my...wife." Maybe not legally yet, but in every other sense. Hopefully, Becky didn't notice his hesitation and Millie wouldn't dispute the relationship. At least the pressure on his arm lessened.

Millie gave a regal nod and shifted closer. "Nice to meet you, Miss Varner."

Becky's eyes widened and then narrowed. "Wife? Well, that was sudden, wasn't it?"

"Not really," Millie answered before Troy could open his mouth. "We've been making plans for years. Unfortunately, the Union Army—and Troy's broken leg—kept us apart."

Becky stared at Troy. "But you never mentioned it last spring."

If Troy didn't know better, he'd be taken in by the hurt expression she put on. Good heavens, why did she have to show up here now? What would Millie make of this?

"I believe Uncle Henry told you about Millie while I was laid up." He pulled Millie to the side of the walkway to let another couple slip past them. Becky followed.

Desperate to get away from the chatterbox, he glanced around. "But where's your family? How did you come to be here?"

"We got word Pa was bein' released, but he's not able to travel alone, so Mama decided we'd come to get him."

Someone down the street hollered Becky's name. They all turned in that direction, and Troy tilted his head. "I believe your sister needs you."

"Yeah, I gotta go now. We're stayin' in the building across the street from the Union Army prison. You know where that is? You should come see us."

Becky hurried away, leaving Troy with a sick sense of dread. Much the way he'd felt when his brother Paul had convinced him to try some chewing tobacco and then tattled to Ma. Was Millie the type of woman to act out her jealousy? Not that she should be jealous. Troy barely tolerated Becky, and Millie was a sight prettier, anyway.

He tried for a casual comment. "Whew, that girl can sure talk, can't she?" He dared a glance in Millie's direction as they resumed their walk.

She smiled at him. Thank heavens.

"Do you plan to visit her family?"

"What? No. Why would I want to visit them and give Becky ideas?"

"What kind of ideas would she get? After all, you're married to me."

"Now, Millie." Troy patted her hand. "I'm sorry to have told that little lie. It was the easiest way to introduce you. It would be just as untruthful to say we're only friends or we're betrothed, wouldn't it? And neither of those would keep Becky away."

"Of course, I see. But it's quite easy to turn that little lie into truth, and then you'd never have to fend off forward females again." Millie pulled him to a stop at the corner. "Troy, I think you knew when you said we were married that's what we should be. We'll figure out our living arrangements when you get your assignment."

"You'll be all right with that? Livin' apart, I mean?"

Why had he thought he needed to have all the answers? Because the responsibility of ensuring the safety of Millie and Amy was a huge one, and he didn't want to botch it.

"It's what we've been doing. At least, now you know where I am, and I know where you'll be." She batted those powerful blue eyes at him. "Troy, more than anything, I want Amy to have a right to your name."

"And I want to give it to her." He lifted a hand to stroke Millie's cheek. He'd hoped for a clear path before setting their direction, but Millie wasn't going to wait for that.

"Do you know where we could find a preacher to make that happen?"

∾

*F*inding a preacher was the easy part. Reverend Holland talked with them and agreed to come to Mrs. Coker's for a small ceremony on Saturday. By the time they reached the house, Millie had thought of a dozen things she needed to do before the day arrived.

She wanted to make an announcement when they walked in, but the group that went to the prison with Seth hadn't yet returned. She thanked Mrs. Coker and Hattie for tending to Amy and lifted her from the cradle. The baby reached for Troy.

"Will you look at that?" Hattie beamed as Troy took the baby. "Only two days since he got here, and she's demanding her pa's attention."

Mrs. Coker nodded. "Just like my girls always did. They know who will give in to their wishes. Well, I enjoyed tending to her, but I'm worn out." She patted the baby's head. "Time for a nap. Don't you agree, Miss Amelia?"

The older women left Millie and Troy alone in the parlor. Millie made a few notes while Troy entertained Amy. When the baby became fussy, Troy handed her over. "I need to return that carriage to the livery, then go to the mercantile and set up an account you can use for purchases till I return."

He kissed her on the forehead and left, and Millie carried Amy upstairs for her nap. A little later, voices from below let her know the others had returned. Millie eased out of the bedroom and went to discover the outcome of her friends' day.

Celeste placed the tea tray on a low table and passed cups to Lydia and Rose as Millie entered the room. "I thought I heard your voices down here. How did the meeting go?"

Rose answered without looking up. "Seth was cleared, at least as far as the Union Army is concerned."

Millie regarded each solemn face. "Then what's wrong? You don't act very happy about it."

Celeste cleared her throat. "Something else happened as we were leaving. Something that affects you and Lydia."

"I don't understand."

Lydia smoothed her skirts. "As we were leaving, a guard called my name, said someone wanted to speak to me, claiming I was his wife."

"His wife?" Millie scoffed at the idea. "Why would someone want to...Lydia?"

The glimmer of tears in Lydia's eyes set off an alarm. Celeste sprang to Millie's side and drew her to the settee.

Lydia took a deep breath and answered. "Cal survived Chickamauga, after all. I don't know how or where he's been the last year, but I glimpsed his face and heard his voice before I swooned."

Rose took up the narrative. "Seth caught her and whisked her to Lucas's carriage. Lieutenant Hart drove us here, then returned to the prison for Seth and Lucas. They should be back shortly."

Millie turned to Lydia. "What will you do? You can't go back to him, Lydia. You know how he is."

"I know, but he has legal authority over us, you and me, and now Amy, unless you marry Troy."

"Well, you can set your mind at ease on that. Troy and I have arranged for Reverend Holland to conduct the ceremony on Saturday. He'll have to return to Ohio alone, but at least we'll be married."

~

"*M*illie and I are getting married at the end of the week." Troy repeated the phrase to himself as he walked to the mercantile with Luke Turner's name on the window.

The wind picked up as the sun sank toward the horizon. He

turned up the collar of the borrowed clothes. He was grateful for the loan and the offer from Luke's housekeeper to clean his uniform, but the fancy duds felt strange. At least his uniform would be ready for the wedding.

His wedding. The word brought him back to his new reality. How was he going to handle this? In a month, he'd gone from a single soldier to a father and family man. And just turned twenty years old. Not that he felt too young—just unprepared for such important responsibilities.

If he could have seen the future on that January day last year, would he have acted differently? Could he have controlled his emotions? The anger had so consumed him, it was unlikely. Subduing Millie's attacker had been necessary. What happened afterward, however, he should have avoided. He had to figure out how to control his carnal desires before life got even more complicated.

At the mercantile, he put half of his cash on an account for Millie's use and arranged to send more each month. "I'm staying at Mr. Turner's house until I return to my post. You can contact me there if needed."

Knowing the store's proprietor had benefits. The clerk's eyes widened. "Yes, sir. I'm sure everything will be fine."

Troy smiled to think he garnered such respect, after all the mistakes he'd made. Meeting Doctor Spencer in the prison hospital a few weeks before had signaled a change, the most recent in a series of significant events. Besides reuniting him with people he loved, it had opened the door to new relationships. Was he ready to face the future with its unknown possibilities?

"What a stupid question." All these thoughts tumbling through his brain led to nowhere, like a dog chasing its own tail. It didn't matter if he was ready or not, life kept coming at him.

He arrived at the Turner house to find all the men

ensconced in Seth's upstairs carriage apartment. Lucas pushed a glass of something strong into Troy's hand as he walked in the door.

"Come in and join the discussion, McNeil. You're likely to have information we can use." Lucas sauntered to the table where Seth and Gideon each held a spread of cards. A half-empty bottle and a tray of glasses sat at Gideon's elbow.

Troy held the drink aloft and spun a chair around to straddle it. "Can't imagine what information I might have for you. How did matters go at the prison today? Since Seth is here and appears no worse than usual, I guess the major was convinced he told the truth?"

Gideon slapped an ace of spades on the table and drew another card from the stack. "Yeah, it looked bad for a while, but we found a way to prove he was in the right."

Seth saluted Lucas with his glass. "Thanks to Luke's brilliant legal mind."

Lucas ignored the praise as he resumed his seat. "However, another ugly problem arose before we left."

Seth snorted as he added a card to Gideon's. "Ugly is right. Ugly as in mean."

"Uh-oh." Troy glanced at each man. "What happened?"

"We met your Uncle Cal," Lucas muttered while he peered at his cards.

"What do you mean? He's dead." A shiver of apprehension prickled Troy's spine. "You're telling me he's alive?"

Gideon tilted his chair back and lifted his glass. "Alive and breathing, but he didn't look so good. More like death walking."

"Alive enough to upset Lydia." Seth speared Troy with his gaze. He motioned to the others. "We decided we should put our heads together and make plans to protect her."

Lucas flipped a card to the table. "Her and Millie. Since she's unmarried and underage, Mr. Gibson is her legal guardian."

Troy swallowed the sip of drink he didn't remember taking. It burned his throat, and he coughed. "As to that, he won't be her guardian come Saturday. Millie and I visited the preacher and made the arrangements today. We'll be gettin' married before I leave." He raised his chin.

Lucas reached over and pounded his shoulder with a hearty, "Congratulations."

Gideon raised his eyebrows in that aristocratic way he had.

Seth nodded his approval. "Good man. Then Lydia will be our primary concern."

"I trust you'll watch out for both of them, though, while I'm away?" Troy directed his request to each man in turn.

"Certainly," Lucas said, "but I have my own houseful of women to see to, as you might have noticed. So, most of that will fall to Seth when Gideon returns to the field."

"A charge I will gladly accept." Seth raised his glass again, and Troy released his breath in a sigh. Seth would be true to his word. But Cal Gibson wouldn't be easy to keep at bay.

CHAPTER 15

*M*illie cleaned Amy's face after she'd had her fill of the thin gruel. "At least we got more inside you today than yesterday." She placed the baby on the rug in the dining room corner with her red yarn ball and rag doll. Lydia helped Millie arrange the pillows to create a safe area where they could see her while the adults ate.

Hattie set a basket of biscuits on the table as everyone took their places. Gideon Hart assisted his grandmother, then pulled out the seat at the end for himself. His movements seemed almost painful and much slower than normal. He avoided eye contact, even when someone spoke directly to him, and instead concentrated on the helpings of food on his plate.

Hopefully, Troy hadn't imbibed to the degree the lieutenant had last night during the men's "planning session" to keep Lydia safe from Cal Gibson.

Mrs. Coker grunted at her grandson. "I don't know why men's brains only work when plied with drink. Seems to me it renders the rest of them helpless far longer afterward."

Millie glanced at Lydia, who covered her smile with a napkin. The lieutenant's report last night rambled and made little sense, so Herbert convinced him to retire and sleep off the effects of his indulgence.

Lydia set down her teacup and voiced the question Millie was reluctant to ask. "Lieutenant, did my nephew join you men?"

Gideon regarded her with confusion. "Certainly. Didn't I say so? His description of your husband's behavior spurred our determination to protect you and Miss Gibson."

"While I appreciate your concern, I doubt there's anything you can do to thwart Cal on my behalf." Lydia held up her hand when he started to protest. "As for Millie and the baby, the best course of action is for her and Troy to marry as soon as possible."

Gideon confirmed the idea with a nod. "I believe that's your nephew's intention."

"Lydia, I told you yesterday about our plans." Millie's brows puckered in confusion. "Are you afraid one of us will back out?"

"No, dear. I'm sure you both intend to honor your commitment." She pressed Millie's hand. "But nothing is certain these days. Just consider all that's happened in the last year."

"I know. But you can't mean to go with Cal when he's released from prison. Where would you go? Not back home, surely. The mill is gone, and likely everything else as well. The mill and the army are all he knows. What would he do? Depend on you to support him?"

Lydia tilted her head. "I've heard there's a mill over in Indiana. He might find a position there. However, I won't be leaving, at least not immediately. I'll tell him he can send for me when he's settled with a job and housing. That will give me time to decide what's best."

She patted Millie's arm. "As long as you and Amy are safe, that's what matters."

"I don't think you have to concern yourself about Mr. Gibson leaving prison anytime soon." Gideon laid aside his fork. "He told us he'd never take the oath, that he'd stay in prison until the war ends."

Millie snorted in disgust. "That sounds like him, stubborn and mean as an old mule."

She pushed away from the table and started collecting the dishes on a tray to carry to the kitchen. Why did Cal have to show up now? His resurrection better not mess up her life now that things were finally going well.

~

FEBRUARY 10, 1865

Troy opened the bakery door and shut it quickly to keep out the cold. He'd promised to meet Lydia there and escort her to the prison for the weekly delivery of pies. She'd protested, but he wouldn't be dissuaded, claiming he wanted to spend time with his favorite aunt. He'd do what he could to protect her.

Lydia slipped into her cloak and flashed a playful smile. "Right on time. I guess army life did you a heap of good."

Troy grinned at her teasing. "Now, Aunt Lydia, I wasn't that bad. Besides, I knew if I didn't get here when I said, you'd go traipsing off by yourself, like the stubborn woman you are, and I couldn't risk that."

She raised her brows. "And who do you think escorted me to the prison before you showed up? Nobody, that's who, and I've never come to any harm these past six months."

"Yeah, but you didn't have a hostile husband inside the prison then." He took the bakery box from her while she pulled on her gloves. Lydia's life hadn't been easy. She'd lost both parents before she turned thirteen, and the relatives decided she should stay with Granny McNeil. That meant working in the cotton mill to support the two of them and later tending Granny as she aged. Lydia must have thought marrying Cal would save her from that drudgery—as it did until Cal left to join the fighting and she returned to the mill.

He shook off his musings as Lydia pulled down the window shade to show the store was closed. She called back to her employers. "Mr. Watford, Mrs. Watford my nephew's here, so I'm leaving now."

They stepped outside and leaned into the wind. The weather prevented decent conversation, so they traveled the city streets in silence. A few flakes of snow swirled in the aura of lights shining from the store windows. The scent of spiced apples drifted from the box and brought back memories of better times on his parents' farm. Troy's months of roaming the countryside made those even more precious.

"Hattie promised a hearty stew for supper." Lydia leaned toward him and raised her voice. "I'll be ready to eat my share as soon as we get to the house."

Troy smiled and jostled the box. "Me too, especially after smelling these pies." He sidled closer to Lydia as they passed the train depot and a group of men emerged from the growing darkness. The cold weather should keep any ruffians off the street, but he'd learned to be on guard. After what Millie had gone through, he viewed any stranger as a threat.

As they neared the prison, Troy recalled running into Becky Varner earlier in the week. She'd said her family was staying across from the prison.

"Do you know Henry's neighbors, Thaddeus and Velma Varner?"

Lydia's teeth chattered as she shook her head. "I never ventured as far as Henry's place. What about them?"

"Millie and I saw their daughter, Becky, the other day. She

said her pa's at the prison and they're staying in the refugee house until he can go home."

"That's where the Union Army put us when we first came to Louisville. Some of our friends are still there. Maybe Millie and I can visit them if they're still here when it warms up."

At the corner of Tenth, they waited for a wagon to pass before crossing to the prison. "Do you think Cal knows you're the one who delivers the baked goods to Major Sullivan?"

Her head bobbed. "Probably. I'd imagine he heard some of the guards call my name the other day. They had no reason not to tell him who I was. They probably thought it a funny coincidence that both our names were Gibson."

Hopefully, they could be quick enough to avoid encountering Cal Gibson today. Cal had never liked Troy and often belittled him in front of others. Of course, Troy had been a kid and taught to treat his elders with respect, so he couldn't fight back. But he'd grown up in the years since he'd seen Cal. More than that, Troy now knew how he'd respond to anyone who threatened his family. He didn't fancy risking his new career by getting into a fight with a prisoner.

Sergeant Dunn must have been watching for Lydia. He stepped in front of the gate and spoke in a low voice. "I'm real sorry, ma'am, about the way you discovered Mr. Gibson here. I couldn't imagine that you was married to him. He's such a..." He paused and worked his jaw. "Well, suffice it to say you deserve better than what I've seen of him. 'Course, the war probably changed him. It does that to a man. I seen—"

Lydia stopped him with an upraised hand. "It's all right, Sergeant. You couldn't have known. Now, if you'd have someone take this box up to the major, I'll be truly grateful to get on my way home."

The guard whistled and motioned for the man at watch on the wall to join them. The soldier scrambled down, and Dunn thrust the box in his hands. "Take this to the major and be quick about it."

Lydia gestured to Troy. "By the way, Sergeant Dunn, this is my nephew, Troy McNeil. You remember how I'd asked everyone to let me know if they saw him?"

"Oh, yeah, I saw him the other day when you brought that Morgan fellow here. We thought he might be a prisoner, but here he is, a member of the Union Army, huh?" He shifted his rifle and thrust out his right hand. "Good to meet you, Private. I guess you surprised everyone when you showed up, huh?"

Troy accepted the gesture of welcome. "That I did. Well, our job here is done. We should get on to the house." And he had something important he needed to discuss with Lydia on the walk home. If he could get up the courage. Hopefully, she would understand his concerns.

~

FEBRUARY 11, 1865

*M*illie chided herself as she regarded her reflection in Mrs. Coker's mirror. Why should she be nervous? For pity's sake, this was Troy, not some stranger. She'd known him for years. But it wasn't Troy who provoked her nerves. It was the step they were taking and the secret she hadn't shared with him. Had she been wrong to insist on having a wedding before he left Louisville?

No, she hadn't done it for herself. They needed to marry for Amy's sake. So what if she'd discovered Cal wasn't her real father? At least he hadn't turned her out, and he'd provided for her all those years. The truth of Millie's birth had nothing to do with her and Troy. Cousins married all the time. She'd explain her background when she had the opportunity.

She picked up the pink-and-silver reticule Lydia had made

in lieu of a bouquet and went to meet Herbert at the foot of the stairs. The dear man had nearly busted his buttons when she'd asked him to serve in the place of a father. He positioned her hand on his sleeve and led her to the parlor, where the furniture had been rearranged to create a short aisle.

Mrs. Coker, Rose, and Celeste occupied the settee while Lydia spoke with Reverend Holland. Amy sat in Rose's lap and chewed on the ever-present rag doll. On the opposite side of the room, Lieutenant Hart and Sergeant Morgan flanked Troy. Herbert's warning "ahem" snapped everyone to attention, and the hum of conversation ceased while he escorted her to the minister. Millie's gaze met Troy's. At last, they'd make everything right.

In a matter of minutes, it was over. Reverend Holland made his final pronouncement and turned to Troy. "You may now kiss your bride."

Troy framed her face with his hands and brushed her lips with his. She opened her eyes as he pulled away, disappointed and surprised by the cursory gesture. Was it because of his natural hesitance to display affection in public, or did he regret their decision?

If the others noticed, they said nothing as Herbert directed them to the dining room for refreshments. Reverend Holland stayed long enough to have cake and coffee, then apologized for leaving early. "I'm afraid that I have another, less joyous occasion to preside over."

As the minister collected his coat and hat, Seth approached to shake Troy's hand. To Millie, he said, "Did you notice we always congratulate the husband and offer our best wishes to the wife?" He grinned and kissed her hand. "We know who's getting the better deal." Then he whispered something to Lydia and ushered Rose to the carriage to return to Lucas's house.

Their departure left only the household members, who began to clear away the party fare. Lieutenant Hart helped

Herbert move the furniture again, while Celeste and Lydia assisted in the kitchen.

Troy tugged on Millie's arm. "Care to walk with me in the garden, Mrs. McNeil?"

Millie's heartbeat raced. She peeked at the baby, happily occupied with her doll in Mrs. Coker's lap, then gathered her shawl. In all their hurried planning, she and Troy hadn't discussed arrangements beyond the ceremony. What did he have in mind?

All the flowers lay dormant beneath the ground, but the garden exuded an aura of peace and offered them a degree of privacy. The setting sun sent streaks of pink and orange across the sky but provided little warmth, and Millie shivered. Troy pulled her into his embrace and met her lips with his own.

Ah, this was how it had been that day when they'd first discovered their mutual attraction. She'd relived those moments many times, but the memory didn't match the reality.

After several minutes, Troy relaxed his hold and looped his arms behind her waist. "Do you have any idea how difficult it's going to be to leave you?" He pressed his lips to her brow.

Millie swallowed. "I think so. But at least we have a couple of days and nights to be together."

He dislodged a curl at her temple as he shook his head. "Not the nights, Millie. I won't leave you in the family way again. We'll wait until we can live together, wherever that may be."

Millie gaped. After the months of longing, how could he so calmly push her away? He wasn't harsh as Cal had been, but his casual indifference cut just as deeply. The sting of tears burned the back of her eyes, but she wouldn't let him see them. From somewhere inside, she stirred up her anger.

"I truly think this is best for now." He rubbed her arm. "I've already mentioned my worries to Aunt Lydia and Seth, to see what they might suggest, and both agreed this was the wisest course."

She pushed out of his arms and adjusted her shawl to keep from looking at him. "How do you propose to go on, then?"

"I'll stay here until everyone retires for the night, then I'll go back and stay in the carriage house with Seth. There's a train bound for Cincinnati in the morning. I'll take it and head on back to Camp Chase."

Millie's heart dropped, and she whirled toward the door. "Fine. I should check on Amy. She's probably gettin' hungry."

"Millie, I'm sorry—"

"It's all right, Troy." She spoke without facing him. "I understand. You really didn't want this marriage, but you agreed to it for Amy's sake."

She reached for the doorknob, but he grabbed her arm and spun her to face him. His brows lowered. "I never said I didn't want to get married. I just thought we oughta wait a while."

Millie sighed, letting the anger flow away as weariness set in. "That's all I've been doing for the last year, Troy. Waiting to hear from you, wondering if you'd been hurt or taken sick or…"

The baby's cries came through the door. "I have to take care of our daughter. You can stay or go as you like. I reckon I'll be here whatever you decide."

⁓

*T*roy didn't follow her straightaway. He had to cool off. Lydia had warned him Millie might not like his decision.

He recalled his conversation with his aunt after they'd left the prison the day before. "She's not sure of your feelings," Lydia had said. "She might take it as a rejection. Cal didn't give her much affection, and I think she's afraid to trust you to be any different."

Seth's advice had focused more on what Troy could do to win Millie over after he left. "Write her as often as you get the chance. Get your pal Walter to help if you need to. If you can find a way to send her a gift, that'd be good. And let her know as soon as you find out about your orders, so she has time to make plans. Meg always chided me about making plans without askin' her opinion."

But how could he consider leaving with her angry and hurt?

Troy circled the dark garden twice, then gathered his courage and slipped in the back door. Soft voices came from the parlor, but the kitchen was deserted. He poured himself a cup of the still-warm coffee and strolled to the front room. Only Lydia and Celeste were there, each working on small clothing items.

Lydia glanced up with a smile. "We're trying to get ahead of Amy's growing. Seems like she hardly wears a gown twice before it's too little. Millie's still upstairs with her. Go on up if you want."

Celeste added her encouragement. "Hers is the room behind the stairs."

Troy returned his cup to the kitchen and climbed to the second floor. He followed the sound of humming and paused at the threshold. Millie lay on her side, Amy cuddled beside her. He tapped on the half-closed door.

Millie lifted her head, eyes wide above tear-stained cheeks. "I thought you'd left." Her voice wavered, but she seemed calm.

He stepped closer. "I told you I'd come back inside. I didn't mean to wait so long. Looks as though everyone's retired but Lydia and Miss Carrigan."

"Mrs. Coker always goes to bed early. Hattie and Herbert have their own sitting room in their apartment. I think Lieutenant Hart went out somewhere."

Troy peered at the baby, whose face snuggled close to Millie's belly. "Is she asleep?"

"Yeah. I try to keep her on a schedule, but you can wake her up if you want." Millie eased away and sat on the side of the bed.

"That's all right." Troy sat beside her and picked up her left hand. He fingered the ring he'd given her. Just a plain circle of gold. She deserved better than he could afford. At least he could be honest with her. "I'm sorry I didn't discuss my concerns with you earlier. Guess I have to learn how to think like a married man now. I've been so used to being alone and making quick decisions, it never occurred to me to ask you."

Millie didn't answer or even raise her face.

"I set up an account for you at Turner's mercantile so you can buy whatever you need for you and Amy."

Millie regarded their joined hands and sighed. "Thank you. I promise I won't buy any more than what's needed."

"Don't worry about that." Troy lifted her hand and kissed the knuckles. He shifted and brushed a stray lock of hair away from her face. "See if you can find a ribbon to match your eyes and maybe a new bonnet for this sunshine hair. I don't want to leave with you sad, sweetheart."

When Millie's eyes fluttered and closed, he was lost. He leaned forward and found her lips. Her hands slid up his chest to clutch his shoulders, and he deepened the kiss. He groaned, murmured her name, and pressed her back against the bed, all his good intentions thrown to the wind.

A snuffling sound beside him made Troy raise his head. Amy had rolled toward the dip in the mattress where Millie lay beneath him.

He sprang from the bed.

She sat up. "Troy—"

"Does she have her own bed?" He motioned to the baby.

Millie pointed to the cradle in the corner. Troy slid his

167

hands under the child and lifted her to his face. Her soft features exuded peace and perfection. He glanced back at Millie and saw his wonder mirrored in her expression. Amy huffed a sigh as he snuggled her close, then tucked her into the tiny bed. He gazed at her a moment longer, then strode to the door.

"Troy?" Millie's voice quavered.

He shut the door with a firm push. "I'm not leaving yet, if that's all right with you."

She nodded, her eyes wide.

He tugged at the buttons on his jacket as he walked back to her side. "After all, we're married now."

CHAPTER 16

February 12, 1865

*M*illie couldn't move. Amy slept in the crook of her arm, which was normal after she'd nursed toward dawn. The warm body that snuggled against Millie's back didn't budge when she tried to put space between them. Instead, the heavy arm across her waist tightened.

Memories of the previous night elicited a smile. The call of nature, however, made her desperate to break free of the confinement. Millie whispered his name but got no response. She turned her head and said it louder. His breath grazed her neck, making her shiver. This wouldn't do.

"Troy Harrison McNeil." She used her sternest voice of command.

The arm lifted, and she slipped free enough to sit up, taking the blanket with her.

"Hey!" Troy's eyes opened as she climbed over Amy and set her feet on the cold floor. She pulled her everyday dress over her gown for an extra layer, then slipped the knitted slippers on her feet. Troy's gaze followed her every move, a lopsided smile on his face. "You goin' somewhere?"

"I need to help with breakfast. You can stay here with Amy. If she wakes up before I get back, call me."

"Wait. Come here."

"Can't." She opened the door and shut it behind her, breathing a sigh of relief. Troy had been right. Spending the night together had been a bad idea, and not just because of the risk of another pregnancy. Because now, at least for her, it was going to be much harder to say goodbye.

"Now, Millie, what do you mean comin' down here this mornin'?" Hattie looked up from placing circles of biscuit dough in the pan. "You should've stayed upstairs with your new husband."

Millie turned to wash her hands and hide her blush. She searched for a simple explanation. "He's spending time with Amy before he has to leave. Are we having grits or potatoes this morning?"

A half hour later, the aromas of coffee and fried ham drew the rest of the household to the kitchen. Millie set Amy's plate on the table and removed her apron. "I'll go get the baby." But she met Troy at the foot of the stairs with their daughter in his arms. Both were fully dressed and wore twin grins.

"There's your mama," Troy said, but he swung the baby away when Millie reached for her. Instead, he leaned toward Millie and whispered in her ear. "You forgot to give us our good morning kisses before you rushed out the door." Without waiting for her response, he pecked her cheek and then held Amy close to her. The child placed both hands on Millie's face and a slobbery kiss on her chin.

Troy transferred the baby to Millie but grasped her wrist before she could turn away. "Are you well?" His hazel eyes gleamed with tender concern, holding her more surely than his hands.

Her heart fluttered. "I'm feeling quite well. Are you?"

His mouth quirked to one side. "Just wishin' I didn't have to go."

Millie gulped to keep the tears from surfacing. "Go on and eat your breakfast while I feed Amy." She lowered her face to the baby's and tickled her. "Are you ready to put some food in your belly, little one?" Amy giggled, and Troy circled his arm around Millie's shoulder to turn them all toward the dining room.

Lydia's questioning gaze passed over Millie before she greeted Troy. "Would you like coffee?"

"Um, yes, please." He glanced about the room as Lydia hurried away and the other women brought in dishes and bowls to set on the table.

Millie chuckled as she tucked a dish towel under Amy's chin. Everyone pitched in for their first meal of the day, and the activity must present quite a spectacle to a newcomer. "Just take a seat anywhere. We're not too particular about who sits where."

He sat beside her, watching in fascination as she spoon-fed Amy. "She sure gobbles it up, doesn't she?"

"I guess she's glad to get something besides milk."

Lieutenant Hart and Mrs. Coker took their places as Lydia and Celeste brought in the coffee and biscuits.

Amy turned her head away to the next spoonful, so Millie wiped her face and settled her on the corner pallet. She returned to find Troy had filled her plate.

She looked from the plate to Troy as a memory surfaced. "Thank you, I think. Did you spit in it?"

Troy grinned at the reminder of days when war was only part of history lessons.

Lydia laughed outright while the others stared and sputtered.

Millie waved away their concern. "An old jest from years

ago." Something she'd forgotten, but the words had slipped out. The memory was oddly comforting and tightened the bond between them.

∾

*T*roy tucked away his feelings and finished his meal. It might be the last opportunity he got enough to fill up for a while. He'd have plenty of time to sort out his mixed emotions on the train ride. He'd best get moving.

"Lieutenant Hart, could I trouble you for a ride to Lucas Turner's house? I left my stuff in Seth's apartment there."

Beside him, Millie tensed. He tried to ignore it.

"I can do that. I want to see if I can find a New York newspaper. Maybe Lucas will have one." The lieutenant rose. "Grandmother, ladies, is there anything I can do for you while I'm out?"

Mrs. Coker answered Gideon's question as she followed him from the room, and the other women began to clear the table. Millie paused with a stack of dishes. "What time does your train leave?"

"Half past ten. I figured you'd be in church, and I'd rather say our farewells in private."

Millie nodded toward the baby. "Would you take Amy upstairs so I can change her nappy? I'll be there as soon as I finish helping here." She left without waiting for an answer.

Troy couldn't tell whether she was angry or simply tired, but he bowed to her wishes. He lifted the baby from her blanket and snuggled her neck before he caught a whiff of a different odor she brought with her. "Oh, your mama is a sly one, ain't she, Amy? I think she's punishing me for leaving y'all."

He continued talking as he climbed to the second floor and entered the bedroom. Too bad the baby couldn't offer him any advice on how to deal with her mother. He laid Amy on the bed, and she rolled over to her belly. "No, no. I think you have to lie on your back." He turned her face-up once more, only to have her roll over again. She giggled as they repeated the process. "Come back, you little stinker."

Millie breezed into the room and grabbed a basket of items from the bureau. "She thinks it's a game. Here, Amy, hold your doll."

To Troy's surprise, the baby lay still and gnawed on the soft toy while Millie made quick work of cleaning and diapering her bottom. She handed the child to Troy. "Now all clean, so you give Papa a kiss before he has to leave."

Lydia tapped on the open door. "Lieutenant Hart is bringing the carriage around. Do you want me to take Amy down?"

Troy nodded. "As soon as I get another hug." He snuggled the baby, then wrapped one arm around Lydia as they made the transfer. "Thanks for everything, Aunt Lydia. I hope you'll write."

"You know I will. Be safe."

She proceeded to the staircase, and Troy turned to Millie, who stood with her arms crossed and her head bowed. He'd seen her take that stance before, usually when Cal had scolded her for some infraction. Was it to keep from displaying her tears?

Two steps took him to her side. "Millie—"

"I'm sorry, Troy." No tears, but distress dulled her eyes and pulled her mouth downward. "I shouldn't have reacted the way I did and made you feel like you had to stay."

"You didn't—"

"Yes, I did. I acted like a spoiled child and made you feel guilty for leavin' us again."

He wrapped his arms around her and whispered into her hair. "Don't you know I wanted to stay? I wrestled with myself all week and changed my mind a dozen times. I honestly don't know if it was the right thing to do, but it's done. And we share the blame or the responsibility or whatever you want to call it." He pulled away to peer at her. "We both made our choices, and we'll live with wherever those lead us."

He lifted her chin with his finger. "Now, I don't want my last day to be spoiled by tears and sadness. Let me see that smile or I'll put one there."

Her lips quirked, but he shook his head. "Not good enough." He nipped her lips and danced his fingers across her ribs. She seized his hands and pressed her mouth to his. He enveloped her, then forced himself to let go. "I have to leave now. I'll write as soon as I can."

He held her hand as they descended the stairs. Lydia pointed toward a package on the hall table. "Hattie packed you a box of goodies for the trip." She bounced Amy in her arms and turned so the child wouldn't see him leave.

Herbert helped him with his overcoat and hat, then opened the door.

Troy raised a hand in farewell. "Y'all take care of each other now until I return." His throat ached as his gaze sought Millie's and noticed the sheen of tears. How long would it be until they could be together again?

The cold air penetrated his clothes when he stepped outside. He strode to the carriage and joined Gideon on the bench. They spoke little on the way but shook hands when Gideon halted the horses at Luke's house.

"Appreciate all your assistance, Lieutenant. I hope we meet again before long." Troy hopped to the ground.

"Likewise, McNeil. Don't worry about your family. Grand-mother takes care of those she loves."

"I can tell. Godspeed." Troy snapped a salute and headed to Seth's apartment. Where he expected to get a stiff reprimand for giving in to temptation and staying with Millie last night. He whistled as he climbed the stairs. It was worth it.

~

FEBRUARY 27, 1865
LOUISVILLE, KENTUCKY

*T*wo weeks had passed with no word from Troy. Millie flipped through the letters again. One official-looking envelope for the lieutenant—Gideon, she corrected, remembering his insistence on the less formal address. She found it difficult to comply when he seemed so proper.

She shuffled the other envelopes. Two items for Mrs. Coker and one for Celeste from the Wilson family, her former neighbors who'd moved to Indiana.

Although Troy had written on the train and posted it from the depot in Cincinnati, the lack of answers to her recent letters disappointed her. Mail service was another casualty of war, of course, but she'd expected something by now.

With a sigh, she slipped the mail into her reticule and reached for the post office door. It swung open before she grasped it, and Millie stepped back to allow a young woman to enter ahead of a soldier. An alarm of recognition tingled along her nerves. Becky Varner. Of all the people to run into. She wasn't in the mood to fend off the talkative girl's questions about her and Troy.

"Why, Mrs. McNeil." Becky tittered and raised her hand to cover her grin. "How nice to see you again. But where is Troy? Surely, you didn't come alone."

Good manners forced Millie to reply to the girl's greeting. "Oh, Miss Varner. I'm sorry, Troy isn't here. My, uh, companion is at the mercantile across the street. I came to pick up the mail for my stepmother and friends."

The soldier shifted closer as he removed his kepi, and Millie caught her breath. She knew that face. Eyes the same shade as Troy's and a prominent mole below one eyebrow. Any sound she made was lost in Miss Varner's giggle. "Oh, pardon my manners. May I introduce Corporal Harris? He's a guard at the refugee house, and he offered to show me around town."

Millie ignored the hand he presented and raised her eyes long enough to see the smirk he sent over Miss Varner's head. "How…considerate of him. Well, I must be off before my escort begins to worry. Good day."

The door opened again, forcing the corporal to shift aside. Millie lifted a silent thanks to the Almighty when Seth pushed his way inside. "Mil—

"Seth! I'm sorry I took so long." Millie grabbed his arm and urged him back out the door. She waved as they turned on the walk. "Good to see you, Miss Varner."

Seth cast a backward glance at the couple but assisted Millie up the street. When they were out of earshot, he asked, "What was that all about?"

"That soldier. I think I saw him in Georgia before we went to Marietta. He tried to…" She caught movement at the post office in her peripheral vision. "Can we cross the street?"

Seth took her elbow, ushered her to the corner, and continued to the bakery. "Is Lydia working today?"

"No, she's watching Amy. She encouraged me to get out while the weather was good."

"But your friends back at the post office don't know that, I presume, so this should be a safe place to talk."

The bell over the door announced their arrival, and Mr. Watford greeted them from his wheeled chair. "Ah, Miss Gibson, welcome. I remember you're a married lady now, but I forget the new name."

"McNeil. How are you today, Mr. Watford?"

"Fine as a flea on a hound dog, thank you. And Mr. Morgan. You're not working?"

"It's varnish day, so I get to take a long break between applying coats. I ran into my young friend outside. Can we get a couple of warm drinks and some muffins?" He directed Millie to the array of sweets and told her to choose what she liked.

In a few minutes, they sat at the small table with their refreshments. "Now, you say you saw that soldier at your home in Georgia. Could it really be the same man?"

"Yes, I remembered him well. He has a mole near his left eye and eyes much like Troy's. The soldiers scouted homes in the area, on the hunt for food." She lowered her gaze and fiddled with her cup. "He caught me alone in the house and tried to...kiss me. I punched him in the nose."

Seth's eyes widened, and then he barked a shout of laughter. "I told Lydia she had her hands full with you. Wish I could've seen the fellow's face."

Millie dropped her eyes to hide her dismay. "Yes, well, seeing him here could be a problem. I think the corporal remembered me just now, and he'd promised to get even with me for refusing his advances. Also, that girl who's with him today is an acquaintance of Troy's. I'm afraid those two might get cozy and share their information. Why would the Union Army put someone like him as a guard at the refugee house?"

"Either they don't know how he is, or they don't care. Wasn't it one of those guards who kidnapped Mrs. Griffin?"

"Yes, and she might've been ruined if Major Griffin hadn't found her." Millie nibbled her lower lip. "I wonder if I ought to warn Miss Varner about him."

"That's a good idea." Seth paused with cup raised to his lips. "She might not heed your advice, but at least you won't feel guilty if anything happens."

Millie propped her chin in her hand. "Yeah, but how would

I get past him at the refugee house? Maybe if Lydia goes with me..."

"I have a better idea." He set down his cup. "Write her a note and ask her to meet you somewhere so you can explain."

~

MARCH 1, 1865
CAMP CHASE, OHIO

*T*roy stood firm against the belligerent prisoner facing him. "I ain't gonna meet you on no field of honor, you crazy Hussar. You know that dueling is against the law, and even if it weren't, the commander would have my hide if I was part of such a stunt."

His adversary continued to rant and taunt him, but his fellow prisoners had tired of the game and wandered off to find their dinner. Troy muttered as he walked up the muddy street toward his own quarters. "If he ain't the most ornery, cantankerous human being I ever met, I don't know who is. Why couldn't he be one of the dozens released while I was gone?"

He pushed inside the sparse room. "Meet him on a field of honor during a war? How crazy."

"Your favorite Rebel causing trouble again, McNeil?" His roommate paused in unpacking his knapsack.

"Walter, welcome back." Troy clasped the man's hand. "I'm sure glad to see you again. Did you get your folks settled in Tennessee?"

"Yeah, they're all staying with Ma's cousin. I hated to light outa here so soon after you returned from Louisville, but it meant a lot to Pop and Ma for me to be there. Everything about the same here?"

"Yeah, same routine, same food. Which you're in time to enjoy. Or do you have something special in your pack?"

Walter grinned. "You know I do. A box of sweets, but we'll save those for times when the fare is especially bad." He slapped Troy on the back. "Come on, you can tell me all about your trip to Kentucky over dinner."

An hour later, they divided a small cake while Troy wrapped up his story. "You see why I need you to help me write to Millie? I seem to have a knack for saying things the wrong way."

"Troy, me boy, writin' to a woman is a whole heap easier than being there and talkin' with her." Walter broke off another bite of cake and smacked his lips. "Mostly, she wants to know you're safe and thinkin' of her while you're apart. Tell her about your day and how much you miss her."

"That's all I need to say?"

"Pretty much. O' course, it wouldn't hurt to quote some fancy poetry or maybe a verse from the Bible that she'll like. Did you ever read the Song of Solomon?"

Troy shook his head. "Can't say that I have."

"Read through it." Walter winked. "It might help. Or you could ask your favorite Georgia Hussar for a suggestion. I understand he likes to quote that Shakespeare fellow."

"Is that so?" Troy tapped his fingers on the desk. "Maybe if I ask him about that, he might forget about wanting to meet on a 'field of honor' to duel."

Walter chuckled. "You might even tell him it's a duel of words. After all, people say words are more powerful than a sword."

CHAPTER 17

MARCH 3, 1865
LOUISVILLE, KENTUCKY

*M*illie had debated how to get Becky Varner to meet her without the corporal as an escort, as she supposed the girl's mother wouldn't allow her to wander around Louisville alone. After discussing the matter with Lydia, she settled on having both Becky and Mrs. Varner meet her at the bakery. Lydia would be there also, should Millie need her.

When the day arrived, she prevailed upon Lieutenant Hart to drive her there. Amy had soiled her outfit and had to be changed twice, which made them late, much to her dismay.

Lieutenant Hart pulled the landau to a stop in front of the bakery. He held Amy and helped Millie alight from the carriage. "I'll return in an hour or so. Will that give you enough time?" He pulled Amy's grip from his collar and handed her into Millie's arms.

"Yes, that's fine. If we finish early, I'll walk down to the mercantile and wait for you there. Thank you so much, Lieutenant."

After he tipped his hat and drove away, Millie shifted Amy and faced the bakery.

Becky and Mrs. Varner were approaching the door.

Millie smiled. "I'm so glad you could meet me today. I know Troy would want us to become better acquainted."

For once, Becky seemed speechless while she gaped at the departing carriage. Mrs. Varner suffered no such affliction. "So nice of you to invite us, Mrs. McNeil. And you don't have to tell me who this little one is." She patted Amy's hand. "She favors Troy."

Becky's attention snapped back to the women, but Millie took the lead. "Let's get inside and out of the wind."

The bell over the door jingled when they opened it, and Lydia rounded the counter. "Ah, here you are. I've set up the larger table for you, ladies. You can hang your wraps on those pegs and take a seat."

Millie passed Amy to Lydia and spoke as she removed her cloak. "Lydia, this is Mrs. Velma Varner and Miss Becky Varner. They're neighbors of your brother Henry down in Alabama."

Becky's eyes widened. "Mr. McNeil is your brother?"

"Half-brother. His mother was Pa's first wife, and I'm the youngest of his second wife. When Mama died, all the others were grown and had their own families, so the relatives sent me to live with Granny McNeil in Georgia."

Mrs. Varner nodded. "I remember Henry said something about that. It's good to meet you."

"And I'm glad to know you. It's always pleasant to find folks with a connection to home." She passed the baby back to Millie. "Now, if you want to choose your treats from the display case, I'll bring you whatever you'd like to drink."

They made their choices and settled at the table. Millie did her best to guide the conversation, asking her guests about their life at home and Mr. Varner's prospects for returning to Alabama. She described her own journey to Louisville and experiences around town, skirting the touchier subjects of her marriage to Troy and Amy's birth.

She finally reached her main objective to warn them about the guards at the refugee house. "Is Lieutenant Goodwin still in charge there? We always turned to him with any problems because he was kind and helpful. Some others, though..." She shook her head as she trailed off suggestively.

Mrs. Varner's eyes widened. "Don't tell me they abused y'all."

Millie nodded. "Some of them. One even kidnapped a friend of ours. Thank goodness he's gone, but it makes me wonder how men like that can secure such a post."

Becky trilled a nervous laugh, glancing from Millie to her mother. "Well, you don't have to worry about Corporal Harris. He's been ever so nice to us and even escorted me around town. Why, you met him the other day when we saw you at the post office, Mrs. McNeil."

Millie ignored the subtle warning in Becky's voice.

"Please, won't you call me Millie? We're so near the same age." She tapped her fingers on the table and fixed her attention on the girl. "You know, he seemed vaguely familiar to me. Quite like a soldier who tried to corner me back in Georgia. Lydia," she called, "you remember the one I punched in the nose that day?"

Lydia had lingered close enough to track the conversation. "Yes, although I only saw him from a distance. Would you recognize him again? After all, it's been several months."

Millie pretended to consider. "Hmm. Maybe not. I do remember his eyes were about the same color as Troy's, and he had a mole right about here." She put a finger near her temple.

Becky's face darkened, but Mrs. Varner missed the description entirely as she leaned toward Amy, who was now waking in Millie's arms. *Oh, well, maybe Becky will heed the warning.*

Millie fished in her reticule for the coins to pay for their meal, silently blessing Troy's generosity. "I guess Amy's decided it's time to head home. I've enjoyed our chat and getting to know each of you. Maybe we can do it again before you leave town."

Lydia took the baby so Millie could don her cloak. The other women gathered their wraps and moseyed toward the door. Millie glanced through the shop window to see Lieutenant Hart guiding the carriage close to the curb.

"I believe your ride has arrived, Mrs. McNeil." Becky turned to Millie with a glint of malice in her narrowed eyes. "Lawsy, every time I see you, you're with a different man."

~

March 12, 1865
Camp Chase, Ohio

"*M*ail for you, Private McNeil." Walter joined Troy at the dining table where he tarried over his meal and jawed with two other guards.

Troy laughed. "Much as I like gettin' letters, I don't like having to answer 'em." He held out his hand, and Walter slapped three envelopes in his hand. "Guess I'll go on back to the room and read 'em."

Back in his room, Troy opened the letter on top. It was from his mother, and he skimmed it first, glad to see that his former nanny, Old Liza, had recovered from the ague. "My brother Rupert went home," he said aloud. "Glad to know he's safe at least. Still no word from Simon."

He finished reading that one and reached for the next envelope. Millie's handwriting made him smile. She told how she'd invited the Varner women to tea at the bakery.

I didn't ask them to Mrs. Coker's for this reason: Becky seems to have taken up with a guard at the refugee house, and I'm certain he's the one I punched in the nose back in Georgia. If he knows where I'm staying, he might make good on his threats. Not that I don't trust the women, but he might trick Becky into saying where we live.

She went on to tell about Amy's latest achievements and to assure him that Seth Morgan checked on them regularly since Lieutenant Hart had returned to his unit in Virginia.

Troy wasn't sure if he cared for Millie being so friendly with Becky, but there wasn't much he could do about it now. As for the soldier she mentioned, that fellow would probably tread with more caution in Louisville than he had in Georgia. All the same, he ought to tell the rest of the household to watch out for him.

He picked up the last letter and tore it open. What was this?

Troy,

I guess your wife didn't want us to know that you had joined the Federal Army. Maybe she thought we wouldn't claim you as a friend while Pa is still recovering from his wounds, but we always knew you didn't hold with slavery and secession. On the other hand, maybe she didn't want you to know that we have seen her about town with different men. I don't want to cause trouble between you and her, but I thought you should know. If I knew where she was staying, I would talk to her about how it looks for a married woman to be out with other men. She wouldn't tell me where you were when I asked. I heard that you were at Camp Chase from a guard at the prison across the street here. Maybe you should come back to Louisville and set matters straight.

Your true friend, Becky Varner.

Troy threw the paper down as if it had bitten him. "Doggone you, Becky Varner, sticking your nose in other people's business." And Millie ought never to have tried to make friends with the girl. He ran his hands through his hair. How was he supposed to handle this from a hundred miles away?

Walter looked up from his writing. "Problems with your little family?"

"Nah, just some nosy busybody trying to stir up trouble." Troy stood and paced the narrow room. "Why do women feel they have to tend to other people's business?"

"Good question." Walter put down his pencil. "My Pa would say it's 'cause they have a need to fix everything."

Troy pushed his hands into his pockets. "Yeah, that sounds about right. Millie wanted to warn Becky, a girl we know, about the man she's been in company with, and now Becky's sent me a letter, accusing Millie of going around town with other men."

Walter flinched. "Ouch. That's a serious accusation."

"Except I know who the men are. One's the grandson of the woman they live with. He's been recuperating from an injury and illness, but he helps the women when they need him to. And Seth hangs around because he's sweet on my Aunt Lydia."

Troy picked up the papers and flopped onto his bunk. "Guess I'll have to warn Millie to watch herself. I sure as heck can't write Becky. That would bring on more trouble."

"You're right about that." Walter tapped his pencil on the desk. "Once you're married, the only other females in your life better be family or older than your grandma."

MARCH 22, 1865
LOUISVILLE, KENTUCKY

"*W*hy, that sneaky little wretch!" Millie stormed into Lydia's room and waved Troy's letter in the air. "Do you know Becky found out that Troy's in Ohio and wrote to him? And she accused *me* of cavortin' around town with different men. I oughta march over there and punch her in the nose."

"You'll do no such thing." Lydia picked up her reticule and marched to the door. "I'll do it for you." She was almost to the staircase by the time Millie caught up, laughing.

"You crazy woman. I hope I remember to do that when Amy grows up."

Lydia smiled and patted Millie's cheek. "It works so much better than trying to talk you out of whatever you're planning. Now let's see what we can do about this."

They walked arm-in-arm back to the bedroom. Millie plopped down on the bed. "At the very least, I think Becky should know Troy told me about her letter."

Lydia's eyes widened. "He isn't going to write her back, is he?"

"Of course not. He warned me to watch myself where she's concerned. If he responded to her letter, it would only encourage her."

Lydia paced to the window. "I hate to say it, but maybe you should confront her in front of her mother. That'll embarrass her and make her less likely to repeat such a mistake."

"Should we ask them to the bakery again? We can't let them know where we're staying. It would feel like an invasion of our privacy, and Corporal Harris might find out."

"I'll be taking pies to the prison tomorrow." Lydia tapped a finger against her chin as she pondered. "Why don't I ask Major Sullivan when he expects Mr. Varner to be well enough to leave? If it's soon, maybe we can have a send-off for the whole family at the refugee house, since they're my brother's neighbors."

Millie recoiled. "But Corporal Harris might be there too."

"I'll speak to Lieutenant Goodwin," Lydia said. "Maybe he can send Harris on an errand."

When Seth visited the next evening, Millie told him about the letters. "Lydia thinks I should confront Becky when her parents are present. Mr. Varner has recovered enough to leave for home next week, so that gives us a reason to send them off with our good wishes."

"Lieutenant Goodwin said he'll be on hand, so we shouldn't have any problems with the other residents or guards." Lydia passed out cups of tea to the ladies and handed Seth the coffee he'd requested. "It's too bad Lieutenant Hart already returned to Virginia. He could go with us."

Seth blew across the liquid in his cup. "Do you need me to accompany you? Or would that cause more trouble?"

Millie exchanged a glance with Lydia before answering. "If you can get away on Saturday, we'd be glad for the extra help."

"I will contribute tea and, of course, send Herbert with you," Mrs. Coker said. "Too bad my old joints won't allow me to go and watch the show." Her eyes twinkled as she bit into her scone.

At noon on Saturday, Herbert and Seth carried trays into the kitchen at the refugee house. Besides the Varners, two other families and a handful of single women occupied the building. Celeste and Rose volunteered to help serve, and soon everyone sat at a table, sharing stories of their journeys to Louisville.

The children gobbled up their treats and ventured outside to brave the wind. They recruited a couple of adults to help with the kites Seth had fashioned from cast-off fabric and bits of wood left from his carpentry work.

Millie broke off a piece of muffin and smashed it between

her fingers before offering it to Amy. "I wish Dorcas could've been here."

Rose set her cup back on the saucer. "So do I, but I suppose supporting her young man in his ministry takes precedence over our little gathering."

"When is their wedding?" Celeste asked. "I hope it's where we can all attend."

"Speaking of weddings, Millie..." Becky jumped into the conversation. "When was it you and Troy got married?"

Millie was prepared for the question. "Last February." Which was true, since it was now March, although she expected the girl would take it to mean last year. Millie held her breath, not wanting to lie outright but determined to shield Amy from malicious gossip. And they *had* pledged themselves to each other in the Scottish fashion, though without witnesses.

Mrs. Varner paused with her cup at her lips. "But Troy was in Alabama to help Henry with his planting last spring."

Millie shrugged, feigning nonchalance. "It was easier for him to avoid the conscription if he kept moving and traveled alone. Besides, I had my job at the mill and didn't want to leave Lydia by herself."

"And then y'all was run out of Georgia." Mr. Varner spoke from his place at the end of the table. "I know that happened before General Lee sent us back that-away at the end of the summer."

Lydia nodded. "It was July. They set the mill on fire and put us in wagons bound for Marietta. Troy was on his way to Georgia and caught up with us, but they sent him and most of the men north ahead of us."

"So," Becky said, bringing the attention back to her, "Troy wasn't with you when the baby was born? When was that?"

"Late October." Millie waited for Becky to do the math. "Doctor Spencer's wife said babies often come early when the mother's endured so much hardship." She paused a moment before going on. "Speaking of Troy, he told me you wrote him a letter, Becky. I wonder how you learned he's at Camp Chase?"

Becky's eyes widened as her gaze swung from Millie to her parents, who rounded on her.

"What's that?" her father asked.

"Rebecca Jane Varner, you ought to know better than to write to a man, especially one who's married." Mrs. Varner's frown emphasized her dismay.

"I, uh, thought..." Becky licked her lips and glanced wildly about the room. She finally looked at Millie again and frowned. "As a friend, I thought he ought to know that his wife was running about town with other men."

Seth glared at the girl. "I was one of those men, and I can assure you I have no designs on Millie McNeil. Her husband is a friend who came to my aid. Naturally, I promised to watch over his family while he's away."

"The other gentleman you might have seen was our landlady's grandson." Lydia stood as she addressed Becky. "He was kind enough to accompany us on occasion while he was in town to recuperate from an illness."

"But you didn't answer my question, Becky." Millie transferred Amy to Lydia's arms. "How did you know Troy's location? I'm sure I didn't mention it, since I wasn't sure how you folks would feel about him joining the Union Army."

Mr. Varner scoffed. "Oh, everybody at home knows the McNeils don't always agree on such matters. As I understand it, that's why Henry moved away. He couldn't abide their bickerin' over politics. My thinkin' is every man must decide for himself and hold to it."

"Well, Rebecca Jane, I'd like to hear the answer to Millie's question too." Mrs. Varner stood and propped her hands on her ample hips. "How did you know where to write to her husband?"

Becky squirmed in her seat. "Corporal Harris told me."

"How did Corporal Harris know?" Mr. Varner leaned forward to peer at his daughter. "And why would he even care?"

"He said he had a score to settle with her." She mumbled her answer.

Her father shook his head. "Speak up, girl. I don't hear as well as I once did."

"He said he had a score to settle with her." She pointed to Millie.

"How could that be?" Mrs. Varner set her empty cup on top of her plate. "How would he have an acquaintance with Millie?"

"I can answer that." Lydia meandered closer to the table, bouncing Amy in her arms. "When the Union Army was squattin' in our area, before they burned the mill, the soldiers went out and scavenged food. Corporal Harris barged into my house while Millie was there alone and made improper advances. She punched him in the nose, and he promised to get even."

Becky gasped. "He only said she embarrassed him in front of his friends."

Seth smirked. "I imagine he was embarrassed to come out with a bloody nose when he thought he could brag about a conquest."

"By the way, where is the corporal today?" Millie made a show of looking around for him. "I expected him to be here since he's so devoted to Becky and y'all will soon be leaving."

"He had to go over to the prison." Mr. Varner chuckled. "Something about mindin' the gate. He wasn't happy to miss our little celebration."

"I don't imagine he was." Millie picked up several dishes and carried them to the sink, mumbling under her breath. "He should consider himself lucky to get off so easily."

CHAPTER 18

*T*he bugler's call blasting through the camp in mid-afternoon jerked Troy from the task of cleaning his rifle. He set aside the weapon, pulled on his boots, and grabbed his kepi. The prison summons to assemble didn't happen every day. "What do you suppose it is?"

Walter plopped his kepi on his head and pushed Troy through the door. "Guess we're about to find out." A group of young recruits and other "galvanized Yankees" who'd been training for the field joined the procession of guards.

Speculation buzzed among the soldiers as they followed the growing assembly to the dining hall. General Richardson strode to the front of the building and signaled for silence.

When the murmurs ceased, his voice rang across the room. "I've received a telegram from Washington with some news we've all been praying for. General Robert E. Lee has surrendered to General Grant in Virginia."

The room erupted in shouts of jubilation before he

191

completed the announcement. Troy clapped and cheered along with his fellows, but questions tempered his response. What did this mean for his future?

The general raised his hand to call for quiet. "While other divisions are still engaged in North Carolina and Texas, the Confederacy is on its last leg. I don't have any direct orders yet, but I expect we'll soon begin releasing the remaining prisoners. Those of you with more than a few months left to serve the Union Army will be reassigned."

Walter slapped Troy on the shoulder. "Hallelujah, we may get to go home soon, McNeil." His smile dimmed when Troy didn't respond with equal exuberance. "At least, long enough to collect our family for the next assignment."

"Yeah, that's what concerns me," Troy said. "Where will we go next? You saw a bit of the South when you went to Tennessee last month. How did it appear to you?"

"Sad and beaten down." Walter sighed. "It's gonna take some time for her to come back. But she can do it, McNeil. We can be part of the restoration efforts, us and our families."

Troy dredged up a degree of enthusiasm and whacked Walter on the back. "I reckon we can. Wherever they may send us, whether south or west or even north."

"Nah." Walter laughed. "They won't send you and me north. We might cause them Yanks some trouble."

~

APRIL 14, 1865
LOUISVILLE, KENTUCKY

"What do you mean, you'll be staying at the refuge house?" Millie followed Lydia upstairs and tried to make sense of her stepmother's announcement. Amy, balanced on her mother's hip, held onto a strand of

Millie's hair that had slipped from her chignon. Millie tugged it free before the baby could guide it to her mouth.

"Major Sullivan is moving Cal to a room there so I can take care of him until he—while he's sick." She started filling her carpet bag with clothes from the dresser drawers.

Fear tightened Millie's chest. "But why should you have to do that? Don't they have a doctor at the prison?"

Lydia shut the bag and faced her. "It's lung fever. He needs to be isolated, Millie, so the disease doesn't spread to the whole prison."

"But what about you? Couldn't you get sick by being with him?"

"It's possible, but as I told Seth, I've done this before. I know how to be careful." She slipped her arm around Millie's waist for a side-hug. "I'll be all right. You just take good care of my girl until I get back." She pressed a kiss to Amy's brow and lugged the bag into the hall.

Millie trailed her, desperate to change Lydia's mind but unsure of how to accomplish it. Why did this happen now, when the end of the war was in sight? General Lee had surrendered to the Union in Virginia, and General Sherman ensured the North's victory by blazing a path of destruction across the Carolinas, according to the Northern newspaper reports. Things were finally looking up, but now Lydia was risking her health by tending Cal.

Seth waited in the parlor, ready to escort Lydia back to the refugee house. He stood as the women entered and took Lydia's bag.

Millie appealed to him. "Seth, can't you stop her from doing this?"

"Already tried. She's a stubborn woman."

Lydia gripped Millie's arms. "Sweetie, I know you're worried about me, but I trust the Lord to take care of me. This is the right thing to do. What I need you to do is pray for me and take care of yourself and this baby." She tied the strings of her bonnet and turned to Seth. "I'm ready now."

Herbert held the door as the two exited, but Millie felt as if bricks sat atop her shoulders.

Mrs. Coker rose from her chair and shuffled to Millie's side. "I don't believe she will expose herself unnecessarily, my dear. Some people are blessed with a constitution that doesn't succumb to sickness. Think of all the sick people that doctors and nurses move among in those hospitals. Knowing she's faced this kind of illness before gives me great hope that she'll return to us soon."

Amy squirmed to get down, so Millie trailed the older woman to the settee where the baby could sit beside her. "I guess I'm being selfish. Lydia has always taken care of everybody, it seems. As a girl, she took care of Granny McNeil for years. When she married Cal, she did everything for him and me. Then it was me and Amy. I just don't know what I'd do if anything happened to her."

Mrs. Coker gazed into the distance. "You'd do what we all do. Pick up the pieces of your life and go on." She smiled at Millie. "You'd learn to be thankful for the time you had together, and you'd see that other people can come into your life and give you joy. Like all of you have done for me. I bless the day Celeste and Rose knocked on my door, looking for work. I may have provided y'all a job and a place to stay, but you've given me so much more."

Millie reached over and squeezed Mrs. Coker's hand. "Oh, Aunt Lottie," she said, using the name Mrs. Coker called herself to Amy. "We thank God every day for you. As you say, we have friends now that we didn't even know of a year ago. It makes you wonder what the future will bring, doesn't it?"

∾

APRIL 15, 1865
CAMP CHASE, OHIO

*F*or days after the general's announcement, Camp Chase buzzed with speculation about the war's end. Troy read the Northern newspaper reports of the jubilation from New York to Chicago over Lee's surrender. Businesses closed and proclaimed a holiday in Washington. Two hundred guns fired in Cincinnati and in Indianapolis. In Detroit, people gathered to celebrate with lights and singing. Reading about the terms of the peace agreement, allowing the Confederate soldiers to return home under parole, lifted his spirits. As much as he aligned with the Union attitude toward slavery, he was a true Southerner who loved the land.

With a genuine prospect of peace on the horizon, he shared his thoughts about the future with his friend. "I tell you, Walt, I wouldn't mind going out west and seein' that part of the country. But I don't want to put Millie and the baby in danger."

They left the dining hall after breakfast and prepared to make their morning rounds. Troy blinked as he entered their quarters, dark in contrast to the growing sunlight outside.

"Understandable." Walter shucked off his jacket to brush out a spot. "It's something to consider. I don't know if I could convince Molly to move so far away. Guess I better pray for an assignment close—"

"Assemble in the dining room in five." The voice and the face disappeared before Troy could form a response. He turned to Walter. "What d'you s'pose that's about?"

"Maybe Joe Johnston surrendered to Sherman. That would put another nail in the South's coffin. I didn't like the way Johnston run his men ragged last year." Walter wagged his head. "Runnin' away instead of fightin'. That wasn't my idea of how to wage a war."

For the second time that week, they joined their fellows to

learn what news was important enough to warrant an assembly. Though General Richardson maintained a face carefully devoid of expression, he couldn't mask the dark smudges and bags beneath his eyes. His lips trembled above his generous beard.

"There is no easy way to say this. Last night, someone killed President Lincoln." The general waited until the gasps and murmurs died down. "Vice President Johnson has assumed leadership, and we will carry on as usual. Tomorrow is Easter, so we place our hope in the promise it represents. We'll hold divine services at sunrise."

Sorrow pierced Troy's heart. Unlike many of his Northern and Southern friends, he neither revered nor hated President Lincoln. His perspective wasn't unique. In the last two years, he'd discovered others who shared his view but held their counsel close in a world of sharply divided—and vociferous—opinions. The opportunity for healing the breach was a shaky proposition. Would Lincoln's assassination affect the tenuous prospect of peace?

General Richardson shuttled to a far corner, where he conferred with his senior officers. Around the hall, men sat stunned into silence.

Walter studied his hands while he spoke. "Reckon that'll set back some of our plans, McNeil. I guess somebody wasn't happy with General Lee's decision to save lives."

Troy pushed back from the table and headed for the door. "Might as well tend to our duties, Private Dykes. We may be here longer than we'd hoped."

~

April 16, 1865
Louisville, Kentucky

*N*ever had Millie anticipated attending church as much as this day. The message of hope in observing Christ's resurrection took on new meaning with news of Lee's surrender.

After four years of destruction, the prospect of peace was as real as the expectation of flowers in springtime. Maybe it was becoming a mother that made her reflect on such things. Or the hardships they'd suffered in the last year. Or the revelations of her true father and Cal's unlikely survival.

She paused in arranging her hair and peered at her reflection in the mirror above her bureau. Her larger bosom and peachy complexion attested to a better diet and living conditions since coming to Mrs. Coker's house. But had she truly grown up, or did she still exhibit some childish behavior? Would her mother be proud of the person she'd become? More importantly, did God require more of her?

She recalled Pastor Holland's message last week, which focused on forgiveness. "Before you join in the worship, waving your palm branches, be sure to clear your heart of any resentment," he'd said. "Forgive those who have wronged you, so that you, too, can be forgiven."

Millie pushed the last hairpin into place. "I'll go see Cal after church and make things right, even if he doesn't admit his faults. If Lydia can forgive him, I reckon I can too."

She hurried downstairs, where Celeste occupied Amy. "I'm ready. Are we waiting on Aunt Lottie?"

"She's not up to it, much as she tried to convince us otherwise. Hattie plans to stay with her. Herbert's getting the carriage now so we can take a turn by the park before church."

"That sounds lovely. Would you mind if we stop by the refugee house afterward?" She hoisted Amy to her hip so

Celeste could collect her cloak. "I feel like I should try to make amends with Cal while there's still time."

"Good for you." Celeste tied the ribbons on her bonnet. "I'll be happy to accompany you there, if you like."

Millie tossed a blanket over Amy and started for the door. The child reached toward the stairs and babbled in urgency.

"What's the matter, sweetie? Want your doll?" Celeste retrieved the toy from the settee and waved it so Amy could see. She pushed it away and motioned upstairs again.

"I think she's telling us to wait for Lydia. She's looked for her ever since Lydia left." Millie strode to the door with the sniffling baby.

Outside, Celeste climbed into the carriage first and took Amy while Millie joined her. The child's cries increased. Celeste's eyes revealed her worry. "Maybe we should make that trip to see Lydia at the refugee house before church and visit the park later."

"I think you're right." Millie jostled Amy. "You want to see Nana?"

The cries subsided, and she turned those hazel eyes to Millie.

"It's amazing how much she understands." Celeste rapped on the side of the vehicle and alerted Herbert to the change. When they arrived, they let themselves inside the building.

"Lydia said the room was down the hall from the guard's office." They spotted Lydia as she stepped out a door and picked up a tray of food.

When Lydia caught sight of them, her jaw dropped. "What in heaven's name are you doing here?"

Millie's hold tightened as Amy poked her head around the blanket draped over her. A watery grin broke out on the baby's face.

"She wouldn't stop crying for you, so we thought we'd come by on our way to church."

Celeste took the tray from Lydia's hands, and Amy lunged for her grandmother.

"Oh, sweet girl. I've missed you so much, but you shouldn't be here." Lydia turned to Millie. "However, if you want to speak to him, this is a good time."

All three women edged into the room. Celeste placed the tray at the foot of the cot, and Millie moved closer to the headboard. "Pa?" Seeing him emphasized how close he was to death. Once a robust man, now his frame was so gaunt, the skin seemed to cling to his bones. His face no longer ruddy, but ashen with dark smudges under his eyes.

Cal's eyes blinked, then opened wide. "Millie. You came."

Lydia moved closer so he could see Amy. "And she brought your granddaughter. This is Amy."

Cal focused on her. He whispered the baby's name, then switched his gaze from Amy to Millie. "Pretty. Like you."

Surprise held her immobile. Cal hadn't complimented her looks since Ma's death. Learning Millie wasn't his flesh and blood must have hit him hard, but he'd provided for her as a father should. "I'm sorry, Pa, for what Ma did. I reckon you did your best by me."

His eyes widened. "You know? 'Bout your Ma and McNeil?"

Millie nodded. "I'm sorry."

"No." He frowned and brought his hand to his chest. "I's... wrong." His words slurred together when he tried to rush them. "Sorry. Forgive."

His hand reached out, and Millie captured it between hers. Why did people wait to reach out to others until death seemed close? Cal had been far from perfect, but who was she to throw blame? And she'd almost let the opportunity for mercy pass. Tears slipped down her cheeks, but she forced a smile. "Already done."

Cal closed his eyes on a sheen of moisture. He sighed and appeared to sleep. Lydia wiped her own tears and led them back into the hall, pressing kisses to Amy's jaw. "He'll rest better now. I doubt he'll last another week. You should go, or you'll be late. I may come to the house later."

Outside the shelter's front door, they found Corporal Harris engaging Herbert in a friendly discussion.

The soldier's gaze turned their way, and he shot both women a roguish grin. "Ah, your charges return. Keep your seat, my good man. I'll assist the ladies."

Celeste tossed a nervous glance toward Millie but allowed the corporal to hand her into the carriage with a quiet word of thanks. She reached to take Amy from Millie's arms. Forced to accept his assistance, Millie limited her expression to a frown and a brief nod.

Once she was settled, he leaned against the landau. "I'd hoped to speak to you, Mrs. McNeil. I owe you—"

"You owe me nothing, sir, except to stay away." Millie hissed her warning as she smacked the carriage frame.

"Stay a moment, please..."

But Herbert spurred the horse, and the carriage rolled forward.

Millie took Amy onto her lap and did not look back.

She ignored the niggling impression that Corporal Harris seemed troubled by her refusal to speak with him. And why did his eyes remind her of Troy's?

CHAPTER 19

May 10, 1865
Camp Chase, Ohio

"Confederate Generals Johnston, Taylor, and Forrest have surrendered, which puts the Carolinas, Georgia, Florida, and Alabama in Union hands along with Virginia and Tennessee. For the Confederacy, only those states west of the Mississippi River remain." General Richardson indicated the areas on the wall map. "We've already sent most of the lower-rank prisoners home. Canvass those in your zone to see which areas we need to send them. Unfortunately, some of the railroad lines are not yet repaired, but we'll get them as close as we can."

"Sir," a soldier in the back asked, "when can we expect to get our orders?"

"My guess is most of you will get them by the end of the month. Any other questions?"

When no one else spoke, the commander dismissed the assembly, which had shrunk considerably since many trainees had elected to return home. With their numbers dwindling, they shifted the remaining prisoners to even the numbers among the three prisons. Troy had yet to meet a few who'd been relocated to his area, so he stopped by his room to grab pencil and paper. He crept about so he wouldn't disturb Walter, asleep after his turn at night duty.

Troy covered the line of barracks, making notes of names and hometowns, along with the nearest rail or steam station for each. With warmer days, the grounds had dried out. Maybe someone could coax grass to grow later, once the camp closed for good.

He took a break at noon and made his way to the dining room. Walter wandered in behind him, and they carried their trays to a table where two other guards sat. Troy only knew them by their surnames, Bailey and Young.

Bailey broke his bread and crumbled half of it into his soup. "Most of the new men in my area hail from South Georgia. Ain't that where you're from, McNeil?"

Troy shook his head while he swallowed. "I got kin there, but my folks are in Alabama near the Georgia line."

"Alabama, you say?" Young put down his spoon and thumbed through his papers. "There's a fellow named McNeil came to my area when Donaldson left. He's from—let me see." He ran a finger down the top sheet, then flipped to the next page. "Randolph County. Nearest station is Wedowee, if it wasn't destroyed, he said."

Troy rubbed his nose. "Might be some distant kin. Both my brothers who joined the Confederacy are accounted for. What's the fellow's first name?"

"Robert, but he goes by Ellis."

Troy sat up straight. "Ellis? Well, I'll be. That's Pa's youngest brother."

Walter slapped Troy on the back and guffawed. "Small world, ain't it? You oughta go over and see him."

"I don't know, Walter. He's something of a roughhouser. He might not take kindly to findin' out I'm with the Union."

"Maybe he's mellowed with age." Bailey pointed with his spoon. "What's the worst he could do? Disown you?" That brought a laugh from the others.

Young put away his papers and nodded. "He seemed pretty harmless to me. Besides, he'll be leaving in a few days."

Troy scratched the beard he'd started again. It was supposed to make him appear older, if he could abide the itching while it grew in. Would Ellis berate him as a foolish kid for his idealistic values as Paul had? Troy could always walk away. Lydia would be disappointed if he didn't at least speak to the man.

"All right, I'll mosey over after I finish with my reports."

Troy finished his meal and went back to work. The prospect of going home made the prisoners easier to handle, so it didn't take long to get their information.

He wandered over to Prison Three and found Private Young lounging at the first barrack's door. The guard straightened when Troy approached. "Hey, McNeil. You come to meet your cousin?"

"Uncle," Troy said as he scanned the area. "Which building is he in?"

"Number four over there. They'll be getting ready for dinner." Young grinned. "I'll hang around in case you need any help."

"Hey, if I can manage that crazy Hussar over my way, I figure I can handle an irate relative." He ambled to the barrack and called into the open doorway. "Ellis McNeil in here?"

"Who's asking?" The gruff voice sounded belligerent.

Troy shored up his courage. "Your nephew, John's youngest son, Troy."

MAY 23, 1865
LOUISVILLE, KENTUCKY

"*T*roy's letter said he ought to get his orders any day now." Millie clipped a clothespin over the last diaper on the line and reached for her empty basket. She enjoyed doing laundry for the opportunity to be outside, especially since Mrs. Coker's wringer washing machine did the hardest part.

Celeste tipped over the tub to dump the rinse water near the rose bushes. She pushed the contraption to the tool shed door, then bent to examine a tomato plant in the vegetable plot. "Maybe he'll make it to Louisville in time for the big celebration the town will throw in July."

"Yeah, I hope so."

Celeste headed for the house and opened the back door. "You comin' inside?"

"Not yet. I think I'll sit here a spell and enjoy the quiet." Millie dropped onto the garden bench as the door shut behind Celeste. The warmer weather reminded her of Georgia, with bees droning as they flitted around buttercups and daisies. Summer would soon be here.

A squeal inside the house jerked her out of her pleasant reverie but spread her lips in a smile. Lydia and Amy must have returned from their walk. Celeste liked to entertain the baby by playing hide and seek with her. The scrape of the back door warned Millie her rest was over. With a sigh, she grasped her basket and stepped away from the bench.

Suddenly, strong arms circled her waist, and a beard brushed her nape. She emitted a shriek of her own.

"So, Mrs. McNeil, I caught you loafin' on the job, tryin' to sneak away from your chores." The warm sound of his voice raised surprised delight. "What do you have to say for yourself?"

She dropped the basket and turned in Troy's arms to pull his lips down to hers. After a kiss that didn't last nearly long enough, she said, "Welcome home, Mr. McNeil." Their greeting stretched over a few minutes before she released him.

"Why didn't you send a telegram to warn me? I would've put on a better dress. Did you see how much Amy's grown? I heard her squeal, so I guess you saw her first."

Troy shook his head. "They said Celeste took her upstairs to change her. That was Lydia you heard hollering like a stuck pig."

Millie chuckled. "Well, I guess you have a powerful effect on all the ladies in your life."

"Oh, she wasn't hollering to see me." He brushed aside her hair and kissed her earlobe. "I brought somebody with me who surprised her."

"Really? Who's that?"

"Her brother. I found him at the camp and decided to bring him with me before sending him home to Alabama."

His words pierced the fog of desire and shot alarm through Millie. Dread pooled in her belly. Both Henry and John remained in Alabama, but... "Which brother?"

Troy shifted as she put distance between them. "The one closest to her. Ellis. You might as well go in and meet him."

Meet him? Meet the man whose actions had resulted in her birth but who'd never shown an interest in her existence? But Troy didn't know about that.

A shadow moved across the sky, and the bright afternoon faded. She clutched Troy's arms as the ground tilted.

~

*T*roy's arms tightened around Millie when she swayed. It wasn't like her to swoon, no matter the reason. Millie's feistiness was more likely to produce a roaring fight. His mind went to the attack she'd endured last year. Another woman might have gone into a decline, but Millie had fought back and grasped the first opportunity to wrench beauty from that ugliness. And life from death. Though neither of them had realized it at the time.

The notion jarred him. Had it happened again?

"Millie, honey? Are you unwell? You're not...do you need to lie down?"

She stirred in his arms. "What? No, I'll be fine. Just...let's sit a moment."

Troy guided her to the bench where he'd found her moments earlier. He kept an arm around her and pressed her head to his shoulder.

She released a shuddering breath, then spoke in a small voice. "There's something I have to tell you."

Her fingers moved over her skirt, pleating it into folds and smoothing it out again. He captured the restless movement with his free hand and brought the fingers to his lips. "Don't worry. I'm not leaving you this time. We'll manage. We're not the first couple to have babies so close together. I remember Ma sayin'—"

"Huh?" She snatched her hand away and drew back to face him. "What are you thinking?"

"That we, uh, you're going to have another baby?" Her expression worried him. Wasn't that what she wanted to tell him?

Millie patted his hand. "No, you silly man. I'm not in the family way again..." Her words trailed, and her eyes rounded. "You're not leaving? Did you get your orders? Will we be staying in Louisville?"

He placed a finger against her lips. "I'm not telling you what they are yet. Not until you finish what you were going to tell me."

She dropped her head in a familiar pose. The one that admitted she'd been caught trying to change the subject. If there wasn't going to be another baby, why did she almost swoon? What could be so grievous?

"A while back, I found a letter hidden in the baby clothes my mother left me. She'd been so strict that I shouldn't touch them, I'd forgotten about them for years. She'd said I must wait until I had my own baby. She'd even locked the little chest where they were packed."

She paused, and Troy nudged her. "Go on."

Her head moved back to his shoulder. "She confessed that Cal isn't really my father. Mother left him for a few months and went to visit her aunt in Alabama. While she was there, she took up with another man, and that's when she became pregnant. With me."

Alabama? A sense of dread washed over Troy. His heart beat faster, and his palms started sweating. "Please don't tell me it was my pa."

Millie jerked back and trained wide eyes on him. "What? Oh, no. It wasn't John, but it was a McNeil. His brother, Ellis."

Troy released his breath with a mighty heave. "Thank God. After all Pa's lectures and threatening, I thought... Wait a minute. Ellis? Then that means you and I are cousins."

Her brow wrinkled over troubled eyes. "You aren't upset with me, are you? For not telling you before we got married?"

"We can't change the past. Not our parents' actions nor ours." When she still held that worried frown, he tried to guess her thoughts. "It's all right, Millie. Alabama recognizes a marriage between cousins, even first cousins."

"That's good to know. But what about Kentucky? We got married in Kentucky."

He didn't know what the law here said, but he didn't want Millie to worry about it. "I guess we'll have to ask somebody.

Maybe Lucas knows. But don't worry over it. If necessary, we'll go down to Tennessee or Georgia or Alabama and get married again. My main concern now is to keep our family safe and together, wherever we make our home."

CHAPTER 20

*W*hile Millie appreciated his assurances, her ire rose. Were all men so thick-headed?

"You said you brought Ellis with you."

"Yeah, he's inside now." He grinned. "Lydia like to have busted my ears when she saw him. He's wantin' to meet you."

Millie patted his chest, trying to be patient. "Troy, I don't know if that's a good idea. I don't know if he has any idea that I'm his daughter."

Troy swiped a hand behind his neck. "He never said anything about it if he does. I didn't know he was in the prison camp at all until a few days ago. When he found out y'all were here, he said he'd stay at the camp until I got my reassignment so he could come with me to see y'all before he went home."

"He knows." Millie pushed away and stood. "Ma sent him a letter, but I couldn't know whether she did. How long has he known? Why did he never try to contact me before? Did he think I was a mistake that shouldn't have happened?"

She paced a few steps to the white oak tree that spread its limbs over the garden. The scent of honeysuckle drifted her way. She took a deep breath to inhale the delicate perfume and shore up her courage. When she turned, Troy stood behind her. He caught her in his arms. "Why don't we go inside, and you can ask him?"

"But what if—?"

"Hey, you two," Celeste called from the back door. "Lydia says your tea is getting cold, and your daughter is cranky and wants her mama."

Troy squeezed Millie's arm. "We're coming." He nodded toward the house and urged her in that direction, lowering his voice so only she could hear. "Where's my brave girl who fought off her attackers, traveled two hundred miles from home, and convinced a scaredy-cat idiot to marry her?"

She laughed at the characterization but had to agree with his point. She'd faced more frightening experiences than this in the last year. "All right, but you stay right beside me, you hear?"

"Yes, ma'am. I know who's the boss in this family."

His hand at her waist bolstered her confidence, and they moved into the parlor. Celeste and Lieutenant Hart were sorting through sheet music at the piano while Hattie added more cups to the tea service. Lydia met them with the tearful baby. Millie took the child, soothing Amy with her voice and a gentle back-rubbing. Directing her attention to the baby allowed her to ignore the other man in the room.

When Amy noticed Troy looming close, her face crimped up for another spate of crying until he poked a finger in her belly. She issued a tiny giggle, which made the adults laugh, and Amy responded with more giggles.

"Do you think she remembers me?" Troy jiggled his fingers under Amy's chin to elicit another chuckle.

Millie smiled. "Maybe, but she has so many admirers, she must find it hard to keep up with everyone."

"And here's another admirer to add to her list." Lydia tugged at the older man beside her. "Millie, I don't know if you ever met my brother, Ellis."

The action forced Millie to peer at the man's face. Brown hair brushed the tops of his ears to meld with the graying beard. Dark brows arched above faded blue eyes. No smile warmed his face, but she detected a nervous tic at the corner of his mouth. *This man is my father.*

"Once." The word seemed to force itself from his lips. "I happened to be in Campbell County when Lydia and Cal got married." He turned a shaky smile on Lydia. "Had to be there for my baby sister's wedding, didn't I?"

Celeste led Gideon to the group. "It's good to see you again, Troy, and to meet you, Mr. McNeil." She dipped her head to Ellis. "I hope you'll excuse Lieutenant Hart and me. We need to run an errand for his grandmother."

Gideon's eyes widened, but he agreed. "Oh, yes, I'd forgotten."

As they slipped away, Hattie left to check on Mrs. Coker, who was confined to bed since she'd taken a fall on the stairs a few weeks earlier.

Millie and Troy took the settee, feeding Amy bites of a scone between them. Taking a nearby chair, Lydia passed out cups of tea. Ellis sat across from them.

With a deep breath, Millie pressed her shoulders back and faced Ellis. "We all know the truth."

He peered over his teacup with contrived innocence. "What truth is that?"

Oh, he's a charmer. No wonder Mother fell for him.

She drew a deep breath. "That you and my mother had an affair while she was in Alabama. That you're my true father." She couldn't help the hard edge to her voice. Why had he never tried to see her before?

He peered into his cup. "How long have you known?"

Millie swallowed. "I found Mother's letter a few months ago, hidden in the baby clothes she left me. Troy found out tonight."

"I figured he didn't know when he found me at the camp,"

Ellis said. "At first, I didn't care to have much to do with him. Then I learned he knew what'd happened to you and Lydia."

"You did have a pile of questions about them." Troy directed his smile at the women. "I just thought he was homesick for any word of relatives."

Ellis set down his cup. "I had to work in a few questions about Henry and John's other boys so you wouldn't guess I was mainly interested in Millie. When you told me y'all was married and had a baby, I nearly confessed it all."

He gazed at Amy with a sheen of moisture over his eyes. "I missed so much."

Lydia broke off a piece of her scone and handed it to the baby. "When did you learn about Millie?"

"When I got Polly's letter, a few months before you married Cal. I was shocked. It wasn't like we'd had a lot of time alone together that winter. Her Aunt Myrtle was a sharp old bird and kept an eye on her. But I guess she figured Polly needed some time to come to terms with her marriage. We'd meet when Myrtle went to her quiltin' bee at church."

Millie and Troy exchanged glances. Sadness colored his voice, arousing her empathy. She didn't want to feel anything for this man, but she understood how giving in to a moment of desire could lead to consequences. Her mother's circumstances hadn't been so different from her own.

Ellis looked at his hands. "I loved her, you know. I had a fit when I heard she'd returned to that sorry so and so. If I'd known she was carryin' you, Millie, I would've come after her. By the time I knew, though, Polly had died, and I had my own family to consider."

He turned to Lydia. "I did worry about you and tried to get Granny to persuade you not to marry Cal. But she wanted you to have the security of a husband and your own family. Goin' to the wedding gave me a good excuse to visit and see Millie for myself. I knew Lydia would take care of you, Millie. I prayed Cal would treat you both better than he had Polly."

Amy's fussiness interrupted the adults' conversation. Millie glanced at the clock on the mantle. "It's dinnertime for this little one." And she needed some time to figure out how she felt about this new relationship.

Troy stood and reached for the baby. "I'll take her to your room."

~

*T*roy nuzzled Amy's neck as he carried her upstairs. He loved to hear her giggles. After Ellis's story, he didn't want to miss any more of his daughter's life. Near the threshold of Millie's room sat an odd wooden contraption. Troy motioned toward it. "What's that?"

Millie turned back to see what caught his attention. "Seth called it a baby barrier. He said it's to keep her safe when she starts crawling around. After Aunt Lottie fell, we realized Amy could tumble down the stairs too."

Millie put Amy on the bed and changed her diaper. When she moved to the rocking chair and started adjusting her bodice, Troy turned away. "Do you want me to leave?"

"Not unless you want to. It won't take her long to fall asleep."

He strode to the window that overlooked the street and spoke without turning. "I thought you might want to talk. And we can discuss my orders and make plans for moving."

A soft sigh. "I'd like that. Please go ahead."

The creaking of the rocking chair provided a rhythmic background. On the street below, two dogs chased each other, and a boy slung a long-handled blade across the neighbor's lawn.

Troy contemplated how to start. "General Richardson suggested those of us from the South should be reassigned somewhere near our homes. He thinks people will cooperate better with folks they know." He slid his hands inside his pants pockets and fingered the few coins there. "Others on the committee didn't agree, but they consented to it on a trial basis."

Millie hummed softly. Why didn't she comment? He glanced back, but her chair sat at an angle, and her gaze focused on the babe in her arms.

He prodded for a response. "How do you feel about that?"

"Does that mean you'll be going back to Alabama?"

"Better than that." He grinned and forced a note of enthusiasm into his voice. "It means *we'll* be going where I can cover the farms along the central Georgia-Alabama border."

"I see."

He still couldn't figure out her feelings about it. She seemed so settled here. Would she be reluctant to leave all the friends and comforts she now enjoyed? He couldn't say what they'd find closer to home.

A pause. Then she asked another question. "Just what will you be doing there?"

He turned back to the window and laughed. "A little bit of everything, it sounds like. Visiting farms to see what they need, routing materials and laborers their way, helping the local officials keep the peace. At least I won't be fighting like the units in Texas."

He tried to ignore the whisper of rustling fabric, but he could trace her quiet steps to Amy's bed. "You can turn around now."

Troy pivoted, his eyebrows shooting up when Millie stood inches away from him. She grinned up at him. *The minx.*

She pecked his chin as his arms circled behind her. "Lydia will be sad to see us go. How soon will we leave?"

"By the end of the month. That gives us over a week to

gather what we'll need for the trip." He pulled her closer and pressed his lips to her ear. "What do you think, Mrs. McNeil?"

"I guess we'll do all right, then." She slid her hands to his chest and eased him away. "We need to go back downstairs and break the news to Lydia."

She danced out of his grasp, leaving him no choice but to follow.

~

*F*rom the expression on Lydia's face, Millie guessed she'd already heard the news from Ellis. Her father. It was going to take a while to get used to thinking of this stranger in such a familiar way.

Ellis rose. "I didn't mean to spill the beans, Troy. It just slipped out when we started talking about how I'd get home."

Celeste had returned from her errand and sat beside Lydia on the sofa, their hands clasped together.

Troy pulled Millie close with one arm. "Now don't turn on the tears, Aunt Lydia. You know I can't leave Millie and Amy here. I promise I'll take good care of 'em. Besides, we won't be far from other family. We're like to have all kinds of company visit by the end of summer."

Millie's emotions swirled in response to the other women's upset. After all the events of the past year, it was like ripping a bandage off an open wound each time someone in their group left. She patted Troy's hand and left his embrace to wiggle onto the sofa beside Lydia. Before she could speak her reassurance, a noise at the front door drew their attention.

Herbert ushered Seth and Gideon inside. Seth took one look at the women, and his expression shifted to a frown. "Hey, what's wrong?" He took a chair near the settee and leaned toward Lydia. "Is someone hurt or sick?"

Millie gave a shaky laugh. "Nothing so serious. Amy and I

will be going back to Alabama with Troy in a couple of weeks." She wanted to chuckle when Seth's countenance dropped. He'd also grown attached to the baby.

"At least you'll be here for the wedding, right?" Celeste glanced from Millie to Troy, who stared back.

"When is it?" he asked.

"Next Friday."

"Yeah, we'll be here for that." He glanced around when nobody said any more. "Uh, I guess I oughta ask. Who's gettin' married?"

Millie chuckled. He hadn't been around to witness the growing romances. It might surprise him that Seth had persuaded Lydia to marry so soon after Cal's death. But she'd thought herself a widow for over a year. Millie prayed her step-mother would be happier with Seth.

~

May 29, 1865

*D*ancers swirled around the bare parlor floor, keeping time to the lovely waltz coming from the piano. Millie waited for Lydia and Seth to pass by, then darted across the floor before Gideon swept by with Celeste. The friends had decided a double wedding deserved a grand celebration.

Millie carried a slice of cake to the corner where Mrs. Coker sat, ensconced on her makeshift throne. Playfully executing a proper curtsey, Millie set the plate on the nearby table. "Here you are, your majesty."

To be sure Mrs. Coker could watch the proceedings, the men had built a platform large enough for her chair, a stool, and a table to hold her refreshments. The doctor allowed her to leave her bed for short periods now. She'd declared herself

Queen Charlotte when they placed her there, and all her "attendants" had played along.

The elderly lady beamed from her position. "Thank you, dear. I declare, this house has seen more weddings in the last six months than in the previous forty years. And dancing! Why, I reckon it's been nearly twenty years since we rolled up the carpets and had the piano tuned."

Millie laughed along with her, delighted to see their benefactress enjoying the celebrations. "I'm glad you can be downstairs to enjoy it with us. We've missed you."

Moisture filmed over Mrs. Coker's brown eyes. "Not as much as I shall miss you and Amy when you leave." She swiped a gnarled finger under one eye. "But perhaps there'll be other babies in the near future to ease that pain."

Millie followed her gaze to the couples swaying to the soft music. Lydia and Seth, Celeste and Gideon, Lucas and Emily. Even Olivia and Doctor Evan Spencer had traveled from Frankfort to attend the wedding. Rose and Major Griffin had postponed their move to Indiana to be there. Would Mrs. Coker's prediction come true? She counted six possibilities. "I daresay you may be right, Aunt Lottie." She prayed that Lydia and Seth might have that joy.

As the music swelled, her attention drifted to the piano. How remarkable that Seth's former brother-in-law, Will Larsen, had found him in Louisville last month. He could coax such sweet sounds from the instrument. Troy spun Amy in a circle to elicit a squeal of happiness, making his way to Millie.

Mrs. Coker held out her hand. "Here, young man, let me hold that baby so you can whirl your wife around."

Troy grinned and made the switch. "Yes, ma'am. That's one order I'm happy to obey."

Millie wavered. "I've not danced much. I'm rather clumsy, you know."

"Consider this your first lesson. All you must do is follow me."

"Oh, and you have a good deal of experience dancing, I suppose." She teased, but it occurred to her she didn't know this grown-up Troy so well.

He responded in kind. "Enough to get around."

Troy inclined his head toward Ellis as they swept by him. "He looks lonely. You should at least try to talk to him."

She bristled. "I hardly know what to say. He's a stranger to me."

"You could ask him about your mother. You were young when she died. Surely, you must wonder about her."

Troy knew how to prod her. She didn't like it, but he was right. It might be a long trip back to the Georgia-Alabama line.

CHAPTER 21

*W*ith directions to a house where they could rent rooms, Troy led Millie and Ellis through Rome, Georgia. He'd been here once during his years of rambling, and he remembered it as a pretty town set among rolling green hills. War and lack of care had reduced it to a sad state.

"When you were here before," Ellis asked, "did you make the acquaintance of many people?"

Troy clutched a carpetbag in each hand and wore a knapsack on each shoulder. He scratched his cheek with his only available finger and shook his head. "I kept to the outskirts, didn't want to arouse suspicions since I didn't wear Roswell Gray."

Beside him, Millie carried a slumbering Amy. Keeping the child confined to their small area on the train had worn her down. Troy and Ellis had tried to assist, but Amy always clambered back to her mother. Millie's eyes met his, and her lips curved upward, but her shoulders slumped. The Georgia heat did little to encourage her dragging steps.

The street sign was tilted, but he read the name with relief. "Ah, there's the house. And look, there are rocking chairs on the porch." He led the way up the red brick steps and dropped the bags from his hands. "Why don't you sit here while I check with the owner about our rooms?"

He plied the knocker as Millie sank into one rocker and Ellis took the other. In moments, the door opened to reveal a rail-thin woman in a faded green gown, standing beside a stout man in Union blue. The man was balanced between two crutches, and one leg of his trousers hung loose, its end pinned up to prevent dragging.

Troy snapped to attention and saluted. "General."

The woman shrank beside the balding general, who released his grip on one crutch long enough to return Troy's gesture. Even with the injury, the man's presence commanded respect. His eyes appeared to sink into his head beneath bushy brows on either side of a prominent nose. A generous goatee spread from his chin. "What's your name, soldier?"

"Corporal Troy McNeil, sir."

"Where are you bound, Corporal?"

"Randolph County, Alabama, sir. I'm assigned to work with the Bureau of Refugees, Freedmen, and Abandoned Lands in the rural areas between Wedowee, Alabama, and Campbelltown, Georgia."

"A local boy, eh? Well, glad to meet you. Wager Swayne." He motioned to the woman beside him. "My wife, Ellen. I'll be working out of Montgomery, so I imagine we'll have opportunity to meet again later."

Mrs. Swayne nodded to Troy and prodded her husband aside. "We should let the young man go inside and claim his room." To Troy, she said, "We were just going for a stroll."

"Yes, ma'am. I wish you a pleasant outing." He exchanged

places with them, noting the man's progress down the steps while his wife stayed close but allowed him to navigate without help. Not that she could catch him if he fell.

He found the clerk at a tall desk set at the end of a short hallway. "I'm Corporal McNeil. I sent a telegram requesting two rooms."

"Of course, Corporal. I have number five and number eight for you. Both are upstairs." He handed Troy the keys and rattled off information about the facilities and meals offered.

"Thank you. I'll get my wife and uncle now."

Troy met Millie on her way inside. "I need to change Amy's nappy, and she'll want to eat soon." She shifted the baby and leaned against the door jamb. "Did you meet the couple who just left?"

He motioned to Ellis as he hefted the bags and led the way to find their rooms. "Yeah, I think that's my new commander and his wife. Although he'll be in Montgomery, his rank is too high to be subordinate to someone else. I was surprised to meet him here. Thought it'd be Major Newton, not the general."

"Maybe he's taking his journey slow to rest his body." In the upstairs hallway, she leaned against the wall while Troy fit the key in the lock and Ellis continued down the hall to his room. "It must be hard to be missing a limb like that."

The door swung open, and Troy gestured her inside. "I'm sure it takes some getting used to. Too many men suffer similar losses. Everyone's had to adjust to changes in the last few years, and it ain't over yet, least not for folks in the South."

Millie laid Amy on the bed, tugging to remove the soiled items while she hummed to keep the child from waking. When she finished and straightened at the edge of the bed, Troy captured her in his arms, his fatigue forgotten. "So...while she's asleep..."

A knock at the door interrupted him. Troy groaned but

answered the summons. Ellis stood there, his hand extended. "Uh, you got a key to my room?"

Troy pulled the second key from his pocket. "Here you go. I imagine you'll want to take a nap before the evening meal is ready. We'll see you in the dining room then."

Ellis smirked. "Yeah, see you then."

~

"*J*understand they plan to build a grand hotel a few blocks over." Millie shared the information with Troy and Ellis the next morning while they enjoyed a proper breakfast, complete with grits and gravy. The cook helped them secure Amy to a chair by draping an apron over her dress and knotting its strings in the chair back's spokes. The upside-down pot the child sat upon elevated her to the height of the table. Her joyful babbling ceased temporarily as Millie spooned food into her mouth.

Troy looked up from his meal. "Where'd you hear that?"

"From the general's wife. She sits in on all her husband's meetings so she can keep him from over-taxing his body."

"When did you speak with Mrs. Swayne?" Troy picked up his coffee cup. "I thought they were leaving today."

Millie handed Amy half a biscuit, which she immediately crumbled. "Their train leaves this afternoon. She was in the kitchen when I came to get milk for the cat that adopted us. Mrs. Swayne had questions about living in the area, which I answered as best as I could."

Troy pushed back from the table. "Last night, I realized I should've asked the general if I could take a day or two to check on Lydia's house." He paused when Millie speared him with a pointed look. "Excuse me, *our* house—before we continue to Alabama. If they're still here, I can ask him now."

Millie put out a hand to stop him. "You should sit in the

parlor and read the newspaper. I expect the general will be there shortly, and you can speak to him then, when he's at his leisure."

"But I also need to find a wagon so we can get on our way. That could take a while."

Millie lowered her voice. "Why don't you let Ellis take care of that? He might get a better price than you would in that uniform."

Troy raised his eyebrows at her suggestion. "I get the feeling, Millie McNeil, you are going to be a valuable asset to my government work in the future." He leaned over Amy to touch his wife's hand. "I've always known you were a rare gem."

His praise flooded Millie with warmth. She dropped her gaze as he moved to Ellis's side to discuss what they needed for the rest of the journey. When he started toward the door, Millie cleared her throat.

"Excuse me, Corporal McNeil. Would you care to accompany your daughter and me to the parlor?" Troy was so eager to do a good job. Lydia had advised Millie to be alert for ways to help him and not let him stretch himself too thin. It pleased her to find small ways to do so.

With Troy recruiting Ellis's help, they accomplished two primary goals for the day—getting the general's permission to go first to the house in Campbell County and securing a horse and wagon to transport them there. Troy took the wagon first to the depot to pick up the goods for distribution in his assigned area. While the men loaded their baggage and arranged a place for Millie and Amy to ride in the wagon bed, she worked with the cook to prepare food to carry with them.

By early afternoon, they were on the road. Troy pointed out places he recognized from his travels during the war. What he didn't mention was plain for all to see. Destruction everywhere. The men who represented the government through the Bureau

for Refugees, Freedmen, and Abandoned Lands faced a
daunting responsibility.

~

JUNE 6, 1865
CAMPBELL COUNTY

"*W*ell, Lydia's house is still standing." Troy pulled
the horse to a stop. "I don't see any sign of
squatters, but I think it's best for me to go in alone to be sure."

Millie nodded her agreement, bouncing the baby on her
knee while Ellis surveyed the farm from the wagon seat.

He set the brake and jumped over the wheel. One rocker
rested on its side, and the other lay tipped over with its
runners facing upward. Leaves and twigs littered the porch.
Troy strode to the door and jiggled the knob. It turned easily,
so he pushed his way inside. From the layer of dust on the
furniture, he'd guess it hadn't been touched since last July,
when he'd found it deserted. He walked all through the house
and even pushed aside the armoire to peer into the secret
room. If anyone had taken shelter here, they must have moved
on when they didn't find any food. Millie would be a better
judge of that, but he was pleased to find it in such good
condition.

Troy stepped onto the porch. "You can come on in." He
continued to the wagon and motioned for Millie to pass Amy
over the side. "It's a mite dusty, so you might want to find the
broom before we let this one crawl around."

Millie hurried past him, the tabby cat they'd christened
Sunflower at her feet.

Ellis helped Troy move their baggage to the porch, then
they righted the rocking chairs and sat. Millie called out her
progress. "Found the broom. The pantry needs a scrubbing, but

it can wait. It's a good thing Sunflower came with us. It looks like some rodent tore the flour sack to pieces."

After a few minutes, she came to the door. "You can bring her in now. I'll set her in the wash tub while I clean the kitchen. You two might take the horse to the old barn and see what kind of condition it's in."

Ellis rose. "That's something I can do, Troy. You stay and help Millie."

By the time they'd eaten and prepared the bedrooms, the sun hovered near the horizon. Ellis had gone to bed, leaving Millie and Troy to the rockers. A light breeze brought a faint scent of pine and magnolia. The quiet should have wrapped him in peace, but Troy's thoughts kept circling back to that fateful day last winter. Time and distance had dulled the memory, but being here again brought it all back.

He reached for Millie's hand, trying to gauge her emotions. "Is it hard for you to be here again?"

Millie gazed at him. "I lived here for six months after the attack, remember? Are you having trouble being here?"

He threaded her fingers with his. "I've been thinking I ought to go find where I dumped the body. See if there's anything left that could identify the man."

Millie dropped his hand and turned her face away. "Why? If Mrs. Tucker reported the man roamin' in the woods, somebody would've found and moved the body by now."

"Did you ever hear anything to that effect?"

"No." Millie shuddered. "Do you think it would still be there?"

"If nobody investigated the report, it could be. When Cal showed up at the prison in Louisville, it made me think. What if somebody's waiting to hear about that man? We know he's dead, but maybe nobody else does. Shouldn't we at least try to find out?"

Millie shook her head. "I don't know, Troy. I don't think it's a good idea, but I won't try to stop you." She stood and shifted Amy in her arms. "Is it gonna bother you to sleep in that room?"

He rose and pulled the strand of Millie's hair from the baby's fist before he cupped her cheek. "No more than the past few nights of sleeping with you in a room next to your pa and my uncle." His attempt to shrug away her concern failed.

Both his hands on her shoulders made her look at him. "I'll deal with it. Besides, I reckon we created something precious there." He kissed the baby's blond curls and guided Millie through the door.

~

For all Troy's sweet talk and casual attitude about sleeping in her old bedroom, Millie had her doubts. It had taken her weeks after the attack to quell her panic. She'd often woken from a disturbing dream and lain awake, recalling every moment of that day. So, it didn't surprise her to find Troy sitting on the side of the bed near daybreak. He stared at the fireplace.

Millie scooted over to slide her hand along his back. "You won't rest until you find out, will you?"

He raked his hand through his hair. "I think it's part of the reason God brought us back here. Not just to claim the farm to keep it in the McNeil family or to try to keep peace and help my neighbors." He turned sideways to put an arm around her. "Millie, I have to try."

"I know." She wished she could lighten his burden. Why hadn't she realized before how the incident had affected him? "Do you want someone to go with you, or do you need to go alone?"

"I need to see if I can find anything first. I'll come back and get Ellis to help if necessary."

She kissed him. "All right. I'll get up and put on some coffee. You stay here with Amy while I do that. She'll probably wake up soon."

Millie slipped on the dress she'd discarded the night before and headed into the kitchen. She fed wood into the stove and pumped water into a pot. While she waited for those to heat, she pushed aside the curtain at the window to catch the sunrise. "Lord, please go with Troy and help him find something to settle his soul. You know what happened that day, how it weighs on his mind. Please give him peace about it."

She opened the kitchen door to let Sunflower out. A red bird flew into her field of vision and landed on the clothesline post nearest the house. That reminded Millie she needed to do laundry, since most of their clothes were dirty. Maybe Ellis would help her haul out the mattresses to sun them while the dry spell lingered. No telling when a summer storm might pop up.

Turning back to the stove, she prepared coffee and stirred some grits into the remaining hot water. Sounds from the bedroom told her Amy was awake, so she rummaged in their packs for the jars of jelly and the remaining biscuits she'd brought from Rome. Soon they'd need to check the town and farms in the area to see where they could buy perishable food. Their money would be useless if nothing was available.

Troy carried Amy into the kitchen and set her in the chair as they'd done before. Millie brought him a cup of coffee and gave Amy a broken biscuit. "You want something to eat before you go out?"

"Nah, I'll wait." He sipped his coffee and stared out the open back door for a minute. "What do you plan to do today?"

Millie sat beside Amy and spooned a bit of jelly on a biscuit. "I need to wash clothes and clean out the pantry. We should walk over the hill and see if anything's left in town. We need eggs and vegetables."

"Why don't you wait till I get back from my errand? I should return before you finish hanging the clothes."

"All right."

Troy rose, kissed the top of Amy's head, then slipped over to Millie and cupped her face. "I'll be back soon."

"I'm praying for you."

He nodded and left the house.

CHAPTER 22

*T*roy forced himself to cross the yard while he recalled his actions on that eventful day. As much as he and Millie—and the whole world—had changed since then, aside from the overgrown vegetation, the property looked much the same. He searched for the largest oak tree where he'd set a trap more than once in the past. A few yards farther, he found the quadrant of pines where he'd discovered evidence of the vagrant's camp last year.

He counted off twenty strides, as he had back then. Too bad he didn't have the wheelbarrow and a load to better match the distance. He should have checked the shed for a hoe or shovel before he set off this morning. He might have to do some digging.

A half hour later, he'd walked twice as far as he remembered going the previous year. He marked off an area bigger than the house and used a stout limb to sweep away the layers of leaves and vines, ever mindful of snakes. All he'd uncovered so far was a couple of dry bones from a small animal.

Frustrated, he threw down the limb and raised his face to gaze heavenward. "I could use some help here, Lord. You know

I want to make this right if I can. Please show me what to do, where to look, or even what I should be huntin' for."

No answer came. Troy strained to listen, hoping for a small voice like one of the Old Testament prophets had heard. Still nothing but the distant boring of a woodpecker. He kicked at the base of a bush, then jumped back when a large lizard sprang from its depths and scurried up a nearby tree. Troy monitored the reptile's journey until the creature disappeared behind a leaf-covered limb. Along its path, vines quivered, and a strange object swung away from the trunk, over Troy's head.

Troy peered up at the round item, darker than the leaves around it, more solid than a bird's nest. His heartbeat increased. Was it a canteen? It was too high to grab. Looking about, he found a longer stick. Maybe he could knock it down. The stick made the object spin, revealing an attached strap. Troy changed his angle to hook the strap and slide it over the limb. After a few tries, the object dropped to the forest floor, and Troy nearly cried with relief.

He picked it up to confirm his find. A Confederate-issued canteen. "Thank You, God." The condition indicated it had been there for quite some time, so finding it seemed providential. Under its thick layer of lichen and dirt, would he find any mark to identify its owner?

He rushed to the house to share his discovery with Millie. As he approached, she pinned a dark skirt on the line and picked up the empty basket. Troy dunked the canteen in the tub of dirty water near the back porch. What did she use to scrub the stains on clothes?

"Hey, you found something." She leaned over his shoulder. "What is it?"

"A canteen. Pretty sure it's Confederate because of the way it's made. Where's Ellis? He might know more about it."

"He's on the front porch with Amy. She's finally warmed up to him and doesn't have to keep me in sight."

"Do you have something I could scrub this with?" He lifted the canteen to show her its condition. "The grime is packed in all these grooves."

"The small brush Lydia used to clean the frying pan might still be here." She headed for the kitchen. "I'll see if I can find it."

Troy dragged the tub closer to a stump at the edge of the porch and sat. He'd succeeded in removing the canteen's cap when Ellis came out the back door. "Millie said to give you this and to tell you not to scratch it by scrubbing too hard." He handed Troy a well-worn brush like the kind the army used to groom horses.

"Where'd she get to?" Troy dipped the brush in the water and started sweeping it across the canteen.

"She's gettin' the baby to sleep." Ellis gestured to the item in Troy's hands. "Where'd you find that?"

Troy lifted it higher to give Ellis a better view. "In the woods this morning. You know who might've carried one like this?"

"Yeah, some companies from Alabama had that kind in their gear." He pulled up a stalk of sour grass and chewed on it. "Wonder how it ended up in your woods?"

Troy gritted his teeth. "When I came through last year, I found signs of somebody campin' there. I wanted to investigate the area today and clear it out before we settle in."

"So you're plannin' to stay here. You could work from your folks' house or mine." Ellis walked to the porch and leaned against a post.

"I'd rather keep peace in the family, and that means not bein' around Paul too much." Troy dunked the brush in the water and resumed cleaning the canteen. "For the time being, we'll probably alternate between here and Henry's. That way, I can keep Millie and Amy close by while I make my rounds. Once I finish my time with the army, we'll decide which area suits us best. I want to keep this farm in the family, but I need to be sure we're not too isolated."

"I hope I'll be able to visit from time to time, wherever y'all end up."

Troy avoided issuing an open invitation by pointing to the bottom of the canteen. "Look here. Does it look to you like somebody scratched something there?" He stood and moved closer to Ellis, extending the container his way.

Ellis took the dripping metal and examined it. "Appears to be numbers to me. Maybe the company that made it stamped it?"

"Yeah, I guess you're right." Troy's shoulders slumped. He'd hoped for more.

Soft footsteps announced Millie's return. "You find out anything?"

"Just a number on the bottom. I doubt it'll help much."

"Let me see." She took the canteen and examined it, then slid her fingers over the strap. "What's this? Is that a *P* or an *R*?"

Both men peered at the section she pointed out. "Hmm. I never thought to check the strap. Looks like *RWG*. Somebody's initials?" Troy broke into a grin. "That ought to be enough to identify the owner or at least narrow it down. I'll write a letter to General Swayne and see if he can tell me who to contact."

He turned to acknowledge Millie's help, but she'd turned pale. "Millie? You feelin' poorly?" He guided her to the stump where he'd sat to clean the canteen. He pushed her head down to her lap and squatted beside her.

Ellis's brow wrinkled above anxious eyes. "Can I get you anything? A glass of water maybe?"

Millie raised her head. "Pa—Cal—had an older brother. His name was Raymond, but they called him 'RW.' I never met him, but Pa mentioned him often. He left home when Pa was fifteen, I think. They never heard from him but one time." She gripped Troy's hand. "I think he may have been the man we killed."

~

"*W*hat's this?" Ellis's shout caused Millie to jump. "You killed a man? How could you know it was Cal's brother if you've never seen him?"

She looked from Ellis to Troy. "We might as well tell him." Millie levered herself from the stump. "Let's go inside so we can hear Amy if she wakes up."

She told Ellis what happened, beginning with the day Troy showed up—and they admitted their feelings for each other—and ending with the stranger's attack. "We didn't mean for him to die. He hit his head on the hearth."

Ellis glanced from one to the other, but Millie didn't plan to say any more. Perhaps he figured out what had happened next. "What did you do with the body?"

Troy cleared his throat. "I took it to the woods and dumped it."

"I see." Ellis drummed his fingers on the table. "And today is the first time you tried to find out who he was?"

"It's the first opportunity I had, what with a broken leg that kept me away and then getting caught and carried north by the Federals."

"When Camp Chase closed, I'd planned to ask for an assignment out west." Troy lifted his hands. "But now I believe God fixed it so I could come back here. The closer we got, the more I felt as though I had to try to make things right. I didn't have any idea what I might find when I searched the woods. I must've walked by that canteen a dozen times without seeing it, hanging on a high tree limb."

"And now maybe we can find out who he was," Millie said. "Whether it was Cal's brother or not."

CHAPTER 23

July 5, 1865
RANDOLPH COUNTY, ALABAMA

*M*illie paced the parlor floor with a sleepy Amy, thankful to evade the afternoon's heat and the men's discussion on the porch. The baby's whimper pulled at her heart. "Poor darlin'. Cutting teeth is a miserable business, ain't it?"

About as miserable as the first few weeks of pregnancy. Millie forced back the nausea that threatened and concentrated on the voices on the other side of the wall. If she stepped closer to the window, she could see Ellis and Henry leaning against the porch railing.

After Troy made his initial visits to the homes on the Georgia side of his assigned area, they'd headed to Henry's, which would serve as home base for the Alabama side. Ellis would proceed to his house when Troy made his first trip to surrounding farms. As he met the families there, Troy would seek information about the canteen they'd found. Since it looked to be from an Alabama company, he might get some leads on the owner.

Millie leaned on the window frame as the men's discussion continued.

"You asked for my opinion, and I gave it. I think a family reunion is a bad idea." Henry spat a stream of tobacco juice into the yard as if to punctuate his objection to the proposal. "Unless you want to start the war all over again. Too many mule-headed McNeils who aren't afraid to spout their opinions and not listen to anyone else."

"Now, Henry, we ain't all that bad. Why, look at Troy and me." Ellis gestured in Troy's direction. "We've been gettin' along fine for more than two months, even seein' each other every day and livin' in close quarters."

"You two got more at stake, more reason to set aside your own ideas and get along." Henry tilted his head. "Namely, those two females inside the house."

"But that's part of the reason for the reunion, Henry. To introduce Millie as Troy's wife and explain why he's here with the army."

Amy sighed, the signal she'd fallen asleep. Millie meandered closer to the door to hear if Troy had anything to add to the debate. He'd been conspicuously quiet.

Henry lowered his voice. "I know this had to be your idea, Ellis, but you pushed it off on Troy to bring it up. And you're all set to let everybody know Millie's your daughter, ain't ya? Well, you need to think how that's gonna affect your other young'uns, not to mention Millie."

"I ain't out to embarrass anyone, Henry. I can tell my boys and Sadie in private." Ellis glanced toward the door. "I've come to realize family is the most important part of our lives. The war changed us all somehow, and I want us to get to know each other again. Let bygones be bygones."

Millie abandoned her eavesdropping. She liked Henry. He'd

seemed glad to have them there, but he wouldn't let Ellis charm him into an action he didn't approve. She carried the baby into the bedroom and laid her in the trundle bed. After pulling back the curtain to allow any drifting breeze inside the room, she tiptoed into the hallway.

Troy met her at the threshold of the parlor. "She finally gave up the fight?"

"Yeah. Soaking the cloth in chamomile tea was a good idea. I don't know if it helped with the pain or put her to sleep, but it worked." Millie hadn't known what to do, but both Henry and Ellis remembered their wives using such. It was a far better choice than rubbing whiskey on the baby's gums as she'd heard some parents did. She peeked around the doorframe and found the room empty as well as the porch. "Where'd they go?"

Troy took her hand and led her to the worn sofa. "They went to check Blackie's hoof. I may have suggested she seemed to be favorin' her left front leg. I expect they'll spend twenty minutes debating whether she needs a compress on it."

Millie swatted his hand but couldn't hold back her grin. "You're a rascal, Troy McNeil." She slipped off her shoes and tucked her feet under her skirt.

Troy settled his arm across her shoulders and urged her closer. "I had to get you alone for a while. How are you feeling?"

"I'm fine." *Tired. Queasy. Wish Lydia was here to help.* But she didn't want to concentrate on her feelings. She wanted to know about the discussion she'd overheard. "Why is Ellis so determined to get all the family together? We'll surely meet everyone as we visit around the territory for your assignment."

He turned her face to his. "Because *you* are going to stay here the next few weeks while I make those rounds."

Millie reared back in surprise. "But I thought we decided people might be more agreeable if I went with you."

"That was before you got sick." He placed a finger on her lips when she opened her mouth to argue. "Hey, we've already contacted several families on our journey from Campbell County. I can reach the rest of the area by going a couple of days at a time and coming back here between trips."

He held up her left hand and used his finger to demonstrate. "See, Henry's farm is here." He touched the center of her palm and drew an imaginary line to the base of her hand and across to the thumb. "This is the southern section of the county. This is the western region." He touched the index finger, then moved to the two middle fingers. "And here's the northern section. We've already covered the eastern part."

Millie shivered as he lifted her hand to his lips. "With you here in the center," he said, "I can come back to check on you and Amy, pick up more supplies in Wedowee, and then move on to another area."

"I see you have it all figured out, but I still don't like you going alone."

"Ellis will go with me when I head toward his farm. If possible, I'll get Tom, his oldest, to ride with me some. Someone else might help later."

Millie pondered his plans. Finding no way to argue, she posed another question. "Do you still intend to set up an office in a couple of the towns?"

Troy nodded. "Just as soon as I get more information and materials from Washington. There should be another soldier or a lawyer comin' to help man the offices too. As people learn about the bureau, we'll provide different services. There was talk of using the offices to start schools for the freed slaves or others who want to learn to read and write and cipher."

Millie leaned her head on his shoulder. "Until we went to Marietta, I never realized how blessed I was to get a few years of schoolin'. None of the Roswell women could read except Miss Rose and Celeste, and they'd only worked there a year. Their pa was a preacher, and they'd gone to schools in the other towns where they lived."

The crunch of wagon wheels on the hard-packed drive into the yard drew their attention. Troy patted Millie's hand as he eased away. "You sit still." He stood and stretched, then ambled closer to the window. Whatever he saw elicited a groan.

Millie straightened and found her shoes. "Who is it, Troy? More relatives?"

"That would be bad enough, wouldn't it?" He reached out a hand to help her rise. "No, it's our friend, Becky Varner and her family. The whole, noisy crew."

~

*T*roy plastered on his friendly face. As he reached the front door, Henry and Ellis emerged from the barn in time to intercept the neighbors and delay their entrance to the house. Feminine voices squealed as the women welcomed Ellis with exuberance.

"Ellis McNeil. As I live and breathe, it *is* you." Mrs. Varner moved in for a hug.

Becky scooted to his other side. "Why, Mr. Ellis, I declare you haven't aged a bit since I last saw you."

Millie turned her face into Troy's chest to suppress her laughter, but her giggles ignited his own humor. He summoned his strength to set her away and admonished her to behave. "You are going to get me in trouble with our neighbors, minx. Now let's act like adults and welcome them inside."

Millie pressed her lips together and nodded, then ruined the effect with a snort. "I'd better go check on Amy. All the noise is bound to wake her." She scuttled down the hallway before he could catch her.

"Chicken," he called.

Behind him, Mr. Varner's voice called, "Chicken? Is that what you brought from up north? And here I was hoping you brought some cows for milk and meat."

Troy pivoted and clasped the older man's hand. "Good to see you, sir. No, all they let me bring was staples and canned foods, since we came by wagon. I hope to get some of the other by rail or steamboat in a few weeks."

Troy greeted the others and ushered them into the parlor. He cast a quick glance toward the bedrooms. When would Mille come out? He floundered in the company of women, even those he'd known for years. He needed his wife by his side.

How are you going to survive meeting women on your travels around the county? He stuttered to a stop. Maybe he could delay his departure until Millie was able to travel again.

~

*M*illie hadn't meant to fall asleep and avoid the visiting neighbors. How long was it since they arrived? The low hum of conversation seeped into the hall as she sneaked into the kitchen and nibbled a bit of bread. Perhaps that would keep her stomach quiet long enough to visit with the Varners. If not, she'd find an excuse to slip away.

She peeked into the bedroom and found Amy sitting up. So much for a prolonged rest. "Hey, sweetie. Did you have a good nap?"

A drooly smile preceded her daughter's jabbering. Millie changed Amy's diaper and hoisted her onto her hip. "Come on. Let's go brave the onslaught. Your pa probably needs us."

She crossed into the parlor where the women crowded on the sofa while the men had posted themselves around the perimeter of the room. Henry, Ellis, and Mr. Varner stood by the window, discussing the current drought and need for rain. Near the fireplace, Troy examined a wood carving the Varner boy had brought with him.

Millie started toward Troy, but Mrs. Varner called to her. "There's that sweet baby. Bring her over here, Mrs. McNeil, if you please. I'm longing for the day when my girls give me some grandbabies to love on."

Becky sat at the end closest to the fireplace. She smirked as Millie changed directions. How did such congenial parents produce a schemer like Becky? Despite Mrs. Varner's chattiness, Millie liked the woman and was glad she lived close enough to call on for motherly advice. Too bad Becky was part of that package.

Millie took the chair beside the sofa and passed Amy to the woman's waiting arms. "You'll need this cloth to protect your dress. She's cutting her first tooth and drooling on everything."

"Oh, pish-posh. I've worn my share of slobber before." She directed her attention to the baby as her youngest daughter huddled closer. Something about it reminded Millie of her friends back in Louisville—Lydia, Celeste, Aunt Lottie, Hattie, and Herbert. Millie choked back the tears that threatened with her sudden swelling of melancholy.

Becky leaned toward Troy and whispered something. He raised his eyebrows and handed the carving back to Becky's brother before he strolled to Millie's side. He ran a hand along her arm. "Are you feeling sick? Becky said you look a little pale to her."

"No." Millie pushed down her feelings. "I just had a wave of homesickness, I guess. Do you think we might have any letters from Louisville at the post office?"

He squatted beside her chair. "I'll check when I go to town tomorrow."

Amy squirmed to get to him, calling, "Papa, Papa."

Troy laughed and caught her up in his arms as he stood. "Hey, Punkin. You wanna go over and see Uncle Henry and Grandpa for a while?"

Millie cringed at his blunder, but Troy seemed oblivious. He continued talking to the child as he ambled toward the men.

"Grandpa?" Becky asked. "Who's he talking about?"

Summoning a smile, Millie told the truth—but not the whole truth. "Ellis wanted her to call him that. My pa died from lung fever a couple months ago. Of course, I don't reckon y'all knew Cal Gibson, since he always lived in Campbell County."

Mrs. Varner frowned. "Wasn't he in the prison at Louisville while Mr. Varner was there? Seems I remember Thaddeus mentioning him."

"Yes. After y'all left, the prison moved him to an isolated room in the refugee home to protect the other prisoners. Lydia, my stepmother, tended to him near the end."

"That's right. We met her at the bakery and the farewell dinner for Thaddeus. She was a McNeil, wasn't she?"

"Yes, the youngest after Ellis and John." Millie stood. "And she would be appalled at what a terrible hostess I am. I haven't even offered y'all anything to drink on this warm afternoon. Mrs. Varner, would you ladies care for some tea?"

At their nods, she swept over to the men and nudged Troy. "Let Ellis hold Amy so you can help me carry the teapot and cups from the kitchen."

Widening her eyes to communicate her urgency to Troy, she turned and led him down the hallway. When they reached the kitchen, Millie filled the kettle and set it on the stove. Then she swung toward Troy. "Well, I guess you let the cat out of the bag."

~

Troy stared at his wife. He couldn't resist teasing her. "The cat? Isn't Sunflower in the barn?"

Millie stomped her foot and huffed. "When you took Amy from Mrs. Varner, you said you were taking her to see Uncle Henry and her grandpa."

"And I did. What's—oh." He slapped his forehead. "I called Ellis her grandpa in front of Mrs. Varner. Did she notice?"

Millie gave him that raised-eyebrow look. "I smoothed it over by explaining that Cal had died and Ellis wanted Amy to call him that."

Millie measured the tea leaves and set out cups. She filled four with water and put them on a tray. "Take these out while I finish the tea. And don't linger. I'll need you to bring the tray back."

"I'm sorry, Millie. I didn't mean to put you in such an awkward position."

"I know." She sighed. "But I guess we might as well have that reunion and get everything out in the open. Secrets can be a heavy burden to bear."

On his way to the parlor, Troy debated the best way to convince Uncle Henry to host the reunion. His place was the most centrally located, but he didn't have a wife to take on the responsibility of organizing such an event. Troy gave glasses of water to those who wanted it and hurried back to Millie.

"I think I know why Henry's against the reunion." He set the tray down while Millie gathered the cups and dishes.

"Why is that?"

"He doesn't have a wife to manage the food preparation. Even if his housekeeper had stayed around, it would be too much for her to handle on her own."

Millie bit her lip. "I suppose I could do it, but I hardly know where to start."

Troy shook his head. "Not with a nine-month-old to care for, and especially not if you're expecting again."

"Shush." She swatted his arm. "You're not supposed to know about that, at least not until I know for sure."

He draped an arm across her shoulders and kissed her temple. "I want to share everything about it this time. To make up for missing the first one."

"Good." She loaded the tray and walked toward the hallway.

"I'll wake you up in the morning so you can hold the chamber pot while I throw up."

The immediate queasiness in his own stomach at the mere suggestion made him grimace. He quick-stepped to catch up to her. "How about I just get you a wet cloth for when you've finished?"

She flashed a smile over her shoulder.

All teasing vanished when they stepped into the parlor. Ellis and Mr. Varner hovered over the chair where Henry sprawled.

Becky held Amy and stood apart while Mrs. Varner plied a paper fan over Henry's inert form. The other children—Bobby Ray, Beatrice, and Blanche—huddled on the sofa.

Troy barely registered Millie setting down the tray and taking the whimpering baby from Becky's arms as he rushed to his uncle. "Henry? What's the matter? What can I do?"

Henry lifted a trembling hand to his chest. "Heart." His voice was so weak, Troy had to lean in to hear him.

"I'm going for the doctor." He spun around.

Millie tugged on his arm. "What can I do?"

"Just make him as comfortable as you can." He lowered his voice. "And get rid of all these people."

CHAPTER 24

*M*illie sagged onto the couch, and Troy paced from one end of the room to the other. She'd persuaded their company to leave after Mr. Varner and Ellis helped Henry to bed. Only her promise to keep them informed about his condition convinced them. As wonderful as it was to have neighbors who cared for one another, a crew like the Varners could try a person's patience.

Ellis kept vigil at Henry's bedside until Troy returned with the doctor. Millie fed Amy and put her to bed, then fixed a simple supper for the rest of them, though no one had much appetite. Worry sat heavy on their shoulders.

The doctor emerged from Henry's room, and the three of them gathered around to hear what he had to say. "It could be an acute case of dyspepsia, or it could be dropsy, so I want him to rest and take it easy for a few days. I'll leave some medicine. See if you can get him to take it. And I'd suggest no visitors for a while if it makes him excitable. Not much we can do beyond that."

They all murmured agreement. Millie touched the doctor's hand. "Would you like a bite to eat?"

"No, thank ye, but I'd appreciate a cup of water." His lips twisted into a semblance of a smile. Poor man may not have much reason to practice smiling in his line of business.

"I'll get it."

Surprisingly, the physician followed her to the kitchen. While she pumped water into a cup, he cleared his throat. "Now, Mrs. McNeil, I want you to be careful not to overtax yourself taking care of Henry. With him and the small child you already have, it'd be easy to get run down in your condition."

Millie handed him the cup. "Troy told you about that, did he?"

The doctor chuckled. "He wants to be sure you're taken care of." He gulped his water and set the cup on the table. "I know Troy has plans to travel around the county, but somebody needs to stay here to help you in case Henry has another spell and you need to fetch me again."

He didn't wait for Millie to respond but strode back to the front door and bid them all good night.

Well, this is a fine predicament. Could she convince Troy to wait a couple of days before he left? Maybe Ellis would put off going home.

After she put away the leftover food and tidied the kitchen, she went to discuss the situation.

Ellis and Troy stood on either side of the steps leading off the porch. They ceased talking when Millie joined them. She moved to Troy's side and slipped into his embrace. "I guess any family gathering will have to wait, at least until Henry's condition improves. Will you change your travel plans?"

"We've been discussin' it." Troy shot a disgruntled look at Ellis. "Rather than start on the north side, I'm going to head south to Pa's and see if Rupert will ride with me a couple of days. Ellis will stay here to help with Henry and watch over the farm."

"I reckon a couple days' delay won't hurt," Ellis said. "I'll go check on Henry and see if there's anything in particular he wants me to do tomorrow." He stepped into the house, letting the screen door slam behind him.

When he was out of hearing distance, she peered up at Troy. "Ellis doesn't seem happy. Is he so eager to get home? Is he worried about the children?"

"No, that's not the reason he didn't want to stay. He hasn't taken to the idea of hiring former slaves, and I warned him to watch the way he speaks to the field workers I arranged to start tomorrow. I'll ride out and explain the situation to them before I leave."

"You could hire a housekeeper and cook for Henry. That way, someone will be nearby in case he has another spell like he had today."

Troy shook his head. "He won't like it."

Millie patted his cheek. "If we can feed him well while we're here, maybe it will convince him to hire someone."

"Ah, now I know how you women work. You spoil us so we can't get by without you." He nuzzled her ear and made her shiver.

"Are you complainin' about that, Mr. McNeil?"

"No, ma'am. Not for a minute." He ran his hand down her arm and grasped her fingers. "Let's go see how Henry's doin', and then I'll turn the tables and spoil you with a back rub."

"I like that plan."

JULY 11, 1865

The sun sank toward the horizon as Troy pulled up to his family's farm. Liza, his old nanny, must have spotted the wagon while she was taking sheets off the line. She threw up her hands and hollered. Though he couldn't make out her words, he didn't miss the joy on her golden face. At least someone was glad to see him. Hopefully, Paul would tolerate him for a few hours.

The back door flew open, and his mother joined Liza running to the curve in the drive where Troy slowed the wagon to a stop. He jumped to the ground to welcome their embrace.

Liza thumped his arm. "Mistah Troy, you done growed taller agin."

"Why are you alone, Troy?" Ma sent him a probing stare. "Your last letter promised to bring me a daughter-in-law, did it not?"

He was saved from answering when a young boy skidded around the corner of the house and approached. "Can I see to your horses, mister?"

The women laughed. "This is your Uncle Troy, P.J.," Ma said. "You don't remember him?"

As the boy shook his head, Troy feigned surprise. "This is Paul Junior? It can't be. He's too big." The boy stood taller. "Tell you what," Troy said. "I'll pull the wagon into the barn, and you can rub down the horses."

P.J. took off for the barn, and Troy turned back to the women. "I'll come inside in a few minutes. Ma. Liza, I hope you'll join us." He chuckled at her surprise but didn't wait for an answer.

He maneuvered the wagon inside and to the far corner of the barn. The boy helped him unhook the pair while chattering about the animals he'd seen on the farm. Troy slipped in his question as they led the horses to the water trough. "Who's all up to the house, P.J.?"

The boy rubbed one horse with a worn brush. "Pa and Ma, Lucy, Uncle Rupert, Mawmaw and Pawpaw."

P.J. might be the best person to give him an unfiltered picture of what he was up against. "Jem and Pansy still around?" He'd like to be the one to help his friends get their own place, now that they were free, although it would rile Paul to let them go.

P.J. didn't pause in his brushing. "No. They left a few days ago. Pa cussed and Mawmaw cried."

"Well, if you can finish up here, I'll go on inside and say hello to everyone." Troy reached to ruffle the boy's hair but shifted to grip his shoulder. "See you in a little while."

P.J.'s eagerness to help inspired him. As much as he dreaded facing Pa and his brothers, he needed someone to stay at Henry's so he could cover the county by the end of the month. By that time, he should have a legal assistant and the materials he'd ordered.

He entered the front room and found everyone gathered there. Ma crossed the room to his side and handed him a cup of water. "I figured you'd be thirsty more than hungry, but I've got a plate warming on the stove."

"Thank you, Ma." He gulped the water, then turned to greet the others. "Paul, Jane, that's a mighty fine boy you got there." Troy angled his head toward the barn. "He's a big help. And this pretty girl must be Lucy."

Jane offered him a smile, but his brother merely grunted Troy's name. *Some people still fighting the war, I guess.*

Troy turned to Rupert, the brother closest to him in age, if not in outlook. "Good to see you, Rupert. It's been a while."

Rupert's heavy beard made him seem older than his twenty-two years. He shifted and offered Troy his hand. Troy masked his surprise and gripped it while clearing his throat. He backed away and faced his father.

Pa's strong hand gripped his shoulder. "Good to have you home, son."

The dissension among his sons had troubled Pa and affected all their relationships. Troy found they could manage short periods together, but arguments tended to sprout up over time.

Ma took the cup he still held and pulled him to the chair beside hers. "Now you sit right down here, Troy, and tell me why you've come alone on this trip. Didn't you say you'd married somebody up in Kentucky?"

Troy hoped they'd attribute the warmth in his face to riding in the July heat all afternoon. He wasn't prepared to go into detail about his marriage with an audience. "Yes, Ma. Millie and I got married in February. But Henry had some kind of spell yesterday, so she stayed to take care of him until he's able to be up and about."

The other adults sat forward. For all his gruffness, Henry was a favorite with most of the family. Several voices expressed concern.

"Oh, dear. Did you get the doctor?" Ma asked.

Troy told them about Henry's collapse. "The doctor wasn't real clear on what the problem was, but he said to make him rest for a couple days. Ellis is there, so he'll do the farm chores. He traveled with me from Camp Chase, you know."

"Was that wise?" Rupert asked. "Ellis and Henry don't always get along. I think they enjoy arguing."

"They'll behave themselves with Millie there." Troy crossed one leg over the other and rested his head on the back of the stuffed chair. "I didn't want Millie to run herself down. She's had a little stomach upset, plus she already has Amy to keep up with."

Questioning faces stared back at him.

Ma touched his arm. "Who's Amy?"

He might as well tell the whole story. "Amy's our daughter. You remember when I came home last year, before the Federals pushed so far into Georgia? Well, here's what happened..."

July 17, 1865

*C*urled around her sleeping child, Millie swatted at the mosquito buzzing beside her ear. The summer heat sapped her energy like it never had before. Even those years she'd worked in the mill hadn't been this bad. Of course, then she didn't have a crawling baby to run after.

She eased away from Amy and sat up. By the angle of sunlight spilling across the floor, it was time to start supper. She positioned the chair sideways at the bedroom door and hoped it would keep the baby inside if she wakened. Then she slogged down the hallway to the kitchen.

The sight of a big-boned brown woman brought her to a halt. She'd forgotten about hiring Jewel this morning. When the woman showed up, looking for work, Millie considered her an answer to prayer. The last week had not been easy. Maybe Troy would be better pleased with Millie's boldness than Ellis had been.

"I'm glad you made it back from your friend's house without any trouble. Are you finding everything you need?"

Jewel wiped her hands on a towel as she faced Millie. "Yes'm. I can make do wit' what's here jus' fine."

"And where is your son?" Millie glanced around the room. "I'm sorry, I don't remember his name."

"Levi." The woman's smile lit up her face. "He's right outside the back door. He likes to draw in the dirt."

"He can come in if you like. But it's probably a mite cooler in the shade than in the kitchen. Now, what can I do to help you?"

"Not a thing, ma'am. You rest a while. I'll holler if I'm in need."

Before Millie could respond, a child's shout rang from the backyard. "Wagon comin'."

Ellis yelled from the front porch. "Troy's back, Millie."

Millie scurried down the hall to peek in on Amy, but the

baby slept on despite the noise outside. Amy had missed her pa, but Millie decided not to wake her.

Millie continued past the parlor and joined Ellis on the porch. The trees bordering the road cast the wagon in shadow. Millie shaded the glare from the afternoon sun with a hand cupped over her eyes. "Who's that with him?"

"Looks like Connie and Rupert." Ellis directed his gaze to Millie. "Troy's mama and brother."

Though she was uneasy about meeting his family, her joy at Troy's return propelled her down the steps and into his arms as soon as he left the wagon. He welcomed her with a knee-weakening kiss until someone spoke behind him. "Enough, little brother. You're embarrassing Ma."

Millie ducked her head, but Troy laughed and pulled the offender to his side. "Millie, this is Rupert the Terrible, the youngest of my older brothers."

She peeked around Troy's shoulder to offer a welcome. "Hello, Rupert. Glad to have you."

Ellis called a greeting to Rupert and moved to help Connie descend from the wagon.

Rupert punched Troy on the arm. "I'm impressed that Troy had the good sense to snag a pretty woman." He motioned to the woman who approached them. "And this is our Ma."

Millie tamped down her nervousness and reached out a hand of welcome. "I'm happy to finally meet you, Mrs. McNeil. Lydia mentioned you often."

"Please call me Connie or Ma, whichever suits you." Connie's eyes sparkled. "And Lydia...I haven't seen her in ages. Seems each time John visited, I had to stay home for some reason."

Troy twisted his lips to one side. "You'll have plenty of time to hear all about it." To Millie he said, "Ma insisted on coming to help you with Henry and the house while Rupert and Ellis trade off travelin' with me."

"Speaking of Henry, how is he?" Connie hooked Millie's arm with her own and started toward the house.

"Ornery," Ellis said behind them. "Cantankerous. Y'all go on in and deal with him. I'll tend to the horses."

Troy laughed. "That sounds about right."

"I'd say it's a good sign he's getting better." Connie preceded Millie inside while Troy held the door. "Which room is he in?"

Millie led them to the bedroom but pulled Troy aside. "I have to tell you what I did today." Amy's cry from the other room interrupted her, and Troy reversed directions. Millie clutched his arm. "Troy, I hired a cook."

He stopped and stared at her as if she spoke in a different language. "You hired a cook? I thought I was to bring you one, which is why Ma is here. How will you pay her?"

Millie lifted her hands. "I thought you'd work that out. She seemed desperate."

Amy's cries increased, and Troy pulled away. "We'll talk about it later. After I see my daughter."

What had she done wrong? Wasn't she supposed to help him?

~

*T*roy shook his head, trying to make sense of what Millie said. He was tired after a long day on the road, which included brief side trips to let folks know about his assignment. Responses to his announcement had ranged from relieved cooperation to angry threats. His superiors had warned him this introductory period would be the most difficult. Once people realized his purpose was to ease the way into a new method of doing business, things should settle down.

At the bedroom door, Amy nudged at the chair blocking her way of escape. Her tears of frustration pushed aside his fatigue. "Hey, sweetheart. Did you miss Pa?"

His heart melted when she ceased crying and flashed him a smile. How was it possible to love someone so much? This child's existence had surprised everyone, but she'd enriched his life more than he could have guessed.

He picked her up and bounced her in his arms. "Can you say Pa? Papa?" She giggled as he moved the chair and carried her to the bed.

Millie stepped into the room and set about changing Amy's diaper. "She'll be hungry, as I imagine you are. I went by the kitchen to check on supper. Jewel said it'll be on the table in a few minutes."

"The cook's name is Jewel?"

She removed a pin from her mouth and fastened the cloth's edges. "She fixed supper, and it looks as good as it smells."

Troy tried to retain his anger but felt it slipping away. "Ah, yes, the one we can't pay." He picked up the baby. She giggled and patted his cheeks.

Millie propped her hands on her hips. "Troy, didn't you say part of your work is to arrange contracts between farmers and former slaves? I figured you could start here with Henry and Jewel."

"What does Henry think?" Troy's voice came out harder than he wanted, but he hadn't expected his wife going off and making such decisions while he was gone. *Is that it, or are you really upset that she accomplished something you haven't yet?*

Millie sighed. "I mentioned it to him, but he wasn't up to talking much. Ellis had already worn him out discussing the farm chores."

"And you said the cook is already working? Where's she gonna stay? I doubt she'll want to share quarters with the field hands."

"I got Ellis to help me clear out the storage room off the kitchen for now. It's just her and her son. They can sleep in there until we figure out something more permanent. She only needs room and board she said, but you can talk to her later."

Amy continued patting his face with her chubby hands.

Millie picked up the discarded diaper and tossed it in a bucket.

Troy couldn't think of any other questions to ask. He didn't like being at odds with Millie. Might as well give the cook a try.

She tugged on his arm. "We'd better see if the others are ready to eat. And we'll have to prepare a room for Connie. You think Rupert will mind sharing with Ellis?"

Her touch melted his resistance. Troy pulled her back and leaned closer to peck her on the cheek. "I think you and I need to figure out how to handle this situation. Ma's here to help you with the household chores until I set up the office. I didn't know you planned to hire a cook."

"It's not like I went looking for her. She showed up while I was hanging clothes and asked if we needed help. Ellis wasn't too happy about it, but I think he'll like her cooking better than mine."

"You're a good cook." His protest sounded weak to his own ears.

Millie snorted. "Sweet of you to say so, but my cooking is adequate at best. Jewel cooked for a plantation somewhere south of Atlanta, a house that entertained governors and senators."

"Hmpf. Well, let's see what she can do with greens and cornmeal. I traded some of the coffee and tea we brought from Rome for a few vegetables. Now, I'm sure Ma is ready to get hold of her newest grandchild." He jostled Amy and led the way to the parlor.

"And Henry may have already booted Ma and Rupert out of his room."

As they approached the parlor, Ellis was explaining how he came to meet Troy at Camp Chase.

Troy raised his voice to draw everyone's attention. "Here she is, Ma. Miss Amelia Ruth McNeil."

Connie made room on the sofa and patted the place next to her. "Come over here, Troy, so she can get used to me."

Connie spent a few minutes talking to the baby before she finally convinced her to sit in her lap. "You call her Amy instead of Amelia?"

"I didn't want her to have trouble saying her own name," Millie said. "My full name is Millicent Anne, but as a child I had trouble saying Millicent, so I preferred Millie."

"I hadn't thought of that." Connie cast a fond glance at her sons. "I remember Rupert had difficulty with his *R*'s early on, so he said 'Wupert' and 'Twoy.'"

Rupert ducked his head. "Until Miss Whitaker rapped my knuckles for it during school. Say, what's cooking that smells so good?"

Troy's stomach growled, and Millie laughed. "If you'll excuse me, I'll go see how soon we can have supper. I'm sure you're all getting hungry."

Troy had a feeling he was about to concede defeat on this round. Thank goodness, they'd brought plenty of goods from Rome and had more on the way.

CHAPTER 25

*C*ompliments on Jewel's fine meal dominated the conversation as the men helped Henry back to his bed. The tantalizing aromas had tempted Troy's uncle to join them at the table, but Henry still hadn't regained his full strength. After they got him settled for the night, Troy found Millie leaving the kitchen.

"I see you helped Jewel clean up." He gestured to her damp bodice. "You seem to have half the dish water on your dress."

She laughed and waved him away. "The poor woman was wrung out from her busy day, plus having to double her preparations to feed everyone. Now that she's settled, I'm sure she can handle it by herself."

"Of course, Henry will have the final say once he's able to deal with it." With a hand at her back, Troy escorted her to the front porch. "I suppose Ma has Amy?"

"I think they're quite taken with each other."

They joined the rest of the family on the front porch. Millie sank into the empty rocker, and Troy leaned against the rail beside her. Amy had quieted with a thumb in her mouth while Ma rocked and hummed to her.

Ellis pulled a blade of grass from his mouth and tossed it aside. "How soon do you plan to head north, Troy? I'm a mite anxious to see Sadie and the boys."

Ma looked up. "Is Irene's mother still there, Ellis?"

"Yeah, I sent a letter when we got to Chattanooga and told her we'd come to Henry's first. She sent her reply here." He shot a glance Troy's way. "It was her idea to get all the family together for a reunion before harvest begins."

Ma's eyebrows went up. "A reunion? Where would you have it?"

"This is the most logical place." Ellis turned to Millie. "Especially now that he has a proper cook."

Troy groaned. "Ellis, we've been over this. Henry won't cotton to the idea."

"That's because he thought it'd be too much on Millie."

Millie sat forward in her rocker and peered at Ellis. "Why's that?"

"With taking care of the little one there." Ellis gestured to the sleeping child. "And your...delicate condition. Sorry. Henry guessed it when you were sick every morning."

Color suffused Millie's face. Rupert stood and reached for the door. "I believe it's past my bedtime. You old married folks can stay up late and continue your discussion."

As he disappeared inside, Ma shifted Amy in her arms. "Another baby so soon? I mean...how old is Amy?"

"She's nine months old already." Millie leaned over to brush Amy's cheek. "She's small for her age, probably because of the turmoil we went through on the journey north. She was born in the refugee house in Louisville."

"I don't understand why Troy never mentioned your relationship when he was home last spring." Ma searched their faces. "And you only married earlier this year?"

Troy put a protective hand on Millie's shoulder, but she smiled. "He didn't know about Amy until he met Doctor

Spencer at Camp Chase. I guess February was a time of revelations for both of us."

"Oh? What else did you discover?" Ma's question seemed apprehensive.

Troy used his foot to set Millie's rocker in motion. "Millie found out her real father was Ellis instead of Cal Gibson."

"Oh, dear." Ma's gaze swung from Troy and Millie to Ellis. "How did that happen?"

Ellis shuffled his feet. "Polly left her a letter but hid it where she wouldn't find it for years."

Troy intercepted the glances between his mother and Ellis. "Ma? You knew about that?"

"Yes." Ma sighed with the confession. "I met Polly when she stayed with her aunt years ago. We weren't close, so I didn't know she was increasing when she left. It wasn't until Ellis received her letter that I learned about Millie."

Troy's muscles tensed, his confusion blooming into suspicion as he faced Ellis. "Why would you share that letter with my mother? She didn't know Millie or Cal. She barely knew Millie's mother."

Ellis dropped his head and turned away. "I can't say."

Troy's face burned. He pushed off the rail and curled his fists, straining to curb his anger. "Why not? Did you also have an affair with Ma?"

Ellis jerked around. "What? No!"

Ma stopped her rocker and leaned toward Troy. "Calm down. We've had no relationship beyond the proper one as brother and sister by law. Ellis shared the letter with your pa and me because he wanted our advice." She heaved a deep sigh. "He knew we'd understand his distress."

Rather than calm him, her answer roused Troy further. "How? Why would you and Pa understand more than Henry or someone else?"

"Because our situation wasn't too different." Her voice dropped, and tears filled her eyes.

Ma tapped her fingers on the rocker arms. "Your situation? What are you saying?"

"You know that your pa's first wife died when Rupert was a baby and I was teaching school. I fell in love with someone who left the area before I discovered I was expecting you. Your pa—John, that is—and I were close, so I confessed my condition to him."

Troy struggled to hear her above the roaring in his ears. The world tilted.

Millie sprang from her chair and led him to the chair she'd vacated. "Troy, you need to sit down. Here." She then sat in his lap, holding his hands.

Ma swiped the tears that slipped from her eyes. "I'm sorry, Troy. John and I often started to tell you, but the time never seemed right."

Shock gave way to anger. How dare they withhold such information? He glared at his mother. "Who else knows, besides Ellis? Henry? The whole county? Everyone but me?"

"No. Troy, please listen." Ma swallowed and took a deep breath. "Henry and June had already moved here. Ellis was staying with John to help with your brothers, so he was there when John and I were wed. The boys were too young to realize anything except they were getting a new mama. Ellis was sworn to secrecy. Everybody else assumed you were John's child."

∾

*T*roy's heart pulsed beneath Millie's fingers. His hand gripped her waist. "Did my—the man who left you in that situation refuse to marry you? Or were you attacked?"

It seemed to Millie that she and Troy both held their breath as they waited for the answer.

Connie's eyes widened. "I wasn't attacked, so you can rest easy there. You don't have a violent heritage. Ethan came to the area to help his sister-in-law on the farm when his brother was gored by a bull. He brought his niece and nephew to school, and over time we developed a close relationship. We planned to marry at the end of the school year but kept it secret on account of my job."

She stroked Amy's hair and sighed. "It was early spring, and one week those children didn't show up for school, so I was concerned they might be sick. Their farm was a couple miles out, so it was late afternoon when I arrived, and a storm was blowing in. I found out the children's grandfather had moved them to the northern part of the state. Ethan stayed to handle the sale of the farm. The storm got worse, and the wind and snow made driving back to town impossible."

Ellis interrupted. "Connie, you don't have to continue. I'm sure they get the idea."

"No, Troy should know." She pressed on. "Because of the storm, I couldn't leave the farm for two days. Too much time together with no one else around. The snow prevented all travel. When the roads were passable again, I returned to town. Ethan had to leave to secure his job but promised he'd return in June, and we would wed." Connie's gaze dropped to her lap.

Troy's voice came out low and sorrowful. "He never returned, did he?"

Either Connie didn't hear or ignored his question. She shifted Amy in her arms. "John was recently widowed with three boys to care for, so I figured it would benefit us both to get married. He agreed, and we married after school let out. We suffered some cruel slander, since Rupert wasn't quite two and you were born seven months later, but we've made a good marriage. I couldn't have asked for a better man to step in as your pa."

Troy's grip on Millie had loosened, and he nodded to his mother. "Thank you for telling me."

Millie's poor mother-in-law looked done-in. "Why don't you help me put Amy to bed, Connie? Ellis and Troy can follow when they're ready."

~

*A*s soon as the women walked away, Troy leaned forward with his face in his hands. *Dear God, I almost did the same to Millie as my natural father did to Ma.*

Troy groaned. "How do you reconcile who you thought you were when you find out you're someone else?"

Ellis shuffled his feet. "You're the same man your folks raised you to be. They both made sacrifices for your sake, which is a lot more than I did for Polly and Millie. You can repay them by being a man they'll be proud of."

"In recent years," Troy said, "I felt like I could never please Pa. I guess I disappointed him. Maybe he wondered if he'd wasted all those years. Pa and I never could agree."

"On politics, which isn't everything. That's your ma's influence, and he knows it. Simon shares your views—wherever he is. So does Henry. It's not like you're the only one around here to support the Union." Ellis shook his head. "I suspect many of our Southern boys got caught up in war fever, and you see where that got us."

Troy raised his head. "Why did you join? With Irene gone and three young'uns at home, nobody expected you to risk your life. That bothered Pa too."

"It was a dumb move, I reckon. When Tom turned fifteen, he started talking about joining. I reasoned it'd be better for me to go so he'd stay at home to run the farm. He's the type who shoulders responsibility. In that, he's more like John than me." Ellis sat in the empty chair next to Troy. "In the back of my mind, I think it gave me an excuse to be away for a while and maybe to find Millie."

How would Troy feel if he hadn't known about Amy until years later? Impossible to say for sure, but he had a hunch he'd go to any lengths to find her. Recent days had changed his opinion of Ellis, made him understand the man better. Perhaps it was time to confess his own failures.

"The day Millie was attacked changed me. I'd never felt so much rage as when I saw that man holding her."

He clenched his fists at the memory and took a deep breath to calm down. "I wrestled him to the floor, and his head struck the bricks. Afterward, I tried to teach her how to defend herself. We ended up making love."

"You don't have to explain. I was about the same age when I met Polly."

Troy squirmed. "What I'm trying to say is, our story isn't so different from Ma's or yours. If I hadn't arrived in New Manchester the day the Army moved them out, I might never have found them. Maybe I wouldn't have been caught and sent north. If Doctor Spencer hadn't come to Camp Chase and told me Millie was in Louisville, I might not have learned about Amy for years."

Ellis stood and clapped him on the shoulder. "You are a blessed man, Troy. I'm glad things turned out for you and Millie."

After Ellis went to bed, Troy sat for a while and listened to the katydids' chorus, punctuated by the occasional hoot of an owl. The day's heat dwindled to a pleasant warmth as darkness covered the land. A year ago in this very place, he'd wrestled with guilt and a restless impatience to get back to Millie. He'd been ignorant of the life they'd created, but a sense of urgency had driven him to return.

He stood and stepped to the edge of the porch for a clearer view of the stars splashed across a velvet sky. The faint scent of wood smoke drifted from the workers' cabins. How precious the quiet of peace.

"'I will lift mine eyes to the hills, whence cometh my help. My help cometh from the Lord, the Maker of heaven and earth.'" He spoke into the inky stillness. "Thank You."

~

*A*fter she put Amy to bed, Millie suggested Connie join her in a cup of chamomile tea. While the water heated, Connie sat at the table, and Millie pulled out mugs.

"I'm sorry for Troy's outburst," Millie said. "Having experienced the same shock myself not long ago, I'm sure he'll come around."

She poured the water over the leaves. "Mother's letter stunned me. But I knew how cruel Cal could be, so I understood what my mother did. All I knew about Ellis was from childhood stories Lydia had told me."

Connie propped her chin in her hand. "Unfortunately, I can't tell Troy much about Ethan. I knew so little about him. Troy gets most of his looks from me, but sometimes I can see glimpses of Ethan in him, especially around his eyes."

"Ironic, isn't it?" Millie poured the tea and offered Connie the honey jar. "Troy was raised as a McNeil, but he isn't, and I am." A sudden thought occurred. "Oh! This means we aren't first cousins, after all." She spun toward Connie. "Unless you were born a McNeil?"

She asked in jest, but Connie paused before sipping. "We're related, but not closely. My mother was a McNeil. That's how I got the teaching position, through family connections."

"And why no one suspected Troy wasn't John's son. He favors the McNeils."

Connie regarded her with surprise. "I suppose that's true. I always thought it fortunate he looked more like me. And not many people in the community knew Ethan well because he'd been gone for years and only returned to help his brother's family."

Footsteps shuffling in the hallway told Millie Troy had come in. Connie finished her tea. "I believe I'll take myself to bed, dear."

Millie rinsed their cups and set them in the basin. "Good night. I hope you rest well."

She followed Connie until she reached the door where Troy waited for her. He led her into their room and wrapped her in his embrace.

"How are you, Troy? Do you need to talk?"

"Not tonight. After considering all we learned, I'm grateful Seth and Doc led me to you and Amy. Our daughter will know her father didn't abandon her."

Millie reached up to kiss his jaw. "God knew how to bring us together. Even if took two armies to do it."

≈

JULY 22, 1865

Troy reached one arm around Ma as she held the baby. "This first trip shouldn't take long. I appreciate you staying to help Millie."

He stashed the Confederate canteen under the seat as Ellis gave Millie a hug and climbed into the wagon. Ma wandered back to the porch, keeping the baby's attention away from the loaded vehicle.

Troy slid his hands up Millie's arms. "Are you well? I didn't hear you heaving this morning."

"The sickness seems to be passing. Or perhaps it's waiting until you've gone." She smiled and reached up for a kiss. "You'll be careful asking about that canteen, won't you?"

"Yeah. You take care now and don't do too much while I'm gone. Let Ma take over some of the chores."

"We'll be fine. Don't get into any trouble out there."

He pressed one last kiss to her ear. "I'll be back in a couple of days."

Ellis picked up the reins and clicked to the horses. Troy spun toward the wagon and leaped over the wheel. He grabbed the seat and levered himself into place. "Whose farm is closest to Henry's this way?"

"You mean besides the Varners' house? That would be Callahan, which will make for a real test of your charm, Corporal. Especially with that blue uniform lyin' in the wagon bed." Ellis smirked and winked at him.

Troy pursed his lips and tapped his knee with one finger. "How long will it take us to get there?"

"Half an hour with this full load."

Troy nodded and pulled his kepi over his eyes. "Time for a nap, then." *And some serious praying.*

He didn't know much about the Callahans, except they had a brood of children. Had any of them been old enough to join the military? Did they lose anyone in the war? All he could do was ask for divine wisdom, as he did with every family visit. At least he'd learned his lesson about leaving off his uniform until he introduced himself.

The road took them by cotton fields as they neared the house, where three people—Troy assumed they were the Callahan children—worked with hoes. The workers glanced up as the wagon passed, raising their hands to block the sun. One dropped her hoe and skedaddled toward the house. Troy prayed she wasn't going to fetch a firearm. Maybe she'd seen the crates in the wagon bed and figured they were selling wares.

Ellis slowed the horses as the house came into sight. The girl crossed the yard in front of them, ignored the steps, and leaped onto the wide porch. She disappeared inside. As the wagon came to a stop, she came out again, followed by a big man in coveralls.

"Good morning, Mr. Callahan." Troy leaned forward to see around Ellis and waved.

The man glared at him and focused on Ellis. "What're you doin' here so early in the day, McNeil? If you're lookin' to sell somethin', you can jes' turn around. We ain't got any money to spare on gee-gaws."

The girl dropped her head but peeked up at them through her lashes.

"Not selling anything, Callahan. I'm on my way home from the Yankee prison camp, traveling with my nephew Troy here." Ellis tipped his head toward Troy. "He's got some business to discuss with you."

Callahan's gaze shifted to Troy. "What kind of business? I don't have anythin' of value 'cept the land, and I ain't interested in sellin' it, even if I ain't got enough hands to work it." He turned back to Ellis. "And you can tell that boy of yours to leave off makin' eyes at my girl at church."

The girl blushed and retreated inside the house.

"Can't be my boy, Callahan," Ellis said. "Somebody's told you wrong."

Troy pushed past Ellis and jumped to the ground. "Mr. Callahan, I ain't sellin' or buyin' anything. I'm here to help you and your family."

"We might be poor, but we don't need charity."

Just as I expected. "This ain't charity. It's barterin'. I can provide a few things you don't have in exchange for some things you do have."

The farmer snorted. "Don't know what you think I got that's worth trading."

"It seems you got more land that needs working. What if I can bring you a few extra hands to help work it?"

"Where you gonna get 'em?" Callahan scoffed. "Most everyone I know can't keep up with their own work."

Troy rubbed his face. "Might as well tell you, I'm working for the government to help get the South back on its feet. I brought some goods with me for that purpose."

Callahan's eyes narrowed. "You'd best be careful. Some folks around here would consider it their duty to shoot a Federal man."

"I'll be settin' up an office in a few days where people can come to sign up. We'll match up those who don't have land with those who do and help you work out the details on how they'll be paid." He waited while the man considered his offer.

"Well, that's all well and good, but it don't help me much right now."

Troy grinned. "Which is why I've brought a few items you might be able to use. We've got a few tools, some seeds, wheat berries, and canned foods. You can choose what you need and tell me what you might have to trade, like maybe a sack of okra or tomatoes."

The man's eyes lit with interest, but he held back, likely not wanting to appear overly eager.

"Maybe your missus would like to take a look, see if there's anything she could use?"

Even as Callahan turned to call, a thin woman stepped onto the porch, followed by the girl who'd disappeared earlier. "Hey there, Ellis." She peered at Troy. "Ain't you the nephew what helped Henry last year?"

Troy offered a grin and bobbed his head. "Yes'm, not that I was much good after I busted up my leg."

"Henry was right proud to have you there." She walked to the back of the wagon while they talked. "Now, what kind of goods you got here?"

While Troy showed her their wares and explained the process,

Ellis and Mr. Callahan trailed behind, exchanging gossip about local matters. He forgot about the canteen until they started to leave. Mr. Callahan was walking toward the barn, but he showed it to the man's wife. She shook her head, and he joined Ellis in the wagon. "I'll be in touch about getting you some help in the fields."

As soon as they cleared the Callahan property, Ellis shot Troy a questioning look. "You know what they traded you wasn't worth half the price of what they took."

The wagon lumbered down the road.

"I know it." Troy smiled with satisfaction. "I think we got a real bargain."

"Bargain? You can't keep doin' business like that. You'll wind up with nothin' to show for your work."

"I'm not here to make money, Ellis. By givin' folks more'n what they expect, I show them I'm here to serve their best interest, which will make them more willin' to work with me."

Ellis snorted. "I hope you're right. Did you even say you're working for the United States government?"

"I mentioned it to the missus." Troy propped his foot on the box and adjusted his straw hat. "When Millie hired Jewel while I was gone, it showed me that women may be more practical about such matters. They can accept a helpin' hand from time to time because they're willin' to help others when it's their turn to give."

"I guess men resist because we feel like it's our job to provide."

"Yep. Sometimes it just comes down to our pride. So that's what I'm up against in this job. Maybe if I can get the women to accept our help, the men will follow."

Ellis grunted as he flicked the reins for the horse to pick up speed. "It's too bad Millie wasn't up to comin' with you. She'd probably outshine us both. Lydia did a good job raising her."

CHAPTER 26

"*W*agon comin' up the road."

At the call, Millie smiled. Levi was a better lookout than Henry's old dog Rusty. A lot faster, too, since the hound's age had slowed him to the speed of pond water. Jewel's five-year-old boy moved like a bumble bee, flitting from one activity to another. He was a pure joy to watch.

Millie hefted Amy to her hip and went to front door. "Is it Troy?"

Her mother-in-law cast a puzzled look her way as she approached from the barn. "No, but it looks like a Union soldier and a couple of women."

Millie joined Connie on the porch. "Maybe it's the assistant Troy was expecting. I wonder who directed him here." As the vehicle drew nearer, dread curled in her belly. "Oh, dear. It's Becky Varner and her sister."

"And no sign of a parent." Connie clicked her tongue. "I can't believe Mrs. Varner let those two girls ride off with a man."

269

"Maybe she didn't know." Millie grimaced. "I wouldn't put it past Becky to contrive a way to do that." She passed the squirming baby to Connie. "Guess I'll see what they want."

She sauntered down the steps as the wagon halted in front of the house. "Becky, Blanche, what brings y'all over this way?"

Becky tittered. "Why, somebody had to show the corporal where y'all lived since Troy wasn't there to meet him in town." She gestured toward the soldier on the far side of the seat.

He hadn't turned Millie's way and seemed to be admiring the stretch of land to the south. Becky elbowed him to get his attention. "I think you two have met before, haven't you?"

Millie recoiled when the man turned her way.

Corporal Harris lifted his kepi in greeting. "Afternoon, ma'am. Nice spread of land you have here."

Though he didn't smile, his expression was pleasant. She detected no hint of the mockery she expected, instead a cautious geniality. What game did he play now?

"It belongs to my uncle." She gestured toward Henry, who ambled closer from the barn. Behind him, Rupert hurried from the field, and Millie breathed easier. Thank God Troy's brother had seen the wagon approach. Against her better judgment, she yielded to her ingrained Southern hospitality. "Won't y'all come in? I'll see if Jewel has any tea or lemonade."

Henry reached them, so she fled up the stairs and inside the house. Between Henry and Rupert, their guests would be treated appropriately. She wasn't sure who had the most gall, Becky or Corporal Harris. *To ride up right to the house! Wait, did Becky say the corporal was here to see Troy?*

A wave of dizziness made Millie pause at the kitchen door.

Jewel must've overheard because she was already arranging cups on a tray when she caught sight of her. "You feelin' poorly, Missus?" She sprang to Millie's side and led her to a chair. "Come sit a minute. I'll soon have cool drinks for the comp'ny."

Millie sat, and Jewel pressed a cup into her hand. "Take small swallows now till the sickness passes."

The cool liquid soothed her right away. "Jewel, you are rightly named. I'm glad you came to us."

The woman shared her smile. "No gladder'n I am to be here. Now, you sit there while I take the tray out. I'll say how you's not well."

"No, I'll go. But maybe you should carry the tray, to be safe. I won't have anyone sayin' I'm a poor hostess." *Nor Corporal Harris thinking he can scare me with his threats and insinuations.*

Everyone had settled on the tree-shaded porch. Connie, Becky, and Blanche took the chairs while the men lounged against the railing.

"Here we are." Millie held the door for Jewel to exit and helped pass out the cups.

Becky barely sipped her tea before she picked up the conversation. "Corporal Harris was telling us he'll be working at the new bureau office in town."

Millie chose a chair near Connie and offered some cooled tea to Amy. She raised her eyebrows at the declaration, glancing from the soldier to Henry and Rupert. This was Troy's legal assistant? Did he plan to take over after Troy had done the hard work?

Rupert shifted at the porch rail. "I'm sure Troy will welcome the help once he finishes his circuit of the county. It's important to let everybody know what they can expect the government to do for them."

"Of course." Harris saluted Rupert with his cup. "I'll be happy to handle the paperwork when the people come into the office. Tell me about the crops grown around here."

The conversation drifted from crops to the weather and families in the area. When the talk dwindled, Becky made a motion to Blanche.

The younger sister spoke up for the first time. "Ma wanted

us to be sure you know about the church picnic on Sunday. It's always the first Sunday of the month. After we eat, we'll have some games and contests."

"Now that sounds like a fine time." Connie smiled at the girl. "Maybe Troy will be back by then. He and Rupert always liked to take part in those."

Henry grunted as he pushed off the porch railing. "I'll come for the eatin', anyways. Ain't too much for games anymore."

"That'll give Corporal Harris a chance to meet everyone too." Becky tossed a coy expression at the soldier, and he sent her an answering grin.

Rupert pointed at the corporal's jacket. "You might want to wear somethin' other than that uniform, though. It might stir up some folks. Good to meet you, Corporal, but I got to get back out to the field. Afternoon, ladies." He set his empty cup on the tray and sauntered to the stairs.

Thankful, Millie shifted Amy in her arms. Even Becky knew his retreat meant the visit was over. The girl wore a look of chagrin but gathered her reticule and fan.

Henry offered the visitor a handshake as the women rose from their chairs. "I guess we'll see you around, Harris."

The corporal's face registered surprise. "Uh, there's one problem. I need a place to stay, was counting on Corporal McNeil to help with that."

～

*A*ccording to the calendar, July had melted into August. Troy couldn't tell much difference. Heat and humidity still stifled the land, and too many fields lay fallow. While letting the land rest was a good principle, Troy believed the best way involved planning and rotation. What the South had done, though, was put themselves in a place of poor harvests year after year while the country pulled itself apart.

He swiped at the sweat that gathered around his hairline. Wasn't much he could do with the moisture under his arms and on his back. He focused on figuring up what he'd accomplished in the past week and all the chores that awaited him. He'd left Ellis at his house after visiting several farms along the way. Ellis's son, Tom, rode with him one full day, then they circled back. If he counted right, they'd had successful meetings with two dozen farmers in the state. He ought to consider finding an office site in Roanoke and maybe one in Heard County, Georgia, rather than concentrating everything in Wedowee. That way, they could offer more schooling for the former slaves.

He could start administering oaths of allegiance to prepare for the Alabama state convention in September. Only when the bureau had collected enough of those would each state be able to apply to rejoin the United States.

When he passed the turnoff to Callahans' farm, anticipation rushed new energy to his limbs. He flicked the reins and prompted the horses to a faster clip. He was ready to see his family and rest a day or two before going out again. His assistants couldn't arrive soon enough.

The horses must have caught his urgency, or maybe they anticipated their own food and surcease. In minutes, he rounded the last curve and spied his uncle's house. Jewel's boy dashed from his play in the yard to the back porch. Troy hoped it was a sign of welcome, not fright. He hadn't spent much time with the youngster.

Guiding the horses to the barn, he waved to Rupert, who returned the gesture and hurried over to help him with the team. Troy jumped from the bench and stretched his arms above his head.

"Good to have you back, little brother." Rupert cuffed him on the shoulder while Troy lifted his hat and sluiced the dampness away.

"Mighty glad to be back. How's everything here?"

"Going good." Rupert reached under the wagon bench and handed Troy his knapsack. "You might want to know—"

"Welcome back, Troy." Ma rushed across the yard with Amy, who chattered and flapped her hands. "This young lady is having a fit to see her pa."

Troy's heart lifted as Amy launched herself into his arms, and he snuggled her against his shoulder. "Did you miss me, sweetie? I missed you so much. You, too, Ma." He shifted Amy so he could drape an arm around his mother.

She squeezed his waist. "I think I should tell you—"

"Troy!" His wife pushed out of the house and hurried toward him.

Ma slipped away so Millie could take her place. Without a thought for his audience, Troy met her lips with his. He grinned when Amy leaned in to join them. "Ah, it's good to be home."

He didn't mean the house or land. Through his years of roaming, he'd learned home was any place where a body was welcomed and surrounded by loved ones. He'd claimed home whenever he was at Lydia's or his parents' or Henry's.

And all those places still were, to a degree. But with Millie —that was his true home. He continued toward the house. "How's Henry?"

"He's much improved," Millie said. "We have to hold him back from doin' too much. You'll be glad to know the shipment from Washington came in."

"It did? Well, hallelujah. Now we can—"

Millie put a finger to his lips. "One of your assistants arrived today too. But Troy, you need to know who..."

A figure in a United States uniform stepped from the house onto the porch. Troy briefly registered her words as he transferred Amy to her arms. He sprinted up the steps and reached out his right hand, noting the insignia. "Welcome to Alabama,

Corporal. Troy McNeil. I'm mighty glad to see you made it so soon."

The soldier's eyebrows lifted, and he met Troy's hand with his own. His smile resembled a smirk as he spoke. "Byron Harris. You don't wear your uniform while traveling?"

"Not on these initial visits. I'd prefer not to get shot at before stating my business." Troy gestured to the door. "Let's go inside and get outta the sun." He turned back to the women, who trailed behind him. "Millie, Ma, you comin' in? I could use a tall drink of water, maybe a slice of pie, if Jewel has any set aside. How about you, Harris?"

Odd that neither Ma nor Millie had offered any refreshments.

The corporal entered the house and waited in the hall for the others to follow. Troy examined the women's faces as they approached the door, but he couldn't decipher their expressions. They certainly didn't look happy. He'd never known Millie or Ma to lack in good manners.

Ma brushed past him. "I'll get your water and pie. You ought to see to your daughter's naptime."

"Oh, right." He turned to their visitor. "If you'll take a seat in the parlor, I'll be right with you. Millie will—"

"I'll change her nappy for you." Millie ignored the other man and hurried down the hall, her heeled half-boots clicking on the wooden floor.

Troy caught up with her at their bedroom door. "What's the matter with everybody? You and Ma act like you don't know how to treat a visitor."

illie tugged him inside the room and shut the door. "You'd best sit down for a minute and listen." She pushed him onto the bed and laid Amy beside him. "That man out there is the one that Becky took up with when we were in Louisville." She switched her attention between Troy and Amy, working as she talked. "You remember I wrote to you about him? He's the same one I punched in the nose last year?"

Troy's brow puckered while he digested her words. "Are you worried he's here because of you? But how would he know you'd be here?"

"I don't know. Maybe I'm imagining things, but it's strange to have him here, and I don't like it." Millie fastened Amy's diaper and handed her to Troy. He rubbed Amy's back as she snuggled against his shoulder.

"Maybe he's in love with Becky. Wouldn't that account for it?" He leaned forward and pecked Millie on the cheek. "It's crazy what a man will do to be with the woman he loves."

"Oh, really?" She tried not to smile, but Troy knew her too well. "Well, he's here, so I guess we'll have to see if he'll work out. Although he promised to get even with me, that was a year ago. Maybe he's decided it's not worth pursuing. I just don't feel easy around him."

"Hopefully, you won't have to deal with him. I'll do my best to keep him away from you. Hey, is she asleep?" He moved so Millie could see Amy's face.

"Yes. How do you do that? She's got to where she fights me at naptime."

His mouth stretched into a silly grin. "She loves being close to her pa."

Millie smoothed the blanket so he could lay the baby down. "Now you'd better go out and see to your assistant. I'd hate for him to think you neglected him."

He settled Amy, then grabbed Millie's waist. "I'm goin', soon's I get a proper kiss from my wife."

Several minutes later, Troy escorted Millie to the parlor to join Connie and Corporal Harris. "Pardon the delay, Corporal, Ma. It took a while to get my girl calmed down."

He smiled innocently, but Millie's blush climbed to her hairline. "Amy does love her pa." Maybe that would divert their suspicions from Troy's mischievous comment. "Connie, did Jewel need any help in the kitchen?"

Oblivious to Millie's discomfort, Connie waved away the possibility of escape. "She's got the meal under control." The curious tenor in Connie's voice piqued Millie's interest.

Troy helped himself to the peach pie on the side table and sat beside Millie. "I trust you had an uneventful journey from Louisville, Corporal. I believe that's where you traveled from, wasn't it?"

Millie didn't miss the glance Harris sent her way.

"I was there when the prison released the last of its occupants." He raised his cup and took a sip. "But, as I was telling your mother, I took a few days to check on my family in Tennessee."

"I hope you found them well. My comrade-in-arms at Camp Chase was from East Tennessee. Fellow named Walter Dykes. Don't suppose you know him?"

The corporal dug into his pie. "No, I'm from the south-central part of the state, south of Nashville."

Troy sipped his water. "I thought that area was more strongly Confederate than Union."

Harris nodded. "It is. My Union sympathies weren't too well thought of, even among family members. I guess I owe them to my uncle who helped raise me."

Millie let Troy carry the conversation and tried to observe Corporal Harris with discretion. Voices near the door announced Henry and Rupert's arrival. Both stopped at the parlor threshold. Henry muttered a greeting, then continued to his room.

"We unloaded the wagon, Troy. No need to trouble yourself about it." Rupert grinned as he teased his brother.

Troy slapped his forehead. "I plumb forgot about it in all the excitement of gettin' home and findin' the corporal here. Thank you, Bud."

"Don't worry, I'll find a way you can repay me soon." He lifted his hat to wipe his brow. "Since Ma won't let me sit at the table, dirty as I am, I'll go wash up."

Connie spurred him on with a playful gesture but turned to Troy when Rupert was out of hearing. "He works harder here than when he's at home. He seems happier too."

"Probably because Henry gives him the run of things." Troy stretched his legs in front of him. "At home, he's got both Pa and Paul to order him around. And I don't imagine Paul is easy to be around since he lost a leg."

"You don't live here, Mrs. McNeil?" Harris asked Connie.

"My home is a good piece south of here." Connie seemed reluctant to give much information.

"I see. Then Mr. Henry McNeil isn't your husband?" His scrutiny bounced between Connie and Troy.

She offered a slight smile. "He's my husband's brother."

Troy laughed. "There's too many McNeils in this county to keep up with, Harris. It's easier to go by first names." He pointed to the hall. "Henry's my uncle, Rupert's the brother next to me, then there's Simon, who's still up north as far as we know, and Paul is at home with Pa. There're others you'll meet later."

He picked up Millie's hand and planted a kiss on her knuckles. "I believe you met my Millie in Louisville."

"That's right. Miss Varner introduced us. But I first met her —to be specific, her fist—a year ago in Georgia." He had the decency to admit it and even look abashed by their earlier encounter. "We were foraging around the town while we waited for orders. She socked me in the nose when I tried to push my advantage on her."

~

*T*he corporal's confession shocked him. And made him breathe easier. It boded well for their future association and convinced him the man's character was better than he'd feared.

Millie bristled. "And you promised to get even." She blurted the accusation, then glanced at Troy as if afraid he'd censure her.

Harris emitted a nervous chuckle. "Yes, I did. I deserved the hit, but it surprised me. I pray you'll forgive my poor behavior." He turned to Troy. "You can imagine my embarrassment when I had to face my associates with a bloody nose."

"You told Becky Varner you had a score to settle with me." Millie was like a bulldog with a bone.

Harris shifted in his seat. "It was the first excuse I could think of to explain my interest in you." When three pairs of eyes skewered him, he rushed on. "Not for what you might think. I knew Miss Varner was from this area, and she called you Mrs. McNeil."

He spread his hands. "You see, I was born here. We lived on a farm east of Wedowee until I was five or six. I even started school here."

Ma coughed and jerked as she transferred her cup and saucer to the table. She lifted a napkin to her lips and said, "Swallowed wrong."

The corporal continued. "I wanted to come here and see if I could reclaim the family farm. I'd been told my schoolteacher married a neighbor named McNeil." His gaze went from Ma to Millie. "I thought you might be kin to her."

Troy turned to his mother. "Would that be you, Ma?"

"Perhaps. How, um, how long ago was that?" She fumbled with the napkin in her lap.

Harris tapped a finger against his chin. "About twenty years ago."

Troy regarded his mother, concern niggling through his thoughts. "Ma, do you remember havin' a student named Harris? I'm sorry, Corporal, but what was your first name?"

"Byron. My sister's a couple years older than me. Her name's Jessie."

Ma's smile seemed strained. "I do remember a girl named Jessie."

"Well, how about that?" Troy forced a smile. "Looks like you've found your teacher, Harris. Now you just have to find the old farm."

The corporal opened his mouth but stopped when Rupert leaned into the room. "Jewel says supper's ready, if y'all didn't ruin your appetite with the pie."

Ma sprang to her feet. "I'll check on Amy for you, Millie. Y'all go on, and we'll be there shortly."

Troy exchanged a glance with Millie. Ma's behavior troubled him. Maybe he'd have a chance to talk with her later. He supposed he ought to help Corporal Harris locate his old family farm too. Seemed like more and more tasks piled on his plate.

He rose and held out his hand for Millie and threaded her fingers through his. "One thing I can't fault you for, Byron, is trying to fix your interest on my wife. She's like the woman Solomon wrote about, worth more than rubies. She's got brains to go with her beauty. Just remember, she's mine."

CHAPTER 27

*T*roy's praise and possessiveness brought a blush to
Millie's cheeks. It wasn't what she was used to. Cal
had never complimented Lydia except to get on her good side
when he'd done something she wouldn't like.

No, don't go imagining things, Millicent Ann. Troy is not like Cal.

And though Corporal Harris had roused her defenses, his
explanation for being here was too strangely related to Connie's
story to be disregarded. His appearance had rattled her
mother-in-law.

They still hadn't decided where to put the corporal. Not
likely they could appeal to any of the neighbors. Most of them
had unmarried daughters to consider, and few would welcome
a Union man in their home, anyway.

Henry and Rupert claimed their places at each end of the
table, and Troy sat beside Millie on the long bench. Corporal
Harris took a chair on the opposite side.

Connie arrived as Jewel set the cornbread on the table.
"Amy's still asleep."

Jewel stepped back so Connie could take a seat next to the
corporal, who rose to assist her.

Connie's steps faltered. She murmured her thanks as she sat but kept her gaze on the table.

Conversation centered on the farm and Troy's travels while they passed around the dishes of beans, potatoes, cornbread, and small pieces of beef in thick gravy. Millie was happy to see how Jewel had stretched a tin of beef and made it delicious.

As Troy ended a story about one of his visits, Amy cried from the bedroom. Millie laid aside her fork and rose, but Connie pushed off her chair first. "I'll get her."

Millie mashed a spoonful of potatoes and added gravy for the baby's meal. Henry took up his duties as host to ask after their guest. "Where do you hail from, Corporal?"

"I'd be pleased for everyone to call me Byron, sir." He repeated his story for Henry and Rupert, who'd missed it earlier.

Henry pushed his plate away. "You don't say. That must've been a good while ago. Can't say as I recall a Harris farm hereabouts."

Connie returned with Amy, so Millie passed the baby's plate to her mother-in-law. With Connie to help, Millie enjoyed the luxury of finishing her own meal and attending to the conversation.

Byron continued. "I only learned the full story a couple of years ago. When my father died, my sister and I moved in with my grandparents. My uncle stayed a while longer to close the sale of the farm, as he was part owner. He always regretted having to sell out, but he couldn't run it by himself, though he tried for a while after Pa died."

"Yep, a farm is a heap o' work," Henry said. "Hard for one man to run it alone. All my daughters moved away, but I got two or three fine nephews who come around and help me since my June passed on to her reward." He gripped Troy's shoulder and nodded toward Rupert at the other end of the table. "Guess I'll have to figure out how to divvy it up when I'm gone."

"Now, Henry, you can leave me outta that calculation." Troy bumped Millie's arm with his elbow. "Millie and I will likely put down roots in Granny McNeil's house over in Campbell County after my time with the army is up."

When Troy looked at Millie for confirmation, she faced him with raised eyebrows.

"Uh, that is, we might settle there. We haven't talked about it much. I just figured she'd want to go...I guess I better keep my mouth shut until we make that decision together."

Millie smiled her approval.

Henry guffawed. "You're learning, boy."

Rupert pushed aside his plate and leaned back in his chair. "Well, I hope you're not planning to depart this earth anytime soon, Henry. I'll need to find me a wife so she can tell me where I want to live."

As the laughter died down, Byron agreed. "I guess that goes for me, too, and I hope to make my home here. If I can't farm, I guess I can always open a law office."

"How much longer do you have to serve, Byron?" Troy asked.

"A little less than a year. Maybe we can make good progress with the bureau before my time is up."

Amy banged her spoon on the table and babbled in Henry's direction.

"That's her sign she's finished," Millie said.

She stood to take the baby, and the men pushed to their feet.

Gunshots erupted nearby. Everyone froze as a window shattered. Something bit the flesh at Millie's shoulder, and then she hit the floor.

∿

"*G*et down!" Troy shouted. "Quiet!"

He hovered over Millie. His body thrummed with energy as he concentrated on distinguishing the sounds around him. Harsh breathing and Amy's whimpers were all he could make out. Nothing from outside the room. Reluctant to tempt the perpetrators with another target, he remained still.

"Troy, let me up." Millie's whisper tickled his ear. "I need to get Amy."

She pushed at his shoulder, and he shifted.

"Don't stand," he said. "Crawl in case they're still out there."

She wriggled her way from his embrace and scooted to the end of the table. A thin line of blood trailed her movement. His heart skipped a beat.

"Millie, where are you hit?" He croaked the words, then slid after her.

He met his brother crawling toward the hallway. Rupert mumbled one word—"rifle"—and pointed to the back door. Troy nodded and kept going, his primary focus on his family.

On the other side of the table, his wife cradled the frightened baby. "It's only a graze from a piece of glass." Millie tilted her head toward Connie, who huddled over Byron. "I think Corporal Harris got the worst of it."

Troy edged that way. "Ma? How bad is he?"

Rupert stormed back into the room. "They high-tailed it outta here before I could get off a shot."

"How many?" Troy stood and helped Millie to her feet.

"I only saw two." Rupert gestured behind him. "Jewel was taking clothes off the line. She might've seen 'em. I'll check the barn."

Jewel scurried from the back of the house, carrying a handful of towels. "Anybody hurt? I heard gunshots. Oh, good lordy, Mrs. Millie. Your arm's bleedin'."

Millie grabbed two towels and passed one to Connie. "Where's Levi?"

Jewel nodded toward the doorway. "Hidin' in the pantry."

Troy squatted behind Byron to help him sit up while Connie wrapped the towel around his upper arm.

"Is that the only place you're hit?" Troy rose to check on Henry.

"Yeah. It's a good thing I turned to speak to Mr. Henry, else you might be missing a partner."

Troy frowned at the corporal's attempt at humor. "I think that was the intention." He stalked over to Jewel, who was pumping water into a basin. "Tell me what you saw, Mrs. Jewel."

"Two men totin' rifles come around the barn and run up to the side o' the house. I grabs Levi, and we walk casual-like to the back door." She shook her head and passed the basin to the table. "I shoulda hollered a warning to you folks when I seen 'em walk up. I thought they was going to the front door, and I could beat 'em inside the house."

Connie and Henry braced Byron as he stood and helped him to a chair so Connie could better examine his wound. They pushed dishes away as he leaned across the table.

"I'm afraid I might pass out..." Byron's face met the tabletop.

Henry chuckled. "Yeah, I think you did, my boy."

"Maybe he'll stay out until I finish cleaning his wounds. Looks like the bullet passed through." Connie probed the arm and dabbed it with the wet towel.

Troy surveyed the room. "Where's Millie?"

"Here." She hurried to Connie's side, holding a threaded needle out of Amy's reach. "If you don't need me for anything else, I'll take Amy to the bedroom for a while."

Troy caught Millie as she turned. "Soon as Ma finishes with Byron, I'll have her check your wound." He secured the towel on her shoulder. "I'll be there as soon as I can." He kissed her and Amy, then walked to the broken window.

He never thought he'd face this level of animosity when he took this assignment. How was he going to protect his family?

~

*A*my calmed down quicker than Millie did. Now that the immediate crisis was over, her strength drained away. *The war's supposed to be over. How long will folks keep fighting each other?*

Millie dropped to the floor with Amy beside her and put a few toys between them. She curled her body to keep the child confined to the small area.

Her mind kept replaying the scene, hearing the gunshots and feeling the sting of shattered glass. Thankfully, the injuries weren't serious, which was remarkable. Angels must've been in their midst.

How was Troy going to deal with this development? Millie's concern for his welfare multiplied. If people were bold enough to attack them here in Henry's home, how vulnerable was Troy when he visited other farms?

The door behind Millie opened, and Troy joined them on the floor. Amy's face lit up. She abandoned her toys and crawled over to him.

"How's Corporal Harris?" Millie leaned against him as he lifted Amy.

"Ma says the wound isn't bad, but he lost a fair amount of blood. He'll need to rest a day or two. If he doesn't develop an infection, he'll be fine." Amy pulled at Troy's ears, and he pressed kisses to her neck, making her giggle.

Millie waited for more information, but Troy didn't offer any. "Does that mean you'll stay here until he's able to travel?"

"More or less." He shrugged, but his jaw muscles clenched.

"I aim to find out who attacked us. I'm gonna wire General Swayne and ask for another man, at least for a while. Rupert and I will take turns guarding the house at night until we can figure out who was behind the assault."

She fingered his shirt collar. "I worry about you visiting the farms. Someone could jump on y'all anywhere along the way."

"All we can do is keep up our guard. I'll advise Byron to leave off his uniform coat and kepi like I do. No sense invitin' mischief." He wrinkled his nose and held Amy at arms' length. "I think she needs a fresh nappy."

Troy stood and helped Millie to her feet. He handed Amy her doll as he laid her on the bed. He sat beside the baby but spoke to Millie. "If anything else happens, I'll have to consider taking you back to Georgia."

She looked up, eyes wide. "Do you think that's necessary?"

"I hope not. You never can tell what some folks'll do."

CHAPTER 28

AUGUST 6, 1865

*M*illie hummed the tune they'd sung at the close of the morning service as she stepped from the church into the sunshine. The simple sermon about casting all your care upon the Lord had nourished her hungry heart. It was as if the Lord reminded her that He watched over everyone.

Troy had insisted they attend church for the spiritual encouragement and to present themselves to the community. The pastor allowed Troy to speak and explain his mission. Those he hadn't visited yet expressed surprise to hear that his purpose included helping the farmers as well as the freed slaves. Following the service, he shook hands all around and introduced Millie to everyone he knew.

Becky hurried to impede their progress. "Where's Corporal Harris? Didn't he want to come for the picnic?"

Troy shook his head. "He didn't feel up to the trip into town today."

"We can't stay this time, either," Millie said. "Maybe next month."

As the congregants scattered, she followed Troy to the wagon. Henry lingered to talk with the pastor. Rupert engaged in a conversation with Mr. and Mrs. Varner while the couple's youngsters visited with friends.

"Why didn't you say anything about the attack?" Millie thought he might use the opportunity to put folks on the alert and warn that such actions would bring punishment.

Troy hoisted Amy higher in his arms. "I wanted to see if anyone acted as though they knew about it. That would tell me where to start digging for information."

Millie climbed onto the wagon bench and turned to take Amy. "I didn't hear anybody mention it. What makes you think they'll say something to you?"

Troy sat beside her. "People like to be the first with news. If word comes back to one of us, we'll find out where that person heard it and follow the trail back, hopefully to the guilty party. Henry's telling the preacher what happened, and Rupert's filling in the Varners."

Millie swung around. "The Varners? Is that wise? You know how Becky likes to talk."

"The Varners are Henry's closest neighbor, so they need to be warned." He poked Amy's belly to make her giggle. "And they have an acquaintance with Byron, so they might feel protective of him. Who knows? Becky's tendency to talk might even prove a benefit in this situation."

"Here comes Rupert now, and Henry's right behind him." Millie tucked her skirts close as Amy crawled to Troy's lap. Four on the seat was tight, but the ride would take less than an hour.

Henry climbed up next to Millie while Rupert sat on the other side of Troy. They rode in silence out of the churchyard. Millie stayed quiet until her patience ran out. "Well? Did you find out anything?"

Henry grunted. "Preacher hadn't heard anything, but he'll put his ear to the ground and let us know if he does."

"Same with Mr. Varner," Rupert said. "I wrangled an invitation to supper on Wednesday, though. Thought it might help to have the whole family there. Sometimes young'uns hear things adults don't."

Troy gaped at him. "How'd you manage that?"

A grin spread across Rupert's face. "Oh, I might've hinted at an interest in one of the daughters. Mrs. Varner nearly leaped for joy."

Henry guffawed, but Troy's expression mirrored Millie's concern. "I hope you know what you're doing, brother. I'd hate for you to get trapped in a sticky situation."

"Oh, come on, Troy." Rupert nudged his side. "Don't tell me you never used sweet words to your advantage. I can't imagine how else you convinced Millie to accept your suit."

Troy cut his eyes to her and slanted that crooked grin. "I'll never tell."

But a thread of worry laced his voice.

~

*A*fter lunch, Ma tugged on Troy's hand. "Can you take a walk with me?"

Her voice held a note of concern, so he set aside his plans for a nap. Maybe he could catch up on sleep later when the prospect of violence subsided.

"Let me tell Millie, and I'll join you on the porch in a minute."

She wandered to the front door. Troy's puzzled gaze followed her. Now what? It wasn't like Ma to share her burdens. She was the one who helped others.

Troy let Millie know where he was headed and joined his mother. She took his arm and guided him onto the road leading away from the house. She didn't say anything at first, making him uneasy.

"Are you ready to go home, Ma? Since Jewel's here to help Millie, I think she'll be fine when I leave again."

"I can stay a few more days till you or Rupert can take me home or John comes to fetch me. That's not what I wanted to discuss." She took a deep breath. "While I've been taking care of Byron, we've spent a good deal of time talking. He's shared more about his reasons for coming here."

"He said he wants to find the old family farm and try to get it back."

"There's another reason he returned to Alabama. He learned some family history during his visit at Christmas. His uncle asked him to check on someone if he should come here. That's why he requested to spend his last months of army duty here."

A strange sense of foreboding sent a chill through Troy. "Where's this leading, Ma?"

She stopped walking and turned to face him. Her eyes seemed to plead with him. For what? Patience? Understanding?

"It took me a while to face my fears. Troy, as you guessed, Byron and his sister Jessie were students during my last year of teaching. They moved away that spring. Their uncle stayed behind for a few weeks." She took a deep breath and blew it out. "Byron's uncle is Ethan Harris. Your natural father."

"So, Byron came to find you? But he knew you'd married Pa."

"He came to find out whether Ethan had a child he didn't know about."

"But why would he think so? Didn't he leave before you knew you were expecting?"

"He did." Her attention turned to her hands. "But a few months later, he came back on business—to collect payment on the farm, according to Byron. I was about six months along with you. We passed on the street in front of the bank. I stumbled, but John caught me. I'm sure I glared at Ethan before I turned away. For days I worried that he might confront me, but he never did. I figured he was relieved to find me married to someone else. It let him off the hook. I never had any more contact with him."

Troy paced away from her, processing this information.

"When Byron heard Millie was a McNeil," Ma continued, "he asked questions about you and your next assignment. He thought it would take him a while to find the right people. He had no idea coming here would put him in direct contact with me or you. Ethan asked him to make discreet inquiries to determine whether the child I was carrying then could have been his. Ethan has his own family now. He's not out to cause trouble for us."

"So he's just curious?" Troy spun back to face her. "I suppose he wants to be sure nobody will upset his family or make demands of him if he comes back to the area."

"I don't think he plans to return, Troy. Of course, he might visit if Byron stays." She placed a hand on Troy's shoulder. "Byron says Ethan has a successful business, and he's done well, even with the war. He wants to pass something on to his son."

"Then let him do it." Troy threw up his hands. "I won't be knocking at his door, asking for a handout. He can go on with his life, and I'll go on with mine."

"Troy, he only has daughters from his marriage. You're his only son. I believe you should think and pray about your answer."

Although he wanted to ignore anything to do with Ethan Harris, he gave in. "All right, I will. But don't expect me to change my mind anytime soon."

~

"*S*o you and Corporal Harris are cousins, then." Millie darted around the clothesline post as Troy paced the backyard. His version of the conversation with Connie had rambled between past and present as he strode from side to side.

Her husband stopped pacing and stared at her. "Yeah, I guess we are. Dang, can this family get any crazier?"

His expression made Millie giggle, then laugh outright.

"It's not laughing matter."

She tried to contain her humor, but she couldn't stop. Then his lips twitched, and he started laughing too.

"It's a good thing..." Millie finally calmed herself. "A good thing we came outside to talk."

"Yeah, we wouldn't want to wake Amy from her nap." Troy looped his arms around Millie's waist and kissed her brow. "What a strange woman you are, Millicent McNeil. To laugh at me in my distress. No wonder I love you."

He dipped his head for a proper kiss, but she held him away. "Not here, Troy. Anyone could come up the road. Besides, you need to decide what you're going to do about this unusual situation."

"I know. You just distracted me for a minute. Let's go sit."

Millie's mind churned as he led her to the back porch steps. How could she help him? The poor man already had so much on his mind with the recent attack and trying to help folks adjust to a new way of life. Troubles bombarded him from all directions.

She leaned against Troy's shoulder. "Let's go back a few days. Before the attack, what were your plans?"

He sighed. "I thought I'd take a day or so to rest and get to know Byron. I want to explain my methods to him, see if he has any ideas to share. Then we'll head to the farms on the west side of the county. There's a constitutional convention in

September to start the process of Alabama rejoining the union, so we need to be ready to help with that if called upon."

Millie turned her face up to his. "If you want my opinion, I think you should do what you planned. It might be good for you and Byron to have that time traveling to get to know each other. Maybe you can learn more about his family and get an idea of what Ethan Harris expects from you."

He shifted to lean against the porch rail. "Here's what keeps botherin' me about all this comin' up now. I wonder about Pa. How will he feel if I go lookin' for Ethan Harris? After all he's done for me, treatin' me like I was his own flesh and blood, never givin' any sign I wasn't his true son. We've had our disputes, but he did his best by me. Will he take it as an insult if I try to build a relationship with a man who isn't even sure I exist?"

Millie stretched out her hand to catch a few raindrops from a passing cloud. "Those are good questions, Troy, and I understand your hesitation. My situation was different, of course, but I'm glad I learned the truth. It gave me the opportunity to see Cal in a new light, so I could forgive him for the way he treated me. I believe he did his best, even if I didn't realize it while I was growing up."

She squeezed Troy's hand. "I'm still figuring out how I feel about Ellis. He's good with Amy, and I'm glad she has him as a grandpa. But Ellis and I have years apart to overcome. I daresay the same would be true for you and Ethan if you decide to meet him."

The rain gained intensity, and Millie stood to duck under the porch roof. "Let's pray you'll get a clear sense of what to do. There's no reason to rush a decision you might wish undone later."

CHAPTER 29

AUGUST 9, 1865

*T*roy threw his knapsack into the wagon and climbed up beside Byron. He hated to leave again, but this trip should be the last one for a while.

They hadn't learned anything about their attackers, but there'd been no further trouble. Millie had pointed out that lights in the house would have clearly revealed Byron in his uniform. He'd been sitting closest to the window, so they figured the perpetrators had aimed for a Union man. With Troy and Byron out of the house, there should be no threat to the others, and Henry and Rupert were on alert. Troy wanted to draw out their opponents, make them come after him. A moving target was harder to hit.

"This western part of the county isn't heavily populated." Troy pointed toward the unending vision of green fields dotted with thick stands of trees. "We'll be doin' more ridin' than talkin' to folks, so you can crawl in back and sleep if your shoulder pains you sittin' up. I don't know many people out this way, so I'll have to be on guard for a hostile reception."

Byron cleared his throat. "Before that becomes our primary concern, I feel like I ought to explain a couple of things. I've been waiting for a time when we could talk without being overheard or interrupted."

Troy felt the other man's gaze on him. "Go ahead."

"First off, last summer when my unit was camped out in Georgia, when I, ah, first saw Mrs. McNeil, your wife."

"You can call her by name, Byron. I think Millie's put that incident behind her."

"I'm glad to hear it. What I didn't want to say in her hearing was what led up to my, er, inappropriate advances. The fellows with me that day were a couple of rough characters. We saw Millie from a distance while she was taking clothes off the line. They started planning...well, you can imagine what they said."

What Troy imagined was bashing in a couple of Yankee heads, but he held his peace.

"Anyway, my sister was also in the family way at that time, and I wouldn't want either of those fellows to set his sights on her. So I convinced them to let me approach Millie."

"She said you insulted her." Troy's hands had tightened on the reins, causing the horses to slow down. He flicked the leather strands to pick up the pace.

"I'm sure I did. Since I didn't know whether they listened near the door, I had to make it seem as though I played their game. That's why I threatened to get even." Byron chuckled. "I never thought I'd be glad to be punched in the nose."

"That's my feisty Millie."

"She packs a wallop." He touched his nose as if it still ached. "I never volunteered to forage again."

They rode in silence for a few minutes, then Byron spoke again. "The other thing I wanted to mention..."

Troy glanced over. He had no doubt about the subject. "Your Uncle Ethan."

His companion nodded. "As soon as I saw you the other day,

I figured it was you. Ma has a picture of him about the same age you are now. However, I didn't know whether you'd been told about him."

"I learned the truth a couple of weeks ago. It was quite a shock."

"I'm sure. I was surprised to hear it myself."

"When was that?"

"Last Christmas." Byron removed his foot from the box and directed his gaze across the fields. "The second battle for Nashville seemed to shake up Uncle Ethan. Made him take stock of his life, I suppose. Then we had a snowstorm that kept us confined to the house for a few days, and he got to reminiscing about a storm in Alabama."

"He shared this with the whole family?"

"Just me and my stepfather."

"Ma said she'd gone to see why her students had missed school. That was you and your sister, I guess?"

"Yeah. I remember Jessie was sad she didn't get to tell our teacher goodbye, but Grandpa was in a hurry to get his crops in the ground. Afraid the weather might turn."

Troy snorted. "He was right, I guess. According to Ma, it was two days before she could leave the farm. You should know she doesn't lay all the blame at your uncle's door."

"Maybe not, but Ethan does. He said he should've taken her to town as soon as she arrived. The snow was already piling up, but he figured it wouldn't last. He'd never known this area to get that kind of weather."

"It's unusual this far south. Until I went to Ohio, I'd never seen more than an inch or two of snow."

Byron cleared his throat. "Ethan said they'd talked about marriage. I guess being alone like that was too much temptation."

"It never occurred to him—?" Troy stopped. Consequences

had never occurred to him either. *Like father, like son?* Something to consider if he ever had a son.

Byron shook his head. "When he saw your mother several months later, she was already married to Mr. McNeil. He wouldn't have caused them problems unless she'd appealed to him for help."

Untended farmland gave way to a field boasting rows of unpicked cotton. As they rounded a curve in the road, a cleared path led to a sprawling house and barn.

"Looks like we're about to meet our first customers of the day. Why don't you sit back and watch for now? I'll be happy for you to offer any suggestions after we leave."

As the day wore on, surprisingly enough, he and Byron fell into an easy routine. Maybe he could get used to this new cousin. Perhaps they shared more than the same eye color.

∿

AUGUST 15, 1865

*W*ith Troy and Byron gone, the house seemed empty to Millie. Rupert and Henry went about their tasks, which kept them outside most of the time. The afternoon heat spurred everyone to seek the shade or a dipper of water to cool off. Millie's energy ran low, and she blessed the Lord for sending Connie her way for this season.

Even the birds seemed to save their songs for the cooler evening hours. Or they could be wary of Sunflower, who followed the women to the porch.

She and Connie settled in the rocking chairs and snapped beans while the cat curled up beside Amy on a blanket between them. Millie startled at a sudden noise. Rupert rounded the corner, his hair dripping water and his clothes damp.

"What happened to you?" Millie asked.

Connie laughed. "My guess is he took a dip in the creek. His favorite method of bathing."

"It beats trying to fill up that tin tub you ladies prefer." He continued across the porch toward the front door.

"Maybe," Connie said, "but it's easier to add scented soap to a tub. You might try using some once in a while."

Millie chuckled. "You goin' out somewhere?"

He stopped in the doorway and tossed them a grin, but he blushed beneath his beard. "Supper with the Varners. Gotta change and head out." He whistled as he went in.

"Wipe the floor behind you if you're trailing water," Connie called. She turned to Millie with a sigh. "As difficult as it is to understand, I think he's taken a likin' to Becky. How do you feel about havin' her for a sister?"

Millie choked back a laugh. "Probably the same as you do havin' her for a daughter."

A couple of hours later, after a peaceful meal, the women joined Henry on the porch. The chirping of cicadas vied with the singing that drifted across the fields where the hired workers gathered. Millie and Connie had shooed Jewel out of the kitchen so she and Levi could attend the weekly prayer meeting.

Connie paused in her game of pat-a-cake with Amy as a figure ambled toward the house. "Is that Rupert comin' back already?"

Millie slapped a mosquito on her arm before she glanced up. "I don't know who it is. Henry, do you recognize that man?"

"Looks like George Callahan." Henry levered himself from the rocker and met the visitor at the base of the steps. "George? Surprised to see you this time of day."

"Brought back the axe I borrowed from you. And I've a letter the mercantile owner had for Troy. He thought it might be important and asked me to bring it."

Henry accepted both items. "Appreciate that. Why don't you sit a spell?" Both men took a chair as Henry continued. "Don't know if you remember my sister-in-law, Connie." He gestured toward the women. "And this is Troy's wife, Millie, and their baby."

Mr. Callahan greeted them, then turned back to Henry. "I heard y'all had a little trouble here back, somebody shootin' through the window?"

Millie focused on the visitor. Did he know who'd done it?

Henry didn't appear distressed. "Yep. I guess someone took exception to me havin' Union men here."

Mr. Callahan rubbed his hands along the rocker arms. "I seen two boys runnin' past my fields about that time. It might not be the same ones, but when I learned your house was shot at, I went to the sheriff and gave a report."

At last, maybe the culprits would be caught. With a glance at the sleepy baby in Connie's arms, Millie rose. "I need to put the little one to bed. Could I bring y'all any refreshments when I come out?"

"Not for me." Mr. Callahan stood also. "I'd better get on to the house before it gets too dark to see the way. Just wanted you folks to know I'll be watchin' out for you." He started down the steps. "Oh, and let Troy know the workers he sent me are doin' a good job."

Henry stood and followed the other man. "I'll put the axe away. Let Connie take care of the baby." He passed Millie the letter. "Maybe you should see what that's about."

Millie gazed at the sealed paper, vacillating between a desire to know and dread of what she might find. What would its contents reveal?

～

AUGUST 16, 1865

"*H*allelujah, home again. Nothin' sweeter after a week of travels." Troy guided the wagon around the last curve that led to the farmhouse. The setting sun gilded the view in gold, calling to mind tales of riches at the end of a rainbow.

"Maybe nothing except knowing we won't have to travel again for a while." Byron flashed a grin. "Now I can set about finding my own place so Rupert won't have to put up with me."

Levi's announcement rang across the yard. "Mistah Troy home." Moments later, the porch filled with family members, Millie with Amy in the forefront. Henry and Rupert followed, and Ma pushed out the door, pulling Pa by the arm.

"Pa's here?"

Rupert sprinted ahead and caught the nearest horse's bridle. "Y'all go on in and eat. I'll tend to this."

Troy didn't have to be told twice. He hopped off the wagon and took Millie in his arms.

They crossed the yard to the house. Ma reached for the baby, but Amy clung to Troy. He shifted her so he could hug Ma, then extended his hand to Pa.

"Surprised to see you here, Pa. I guess you've come to collect Ma?"

"I thought she might be ready to go home." Pa tugged her to his side.

"I hope you'll stay a day or two. I'd like a chance to visit with you."

"Yes, please stay," Millie added.

"I think Paul can manage the farm that long."

"Good." Millie turned to Troy. "You and Byron should go have some supper now. The rest of us have eaten, but we can keep you company."

Millie coaxed Amy away from Troy by sitting on the bench beside him so the baby could lean against his arm.

Jewel set filled plates before him and Byron while Ma poured their tea. The others sat or stood around the table.

"How'd folks to the west take to your offers?" Henry glanced between Troy and Byron.

"Most of 'em were glad to work with us. I think the rest will come around soon." Troy popped another bite of cornbread into his mouth. "How's everything here?"

His question met with varied degrees of concern. His family seemed to look everywhere but at him. Laying down his fork, Troy swallowed a lump of worry. "What's happened?"

Millie touched his arm. "First, we've discovered who the canteen belonged to."

"You have?" A knot formed in his gut. "Who was it?"

She pulled a letter from her pocket and handed it to him. "General Swayne's men found that Cal's brother, R. W., who joined the Twenty-sixth Alabama Infantry, was wounded at Gettysburg, and sent home to Tuscumbia. He died on October first, 1863, of lung fever."

Troy opened the letter, puzzled by her words. He skimmed the writing. "According to this letter, he claimed all his things were stolen on the way home. He blamed the man assigned to assist the wounded."

"A man who never reported back for duty but was found dead in a remote area near New Manchester, Georgia." Millie recited the words she must have memorized.

Byron's eyes went wide. "Isn't that where you're from?" He motioned to Millie. "Where we, ah, met last year?"

Troy ignored Byron and covered Millie's hand with his. "Then it wasn't R.W. but this deserter who attacked you." He was dimly aware of Ma leaning over to whisper in Byron's ear.

Millie blew out a breath. "Yes, thank God. And his family was notified and took him home for burial."

Troy sensed her relief, which added to his own. "Well, I'm glad that's settled."

"As for the other news..." Henry drummed his fingers on the table.

Troy's focus shifted to his uncle. "What other news? Does everything happen when I go away?" He faked a laugh as his anxiety returned.

"George Callahan said he saw some boys runnin' past his place the night Byron was shot. He didn't know about the shootin' till he went to town."

Millie nodded. "He told the sheriff, so maybe they can figure out who did it."

Troy blew out his breath. "Y'all had me worried there for a minute. I was afraid it was something bad. Glad to come home to good news." *Let's pray it stays that way.*

CHAPTER 30

*M*illie and Jewell tallied the last of the items in the pantry and made a list of what they hoped to purchase or trade for. With John and Connie gone, they were settling into a routine. As they returned to the kitchen, Levi's voice rang from the front porch. "Rider comin'."

"Wonder who that could be?" Millie set aside her list and meandered to the front door.

Troy and Byron had gone to town while Henry and Rupert tended to farm chores. Millie blessed this peaceful day filled with ordinary tasks. She prayed this visitor wouldn't disrupt the calm.

She didn't recognize the boy on the bay mare. He rode right up to the porch steps as if he were being chased. "Mrs. McNeil! That's you, ain't it?"

Millie crossed her arms. "Yes. How can I help you?"

"Well, missus, it's your husband, the McNeil what's a Union man. It looks like somebody beat him up bad. I seen him in the meadow when I cut across goin' to my friend's house. You need to come now."

Millie's pulse and mind raced. How could she get to him quickly enough? Troy had the only transportation. "How far is it? I don't have a horse."

"You kin ride with me here on Freckles." He patted the animal's neck.

Millie turned as Jewel stepped onto the porch. "Jewel, Troy's been hurt, and I have to go to him. Maybe Amy will sleep until we get back."

"Don't you worry 'bout the baby, ma'am. I'll watch her. You go get Mr. Troy."

With the boy's help, Millie clambered behind him on the horse's bare back and held on as he clicked them into motion.

They'd not traveled far—a handful of miles, she supposed —when the boy cut across an empty field toward a ramshackle building. He pulled the horse to a stop and slid off, then turned to assist her.

She glanced at the shack. "But where is Troy? I thought you said he was on the road."

"Inside." He shoved her toward the building. "You'll see him."

Millie stumbled, sensing a change in the boy's voice and manner. She whirled to face him. He grabbed her arm in a painful grip and wound a rope around her wrist. When she struggled, he jerked her against him with a harsh laugh. "Dumb Yankee lover. You were so easy to fool."

"Harlan," a voice called from the shack behind her. "Bring her in here afore somebody sees."

Harlan spun her around and pushed her toward the building. Panic seized Millie, and she twisted, trying to get free. The other man jumped to the ground, and together they wrestled her inside. "Troy! What have you done to Troy?"

The second man chuckled. "Nothin' yet. We needed some bait, and you're it."

Millie dropped to the floor. Dear Lord, she'd walked right into their trap, and now Troy would pay the price for her foolishness.

～

*I*t was late afternoon when Troy arrived to find the house in an uproar—Henry yelling at Jewel, who was trying to quiet a squalling Amy while Levi whimpered into her skirts. Where was Millie?

Rather than try to shout over all the noise, he crossed the floor to take his daughter from Jewel. Amy's tears stopped as she lunged into his arms. Henry and Jewel turned to Troy with open mouths.

Levi peeped around Jewel with wide eyes. "Mistah Troy? You ain't hurt?"

Henry lumbered over to hug him, then pushed him away. "Where's Millie?"

"That's what I'd like to know—"

"I didn't see—Troy!" Rupert skidded to a halt from the back door. "You're here. So I guess Millie found you?"

"Found me? Why would she...where is Millie?"

The others started speaking at once. Troy raised his hand. "One at a time, please." His brother might be easiest to understand. "Rupert, what's happened?"

"Jewel said a boy rode up on a horse, telling Millie you'd been hurt and needed her. He helped her on his horse, and they took off, headed toward town."

Dread filled Troy's veins with ice. Amy clung to his neck, quiet for the moment. He didn't want to upset her, so he spoke in a normal tone to Rupert. "Will you see if Blackie will take a saddle and get her ready for me?"

As Rupert walked away, Troy addressed Jewel. "Can we get this baby something to eat? I suspect Levi's hungry too."

The wise woman nodded and led Levi to the kitchen. "Let's see what we kin find."

Henry asked, "What can I do?"

"Maybe you can distract Amy for a minute. I'll need a rifle. Tell me, how long has Millie been gone?"

~

A couple of hours must have passed since Millie's captors brought her to the one-room building. Her fingers threatened to go numb with the blood restricted by the rope around her wrists. She endured the painful pinpricks to flex them every few minutes. Worse than those, however, was the tightness of her bodice and the knowledge that Amy would be crying for her.

How long would it be before Troy came after her? She had no doubt he would, but daylight was fading, and it would be difficult to track them in the dark. Her constant prayer pleaded for his safety and wisdom to realize this was a trap.

From her seated position on the floor, she eyed the man slumped in the lone chair. His hair hung to his shoulders, and his beard was unkempt. The clothes bagged on his lean frame, and she judged him to be no more than twenty. She'd tried to get him to state his grievance with Troy, but all she got was mumbles about Union men and prison.

The boy who'd tricked her sat in the doorway, watching for Troy's arrival, the meadow visible beyond him. If she could stand, perhaps she would catch sight of Troy before Harlan did. Wriggling to bend her knees under her skirts, she pushed against the wall at her back and rose to full height. Her grunting roused the man at the table.

He shifted around. "Here now! What're you doin'?"

"My legs're cramping. Not used to sittin' on the floor like that."

He leered. "Too bad there ain't a bed in here. We could have some fun while we wait on your man." He stood and inched closer.

Millie couldn't control the shudder that racked her as the image of another man looming over her filled her mind.

Please, God, not again.

She closed her eyes, and the vision swept in swift succession from the other attacker to Troy's entrance, the men's tussle, and finally, to Troy's instructions in fighting. A sudden peace filled her. This time, she'd be ready.

From the sound of his movements and the pungent body odor, he was only a step or two away. She inhaled and opened her eyes. Keeping her gaze on his face, she waited till he lifted one hand to her hair.

She drove one knee into his groin. He gasped and doubled over. Her bound hands met his chin and plowed him backward. Before he could regain his feet, Millie gripped the ear of the chair-back with her right palm and forced her hand out of the rope.

Her hands were free, but Harlan had heard the scuffle and stood in the doorway as Clint gained his feet. Suddenly, Harlan pitched forward, and a rifle pointed at Clint.

"Touch my wife again, and you're a dead man."

Millie had never heard sweeter words from Troy McNeil's mouth.

≈

That evening, Troy nestled his chin in Millie's hair and inhaled the scent of lavender. She leaned back in his arms and set the rocking chair in motion as she sang a silly rhyme to the child in her lap. Moonlight shone on the yard beyond the porch. A mockingbird vied with Millie's song and the creaking of their rocker. Henry and Rupert had finally gone to bed, but Troy enjoyed the peaceful atmosphere and holding his family.

Amy hadn't let Millie out of sight since they'd returned. He couldn't blame the baby. Even his uncle had hugged Millie for long moments when she arrived. Jewel's tears of joy had spilled over as she watched the reunion and urged everyone to eat the food she'd prepared during the wait.

At last, Amy's soft snores replaced Millie's singing. "So...tell me how everything went on your trip to town."

Surprise forced a rumble from his throat. "Was that just this morning? Seems it was days ago. Let's see, Byron found a room to rent, and we got the office set up. He's close enough to open it every day, and I'll check with him once a week, as I will the one we put in Roanoke. I need to go back to Georgia soon and see if Preacher Dan needs any help with the office there."

Millie poked her elbow in his ribs. "You mean *we* need to go to Georgia."

He guided her face to his with his finger. "Are you getting homesick or just tired of being here?"

"Neither. I'm all right with either place as long as we're together." Tears formed in her eyes. "When I thought you'd been hurt, my heart dropped. I should've questioned Harlan more, but all I could think was to get to you."

"I know the feeling. It was the same for me. Thank goodness, Henry and Rupert pitched in to help."

"I was surprised to see Rupert get there right behind you."

Troy chuckled. "He runs faster than anyone I know. What I can't believe is that the Federals ever caught him and got him into prison. All the other boys at home gave up racing him. He also got Harlan and Clint to confess they were the ones who shot into the house."

"How did Mr. Varner happen to be coming that way so late in the day?"

"Bobby Ray has an old spyglass and likes to climb trees and pretend he's a sailor. He saw activity at the shack and told his pa, who figured someone was up to no good."

"Ah, I'll have to get Jewel to bake that boy a pie. Thank God for boys who climb trees."

"I'd say you did a pretty good job yourself, knocking Clint to his knees. How'd you do that?"

"I recalled our lessons after the first attack. Right after I prayed."

"Several prayers went up about that time. Thank God, He hears and answers."

EPILOGUE

*M*illie dropped to the rocker on the porch, ready for a rest after doing laundry and chasing Amy as she toddled around the yard. With supper simmering on the stove, she could sit and wait for Troy to return from the Campbell County Bureau office. She blessed Jewel for the cooking lessons she'd shared so that Millie could feed her little family better.

The sunshine had almost lulled her to sleep when Troy rode into the yard. She cracked one eye open to verify his identity. He leaned over and kissed her forehead. "What's the girl's name in that story you tell Amy? The one where the prince wakes her with a kiss?"

"Sleeping Beauty."

"No, her name. Doesn't she have a name?"

"Aurora."

He winced. "That might be hard for Amy to say. How about we rename her Millicent?"

"Hmm. Not much better, but I'll think about it." She straightened as he sat in the chair beside her. "How was your trip?"

"Good. Most folks are settling into the routine. Of course, they're always a couple who complain about the changes. What did you do today, besides run after our daughter?"

"Laundry. Put soup on for supper. Not much."

He frowned and picked up her hand. "You could have waited for me to help with the washing. I thought you're not supposed to reach above your head."

She shrugged. "It didn't hurt anything when I was carrying the first time. Did you check for mail?"

He grinned at her. "I wondered how long it would take you to ask about that." He retrieved the packet he'd dropped beside his chair and pulled out several letters. "Here you go."

Millie squealed and flipped through the pile. "One from the Griffins in Indiana, one from the Spencers in Frankfort, and a fat one from Louisville. Which shall I open first?"

"Hmm. Let's see." He flourished another envelope. "Oh, how about this one from Ma?"

"You already opened it! What did she say?"

"She's going to host a family reunion next month, much to Ellis's delight. And my brother Simon wrote that he's married and living in northeast Georgia. He'll come here on his way to Alabama for the reunion."

Millie bounced in her seat. "How wonderful. We'll get to meet his wife first."

Troy stood and pulled another paper from his shirt pocket. He seemed to brace for her reaction. "There's also one from Ethan Harris in Tennessee."

Her eyes widened. "That was fast. I didn't know you'd written yet."

She sprang from her chair and reached for the paper, but Troy held it away. She moved closer, and he wrapped his arms around her. "You should know by now, when I make up my mind to do something, I move fast, sweetheart. I have to, where you're concerned."

She gave him her saucy grin. "Oh, really? And why is that?"

"It's the only way I can stay ahead of you. Otherwise, you'll run me ragged. You're a managing woman, Millie." He punctuated the comment with a quick kiss. "And I wouldn't have you be any other way."

THE END

Did you enjoy this book? We hope so!
Would you take a quick minute to leave a review where you purchased the book?
It doesn't have to be long. Just a sentence or two telling what you liked about the story!

Receive a FREE ebook and get updates when new Wild Heart books release: https://wildheartbooks.org/newsletter

ABOUT THE AUTHOR

Born into a family of storytellers, **Susan Pope Sloan** published her first articles in high school and continued writing sporadically for decades. Retirement provided the time to focus on writing and indulge her avid interest in history. Her Civil War series begins (and ultimately ends) in her home state of Georgia with references to lesser-known events of that period. She and husband Ricky live near Columbus where she participates in Word Weavers, ACFW, and Toastmasters.

AUTHOR'S NOTE

As with the other books in this series, so much credit goes to Mary Deborah Petite for her excellent scholarly work in *The Women Will Howl* (McFarland & Company, Inc., Publishers, 2008). Her book was a primary source of information for the timeline of events related to the workers' journey from North Georgia to Louisville, Kentucky. She also listed names of people in New Manchester who were Union sympathizers and explained how they assisted young men who wanted to avoid the Confederate conscription.

It was not uncommon for prisoners to join the opposing army, and these were called "galvanized Yankees." Since Troy considered himself a Unionist, he assimilated into the northern army with the understanding that he would serve as a guard and not be forced into combat.

Information on the short-lived Bureau of Refugees, Freedmen, and Abandoned Lands provided general descriptions of the work involved but no details on how it was carried out. The first agents were drawn from the military, so it seemed logical that Troy McNeil would return to the area he knew best to provide aid. His implied friendship with a couple of former slaves and his attitude toward the Confederacy added weight to that decision.

Here are a few websites where I found useful information:

http://38thalabama.com/camp-chase.html

https://www.mycivilwar.com/pow/oh-camp-chase.html

American Civil War Prisoners of War History (thomaslegion.net)

Civil War Index - Civil War Battles from the Official Records - Volume 32, Chapter 44

A Reasonable Captivity: Soldier Experiences in Camp Chase – The Gettysburg Compiler

www.history.com/topics/black-history/freedmens-bureau

www.archives.gov/research/african-americans/freed-mens-bureau

I tried to stay as true to the timeline as I could, but sources vary on what happened when. Also, I could only speculate on some particulars, such as how the women obtained water at the refugee house, how they prepared meals, how many stayed in one room, and how much interaction they had with the guards and men in the Union army prison.

As the war dragged on, the Confederate army had trouble with deserters and stragglers, such as the man who attacked Millie. Another problem was the pockets of Union sympathizers who protected its "draft dodgers" as best they could.

There really was an unusual snowstorm in Alabama in the 1840's like the one that led to Troy's birth. Perhaps you'll read about it in Connie's story later.

If you love historical romance, check out the other Wild Heart books!

Marisol ~ Spanish Rose by Elva Cobb Martin

Escaping to the New World is her only option...Rescuing her will wrap the chains of the Inquisition around his neck.

Marisol Valentin flees Spain after murdering the nobleman who molested her. She ends up for sale on the indentured servants' block at Charles Town harbor—dirty, angry, and with child. Her hopes are shattered, but she must find a refuge for herself and the child she carries. Can this new land offer her the grace, love, and security she craves? Or must she escape again to her only living relative in Cartagena?

Captain Ethan Becket, once a Charles Town minister, now sails the seas as a privateer, grieving his deceased wife. But when he takes captive a ship full of indentured servants, he's intrigued by the woman whose manners seem much more refined than the average Spanish serving girl. Perfect to become governess for his young son. But when he sets out on a quest to find his captured sister, said to be in Cartagena, little does he expect his new Spanish governess to stow away on his ship with her six-month-old son. Yet her offer of help to free his sister is too tempting to pass up. And her beauty, both inside and out, is too attractive for his heart to protect itself against—until he learns she is a wanted murderess.

As their paths intertwine on a journey filled with danger, intrigue, and romance, only love and the grace of God can overcome the past and ignite a new beginning for Marisol and Ethan.

~

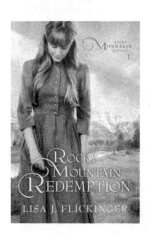

Rocky Mountain Redemption by Lisa J. Flickinger

A Rocky Mountain logging camp may be just the place to find herself.

To escape the devastation caused by the breaking of her wedding engagement, Isabelle Franklin joins her aunt in the Rocky Mountains to feed a camp of lumberjacks cutting on the slopes of Cougar Ridge. If only she could out run the lingering nightmares.

Charles Bailey, camp foreman and Stony Creek's itinerant pastor, develops a reputation to match his new nickname — Preach. However, an inner battle ensues when the details of his rough history threaten to overcome the beliefs of his young faith.

Amid the hazards of camp life, the unlikely friendship growing between the two surprises Isabelle. She's drawn to Preach's brute strength and gentle nature as he leads the ragtag crew toiling for Pollitt's Lumber. But when the ghosts from her past return to haunt her, the choices she will make change the course of her life forever—and that of the man she's come to love.

∾

Lone Star Ranger by Renae Brumbaugh Green

Elizabeth Covington will get her man.

And she has just a week to prove her brother isn't the murderer Texas Ranger Rett Smith accuses him of being. She'll show the good-looking lawman he's wrong, even if it means setting out on a risky race across Texas to catch the real killer.

Rett doesn't want to convict an innocent man. But he can't let the Boston beauty sway his senses to set a guilty man free. When Elizabeth follows him on a dangerous trek, the Ranger vows to keep her safe. But who will protect him from the woman whose conviction and courage leave him doubting everything—even his heart?